Whispers Most Deadly

Whispers Most Deadly

EMMA MacDONALD

MICHAEL  JOSEPH

PENGUIN BOOKS

UK | USA | Canada | Ireland | Australia
India | New Zealand | South Africa

Penguin Michael Joseph is part of the Penguin Random House group of companies whose addresses can be found at global.penguinrandomhouse.com

Penguin Books, Penguin Random House UK,
One Embassy Gardens, 8 Viaduct Gardens, London SW11 7BW

penguin.co.uk

First published 2025
001
Copyright © Emma MacDonald, 2025

The moral right of the author has been asserted

Penguin Random House values and supports copyright. Copyright fuels creativity, encourages diverse voices, promotes freedom of expression and supports a vibrant culture. Thank you for purchasing an authorized edition of this book and for respecting intellectual property laws by not reproducing, scanning or distributing any part of it by any means without permission. You are supporting authors and enabling Penguin Random House to continue to publish books for everyone. No part of this book may be used or reproduced in any manner for the purpose of training artificial intelligence technologies or systems. In accordance with Article 4(3) of the DSM Directive 2019/790, Penguin Random House expressly reserves this work from the text and data mining exception

Set in 13.5/16pt Garamond MT Std
Typeset by Six Red Marbles UK, Thetford, Norfolk
Printed and bound in Great Britain by Clays Ltd, Elcograf S.p.A.

The authorized representative in the EEA is Penguin Random House Ireland, Morrison Chambers, 32 Nassau Street, Dublin D02 YH68

A CIP catalogue record for this book is available from the British Library

HARDBACK ISBN: 978–0–241–71522–2
TRADEPAPERBACK ISBN: 978–0–241–71523–9

Penguin Random House is committed to a sustainable future for our business, our readers and our planet. This book is made from Forest Stewardship Council® certified paper.

To everyone who's ever wondered who they would become if the world would simply let them be

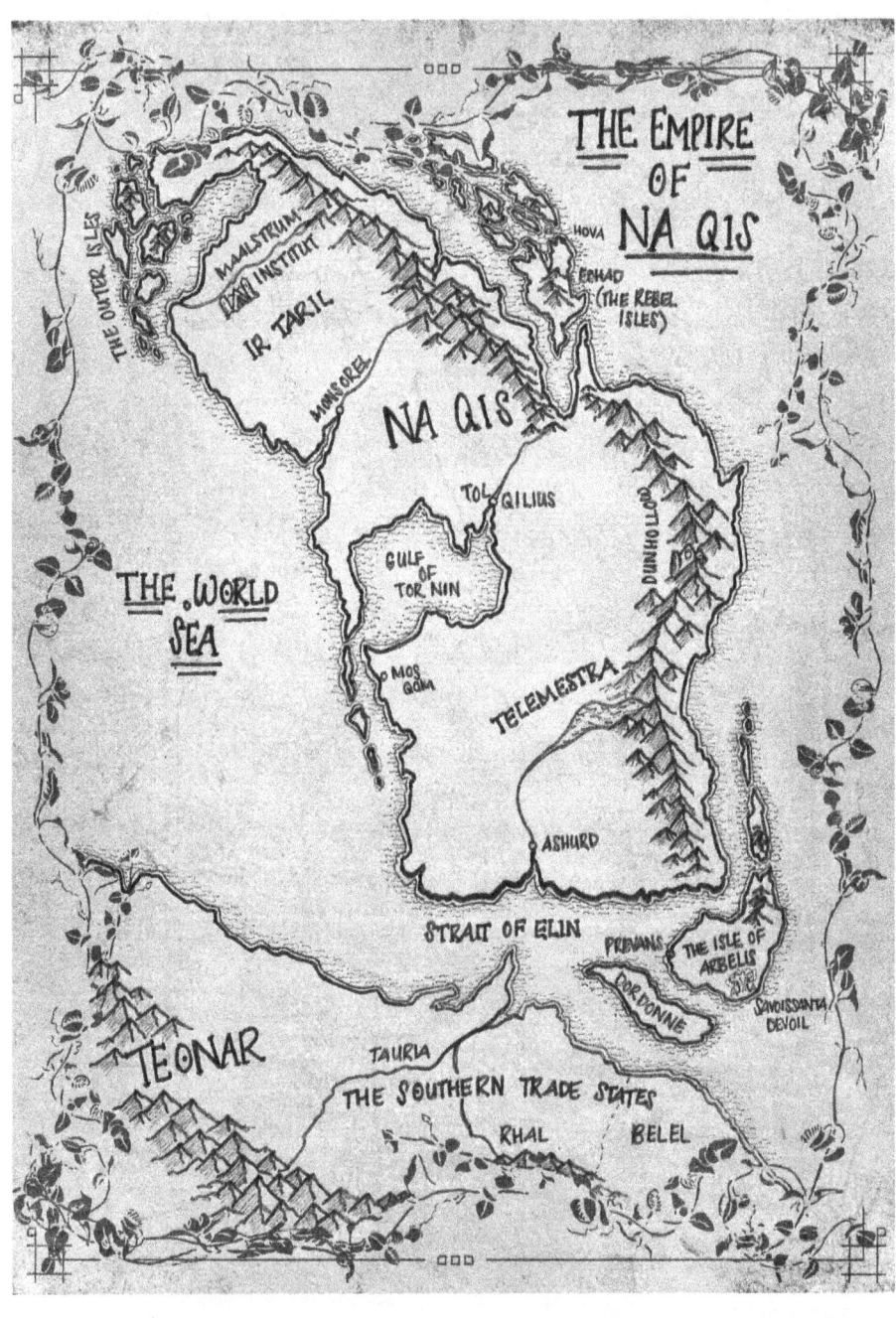

1. Like a Tether

There was something gentle about the scent of death. Not the fetid stench of decay, nor the sterile aroma of embalming halls. No, this was earthy and somewhat sweet, lingering always at the edge of life. A promise of inevitability – like a knot coiled at the end of needle and thread, holding them ever steady.

Rose watched her life source weave through her outstretched fingers. It ebbed against her skin in glowing silver tendrils, pulling at her pulse like the moon on the tides. Soothing in some way.

But, at the moment, utterly useless.

She dropped her hand, eyes scanning the fleeting landscape beyond the compartment window of the cavalcade. The mountains surrounding Dunhollow crept ever closer in the distance, fog hanging low over the sloping pine-hemmed peaks. Her stomach sank as she leaned back against her plush seat.

Nine months. Nine whole months of travelling to the furthest reaches of the empire. To the grandest libraries of Tol Qilius, and archives far beyond their borders. To mountains that shattered the sky and seas that stretched out into the fading horizon.

And yet, here she was, right back where she'd started. For all those months that she'd left Dunhollow in her shadow, there was some broken part of her that would always reach for its rotten halls. A festering wound that refused to heal.

The cavalcade's thin whistle pierced the air. They would reach the station all too soon. And then what?

Classes, curses and cut-throat smiles? How long would it take for the claws of this place to sink into her flesh once again – to tear away every defence she'd so carefully built? *No.* Rose gritted her teeth. Things would be different this time. *She* was different.

Though still not enough, an insidious voice whispered at the back of her mind.

Rose's eyes flicked to the bag at her feet, then to the compartment door. Soren could return any minute, provided he hadn't got caught by more students eager to welcome him back. Already, half a dozen had stopped by the compartment to confirm he really had returned. Though she could hardly blame them. He *was* Dunhollow's most beloved professor, and she had stolen him away for the better part of a year.

Still, something gnawed away deep within her heart, drawing her back to her satchel. To the unsuspecting tome lying buried in its leather folds. Rose tugged at the edges of her pleated skirt, glancing once more at the door before she pulled the book from her bag.

Its spine was worn and frayed, the leather blackened with age. Rose stroked its faint gilded filigree. *Bearath: Studis ab Mord ed Necromancie.* Her breath hitched. *Studies of Death and Necromancy.*

It had been pure chance that she'd stumbled upon it at all, tucked away in the hollows of the Imperial Archive. She and Soren had found countless other books – tomes on the long history of necromancy, scroll after scroll on the dangers and abuses that had led to its prohibition. Terrible tales of its horrors and tragedies, even past the borders of Na Qis, where it was less reviled.

All were dull and aged, telling her hardly anything she

did not already know of her newfound power. Nothing on life source itself. Not a single lesson or legend to be found on healing or revivals. No mention at all of any good that necromancy could do.

But this one was different. It seemed more grimoire than anything else, its browning pages etched with dulled illustrations and spells. Yet there was only one Rose cared for, scrawled into the very end of the tome.

The Spell of True Revival.

Flipping to the last page, the images swirled beneath her fingers. A body rising out of ash, remade and unmarred. *Alive.* Tears pricked her eyes as memories of Fen's corpse flashed through her mind.

Her fingers tightened around the grimoire. It wasn't what she'd set out to do on her travels. She'd only wanted to learn more about her power – strengthen it, so that death could never again touch those she loved. She'd truly been content to let her friend rest in peace. His choice made, his sacrifice honoured.

But finding this had felt like fate, if she'd ever believed in such a thing. A glimmer of hope that held her like a tether. For this spell required no sickening alchemical solutions nor the blood of innocents, like the one that had torn Fen from her last year. Rose's mouth grew dry as her thoughts swept back to that cold, dark basement. To Hollis's twisted cruelty and Fen's tearful goodbye as his life faded away before her.

Squeezing her eyes shut, she shook away the memory. This wasn't the same. Hollis's spell had traded three stolen lives as the price for one, but this one required nothing more than the very thing she now held in the palm of her hand. Silver tendrils pulsed against Rose's skin almost eagerly. With such power now in her grasp, how could she not even *try* to restore what was lost? So she'd secreted the tome away from

Soren, quietly gathering ingredients for the spell along their travels.

Hair stolen from Fen's bedroom at his mother's villa. Amber from the scorched shores of Old Pelanghe, and pyrite from the markets outside the mines of Rhal. It had almost been a macabre form of motivation for her. An impossible dream dangling just out of reach, driving her to hone her power, fuelling her lessons with Soren. And yet, she still couldn't say with any certainty that she was ready.

Rose rubbed the bare spot on her left forearm, the scars of her familiar's tattoo a faint memory upon her pale skin. It was a strange thing to be free of it. For so many years, she'd craved one – to be like the rest of her peers, to have that proof of her casting etched into her flesh.

The familiar's bond wasn't true life, just a scrap of magic made manifest in the shape of the caster's desire. But Rose had made it so. Imbuing her little crow with her source, setting her free from their bond and watching as she'd flown off to some far corner of the world. And never returned . . .

At least she'd been saved the fate of coming back here. The thought struck Rose with acridity as the cavalcade slowed, but she shook it away. She didn't need to run any more. She could face Dunhollow, even with all its scheming and pretension. She could wade through whatever spells and incantations she needed to. And she *would* revive Fen. Soon.

Her throat tightened. What would it be like to see him again? To hold him in her arms and bask in the warm glow of his easy smile? It stirred something within her. Some shattered, desperate part of her heart that leached into her magic.

Before she could stop it, source leapt from her fingers, silver tendrils swirling against the pages, bleeding into them. The tome bowed, groaning beneath her touch, as if she might draw life from the very depths of its dry, shrivelled pages.

But it was too much. *Too soon.* Her pulse skittered as she slammed the book shut. The gentle threads of her magic recoiled, rearing back with a searing heat as life morphed into flame.

'Shit,' Rose hissed, shaking the source away with a soft sizzle.

Her heart pounded in her ears as she stared down at her singed hands. Life was a familiar form. Wrapped in the scent of amber and honey, it flowed out of her easily, utterly her own. But flame?

She didn't quite understand how she'd stolen it from Fen. Perhaps it was the strange, untested magic of his orb that had fuelled her with his final breaths. Or maybe it was simply her connection to him as he'd threaded that line between life and death. Either way, it was his.

And yet, this power remained within her, volatile and unpredictable. So unlike him in that regard. But, in the haphazard moments that it flared out of her, she could swear the faintest hint of red wine and worn leather still held upon it. A last spark of him that refused to burn out.

'Careful.' Soren's voice made her jump, and she glanced up with a start.

He leaned against the doorframe, a kind smile on his lips. She could almost hear his lecture forming, warning her of the dangers of source left untamed. Yet no remonstrance came, Soren's gaze fixing instead on the tome in her lap.

Rose's heart leapt, but she resisted the urge to hide the book. If she did, it would only sharpen his questions, force answers she wasn't yet ready to give. Straightening, she cleared her throat.

'I didn't think you'd be back for a while yet.' She raised an eyebrow at him. 'Not with your gaggle of well-wishers.'

Soren ducked his head, a small smile pulling at his lips. *Perfect.* She forced herself to move slowly, tucking the book back into her satchel at an almost leisurely pace. Soren said nothing, if he even noticed at all. Whatever questions he'd had seemed to have fled as his dark eyes strayed out the compartment window.

A pang of guilt twisted Rose's stomach. It felt wrong, keeping the truth from him. But their travels had revived him as much as they had her, and she couldn't be the one to steal that away.

Though his curse kept him ever young in appearance, the years Soren carried with him had almost fallen away the further they went from Dunhollow. Rose eyed his umber skin, sun-kissed and glowing, even bathed in the dim light of the academy's perpetually pallid skies. There were no bags hanging beneath his eyes now, and his scars seemed lessened too, drawn in faint memories rather than etched in jagged lines. Even his hair was somewhat loosened from the tight thin braids he'd once worn, hanging now in long twists that glimmered with gold cuffs fastened throughout.

Watching him take to the grand libraries and archives like a fish to water hadn't exactly been a shock in the early days of their journey. But seeing him come alive under starlit skies, dancing on beaches and charming locals with his truly staggering linguistic knowledge had been such an unexpected pleasure. She'd always thought of him as vibrant – a rare star amid Dunhollow's bleak skies – but she'd never realized how much the place had dimmed his fire. Nearly as much as it had hers, as it turned out.

Yet his usual tweed jacket had already made its return, draped over an ochre cable-knit sweater and a pair of corduroy trousers. A crisp white blouse peeked out beneath his collar, and, though he'd stopped short of a full tie, there was a stiffness about him now that Rose hadn't seen in many months. The effect of Dunhollow, she supposed.

'This arrived for you,' he said finally, tossing a letter on to her lap.

'Who from?'

'Your mother. Since you're ignoring her letters, she's decided I'm the next best thing.'

Rose snorted, handing back the letter, unopened. 'You can burn it then.'

'I tried already.' His lips quirked. 'Seems she's charmed it against that.'

'Wonderful.'

Soren tugged at his collar. 'Perhaps you should read it. She's not there any more, you know. It could be harmless.'

Rose turned to the window as the station drifted into view. She very much doubted that.

By some small mercy, the consequences of her mother's negligence had finally caught up with her. In the wake of Fen and Aveline's deaths, the board – or, rather, Imrys Elaegius – had stripped her of her position as Dunhollow's chancellor and urged her to retire quietly. As far as Rose knew, she'd been relegated to living with some distant aunt in the Outer Isles of Ir Taril. Far too kind a fate, all things considered. Though it *would* torment her mother.

Cut off from the world she'd once carefully controlled and utterly forgotten? Rose almost grinned. It would eat her alive.

But, even from the tail end of nowhere, her mother would not retract her claws so easily. She would only sink them deeper, were she given even the slightest purchase. The desperation of having no other avenue of control driving her to fall back on old habits, and Rose had always been her favourite target.

Likely, it was only more complaints about her chosen degree field. She'd known her mother would hate that she'd selected a major from the School of Magical Theory; it had almost been an added bonus, even. Until she started sending cursed letters. Rose shifted in her seat. It was all poison, in the end, distilled to keep her small and contained.

'It's nothing I haven't heard before, I'm sure.'

Soren heaved a short sigh that sounded dangerously close to a scoff, before pushing himself off the doorframe. 'Any news from Sylvie?'

Sylvie. Rose's heart leapt. The only bright thing waiting for her at Dunhollow. Though Sylvie was hardly the sort to sit around, quietly pining for Rose's return. If her letters were to be believed, she'd wasted no time reclaiming her spot as top student. Rose could only imagine that meant she once again had the entire school wrapped around her little finger.

Power had always suited Sylvie. And, after spending the best part of the last year lost in shadow and blood, she deserved to spill some of her own. Metaphorically, at least . . . Rose hoped.

But, gods, she couldn't wait to see her. Sylvie was, perhaps, the only reason that she'd even resigned herself to returning and finishing her degree. The thought of seeing those warm amber eyes once more set alight a heat in Rose that even her flames could not match.

'Not since last week,' she said finally.

'She knows you're coming back today?'

'I told her in my last letter.' Rose glanced at the darkening sky outside the window as the cavalcade lurched to a stop. 'Though I'm sure she expected us earlier.'

At this rate, they might miss the welcome feast entirely. Not that it would be the worst thing in the world.

Soren flashed her a sheepish grin and reached for his luggage. 'Well, can't help a few delays.'

Rose shook her head. 'Delays' was an interesting euphemism to describe his panicked shopping spree for last-minute gifts. She'd never seen anyone quite so frantic over luxury Telemestran scarves and fine Arbelian perfumes. Soren grunted beneath the weight of his new satchel as he pulled it down from the rack above.

It took some time to gather all their luggage together – mostly Soren's – before they finally trudged off the cavalcade and into the station. It wasn't too busy this late in the evening, with only a few stragglers weaving past, charmed luggage bobbing over their heads.

Muttering a spell under his breath, Soren whisked all their bags up in a charm before leading Rose off towards the grand doors. The sun had almost set when they exited the station, fog hanging low between the lamp posts that dotted Dunhollow village in a hazy glow.

Rose's breath hung on the air as she sighed deeply. There was a heaviness to being back. An ill-worn weight to the familiarity of slick cobblestones and leaning wood-slatted buildings. The gambling den and smokehouse still stood in lit anticipation of the first-night festivities. The river churned along as always, water gurgling faintly over the rocks, and starlight remained dimmed and hidden behind ever present clouds. Not a single thing had changed in her absence.

No. Rose's eyes strayed to one building, dark and dour among the rest. One thing had changed. The pub stared innocently back at her, a dilapidated echo of the haven it had once been. The lights along the trim of its thatched roof sagged from its frame, burnt out and battered. Around its shuttered windows, gnarled tangles of dead flowers rustled in a light breeze, and the rickety wooden sign hung askew over the doorway, almost as if dejected by its downfall.

A large sign was plastered across the front door with neat bold letters. UNDER NEW MANAGEMENT, it read. Below that was another word, this one in crimson lines that had been scorched into the wood.

MURDERER.

Rose's throat tightened. Damp, musty stones clung to her memory. Listless forms sprawled out in a sickly green light, and Fen's blood pouring between her fingers, not even slowed by the razing heat of her magic. Her breath came out in short, shallow gasps as she stumbled back.

'Rose?' Soren's voice broke through her reeling thoughts. 'Are you all right?'

She swallowed hard. But when she turned to face him, his eyes were fixed firmly on the pub behind her. His kind features twisted, flitting between pain and sorrow almost too fast for her to catch. Her heart sank, pricked by the keen sting of pity.

He'd lost just as much as she had in the depths of that place. His life, his friend, his love – all over again. Her nails bit into the skin of her palms. It held ghosts enough for them both.

She forced a thin smile. 'Fine.'

Soren's gaze lingered on the pub a moment longer before his eyes flicked to their luggage. With a frown, he pulled his watch from his pocket. 'We should get going.' He scratched at his neatly trimmed beard. 'Mind bending the rules?'

Before Rose could answer, Soren mumbled an incantation with a twist of his hand. A shimmering pane sprang forth before them, almost as if he'd conjured a mirror. But its edges faded into smoky stardust, its surface carved from molten silver. *A portal*, she marvelled. Not usually something most would cast as an afterthought, but Soren was never one to be bogged down by convention.

Shaking her head, Rose took his hand as he led her through the glassy surface. It shifted and wavered around them with a soft *pop* before depositing them on the stone steps of Dunhollow's main hall. Rose's head spun, and she swayed slightly as she straightened.

'Sorry, been a while since I've cast that – might leave you a bit wobbly.' Soren brushed off his jacket.

Rose shook her head, eyeing the bags at their feet. 'What about our luggage?'

'Ah, yes.' He paused, casting another charm before their valises simply floated away. 'Now, are you ready?'

Rose sucked in a sharp breath, glancing up at the clock tower looming above the grand doors of the main hall. Nearly seven o'clock. At least the open bar would be over by now. The start-of-term speeches too if the new chancellor were at all merciful. With any luck, her peers would just be tucking into the feast and they could slip in relatively unnoticed.

Yet Rose couldn't force her feet to move. She stared up at the oaken doors before her, but the thought of shoving them open sent a shiver down her spine. With a sigh, she turned back to the courtyard.

Golden leaves rustled upon the breeze, caught in the dim glow flickering out of the halls that surrounded them. Ancient gargoyles glared down at her from the gutters, barely visible at this hour. But she knew they were there. As they always would be. Entirely unchanged, like everything else in this damned place.

All of a sudden, it felt stale and cloying. Like a cage crushing her behind its bars, locked tight and chained with the scars of aching memories. Rose wanted nothing more in that moment than to turn and flee back.

But she couldn't. Not any more.

'Yeah,' she said finally. 'Let's get this over with.' Straightening, she glared up at the doors and shoved them aside before she could think better of it, stepping into the hall.

Almost immediately, Rose stumbled to a stop.

She'd expected the boisterous din of a feast, platters whizzing about faster than gossip and her peers trading insipid tales of their summers. But the aged wooden walls held in utter silence, ensconced in the warm glow of flickering candlelight.

The new chancellor glowered down at Rose and Soren from the dais at the front of the room, and long tables stretched out across the hall between them, packed tight with students. Her peers' plates were picked over, and their wine glasses full, but no idle chatter flowed between them. Instead, they all turned in unison to stare.

Rose's heart sank into the pit of her stomach. *Shit.*

Her eyes flashed to Soren, who gave her a small shrug before slinking off to the professors' table. Rose swallowed hard, gazing out over the ranks of her peers. Until she met a pair of familiar amber eyes across the room and the rest of the hall all but faded. *Sylvie.* For a moment, Rose was struck by the urge to race across the room and embrace her. Lose herself in the floral notes of orchid and musk and the soft curve of Sylvie's lips.

But then those very same lips quirked in a sly smirk, jarring Rose from her thoughts. Heat crept up her cheeks and her heart pounded against her ribs. Straightening her shoulders, she schooled her features into a mask of condescending superiority that would make even Sylvie proud and marched over to the nearest table.

The students at the end of the bench parted as if she had the plague, and she settled between them with a wan smile. Glancing back at Sylvie, Rose winked, making her roll her eyes. But then the chancellor cleared his throat, drawing Rose's attention back to the front of the room.

'Welcome, Messere Thenlif.' His dull eyes narrowed at her. 'Thank you for joining us.'

Rose gave a curt nod, eyeing the chancellor. Woodstone, Sylvie had called him in her letters. Rumour was that he'd come straight from the ranks of the empress's court to take over the position, though he didn't really look the part. Most imperial courtiers dressed more like Ewan or their father. Features smoothed out or sharpened by glamours and the latest fashions enhanced by increasingly gaudy accessories. Dyed hair or eyes, jewels dripping off every bare bit of skin – that sort of thing.

Even now, Rose spotted Ewan's gold-streaked hair catching in the candlelight from where they sat beside Sylvie. But Woodstone was rather plain in comparison. Dull brown hair lay slicked back behind his ears, streaked with grey, and his hazel eyes did not shimmer. Even his robes were a simple charcoal, covered with the aged sapphire chancellor's shawl that her mother wouldn't have been caught dead in, even if it was tradition.

By appearances alone, he seemed her mother's complete opposite. Rose's jaw tightened. He was willing to take over Dunhollow, though, so they must at least share in their corruption.

'Thank you, Chancellor.'

A few whispers and snickers went up from around the room, but Rose ignored them. Instead, she plucked some sandwiches from the sparse platters passing by. Her mother never would've saved the speeches for after the feast. She would have had them all sit in her thrall until they starved before giving an inch.

'As I was saying, now that you're all here and mostly sated, we have a very special announcement to start off the term.' Woodstone adjusted some papers on his pulpit. 'Many of you already know, I'm sure, that Dunhollow will be hosting the decennial Ashwood Tournament this autumn semester, and tonight we will be choosing three students to represent us against our rival academies, Maalstrum Institut and Savoissanta DeVoil.'

The Ashwood Tournament? Rose blinked. The last time it was held, she'd been only twelve, and it had been hosted by DeVoil, far away on the Isle of Arbelis. Soren had taken a sabbatical that semester to advise, given that he was the only professor on the roster from the Isle. She remembered her tear-stained farewell to him, begging him not to leave her alone with her mother.

Rose gritted her teeth. That was a long time ago now.

Honestly, she'd never cared for the tournament, really. For the most part, it was only an excuse for the three academies to leverage their prestige against each other. With Dunhollow priding itself on moulding the empire's next generation of pedigreed prats, it almost always won anyway.

'Before you all get too excited, competitors must be twenty-one or older in order to qualify and will be selected only from the top ten students.'

With a wave of his unadorned hand, the candles dimmed and fluttering sheets of paper sprang forth from seemingly nowhere to dance around Woodstone's head. Ten sheets for ten students. *Top students.*

Rose's heart sank and her eyes flew to Sylvie. When she'd left, they'd both been at the head of their class. But, after everything, surely that didn't still count? Gods, she hoped not. The tournament wasn't usually deadly, but then she would've said the same of Dunhollow once.

'Of those chosen, you will have the chance to accept or decline the opportunity. If the latter, then another name will be picked in your stead. Now, without further ado . . .'

Woodstone eyed the swirling names solemnly, as if this were some great burden he bore with the utmost care and respect. Rose rolled her eyes. So he did have some love for theatrics then. Finally, he reached for a name, unfurling the sheet with agonizing leisure.

'For our first competitor: congratulations to Arden Osiander!' The room filled with tepid applause as the paper leapt from Woodstone's hands and burst into sparkling letters that spelled Arden's name above the chancellor's head. 'Do you accept or decline the honour?'

The boy's flaming-red hair shone in the candlelight as he got to his feet, a smirk marring his sharp features. 'I accept.'

The applause tapered as Arden sauntered to the front of the room, and Rose wrinkled her nose. Clearly, the selection wasn't as impartial as Woodstone claimed. Arden hadn't even met the qualifications to graduate last year; he could hardly be considered a top student.

The hall fell back to silence as Woodstone lifted a hand. The sheets scattered around him, and he made a great show of grasping for and failing to catch a few of them. Some gasps rang out as the students watched, but most seemed content to sip away at their wine, their eyes glazed and gazes drifting.

Rose glanced down at the empty plates beneath them. No wonder Woodstone decided to feed them first – they might have eaten him alive for wasting all this time otherwise.

Slowly, Woodstone unfurled the next name. 'For our second competitor, congratulations to Sylven Belliaris!'

Rose froze as the hall broke into rapturous applause, the glimmering letters of Sylvie's name hanging over Woodstone's head like a curse. *No.* Her gaze locked on Sylvie again, who beamed widely as she stood. But her smile wavered, something dark dancing behind her eyes as they met Rose's. Something she couldn't quite place.

Her heart hammered so loudly in her ears she could barely hear Woodstone. 'Do you accept or decline the honour?'

Rose stared at Sylvie as if they were the only two in the hall. She silently willed her to decline, to be safe and sound and not put herself in undue danger. But there was a fire in Sylvie's eyes. A flame that could not be doused by fear. It was one of the reasons Rose loved her. But, in that moment, she'd never detested anything more as Sylvie's gaze flicked up to Woodstone.

'I accept.'

No. Rose's breath caught in her throat. She couldn't stop her mind reeling to the darkened, eerie corners of the pub basement. To Sylvie's crumpled form on a stone slab, drained and depleted to mere inches from death. It was rare for the tournament to claim a life, but it wasn't unheard of. She couldn't lose her again.

Rose tried to meet Sylvie's gaze, but she ducked her head as she took her place beside Arden. Why would she do this?

'And now, for our final competitor . . .' Woodstone's voice broke through her thoughts as he reached for the third and final name. But he paused as he unfurled it, shock flashing across his features. 'Rosera Thenlif.'

2. The More Things Changed

The entire hall fell into stunned silence, as if Woodstone had frozen them all with some spell. In fairness, he seemed more shocked than anyone, eyeing the paper he held as if sure he'd read it wrong. Perhaps he had.

But, as the paper slipped from his fingers and twisted itself into sparkling letters, Rose's stomach sank. For it was her own name staring back at her, so bright and cheerful despite the dread coiling within her. Finally, the chancellor lifted his gaze to fix Rose with a hard stare.

'Well, Messere Thenlif?' His eyes narrowed. 'Do you accept or decline the honour?'

Rose's heart pounded loudly in her ears. Just below Woodstone's pulpit, she could feel Sylvie's gaze nearly boring a hole through her flesh. Soren's too, she imagined. But she refused to meet either of their eyes. Did they fear for her? Doubt her, perhaps?

After all, how could she ever hope to compete? Yet the thought of it burned at her. Some shred of spite that refused to be cowed by their judgement and buried beneath the weight of expectation. She couldn't do it any more.

'I accept.'

'Very well.' Woodstone's lips thinned. 'Then congratulations to our three competitors. I look forward to seeing you compete.'

A burst of rather muddled, unsure applause broke out over the hall, but Rose didn't move to join the others at the front of the room. Somehow it felt wrong. Like a doorway had been left open to her, yet she could not bring herself to cross the threshold.

'As for the rest of you, please enjoy your evening, and I hope to see you all at the welcome breakfast tomorrow morning.'

With one last flick of his wrist, the papers zipped back into Woodstone's pocket, and he swept out of the hall without another word. Rose stared after him, a hollow weight taking root in her chest. Somehow, she couldn't shake the feeling that she'd already made an enemy of him, like she was a flaw in his otherwise immaculate performance, and there was nothing a showman hated more than having their spotlight stolen.

She let out a small sigh. Around her, the other students settled back to the remnants of the feast, the selection results already fuelling their gossip. Most eyed her over the rims of their goblets, hushed whispers hissing between their ranks. Others ambled out of the hall, snickering as they went. Rose's throat tightened, her fists curling at her sides.

She couldn't stand to be there a moment longer. And yet she was loath to give them the satisfaction of watching her flee. Not this time. Shifting her shoulders back, she straightened out the pleats of her skirt and turned primly on her heel, marching out of the hall. Which wasn't all that much more dignified, she supposed, but it was something.

The cool night air hit her with an almost soothing chill as she stepped outside. But it didn't stop the heat creeping up her skin, burgeoning into flame. Swallowing back tears, she hurried past huddled packs of her peers, coming to a stop behind one of the pillars of the colonnade lining the courtyard.

She sucked in shuddering breaths, trying and failing to douse her magic. What had she been thinking? For every ounce of strength and skill she'd wrested for herself, this place stole it all in an instant. Rose gritted her teeth as fire licked at the soft hairs of her forearm. She never should have come back here.

'Thenlif!'

Rose's source cut off with a jolt, the cool breeze aching against her raw skin as she turned. A blur of dark plaid and gossamer hair stormed towards her, slamming into her soundly. Warm lips pressed against hers, familiar floral scents of orchid and musk swimming through her muddled mind. *Sylvie.*

Rose leaned into the kiss, her fingers tangling through Sylvie's soft hair. All at once, every stray doubt, every fear simply vanished, like a flame snuffed out. Whatever poison these halls held, standing there, wrapped in the warmth of Sylvie's arms, felt like home. A small smile tugged at her lips as Sylvie leaned back, brushing a curl from Rose's forehead.

'Gods, you're a sight for sore eyes.' The words fell softly from her tongue, yet anger lingered in her eyes – hot and piercing. 'But what were you thinking?'

Rose's heart leapt, words stuck on her tongue. Sylvie's gaze held her as if in some spell. Her dark hair fell gently around her face like a curtain, tawny skin flushed. She hadn't changed a bit. And for the first time that night, Rose was utterly glad of it.

She was still achingly beautiful. So fierce and fiery in her fury. Yet utterly reckless. Rose's pulse faltered as the vibrant visage before her flickered, fading to Sylvie lying flat on the slab in the basement of the pub, skin pale and hair matted, her life slowly drained from her. Bile bit at the back of her throat.

'Me?' she spat. 'What about you? You could have declined.'

Sylvie's brow furrowed. 'Why would I do that?'

Rose blanched. She couldn't be serious. 'Because it's dangerous? If anything happened to you again, I—'

'Is *that* what this is about?' Sylvie's eyes softened, but her tone lost none of its edge. 'Thenlif, that was a year ago, and I'll be fine. The Ashwood Tournament is rarely lethal.'

'How reassuring!' Rose scoffed, her eyes flicking away from Sylvie.

Even in the dim light, she caught their peers' gazes sliding over to the pair of them, whispers and smirks running rampant through their vapid little cliques. Shameless, every last one of them. And yet, when she glanced back at Sylvie, there was a flash of something in her gaze as it flitted between Rose and the others. *Humiliation*. There and gone – almost imperceptible before it hardened into resolve.

Rose's stomach sank. Was *that* why she'd done it? The judgement of their peers? No, Sylvie only kept herself on top so none of them would bother her. Yet maybe it wasn't about what she wanted to prove to them, but rather to herself. That she was still strong; that even death could not quell her. Rose bit down hard on her tongue. That, at least, she could understand.

'You don't need to prove anything.'

Sylvie's eyes flashed, then hardened. 'Do you? You're so worried that the tournament will be too much for me, but what about you? You can't even—'

'Can't what?' Rose snapped, the words burning against her tongue with a searing acridity. 'Cast? Protect myself?'

'I—' Sylvie's eyes widened just for a moment before her expression darkened. Crossing the space that had grown between them, she pulled Rose aside and lowered her voice. 'Look, all you have to defend yourself is necromancy and fire source you can barely control. It's too risky for you to compete.'

Rose recoiled. She was right, of course, but that didn't make it sting any less. That Sylvie still saw her as helpless, unable to survive on her own merit.

'And here I was thinking we might work together.' She bit out the words through an empty smile. 'But I suppose it's too much to ask that Dunhollow's star student share in her glory.'

Glaring up at Sylvie from beneath her lashes, Rose held her gaze a moment longer before turning on her heel. But Sylvie caught her sleeve, drawing her to a sharp halt.

'Rose, wait—'

She whirled, words poised like poison against her tongue, when a black-clad figure stepped forth from the crowd behind them. Their gold-streaked hair caught in the light, their blue eyes dulled by boredom, even at this distance.

'As entertaining as this is, perhaps you two could air your dirty laundry privately?' Ewan sighed, waving a hand blithely at the students gathered round. 'You're attracting flies.'

Rose almost rolled her eyes as they flashed her a crooked grin. As if she should have been graced by their presence. But she had no patience for it now.

'Don't worry.' She yanked her arm away from Sylvie. 'The show's over anyway.'

Before either of them could utter another word, Rose turned and tore off down the colonnade. She brushed away tears as she darted past the library, heading for Crannaigh Hall. She wasn't even sure her dorm was still there, but it would hardly surprise her. Nothing else in this damned place had changed, why should that?

She pushed through the dorm hall doors without slowing. Storming up the wooden staircase, Rose ignored the first-years who practically dived out of her path. Dunhollow was nothing more than an ageing, festering rot, held on the edge of demise yet stubbornly refusing the inevitable fall into the abyss. Anything that grew here did so from poisoned roots, even her and Sylvie.

Gritting her teeth, she blinked up at her dormitory door, still the plainest one in the hall. Shaking her head, Rose threw it open and then stilled.

She'd expected nothing more than dust and dark corners, yet the room looked almost untouched. Candles flickered gently beside her four-poster bed as she stepped inside, nearly tripping over her luggage. Straightening, she eyed the neatly stacked books within their shelves and the tidy desk across the way. Even her plethora of plants still hung, vibrant and ever growing in their baskets. As if some intrepid hand had wrapped it all in a preservation charm like some sort of shrine. Sylvie, probably. The thought brought fresh tears to her eyes.

Gently closing the door, Rose tossed her satchel down beside her dresser and sank into the warmth of her bed. Her sheets smelled of oakmoss and fresh linen, but they were soon sullied by the stain of her tears. Of all the people she'd expected to discredit her, Sylvie hadn't been among them.

Once, she would've counted her as chief among her critics, but now? Rose sniffled. How quickly things fell back into familiar, rotten patterns. She'd travelled halfway around the world, and yet here she was, once again found wanting by her peers. Still weak, still strange. Still broken. *Never enough.*

Just like she wasn't enough to save Fen.

Rose jumped as a tapping on her window jarred her from her reverie. For a brief, wild moment, she assumed it was Sylvie. But the thought fled as quickly as it came as she squinted at the feathered figure flapping beyond the panes.

'*Prea?*' she gasped. *It couldn't be.*

She should've been leagues away, released into the protected forests of northern Ir Taril. And yet, there she was, staring back at Rose, head tilted as she watched her keenly. She darted over to the window and yanked it open. The little crow clicked her beak before hopping on to Rose's outstretched arm and cawing loudly.

Rose flinched, but Prea's form didn't waver or sink into her skin now. She was solid and bright – altogether her own. And so *alive*.

Her mind spun as if she'd downed a bottle of wine. *She'd done it.* Her magic had actually been strong enough. Threads of source woven into life where none had been before. And it still had not faded.

Nor had any other life. Her heart leapt. She hadn't stolen anyone's life force, like Hollis had. She hadn't even harmed anyone, besides maybe a slight headache on her part after the casting. And, if that was all it cost, then what else was she capable of?

The Spell of True Revival.

Setting Prea down on the windowsill, Rose scrambled over to her bag, wrenching the tome from its depths. The crow prattled from her perch as the book flipped open to the final page, almost of its own accord. But Rose didn't slow at all, shuffling through the bag for her ingredients and settling them around her as the book instructed.

Amber on her right, to strengthen the bonds of life. Pyrite to her left, to ward away the cold grip of death. And Fen's hair just before her, to bring him forth into this world. To bring him *back*. The only thing missing now was her.

Rose's throat tightened painfully, her hands shaking as she reached for the tome. What if this didn't work? Creating life like Prea's was one thing, but what if she couldn't return one? What if she wasn't strong enough?

No. She shoved the thought away. She may not have been enough to save Fen then, but she could be now. She had to be.

Sitting back on her heels, Rose sucked in a steadying breath and sank fervently into the depths of her magic. It sprang to life almost instantly, silver light curling and coiling around her in shimmering strands. With one final glance at Prea, she placed her palm against the rough parchment of the tome, let her source seep into the pages, and cast the spell.

3. True Revival

A harsh pounding grated Rose's ears. Distant and dull, it beat in tandem to the throbbing pulse at her temples. Her eyes fluttered open to dim daylight, and she found herself staring up at her mossy ceiling, her back pressed firmly against the cold stone floor.

Rose sat up with a jolt, blinking away stars as her head spun. She scanned the floor around her, littered with ash and scorch marks, her memory flickering dimly in recognition. *The Spell of True Revival.*

The incantation still sat heavy on her tongue, the stale stench of decay hanging over her like fog over a river at dawn. And yet, she was utterly alone. The bitter taste of bile soured at the back of her throat. Prea was gone, the window wide open, and Fen was nowhere to be seen.

Rose blinked down at the ritual circle beneath her. The lock of Fen's hair still sat at its centre – singed and matted but nothing more than a lifeless remnant. Pushing herself on to her knees, she searched frantically for the grimoire. But all she could find in its place was a pile of ash. Her heart sank. The spell hadn't worked. And any hope of recasting it lay shrivelled before her.

Rose ran her fingers numbly over the residue of amber, thick lines of soot crawling up her arms. The result of the spell backfiring, no doubt. Her throat tightened.

All that effort, all that time spent growing her power, and none of it had mattered. Tears pricked her eyes, but she wiped them away with the coarse edge of her sleeve. The pounding echoed again, and her gaze flew to the door.

'Rose?' A muffled voice crept through it. *Sylvie's voice.* 'Are you in there?'

Shit.

Rose's heart fluttered like a caged bird as she stood and brushed off her clothes. She couldn't see Sylvie like this. Stepping back quietly, she cringed when her heel connected with the charred remains of her pyrite, sending it clattering across the stone floor.

'Come on.' Sylvie's voice grew softer. 'I know you're still angry, but we need to talk.'

If only that was all it was. Rose groaned inwardly. She knew Sylvie wouldn't be easily deterred; it simply wasn't in her nature. And she was far too clever to be fooled by any paltry excuse Rose might give for her current state. An unfortunate side effect of their long-standing rivalry, she supposed. They knew each other's patterns – every feature and every fracture of their facades. The truth could not be contained by any mask either of them wore. Not any more.

Cursing softly, Rose glanced down at her scorched travel clothes and then to her wardrobe. Rushing forth, she hastily grabbed a change of clothes and ducked into her washroom. Better to face the inevitable head on. She eyed her hiding place with a grimace. Somewhat, anyway.

'Fine, come in,' she called out. 'I'll be out in a minute.'

Rose turned the tap of her sink with a squeak, running her soot-stained arms beneath the cool water. Vaguely, Rose heard Sylvie's soft footfalls over the sound of the gushing tap as she entered the bedroom. A shiver skittered down Rose's spine, and she scrubbed harder, until her pale skin was pink and mottled.

Risking a glance in the mirror, she grimaced. Her eyes were

a sunken mess, and her auburn curls lay flat against her head, frayed and frizzed at the ends. She'd meant to bathe last night. To wash off her travels and the strain of being back.

A snort slipped from her lips before she splashed water over her face. How naive she'd been, thinking all would go according to plan. Now all that remained of the previous night was little more than ash and blank memories. What had she *done*?

Rose lifted her head, patting her face dry. She remembered Prea's return, desperately casting the Spell of True Revival. But after that? Only flashes. The silvery light of her life source enveloping her, burning against her skin. Fen's warm smile rising out of cool depths, and then nothing. Just shadows and smoke.

A wave of nausea rolled over her, and Rose steadied herself on shaky arms. She should never have cast it. Not like that anyway.

Ruining her only chance in a haze of anger and bruised pride. *Fen's* only chance. She bit back tears, reaching instead for her comb. Though the pain of its teeth catching her curls did little to soothe her. She was lucky that the worst she'd done was seemingly knock herself out. Rose checked over her arms and legs as she removed her skirt.

Her hands and wrists were pink and raw, but by some miracle there were no scrapes or bruises to speak of. None visible, anyway. But her heart ached beneath the weight of old scars, wrenched open all over again.

Pressing her lips thin, she pulled on her blouse and trousers. There was little she could do about it now. Turning, she examined her reflection in the mirror, checking briefly for any fault or fracture that Sylvie's keen eyes might find. Fissures that had been mended by her time away still lingered beneath the surface.

Rose's skin was somewhat darker beneath the sun-kissed glow from the white-sand beaches of Belel, her nose and cheeks dusted with chestnut freckles. Her hair now fell just beneath her shoulders – a style that was all the rage in the salons of Tol Qilius. Even the blouse she wore was in the Salirellean fashion, a high collar that sat snugly against her neck, threads of silver weaving down the dangerously low neckline, almost to the high waist of her slim black trousers. It was a far cry from the oversized sweaters and gaunt visage she'd sported at the start of term last year.

But something sharp and shattered lingered in the whiskey-brown hue of her hazel eyes. Like a mirror that showed only dark reflections of the past. She sighed, brushing a curl from her forehead. It would have to do.

Bracing herself, she threw open the door. In spite of everything, her heart leapt, hammering erratically against the cage of her ribs as she caught sight of Sylvie. She sat upon the edge of the bed, staring out the window. Until she turned, and her amber eyes widened, rust-red lips parting in a small gasp.

Her ink-black gossamer hair coiled around a cream turtle-neck, which cinched into a brown plaid skirt around her slim waist. Her tawny skin practically glowed in the dim morning light, making her look like some ethereal work of art. It was all Rose could do not to stare. For her part, Sylvie stared right back, her cheeks flushing as she looked Rose up and down.

'Oh,' she said finally. 'Erm, hi.'

'Hi.'

Rose ducked her head, staring down at the pointed silver toes of her black heels. How strange it was that for most of their years together being at Sylvie's throat had been a familiar comfort. Yet now a few sharp words hung on the air between them like a sea of knives – cutting and impenetrable.

After a long moment of silence, Sylvie cleared her throat, her eyes darting to the floor. 'Look, I – I wanted to apologize.'

Rose blinked in surprise but then sighed. 'Me too.'

'No, you were right.' Sylvie sank back on to the bed. 'I could've declined – should have, probably. The tournament doesn't really matter to me, but when my name was called it felt like . . . I don't know . . . a chance to prove myself, I guess?'

Rose bit the inside of her lip. That was something they had in common, she supposed. But Sylvie had never had anything to prove to anyone, save perhaps herself. And she could hardly judge her for that now.

Rose moved to her side, the mattress shifting beneath her. 'You were right too. Accepting was impulsive, and I shouldn't have.'

'No.' Sylvie tucked a curl behind Rose's ear, the scent of her perfume lingering between them like a soft promise. 'I think you *should* compete.'

Rose scoffed. 'You can't be serious.'

'I am.' Sylvie leaned back on her hands, staring up at the ceiling with a tired sigh. 'This place has made us feel small for too long and always pitched us against each other. It would be nice to fight on the same side for once.'

Rose stared at her. How cruelly ironic it was that the moment Sylvie decided to agree with her, she realized the foolishness of her own stance. As if some petty deity conspired to keep them always at odds. But Sylvie had been right last night – competing *would* be more dangerous for Rose.

As much as she'd grown in her magic, any charge of necromancy would strip it all away. Besides, how could she hope to keep up with competitors who'd practised magic their whole lives when she had only a few paltry months under her belt?

She shook her head. 'Don't you mean "again"?'

'Do I?' Sylvie's tongue caught between her teeth in a cheeky grin.

'Regardless, I may not get a choice. I don't think Woodstone meant to call my name last night – who knows if he'll even let me.'

'Yeah, he sent a summons.' Sylvie held up a snarling slip of paper. 'I found this chewing on your door.'

Rose's stomach sank. 'Oh.'

'Don't worry.' Sylvie's smile slid into a smirk as she leaned in closer, her eyes darkening. 'Whatever nonsense he tries, I'm sure you can be suitably convincing.'

Rose's pulse leapt as Sylvie caught her bottom lip between her own, as if her touch had lit a fire in her veins. She trailed kisses along Rose's jawline, the tantalizing aroma of her perfume drawing her in like a fresh spring bloom.

She caught Sylvie's earlobe between her teeth, eliciting a sharp gasp that sent heat pooling straight between her thighs. Her fingers tangled through Sylvie's hair, and her lips dived ever lower, gently caressing the delicate flesh of Sylvie's neck. And what a pretty neck it was. So soft and fragile. *So easy to snap or slice.*

Rose pulled away with a start. What was *that*?

'Rose?' Sylvie's eyes searched hers, her thumb grazing her bottom lip gently. 'What's wrong?'

'Nothing.' She swallowed hard, pushing off the bed. 'We should, er, go see Woodstone.'

Sylvie caught her hand. 'Are you sure?'

No. The truth almost tumbled out, but she held it against her tongue like a bitter poison. 'I'm fine – really.'

Sylvie stared at her for a long moment but said nothing, instead turning for the door. Yet, as Rose followed behind her, whispers of source reached out to her. *Sylvie's source.* Those thin threads woven between life and death. How easy it would be to snip right through them. Her pulse throbbed with an aching hunger. One clean cut was all it would take to silence those whispers for ever.

The ornate obsidian door of the chancellor's office stared down at Rose – dark with jagged swirling edges carved along its surface, as if it had been pulled from the very depths of a volcano. She'd stood before it countless times, though it had always been her mother's door then – as sharp and austere as she'd been: a towering threshold that hid behind it every dreadful memory her mother had left her with.

And yet, now it was nothing more than a relic. A reminder of what no longer was.

'She's not there any more,' Sylvie said gently, as if she'd read Rose's mind.

Rose startled, but then nodded. 'I know.'

Though, somehow, there was a part of her that almost wished she was. That her mother still sat within, insidious and mesmerizing, her tongue poised with poison. How delicious it would be to tear it from her wretched mouth, leaving those vapid lips of hers painted red only with her own blood.

Rose's pulse skittered beneath her skin, her breath catching in her throat as she bit back the brutal urge. It came from some dark part of her heart and crept out of her with startling acerbity. Some residual effect of her spell backfiring, perhaps?

She shuddered. At least, turned against her mother, it made a cruel sort of sense. But it did nothing to loosen the cold, hard dread coiling in the pit of her stomach.

Sylvie gave her a gentle nudge. 'Ready?'

Rose squared her shoulders, shaking off her macabre thoughts. Whatever this strange urge was, she could do nothing about it now. 'As I'll ever be.'

Sucking in a sharp breath, she raised her fist, rapping her knuckles primly against the door. For a moment, there was nothing but silence, pricking the doubt taking root within her.

Then, finally, Woodstone's voice rang out. 'Enter!'

Steeling herself, Rose cautiously pushed the door open, then blinked at the brightly lit room. Gone was the dark panelling that had once held the space in an oppressive shroud, replaced instead by light maplewood, glimmering with a gilded glow in the dappled sunshine that flickered through the stained-glass windows. A charm, Rose was sure – even Woodstone couldn't rid Dunhollow of its ever present clouds. Still, it made the space so *warm*. Open and welcoming, it was nothing like it had been under her mother's tenure. No magical trinkets whirred overhead, no alarms and messages trilled from an overfilled calendar. Now the only sounds were the soothing lilt of flute music from somewhere overhead and the soft bubbling of a brook, as if one flowed directly beneath their feet.

It was utterly peaceful. And yet, just as false as her mother's facades – nothing more than a harmless veneer covering sharp fangs. Rose wrinkled her nose at the sickly sweet aroma of caramel, a faint acrid stench lingering beneath. The signature of Woodstone's magic, she assumed.

Her eyes flicked to the ornate desk at the centre of the room, where the man himself sat alongside Ewan and Soren. Rose faltered, drawing up short just over the threshold. Woodstone she'd expected, of course, but she couldn't fathom what the other two were doing here. Soren flashed her a brief smile, but his eyes didn't quite meet hers. Ewan did not even move from where they reclined in one of the chairs, a roll-up dangling between their fingers, a thin thread of smoke trailing up towards the arched ceilings.

'Ah, Messeres Thenlif and Belliaris.' Woodstone waved a

hand, calling forth two more chairs from the upper level of the office. 'Thank you for joining us. Please, have a seat.'

Flashing a glance at Sylvie, they both sank slowly into the leather chairs. Rose's jaw clenched as a platter of cloudy silver drinks swept in front of them. She took one politely but didn't sip it. Whatever semblance of peace this place promised, she didn't trust it for a moment. Yet Woodstone's features betrayed nothing behind his amicable smile.

'Well –' Ewan's bored drawl broke through her thoughts – 'now that we're all here, perhaps you'd care to explain why, Chancellor?'

'Of course.' His eyes shifted to Ewan before he leaned forward in his chair. 'You're here because last night, yours was the final name that should have been called.'

'Should've been?' Sylvie echoed, setting her untouched glass on the edge of Woodstone's desk. 'So you're saying the selection was rigged?'

'Calculated, Messere Belliaris – not rigged.' A flash of annoyance danced across the chancellor's features. 'Messere Thenlif may meet the academic requirements to qualify, but her practical skill is still lacking. After consulting the tournament rules with Professor Sylverfir, we decided to begin by alerting all parties.'

Rose's gaze slid towards Soren, but he avoided it. Was he actually working with Woodstone and his 'calculations'? Why?

Ewan's dark brows inched up their forehead. 'So you're still giving me the chance to accept or decline, even though my name was never called?'

'It seemed only fair.'

'And if I were interested, what then?' Their gaze flicked to Rose. 'The two of us would have to duel for the opportunity?'

'No,' Soren blurted out. 'We were thinking a simple show of skill, should both parties be willing.'

Ewan's blue eyes narrowed as they leaned forward, taking a deep draw from their roll-up. 'Because the chancellor is hoping a little test of power will scare off Rose so he can quietly sweep his mistake under the rug, is that it?'

Rose almost snorted as Woodstone's eyes widened. Clearly, he wasn't familiar with Ewan at all, if their bluntness shocked him. More than likely, Ewan considered the tournament either a dreadful bore or a waste of time. Probably both. Besides, they already had power and prestige in spades; they hardly needed to fight for it, or the post-graduation opportunities that winning the tournament usually secured. All of that was surely beneath them.

Though that might not be entirely fair, Rose had to grudgingly admit. They had improved vastly after the events of last year if Sylvie's letters were to be believed. Still a pretentious arse half the time, but an amusing one, at least.

Finally, Chancellor Woodstone frowned, tenting his fingers beneath his chin. 'It is a matter of safety, Messere Elaegius. We cannot, in good conscience, send someone to represent Dunhollow unprepared for the trials of the Ashwood Tournament, and . . .' He faltered, clearing his throat. 'Well, your father made clear he wished to see you participate.'

Rose raised an eyebrow. So *that's* what this was really about. Woodstone didn't care about her safety – this was just a chance for the great Imrys Elaegius to ensure his heir still danced to his tune. Or to prove his own power over this place hadn't waned. Why, she couldn't fathom. It wasn't like he'd lost any standing last year. Though the Order of Salix had been firmly dismantled after Hollis's crimes became known, Imrys's multitude of misdeeds had conveniently never seen the light of day.

'I see.' Ewan tapped their roll-up into the floating ashtray beside them, lips quirked in a wicked grin. 'In that case, I'm afraid I'll have to decline the "honour", Chancellor. The position is all yours, Rose.'

Shock rippled across her own face. 'Er – thanks?'

'But, Messere, you can't—'

'I think you'll find I can, Chancellor.' Ewan heaved themself out of the chair, tossing their coat over their shoulder. 'Oh, and tell my father that he can choke on his wishes for all I care.'

Without another word, they swept out of the room, leaving a cloud of foul-smelling smoke and a thick silence in their wake. Rose blinked at the space they'd left behind, her mind reeling. She never thought she'd see the day they went against their father so blatantly. But then her eyes slid to Sylvie, who was beaming proudly, as if she'd been waiting for this moment.

'So –' Sylvie turned back to Woodstone, folding her arms over her chest – 'does that mean Rose can compete then?'

Woodstone coughed, waving away the remnants of Ewan's smoke. 'I, well, that's—'

Soren cut across him. 'Are you sure you want to, Rose? You can still back out.'

Rose recoiled, sharp words dancing along her tongue. Did he truly doubt her so? His deep brown eyes met hers now, swimming only with concern, but she wanted none of it. What had been the point of him helping her cultivate her magic if he was so afraid of her using it?

'Yes,' said Woodstone, a wan smile pulling at his lips, 'the professor mentioned that your casting has improved somewhat on your travels, but that your skill may still be ... deficient for the Ashwood Tournament.'

'Deficient?' Rose's voice inched up an octave as she rounded on Soren.

'No, Rose. I didn't—'

'And the competitors from Maalstrum and DeVoil will be among the best.' Woodstone got to his feet, gliding around the desk to lean against its edge. As if they were old friends having a chat, and he was not tearing apart her merit. 'There would be no shame in retracting your acceptance.'

Rose's skin prickled. Perhaps he was right. Perhaps he saw the truth she was content to ignore. That, for all the strength of her power, she was driven only by the need to prove a skill she did not possess. Like a child demanding praise for art that was nothing more than scribbled lines. Did she really think she could go up against the best the other academies had to offer? That she could contend with them when she had only paltry flames at her command and life source she couldn't even use freely?

Yet there was a part of Rose that rankled at dismissing herself so easily. It was what she'd always done, after all. But she had survived without magic this long. Surrounded by those determined to keep her small and contained, she had scrounged and scraped for every ounce of power she now held. She had fought for it, every step of the way, and she wouldn't let them cow her so easily this time.

Flames licked at the back of her mind, pulling heat from the air around her as they coiled at her fingers. Yet they did not burn her now. Did not sear or sizzle against her flesh. They were fierce, bright and altogether her own. Until the soft scent of red wine and worn leather washed over Rose, taking her back to stolen kisses and easy smiles. To the warmth of Fen's embrace fading to listless limbs. To death.

Her flames flared, hungry for every stray musing of grief, every ounce of rage her heart could bear. And they fled just as quickly, slamming into a nearby display case. It shattered with a great clatter, fire licking at its wooden frame and reaching all too quickly for the rug beneath. A cool blast of ice doused them in an instant, but it did nothing to settle Rose, even wrapped in Sylvie's signature of plum and lilac.

For a moment, the room was held in utter silence once more, broken only by the crackling of scorched wood and crumbling glass. Rose straightened, her eyes drifting slowly from the blaze she'd ignited. Sylvie's face was almost unreadable, drawn somewhere between shock and pride, though the faintest stirrings of concern danced beneath. Soren's, on the other hand, was crestfallen. But it wasn't sorrow that filled his gaze – it was fear.

Rose's chest tightened, her hands shaking as she tucked a curl behind her ear and turned back to Woodstone. 'I think you'll find, Chancellor, that I can manage just fine.'

Sparks danced within Woodstone's gaze as it slid back to her, a twisted, insidious smile creeping across his lips. 'Very well, Messere Thenlif.' He stuck out a hand to Rose. 'Welcome to the Ashwood Tournament.'

4. A Dunhollow Welcome

The arching heights of the assembly hall stretched out before Rose in a gaudy display. Elaborate chandeliers cascaded down from the ceiling, their dancing light flickering over the portraits and plaques upon the walls, paying tribute to Dunhollow's most revered scholars, distinguished alumni and benefactors. A scoff burned at the back of her throat. It was little more than a vulgar show of pride.

A sea of her fellow fourth-years dotted about the hall, crowded together in haphazard clusters. Their excited chatter ran rampant, buzzing about as if the hall were full of bees. Laughter bounced off the soaring ceilings, but it felt empty and hollow to Rose's ears. Still, it was rare to see her peers this excited about anything, and that it was due to something entirely outside their petty pedigreed cliques made it that much stranger.

They all waited with bated breath for the arrival of the other academies, preening like peacocks in their finest wear. Well, not full formal wear, perhaps, but their linen blouses were cleaned and crisp, waistcoats freshly pressed, and cravats artfully loosened. Rose rolled her eyes. It was all a game to them, she supposed. Maalstrum and DeVoil would only be bringing so many students, and any Dunhollow resident that managed to ensnare one in a romantic entanglement would likely get bragging rights for the rest of the year, if not for the remainder of their academic career.

Rose pressed a nail into the bed of her thumb. For all their insipid gossip, there was a part of her that wished she was with them. Any other year, she would've been, jaded to the display and desperate to depart the charade. But now she was a part of it.

Doomed by her own reckless hand to play the role of proud Dunhollow attendee, Rose found herself trapped upon the grand stage at the front of the hall with Sylvie and Arden. The thought of it soured on her tongue. Sapphire velvet curtains flanked them, adorned with the academy's crest, which was echoed in dancing patterns along the charmed stained-glass windows.

Beside her, Sylvie looked every bit the part – elegant and ornate with a dark starlit dress that skimmed her knees in shrouded wisps. A silver circlet crowned her head, dangling down in delicate jewelled threads atop the ink-black strands of her gossamer hair. Her full lips were painted a deeper red than usual and pulled in a strained smile, though her amber eyes were bright and alert as she watched the hall. She was beautiful and insidious, like a spider drawing its prey right into its web.

Her radiance was somewhat spoiled by Arden, however, who stood on Sylvie's other side, looking like a walking advert for prospective attendees of the academy. He sported an extravagant silver vest that glinted in the warm light, but was marred by a garish blue-velvet sash across his chest, Dunhollow's crest stitched into it. As if he'd elected to wear the curtains. A cruel smirk tugged at Rose's lips. His orange hair stood inches above his freckled forehead, caked with foul-smelling pomade. Perhaps that was the reason for his pinched mouth and furrowed brow.

Rose fidgeted with the sleeves of her own sapphire dress. It was a remnant of the year before, but one she was loath to be rid of. Sylvie had always loved this colour on her, after all.

Still, it fell about Rose stiffly now, like a costume that didn't quite fit.

Yet, next to Sylvie, it matched perfectly. Two gems alight in the night sky: Rose in the star-dusted sapphire of a late evening, while Sylvie was draped in the rich hues of an obsidian midnight. If the other academies were content to look only upon the surface, they would see nothing but the gilded facade. Which was, she supposed, the point of all this. They would never see the horrid shadows lingering around every corner. They would never know the secrets of these halls. They would never feel the cool grip of death that etched itself into every last stone.

After all, the last time the assembly hall had been decked out like this was to announce Aveline's untimely demise and that sham of an investigation. Not that any trace remained. Rose wasn't even sure the residents of Dunhollow remembered it. Her stomach sank. How easily the poor girl had faded from everyone's memories.

Her mind burned beneath the thought, and hungry flames crept from her fingertips. But a cool grip wrapped around her hand, laced with ice. Rose flinched as steam curled up between their fingers, her eyes catching Sylvie's with a soft gasp. They held her steady, soothing her.

'Thanks,' Rose muttered after a moment.

Sylvie nodded and turned away as Rose eyed the back of her bejewelled head. She too had witnessed the worst of Dunhollow, and yet she'd remained. At the time, it had been fair, of course, making up for what was stolen so cruelly from her. But now? It was a sad truth that there was a part of Sylvie that thrived here, and she seemed in no great hurry to let that go. *Perhaps not ever.* The thought made Rose's heart flip.

Suddenly, the room fell quiet, and Rose turned, her eyes

locking on Woodstone as he entered. Dressed once again in plain clothes and that awful shawl, he glided up the stage, taking to the podium languidly, as if he had all the time in the world. With a flick of his hand, the chandeliers' flames shifted to a sapphire hue, casting the room in a pallid glow that pricked Rose's unease. Sickly green flashed behind her eyes as she squeezed them shut, her heart hammering in her ribs.

'Good afternoon, everyone.' Woodstone's booming voice made her jump, her eyes flying open. 'Our friends from Maalstrum and DeVoil will be joining us shortly. Per Ashwood tradition, Dunhollow will have three competitors as the host academy, while the others will put forward only two of their best. But I expect you to give them all a warm Dunhollow welcome.'

Rose rolled her eyes. A Dunhollow welcome was more likely to include backstabbing and venomous rumours. Though perhaps the chancellor preferred to understate the truth of things as much as he did his own appearance.

Reputation was everything, after all. That, above all else at Dunhollow, would surely never change. She wondered briefly if it was some sort of prerequisite when the board considered a chancellor, that they be singularly concerned with the university's standing. Perhaps it was just an unhappy accident.

'Now, without further ado, from the forested shores of Arbelis: Savoissanta DeVoil!'

The words were barely out of Woodstone's mouth before the doors burst open, the floor erupting beneath the grip of shimmering green vines. The Dunhollow students leapt back, all wide eyes and nervous giggles as the DeVoil cohort glided past, glimmering with jewellery that looked to be crafted by vinewood and sea gems. They were sun-kissed and almost glowing – everything one might expect from DeVoil's rather nonchalant reputation. But it was the figure at the rear who stole Rose's attention and the very breath from her lungs.

They strode forth behind their students, a vision of pure beauty in an azure gown that popped against their golden-brown skin, flowing behind them like a train of rippling waves. Like Soren, they appeared far too young to be a professor, but their cerulean eyes were piercing and shrewd, belying years that their skin did not betray.

Long thin braids hung down to the lower curve of their back, plaited through with looser curls. They swayed as they sauntered to the front of the room, the dark roots fading into sandy ends that looked as if they'd been woven with strands of pure gold.

Shaking herself from her reverie, Rose glanced about to see she wasn't the only one who'd been caught in their thrall. Several other students stared unabashedly, their whispers pointed and rather heated. Even Soren's gaze had caught upon them from the professors' post on the other side of the stage. Rose almost grinned. *Interesting.*

Woodstone cleared his throat, trying in vain to hold the room's attention as the DeVoil students stole centre stage. 'Please welcome their champions Peiren Havillande and Azalaïs L'Espina, who will be led in their efforts by the illustrious Mamsella Fiorella de Prevath.'

The two DeVoil competitors stepped forward, where names appeared as if from thin air for each of them, glittering with their pronouns. Rose eyed the trio as they fastened the pins to their clothes. Peiren was almost shockingly nondescript, with hair the colour of tree bark, freckled pink skin and kind hazel eyes that looked rather dazed, as if he weren't quite sure where he was. The faint smell of weedsmoke wafted off him, making Rose grin.

But the other student, Azalaïs, bore the applause more graciously. Dark hair cascaded down her back in luscious waves, dotted through with little white blooms, and her skin was a bright sun-kissed copper, save for her right forearm, which looked to be made of the same vinewood as her jewellery. Rose raised an eyebrow as the woman flashed the crowd a dazzling smile and dipped in a low bow. She wasn't quite as alluring as Mamsella de Prevath, but she was more of a showman than Peiren. Perhaps she would get on well with Woodstone.

As if summoned by her thought, the chancellor herded the DeVoil students back to the wings of the stage and fluffed out his robes. 'Now, from the shattered mountains of Ir Taril, please welcome the students of Maalstrum Institut, who—'

Woodstone's words were swallowed up once more as the doors flung open in a cloud of indigo smoke. Gasps rippled through the room as the Maalstrum delegates swept through, shrouded in shades of deep purple and midnight blue. The candlelight flickered and dimmed around them, as if bent to their will. Rose shivered, yet she couldn't tear her eyes away from them. They were utterly beautiful, mesmerizing proof of perfection, flawless shards of starlight, bewitching in their elegance.

But a rancid feeling took root in Rose's chest, some desperate craving to mar such immaculate faces with a touch of flame. Her stomach sank and she sucked in a sharp breath, shoving the impulse away. Yet it cleared her mind somehow, returning to her just the smallest shred of reason. *Compulsion.* The thought pierced her. *Maalstrum's specialty.* Her head spun as she shook herself free of it, the glow surrounding the Maalstrum delegates fading as she did.

They were almost plain without it. Still stunning, but

lacking that spark that the illusion seemingly gave them. Save for the student at the back, who had an air of effortless beauty, if not entirely conventional. They stood nearly a head taller than the student in front of them, and a shock of loose silver curls gleamed against their cool brown skin, though ink-black strands still peeked through at the roots. Dyed, Rose supposed, but not recently. Their thick brows were dark as well and pulled in an amused scowl. But when their obsidian eyes slid towards Rose, no humour lingered within. They were cold and empty. Until something flickered to life behind them: some shred of a mask they had not prepared under the guise of their illusion, perhaps. All too easily, a wicked smile split their lips and they winked at her. Something deep within Rose stirred. That unknown and unfathomable hunger wrenching at her heart.

Woodstone coughed, waving the haze of smoke away from his face. 'Please welcome Oliv Ivyssen and Callum Avenhart, led by Professor Arvir Mistralus.'

Rose could almost smell the entitlement rolling off them as they stepped forward for their name tags. They might yet give Dunhollow a run for its money. She shook her head, glancing at the silver-haired boy. Callum, his name tag read. He hung back from Oliv, still a picture of casual elegance, but not so committed to putting on the air of condescending superiority. Instead, his gaze flicked to the side, as if he could feel Rose's eyes upon him.

Woodstone held his hand up, quieting the crowd. 'Thank you all for coming – we are honoured to host you for the thirtieth running of the Ashwood Tournament. It is my hope that you'll find your time here most riveting and our student body most welcoming.'

Rose bit her tongue. Normally, she would decry the notion as utter drivel. But if the way her peers were still staring at their guests was any indication, they might actually manage a shred of hospitality for once.

She turned away quickly before Woodstone beckoned the three of them forward. 'And, on that note, allow me to introduce Dunhollow's own competitors. Arden Osiander, Sylven Belliaris and Rosera Thenlif, counselled by Professor Soren Sylverfir.'

The hall erupted with applause for them – a great show of empty praise. Still, Rose thought as her fingers curled around her name tag, it might have been the first time in her tenure here that anyone had actually cheered when her name was called.

But the pretence of it all turned her stomach, and she glanced away, only to find Callum's dark eyes boring into hers. Her heart leapt, but she felt no tendril of magic slipping between the folds of her mind. He simply smiled, though his eyes betrayed a sharpness. Like a cat toying with its prey.

Rose's blood boiled as his grin widened. If he wasn't careful, she would be all too glad to carve him a second smile straight down to the bones of his tender throat. She doubted he would look quite so lovely then.

The din of insipid chatter pulsed in Rose's ears like a heartbeat. In only a few moments the assembly hall had been utterly transformed. Tidy rows of chairs had been replaced with a staggering buffet table piled high with decadent delicacies, and her peers milled freely throughout the room. Trays of chilled wine floated about, weaving between packs of huddled students. Rose's fingers tightened around her own glass. Yet even such opulence could not wash away the stain of subterfuge and deceit in these halls.

Though the purpose of this gathering was evidently to 'share in the spirit of camaraderie', according to Woodstone, there was very little mingling. Most of her peers stuck to themselves, though Arden prattled on to one of the Maalstrum students, Oliv, whose eyes grew dull and glazed. Not that he noticed. Rose shook her head.

Meanwhile, across the long buffet table, she spied Sylvie having far more luck with their DeVoil counterparts. Though Rose wasn't entirely certain the one called Peiren wasn't just drawn to her shiny circlet, as he reached out to touch it, eyes wide. Beside them, Soren chatted away with the gorgeous Mamsella de Prevath, the picture of charm as he leaned against the wall with an easy smile.

Rose tapped her fingers against her swirling flute of wine with a sly smile. She hadn't entirely forgiven him for conspiring with Woodstone, but it was good to see him so at ease. A gentle nudge at her arm made her jump, and she glared at a floating pitcher, which refilled her glass all too eagerly. They flitted about the room, interspersed by whizzing platters of canapés and charcuterie. It would be far too plebeian to ask attendees to refill their plates and glasses themselves, she supposed.

Such opulence for so little reason. Rose wondered if, at the moment the clock struck the hour, the charm would fade, and all this luxury would simply vanish, leaving bare stone and disappointment in its wake. Her sparkling wine bubbled against her lips as she hid her smile behind her glass, almost chuckling at the thought of Woodstone's face, were that to happen.

He swept around the room now, gliding between conversations like a skilled alchemist keeping all their cauldrons bubbling at the same temperature. Rose sighed, setting her wine on the table. If he caught her hanging back like this, he would chide her for not giving a 'Dunhollow welcome', she was sure. Though there was nothing that sounded less appealing to her now.

'You know,' Sylvie's breath brushed the shell of her ear. 'I think they may have overdone it, just a bit.'

Rose turned, giving her a dry smile. 'It is the Dunhollow way, after all.'

'Well –' Sylvie's voice lowered – 'if you're just going to hang out in a corner instead of mingling, I can think of far more pleasant ways to waste the afternoon.'

A fierce heat crept across Rose's cheeks as her eyes slid to the dangerously low cut of Sylvie's neckline. Gods, what she wouldn't give to leave this farce behind. To take Sylvie back to her dorm and spend the rest of the day tucked away in her warm embrace. Her heart skipped a beat and she took a sip of wine, though it was a poor substitute for the taste she truly craved.

Rose cleared her throat. 'Something tells me Woodstone wouldn't approve of us running off,' she managed finally.

Sylvie pursed her lips. 'Spoilsport.'

Rose shook her head, taking another sip of wine in a vain attempt to cool the razing heat pulsing beneath her skin. Even if she'd agreed, Sylvie wouldn't have left. She fitted right in at events like these, working the room as if she were born to do it.

'Did you find out anything useful from our competition?'

Sylvie shrugged. 'Not that we didn't already know. Besides some rather ... interesting herbal recommendations, the DeVoil competitors don't seem good for much beyond healing.'

'And from Maalstrum?'

'Had little more to offer than small talk.' Sylvie sighed before downing the last of her wine. 'Hard to get a read on them unless you want to risk having your thoughts laid bare.'

'Getting compelled is far more dangerous, I assure you.' A voice behind Rose made her jump. But, when she turned, her gaze caught only empty air. 'And illusions are almost worse.'

She whirled back to find the silver-haired student, Callum, standing before them with a sly grin, one hand outstretched. Two flutes of wine dangled from his fingertips, which he presented with a small flourish. Rose eyed him warily, sharing a glance with Sylvie before they both took the proffered glasses.

Callum straightened and raised his own glass to theirs. 'Though you two look perfectly capable of taking care of yourselves. Cheers.'

Sylvie eyed him up and down before taking a sip. 'Thanks, Callis.'

Rose nearly snorted into her wine. Sylvie knew perfectly well what his name was; it glowed brightly at them from the name tag on his chest. Though she couldn't blame her for aiming a blow at his ego. From the look of him, it didn't need any more preening.

His streaked silver hair glowed in the candlelight, eyes all too shrewd as he beamed down at them. He held himself as if he came from the heights of the imperial court, dressed impeccably in deep amethyst robes that came to a point at a jewelled collar. A velvet cape hung artfully from his shoulders, held by a delicate chain across his chest, and shimmering as if the night sky had been mapped upon it. He looked more like Rose had imagined Woodstone would – as if the world was made to fall at his feet. It could've all been an illusion, she supposed. Some vain attempt to make himself grander and more imposing, though she caught no scent of a signature to betray his casting.

'Callum, actually.' He stuck out his free hand, his smile undimmed by Sylvie's slight.

'Sylvie.' Her eyes hardened as her mask fell firmly into place. 'And this is Rose.'

Rose forced a wan smile, still eyeing him suspiciously. But he hardly seemed perturbed, grinning as if this were all a mere game to him. Perhaps it was. Though, if that were the case, she wouldn't recommend he choose Sylvie as an opponent.

'Yes, your cohort over there had quite a lot to say about you two.' He jerked his head towards Arden, who still chattered away to Oliv. Rose noted her figure glimmered at the edges. 'Nothing particularly kind, of course. Not much camaraderie here at Dunhollow, is there?'

Rose snorted. 'Sorry to disappoint.'

'Oh, hardly.' Callum ran a gloved hand through his curls, leaning in as if about to share some riveting piece of gossip. 'Dunhollow has a reputation for being more cut-throat than close-knit. Though you two seem quite cosy. I hear you're the academy's power couple.'

Sylvie's red lips pulled in a smirk. 'Did Arden tell you that too?'

'More or less.' Callum tugged at the chain of his cape. 'Though he wasn't quite as forthcoming on your specialties.'

So *that's* what he wanted. He didn't care for Dunhollow gossip or petty enmity – he simply was trying to gain a leg up on the competition. Not a terrible strategy, Rose had to admit. She was honestly shocked more students weren't doing the same, though only Sylvie and Callum seemed to possess the forethought. That said, she was more surprised he couldn't have got that information out of Arden. Rose's eyes flicked to the boy's coiffed red hair. Perhaps he did have at least one worthwhile thought in that empty head of his.

'I'm afraid you'll need more than a glass of wine to prise that from our lips.' Sylvie twirled her goblet between her fingers. 'And I wouldn't recommend peering into our minds either.'

'I wouldn't dare.' Callum's eyes seemed perfectly sincere, but the wry quirk of his lips said he absolutely would.

'I'm sure.'

'Well, since you already know my strengths, there's no harm in guessing yours.' He leaned against the table, his eyes roving over Sylvie in a way that made Rose's stomach twist. 'You look like something of a fortress, so I'd say source magic is your specialty – ice, if I had to pick. Though I'm sure you're a woman of many talents.'

'Mmm.' Sylvie's eyes sparked, though, from the subtle tightening of her lips, Rose was quite sure she hated that he'd guessed so easily. 'None that you'll be privy to.'

'Quite.' He grinned, completely unfazed as his gaze slid to Rose. 'You, on the other hand, you're a bit odd, aren't you?'

Out of instinct, she shrank back. A lifetime of keeping herself small and unnoticeable flooded through the cracks in her facade – burying her in an instant. But then she straightened, meeting his gaze with every ounce of fire she could manage. She'd not come this far to play prey to some entitled, well-dressed prat.

Forcing a taut smile, Rose chuckled. 'With compliments like that, I can see why you need illusions to compensate for your charm.'

'You wound me, *dal*.' Callum clutched his heart in mock pain. 'I'm nothing if not charming.'

Dal. Rose raised an eyebrow. Short for *dalissan*, the Tarilian word for 'darling', if memory served, though she hadn't studied the language in years. Still, in that tone, it sounded less like an endearment and more like a parent scolding an unruly child.

She bristled beneath his gaze. 'If you say so.'

'Well, with a sharp tongue like that, you'd fit right in at Maalstrum, though I'd be shocked if mental magics were your specialty.' Callum stroked his chin as if in deep thought. 'No, there's a spark of something more . . . sinister about you.'

Rose's pulse leapt, and Sylvie stiffened beside her. Could he sense her necromancy? Or perhaps this was all part of his game. A stab in the dark meant to illicit some reaction that he could use to his advantage. Yet, when she met his gaze, his eyes were too keen — too prying, as if they saw every raw and broken part of her. And suddenly, they were far too close.

Her jaw tightened, her heart hammering against her ribs. He had dangerous magic of his own at his beck and call, after all. How easy would it be for him to slip past her defences and lay her every thought bare?

Though, for all the strength of his power, his pretty little skull would shatter just as easily as anyone else's. A fine mind crushed to pulp beneath the heel of her boot. The very idea of it twisted giddily at something deep within her.

Bile crept up her throat as she forced the thought back. Whatever sick impulse it was that urged her on, she could not indulge it here. *Not now.* Flashing a glance at Sylvie, Rose forced the searing heat of her muddled mind into the palm of her hand. Callum blinked as flames licked up her skin, twirling between her fingers.

Rose hummed with a mirthless smile. 'Guess you're not as insightful as you thought.'

Her flames danced in Callum's eyes, their glow catching the faint slivers of silver within. Yet they only made his smile widen. 'Well, aren't you full of surprises?'

Sharp words bit against Rose's lips, but she swallowed them. He'd gotten what he wanted, after all. And she'd been fool enough to walk right into his trap. With a huff, she cut off her source, the flames dying in her palm. It wouldn't do to give him any more ground by letting her anger betray her.

Sylvie took Rose's hand, squeezing it gently. 'Well, as much as we'd love to stay and chat all day, we really should make the rounds.'

'Of course.' Callum dipped his head in a mocking bow. 'Best of luck in the trials.'

Sylvie flashed a final taut smile before dragging Rose to the other end of the table, putting a plethora of students between them and Callum. 'Are you all right?'

Rose glanced up, recoiling from the intensity in Sylvie's eyes. 'Yeah, fine.'

'Really? You looked like you were ready to rip his throat out.'

'Just nervous.' She shrugged. 'Didn't want him delving into my thoughts.'

'Right.' Sylvie nodded, though her eyes narrowed, as if she didn't quite believe her. 'We should steer clear of him as much as possible. Just to be safe.'

Rose followed her gaze back to Callum, who stood still as a statue, his eyes roving over the room. Watching, waiting – *listening*. Her stomach sank. Somehow, she couldn't agree more.

5. Strategy and Summoning

The skies hung on the last dregs of a muted sunrise as Rose approached the training field. Not that anyone ever saw the sun's daily journey across the sky in this place. The passage of time at Dunhollow was marked only in differing shades of grey and the droning chimes of the clock tower over the courtyard.

Rose fought back a yawn. Why she had bothered with such an early class, she couldn't fathom now, especially Strategy and Summoning. Some overeager part of her that had been spurred on by a summer of successes but that now lay dormant and reticent. She tightened her grip on her satchel. A year ago, she'd have rather carved out her own eyes than willingly rejoin a class in the School of Defensive Arts, and now she was there because of her own foolish pride.

An all too common problem, these days. Rose scowled at the sunless skies, as if her suffering were their fault. Her eyes flicked down to the course list in her hands. At least her other choices were still safe.

SDA: Strategy and Summoning Level 4, 7:45–9:10, Menier/ Wenore/Fenvier

SMT: Magical Assimilation in Early Na Qis: The Qisan Legacy, 11:00–12:25, Menier/Wenore/Fenvier

SMT: Spellcrafting Symbiosis: Language, Culture, Religion and Casting, 10:00–11:25, Tenier/Torier

CHH: Advanced Botanical Sciences, Level 4, 15:25–16:50, Tenier/ Torier

Sighing, she shoved the list into her pocket and approached

the edge of the field, glaring at the thick fog creeping across its verdant ground. It drifted slowly down from the pine-hemmed mountains beyond the forest, seeping out of the looming treeline to a din of faint shrieks.

Rose shivered as a tapestry of ancient gnarled trees stole across her mind. Footsteps thundering through the night as the darkness closed in, the metallic tang of blood heavy on the wind. And Fen's cracked, broken gaze as he reached for her, gone before her very eyes. She swallowed hard, shoving the memories of the forest's cursed depths aside.

Yet the ghosts that haunted her would not be so easily shaken this year. Aveline's claws had sunk deep, her gaunt, milky gaze hanging over Rose's memory, but even she'd faded to flame and shield. Fire now burgeoned beneath her skin, granting her the strength to defend herself, but nothing could protect her from the dark depths of her own mind.

Rose chewed the inside of her lip. It had to be some side effect of the spell backfiring – some shade of a restless spirit that attached itself to her, perhaps? Until last year, she'd never given much thought to the veil between the dead and the living, but there had always been stories.

Tales of necromancers piercing that tenuous shroud to the realm of the dead, just as dreamers could touch the dreamlands of old. Places of higher magic, gods and spirits, if myths were to be believed. Rose wrinkled her nose. She wasn't really one for religion on the whole, but if it *were* true, then, in her hubris, she might've delved deeper into death than most ever would. Or should. It stood to reason that some of it came back with her, even if Fen hadn't. Rose's throat tightened. And for what? Hollow memories and bitter disappointment? She had nothing to show for her mistake beyond regret.

At least Fen's soul could still rest. A small comfort, but a silver lining, nonetheless. It was a mercy that the spell had not worked, rather than bringing him back as some mutilated half-dead version of himself. Rose's nails bit into her palms. She didn't think she could bear the horror of that.

Gritting her teeth, Rose set her satchel on the side of the field. A few of her fellow students gathered around its edges, most bleary-eyed and yawning. *Only ten*, she counted with a frown. It was a higher-level curriculum, but surely there should be more than that. Sylvie, at the very least. That was the main reason Rose had wanted to take this course, after all. A chance for them to finally have a class together where they weren't at each other's throats. Though her stomach only twisted at the thought now. Perhaps they should have picked an elective that they could both excel in. Rose fidgeted with her sleeves, suddenly all too tight against her skin in the damp morning air.

She didn't even fulfil the prerequisites for this course. Her command of her life source had come a long way on her travels with Soren, but flame? She shuddered at the thought of Fen's signature falling over her, his smile lingering at the back of her mind each time she cast. But it was her only lifeline now, if she didn't want to make a fool of herself in the tournament. She had to learn to control it and there was no better place to do so than under the eagle-eyed gaze of Professor Troidilis, as loath as Rose was to admit it.

Warm fingers linked gently through hers, making Rose jump. She turned, for the briefest moment, half hoping to meet Fen's kind brown eyes. But it was an amber gaze that stared down at her. Rose flashed a smile at Sylvie, but she couldn't help the smallest tendrils of disappointment that crept through her heart like poisonous barbs. Not of Sylvie – never about her. But there was a chasm somewhere deep within Rose. Something she'd wrenched open in the cold, dark depths of that basement when she'd let Fen die, and which could never be filled so long as that hung over her. It would be the same if she'd lost Sylvie instead. A wound that festered and seethed within her, furious that such a foul choice had ever had to be made.

Sylvie planted a small kiss on her brow. 'Can't believe I let you talk me into a class this early.'

Rose scowled. The unholy hour was the least of her worries. 'You'll be fine.'

Sylvie's face fell as her eyes flicked over Rose's shoulder. 'Don't look now, but we've got company.'

Rose resisted the urge to turn immediately, but only just. Instead, she slid her gaze slowly to the path behind them, where a familiar shock of silver hair lingered. She groaned. *Wonderful.* That was all she needed.

Unlike the other students, Callum looked hardly perturbed by the early hour, his cool brown skin smooth and glowing, his dark eyes ever alert. He'd traded his finely woven vest for slightly plainer fare, sleeves rolled up to the elbows and collar loosened. He was the picture of casual elegance, yet Rose only wrinkled her nose.

Technically, the students from Maalstrum or DeVoil weren't here for a formal semester, and, thus, weren't restricted by an official course list. They could come and go as they pleased, sitting in on whatever classes suited their fancy, though Rose had rather thought they'd be more inclined to stick to their specialty areas – Maalstrum in the College of Illusion and Invocation, and DeVoil in the College of Healing and Herbalism. Easier to whittle away a useless semester when one barely had to try. Though, clearly, Callum didn't agree.

Yet, as her eyes roved over him, no brutal, murderous thoughts filled her mind. *Strange.* Mere days ago, she'd been ready to tear his throat out just for breathing near her, and now? Nothing. As if the threads of death ensnared her at mere whim.

'Are you all right?' Sylvie's voice startled her.

'What?' She glanced up. 'Oh, yeah, fine.'

Sylvie raised a solitary brow. 'Saying so doesn't make it so, Rose.'

The truth burned against Rose's tongue, yet she faltered. It was an odd thing to unburden herself to Sylvie now when, for so long, she'd been the last person Rose ever would've turned to. As much as she hated to admit it, there was still an old, reflexive part of her that tangled the truth around her heart like a barbed noose, wound only by her own hand. But whatever shred of honesty she had within her fled as the field fell into cowed silence.

Professor Troidilis swept on to the green grass, their emerald robes stark against the dim skies and eyes ever sharp. They had not changed a bit in the last year, still rigid and formidable, their mere presence enough to bind the students, as if in some spell.

Rose's classmates straightened, swallowing their yawns as they lined the field in fearful anticipation. All save Rose, Sylvie and – unsurprisingly – Callum, who idled behind the rest. The professor's eyes landed upon Rose almost immediately, their upper lip curling. But Rose refused to drop their gaze. If they were determined to humiliate her this year, they would not find her so unprepared.

After a moment, Troidilis turned back to the other students. 'Good morning.'

'Good morning, Professor.' A chorus of mumbles rose from the field.

'Before we begin, I'd like to address that this course is focused on the most advanced aspects of source magic.' They raised a thin brow. 'Anyone who feels that they will not be able to keep up with the rigorous curriculum should leave now and save us all the time.'

Nobody moved, though all eyes followed the professor's straight to Rose. Sylvie reached for her hand once more, squeezing lightly. But Rose didn't meet her gaze, a fierce heat creeping across her cheeks.

'Messere Thenlif?' Their eyes narrowed. 'I don't recall you completing your third levels prior to this course.'

Rose gritted her teeth. She didn't think it would take them quite *so* little time to single her out. Perhaps they were still bitter after last year – or just wanted to finish what they'd started. She bit back a harsh response, silently cursing herself once again for ever thinking this would go well.

After a moment, she squared her shoulders. 'I'll manage, Professor.'

'We'll see.' Professor Troidilis gave a curt nod before turning away. 'Now, today, we will be focusing on summonings. Most of you are used to calling your familiars, but what I will be asking of you today is far more complex. Messere Belliaris, step forward.'

Sylvie's head snapped up, her fingers loosening around Rose's as she did as she was bidden. 'Yes, Professor?'

'Please demonstrate for the rest of the class a proper summoning.'

A soft warmth bloomed in Rose's chest for the way a self-sure smirk pulled at Sylvie's lips. With a mere twist of her hand, shards of ice sprang forth, dusting the ground in a shimmering array. For a moment, nothing happened. But then they shifted, twisting and cracking into jagged translucent shapes. Pointed ears, glittering whiskers and teeth all too sharp.

An enormous crystalline cat blinked at them, shaking away stray icicles with a shudder. Sylvie beamed as a chorus of gasps went up from the other students, looking far too pleased with herself. Rose shook her head. Once, that smug smile would've eaten away at her, but now it only set her pulse racing. She could think of so many pleasurable ways to make Sylvie swallow it anyhow.

'Very good, Sylvie, thank you.'

Rose snorted. There was no hiding who the professor's favourite was. Though she could hardly complain about that. Soren made no secret of his fondness for her, and Sylvie had more than earned the praise. Her casting had always been strong – a rare natural talent. She barely ever had to study, which Rose knew now was more because she struggled to focus on texts and scrolls, rather than any arrogance on Sylvie's part, as she'd so long assumed.

'As you can see, the easiest shape for most of you to summon will be similar to your familiars.' The professor cut across Rose's thoughts. 'I don't expect many of you will be at Messere Belliaris's level, but she can demonstrate the basics for you.'

Sylvie gave a curt nod, explaining how she connected to the shape. It wasn't unlike the familiar's bond, but where that was a piece of magic made manifest into the shape of the caster's choosing, summonings were raw source, still pulled into shape at the caster's will, but thrumming with a power all of their own. But the thought only chilled her. What if hers should take the form of life, instead of flame?

A low voice brushed her ear. 'The professor really does not care for you.'

Rose jumped, whirling on Callum. Of course, he wouldn't make keeping her distance an easy prospect. Her eyes narrowed as a perfume of pine and juniper tingled against her nose. Not his signature, she guessed. It was too sharp – too clean. All too like his facade of cutting elegance. The scent of one's magic so rarely matched the mask one wore, she'd found.

'Picked that up from their head, did you?' she snapped, her eyes drifting back to the professor.

'No, they just look at you like you're something to be scraped off their shoe.' He chuckled. 'But now that you mention it . . .'

Rose raised an eyebrow as his dark gaze fixed on Troidilis. Was he really so brazen? 'You can't be serious.'

'Is there a problem, Messere Thenlif?' The professor's voice cut across the field like a blade.

Yes, Rose thought, her eyes flashing to Callum. Could Troidilis feel him peeling through the folds of their mind, or were they blissfully unaware? If they were, they certainly wouldn't be persuaded by her.

'No, Professor.'

They sniffed, as if her very presence was a foul odour they wished to be rid of. 'Then I'll ask you to kindly cease with the interruptions.'

Rose swallowed her protest, the sharp words cutting all the way down. With a soft sigh, she met Sylvie's gaze, which darkened as it flicked between her and Callum. But then the professor pulled her away, leaving Rose at his mercy.

'Yes, Messere Thenlif,' Callum whispered, 'do try to keep it down.'

Rose shot him a withering glare. 'Aren't you in the wrong class? I'd have thought you'd be more at home in the College of Illusion and Invocation.'

Which wasn't entirely fair, she supposed. The mental magics might have had a separate field of study, but they were a source too, of a sort. Not like pulling at fire or ice, of course, but the energy within one's mind held a power of its own and was no less dangerous to manipulate. More so, even.

'Oh, don't worry about me.' He ran a hand through his hair. A flash of blood-red ink caught her eye just behind his ear. His familiar's mark, perhaps? 'I'm somewhat of a prodigy in mental magics already, so I doubt there's much the Dunhollow curriculum has to offer. Better to broaden my horizons, don't you think?'

'If you say so.'

'You're one to talk anyway.' He leaned in closer, his warm breath brushing her cheek. 'Tell me, how *did* you go from not even being able to cast a barrier last year to taking an advanced course like this?'

Rose faltered. Dark dank walls flooded her mind, source crackling from Fen's orb, searing through her veins. And blood – so much blood. Thick and seeping through her fingers. *No.* She shoved the memory down. Whether it was the orb that had granted her his source or just some stray strand of her necromancy, she wasn't sure. Perhaps it was her own desperate will to hold on to a piece of him. His life, his spirit – a ghost all of her own making. Her stomach lurched. Whatever it was, she doubted it was any less volatile in the aftermath of her foolish spell. Either way, it didn't concern Callum.

Sucking in a sharp breath, she gave him a sly grin. 'Magic.'

'Hilarious.'

'Surely you didn't think I would just come out and tell you?' Her smirk widened, and she glanced up at him from beneath her lashes. 'This is Dunhollow – nothing comes easily here. Especially not the truth.'

'We'll see.' His eyes almost danced with amusement. He was *enjoying* this. 'Oh, and don't look now, but the professor is going to ask you to demonstrate.'

'Messere Thenlif!'

Shit.

'Since you can't pay attention, clearly you must already have summoning mastered.' Troidilis glared down the bridge of their nose at her. 'Would you care to demonstrate for the class?'

'Best of luck, dal.' Callum whispered, stepping back from her side.

Her jaw tightened. 'Of course, Professor.'

Rose stepped forward, Sylvie's gaze following her every move. It wasn't as if she could say no. Pass the burden on to some other unlucky soul and be done with it. The professor was determined to humiliate her, and so they would, unless she could manage to conjure up some shred of source.

Surely it couldn't be *that* hard, she tried in vain to convince herself. Simply draw the blaze into some semblance of a shape she was connected to. A crow was the easy answer. And if she had managed to bring life to Prea's iridescent feathers, surely it couldn't take that much more to create an inanimate version out of flame.

Yet her mouth was dry, her heart thudding dully as she lifted her hand. At first, nothing happened, not even a spark flickering to life in her palms. But then she caught Sylvie's steady gaze – full of such surety. In Rose. In her power. And it razed through her with little more than a breath. Like a dying ember revived, her magic surged out of her, tingling down her spine, flaring across her skin, forging itself deep within her heart. As if she herself were made of fire.

Rose blinked down at her arms, utterly entwined with flames. They licked and curled around the edges of delicate plumage, which fluttered to life against her skin. It was almost a cold feeling as the summoning pulled away from her, stretching its wings up into the air.

A soft breath fled from her lungs as the crow took to the sky. Its fiery edges flickered and wavered, slightly raggedy against its flame-gold core. Even so, a smile pulled at the corners of Rose's mouth. She'd really done it.

The weight in her heart lifted, soaring along the wings of her summoning. For the first time, the source felt like her own, the smell of amber and honey enveloping her. The magic swelled within her, not with a caustic grip, but rather a warm hand guiding her – protecting her. Until another scent stole over her, faint and fleeting, but all too familiar.

Red wine and worn leather. Rose's stomach dropped, and she faltered as Fen's eyes flashed through her mind. A kind smile breaking through shadow, a lone hand stretching out from the depths of death itself, stilling just beyond her reach, and then gone.

Rose's breath caught in her throat, source flaring as she stumbled back. Flame seared her skin, drawing her back to the verdant field as her summoning let out a rasping squawk and dived straight into the crowd of her peers.

Rose leapt out of its way, fingers curling uselessly over empty air as she tried desperately to call it back. But whatever bound them had frayed and worn, as if the very magic had rejected her tenuous grasp of it. Her heart pounded in her ears as her eyes flew over the field, her peers shrieking and scattering as the crow's great wings skimmed just over their heads.

Rose scrambled to her feet, but another figure cut across the field ahead of her. *Sylvie.* Swift and silent, her crystalline cat followed her will as if bound to the same heartbeat. Ice trailed in the wake of its enormous paws as it leapt into the air on Sylvie's command, catching the crow mid-flight between its teeth. With a vigorous shake of its head, the crow was wrenched apart, flames splintering into slivers.

But one skewed sideways, catching Sylvie in the shoulder. She cried out, clutching her arm as she fell back.

'Sylvie!' Rose raced forward, tumbling to her knees beside her. 'I'm so sorry. I—'

The words died on her lips as Sylvie propped herself up on her elbows, her hand falling away from her shoulder. Her skin was singed and red, fierce blisters already creeping across the marred flesh. The woollen fabric of her dark turtleneck peeled back in blackened edges, smouldering gently. Bile crept up Rose's throat as she met Sylvie's eyes, which widened ever so slightly.

'It's fine, Rose.' She moved to cover the wound. 'Really, I'm fine.'

'Step aside!' The sharp order parted the crowd.

But Rose didn't move – couldn't. Not even as the professor eased Sylvie back into the grass with a gasp, muttering a healing incantation under their breath. This was all her fault. Tears pricked her eyes. She should never have cast the summoning – should never have joined this bloody class in the first place.

She forced her tears back with a shuddering breath. Already, Sylvie's flesh sealed and smoothed itself beneath Troidilis's care, the pain leaching away from her features. Yet there was something about the way she lay sprawled across the ground, utterly still with her gossamer hair fanning out around her, that clawed beneath Rose's skin.

The last person who'd hurt her like this was Hollis, holding her captive in that rancid cell, growing listless and ever weaker upon that slab. Rose's source had been hungry for vengeance then, roasting away his life until all that remained was a charred husk. Perhaps there was a morbid sort of poetry to her now being the source of Sylvie's pain.

A beautiful reflection – life and death ever caught in their perpetual cycle. Threads mirrored and matched, ever echoed within her own power. And how easily she could pull those strings to her own tune. *Or snip them away entirely.*

Rose swallowed a gag as she leapt to her feet. *No.* She could never.

'Rose?' Sylvie lifted her head weakly. 'Really, it's fine.'

But Rose only shook her head. She couldn't stay here a moment longer, caught in the stench of burnt flesh and the murderous cravings that ensnared her mind. And so, without another word, she turned on her heel and fled.

6. That Broken Line

The smell of damp earth and ferns welcomed Rose back to her dorm, a gentle balm to the fire in her veins. The door slammed behind her with enough force to shake the hinges, but she couldn't bring herself to care. Her heart hammered against her ribs, stoking the flames still clinging to life within her.

Gods, what had she *done*?

A scathing laugh bubbled to her lips. Here she was, thinking she could protect Sylvie, when she might be her greatest threat. And she had no one to blame but herself.

Perhaps it was some sort of curse. Just as Soren had condemned himself to eternal life, she too had to pay the price for toying with that fragile thread. She'd sought out death, and now a piece of it sought her. Trapping her thoughts, her desires, forever beyond that broken line. But any weakness it found purchase in began in her. Some mangled fragile thing born within the twisted makings of her own soul.

She faltered, sucking in a sharp breath. In an instant, it was as if every shred of care and energy fled her, leaving behind only a trembling, weeping husk. She sank on to the floor beside her bed, pulling her knees to her chest as tears streamed freely on to her woollen trousers. She sniffled, wiping her sleeve over her nose, when a knock thudded against her door. Rose stilled as another knock rang out, louder this time.

'Rose, it's me.' Sylvie's voice filtered through the door.

Rose's head snapped up, guilt pooling low in her gut like

molten lava. *No.* She couldn't be here – it wasn't safe. Even so, something pulled her to her feet, drawing her to the door. As if some tether bound them, even now. And Rose didn't have the heart to cut it. Reaching for the knob, she threw open the door.

Sylvie stared down at her, her amber eyes blazing. Rose's own gaze flicked immediately to her shoulder, but Sylvie's tawny skin was whole and healed, with not even the faintest hint of redness. The only evidence that remained were the scorched edges of her sweater, looking somewhat lopsided with only one shoulder bare.

A sigh slipped past Rose's lips. 'You're all right.'

'No thanks to you,' Sylvie snapped, pushing past her.

Rose closed the door behind her, words sticking to her tongue as she turned. 'I-I'm sorry. I lost control of the cast, and—'

'Gods, I don't care about your casting, Rose!' she cut across her, running her fingers through her tangled hair.

'What?'

'Magic is dangerous – that's not exactly news.' She waved a hand vaguely, as if shooing the notion away. 'But why did you run off?'

'It just reminded me too much of, well, last year.'

Sylvie blanched just for a moment before her eyes narrowed. 'No, something else is going on with you. It has been since you got back.'

She circled Rose like a cat stalking its prey, her eyes too shrewd. Too keen. And far too close to the truth.

Rose took a step back, pressing up against the door. 'It's nothing.' She licked her chapped lips. 'I'm fine.'

Sylvie raised an eyebrow. 'You're clearly not.'

Rose swallowed a curse. Even without her swollen eyes and tear-stained cheeks, it would have been a hollow lie. The truth burned against her lips, desperate to be free. And didn't Sylvie deserve that much?

'I cast the Spell of True Revival.' The words fell from her before she could think better of it.

At that, Sylvie went stock still. Shock flickered across her face, warring with confusion before finally settling on grim resignation. 'Oh, Rose,' she muttered. 'Please tell me that's not what it sounds like.'

Rose swallowed hard. 'It is.'

A thick silence fell between them, only broken by a gentle breeze rustling through the foliage above Rose's open window. For several achingly long moments, it seemed all Sylvie could do was stare at her. Her lips parted and eyes wide. But then something snapped, some shred of fury falling over her lovely features.

'Is that what your whole trip was about?' she snapped. 'Finding some godsawful spell to revive Fen?'

'No.' Rose shook her head. 'Of course not! Finding the spell was an accident, but when I did, I just—'

'Decided to do the exact same thing Soren did?' Sylvie's face fell, her voice softening as it cracked over her words. 'Or Hollis?'

Rose reeled back as if she'd struck her. That wasn't the same at all. Hollis had brutally attacked and murdered two people – almost three. So lost in his grief and longing that he saw their lives as a reasonable trade for the one he'd lost. Did Sylvie really think her capable of that?

'That's not fair.' Her fingers tightened, nails biting into her palms. 'You know I would never. But this spell used life source, not alchemy – the only person at risk was me.'

'That's not better!' Sylvie cried. 'You think Fen would be all right with you trading your life for his? Not to mention that I'd prefer you alive. Did you even think about that?'

'It wasn't like that! It was after our fight and I . . .' Rose faltered. 'I don't know. I suppose I wanted to prove I could. And I'd already brought Prea to life.'

'You *what*?' Sylvie's thick brows shot up her forehead.

'It was earlier in the summer.' Rose rubbed the back of her neck. 'I didn't think it'd last, but then it did, and I thought I could do the same for Fen.'

'But it didn't work?'

'Something went wrong.' She pushed away from the door, easing into her window seat as Sylvie's sharp eyes followed her. 'I-I don't remember what happened after the spell, but Fen wasn't there, the grimoire I used was gone, and I keep having these . . . thoughts.'

Sylvie took a slow step back. Not fearful – not yet. But hesitant all the same. 'What kind of thoughts?'

'Brutal, murderous things.' Rose swallowed against the growing lump in her throat. 'Sometimes they just slip in, other times it's when I'm angry.'

'About me?'

Rose nodded, not trusting her voice against the threat of tears.

'That's why you ran.' Sylvie's tone was soft, holding no anger for her.

'I could never hurt you.' The broken whisper slipped between her lips, with some resilient shred of hope that Sylvie might believe that one truth. 'But the idea that there's some part of my mind that wanted to, I . . . It killed me.'

Before Rose could stop them, her tears broke free, streaming down her cheeks. There was nothing that stood between her and Sylvie's judgement. No facade or justification that she could claim. No comfort she could turn to. Nothing.

But Sylvie didn't flee – she didn't even turn away. Instead, she pulled Rose close, her arms wrapping around her shoulders as if she alone could hold all the wretched, shattered pieces of her together. For a moment, Rose hardly dared to move. But then she threw her arms around Sylvie's waist, clinging to her as if she was a lifeline.

'I'll understand if you hate me for this.' Rose's voice was muffled against Sylvie's scorched sweater.

'Gods, you're thick sometimes.' Sylvie leaned back, catching Rose's chin and forcing her gaze up. 'And a hypocrite, but, no, I don't hate you. I love you, actually. And we're going to figure this out – together.'

Rose's breath caught in her throat. Some stubborn, hateful part of her brain almost didn't believe her. It was far more grace than she deserved, after all. But there was no lie in Sylvie's eyes. Her heart swelled, the barbed cord of dread and fear that held it simply falling away.

She pulled Sylvie closer, tucking her head once more just over her softly beating heart. 'Together, then.'

7. The Caster's Cantina

The warmth of the pub had once been a soothing balm to Rose's soul. A cheerful haven beyond the imposing halls of Dunhollow, always filled with kind smiles, easy conversations and a hot meal. But now it was more of an anchor. As cold and hard as lead, it rooted her to these ragged stones, ever tethering her to horrors she might never escape. A shiver crawled up her spine as she stilled in the doorway, despite the horde of bodies swarming around her.

Her breath was tight in her chest, her eyes darting left and right at her peers. Sylvie clung tightly to Rose's hand as Ewan forged through the crowd ahead of them, but neither of them followed, as if some invisible chain ensnared them both, refusing to allow them past the threshold. Finally, Rose sucked in a sharp breath and took a step forward. And then another.

The hairs on her arms still stood stiff, though, as Sylvie followed behind her, both of them ducking through the crowd uneasily. Ewan waved them over to a small table just by the exit, muttering something about her and Sylvie needing an escape route from 'this rotten little hovel' before darting off to get drinks. Rose almost smiled as she sank into one of the stools. It was a blunt sort of thoughtfulness but touching all the same.

Rose ducked forward as a student squeezed past her, struggling to maintain their levitation charm on the drinks they carried. Far too many students squeezed into the space, packed tightly like sardines into a jar. It was a pre-tournament soirée to 'promote amicable relations', Woodstone had claimed. Rose wrinkled her nose. Never mind that they'd only be at each other's throats in the first trial tomorrow morning. Anything to keep up appearances.

Which was all this was, really. A paltry attempt to ensure that any rumours the other schools had heard of a murderous barman remained exactly that. Rose pursed her lips. Either way, it brought her peers out en masse. Likely drawn in by the opportunity to rub elbows with Maalstrum and DeVoil. Or perhaps just excited at the prospect of having their favourite drinking hole finally restored.

Rose's pulse quickened as her eyes roved over their ranks. Most lounged on the couches around the fireplace or at the booths beside the foggy windows. A few meandered about looking for a place to sit and some had simply given up, idling in small packs between the mahogany cocktail tables throughout the room.

Meanwhile, the Maalstrum and DeVoil students mostly stuck to themselves, avoiding the longing glances of her peers. Though she did note there was no telltale silver hair to be found among them. Her brow wrinkled. Of course Callum would've found a way to avoid this charade.

Her eyes flicked to the red-brick wall at the back of the bar and the frescoed floors beneath her. The Caster's Cantina, this place was now called. Decorated in the style of the open-air bars so popular in Tol Qilius, it was more chic than cosy. Twinkling lights danced around the wooden beams, and there was not a mug of ale in sight. Fine wines and frivolous cocktails lined the freshly polished tables, decadent desserts stacked high. It was almost unrecognizable now.

But there were still echoes of the old pub in the cavernous hearth and the uproarious game of Caster's Darts. In the smell of buttery dough wafting through the air or the creaking steps leading to the inn above. Rose shivered. Like flowers blooming from a corpse, it would always have rot at its core.

Rose shuddered. They should have let this place fall to rubble, though it was no great shock they hadn't. Dunhollow itself was built upon the bones of death and deceit – there was no cruelty it wouldn't happily cover up. As if a new coating of paint and a little varnish were all it took to cleanse the stains of sin and sorrow.

Beside her, Sylvie sat staring down at her hands. To the untrained eye, she merely looked thoughtful – the picture of casual disinterest. But Rose was no novice when it came to spotting cracks in Sylvie's facade. The way her hands trembled as she tore apart her napkin, or how her knee bumped the underside of the tabletop. The thin sheen of sweat creeping across her otherwise flawless brow. She was terrified and trying so desperately not to show it.

It wrenched Rose's heart in two. This wretched place had stolen so much from them both, yet Sylvie would rather condemn herself to suffer in silence than admit that. Rose gritted her teeth. She couldn't watch her do that to herself. Not alone, at least.

Sylvie jumped as Rose reached for her hand. 'Hey, you all right?'

A forced smile tugged at Sylvie's lips, but it fell as her eyes darted to the stairs. 'Not really,' she said finally. 'You?'

'Not really.' Rose squeezed her hand tighter. 'We don't have to stay.'

Sylvie fell silent, and a spark of hope flared to life in Rose's chest. But then she shook her head. 'No, it's fine.'

Of course not. Rose pursed her lips. 'Saying so doesn't make it so.'

Sylvie shot her a sharp glance. 'I just can't believe they reopened this place after everything. They should have burned it to the ground.'

'That could still be arranged,' said Rose drily.

Any trace of humour drained away from Sylvie's face, and she pulled her hand back. Rose's stomach twisted. Perhaps it was a bit too soon to jest about it.

'You should talk to Soren,' Sylvie said after a moment.

Rose frowned. 'And tell him what? That I made the exact same mistake he did? He'd hate me.'

Sylvie flashed her a sidelong glance. 'He could never hate you.'

'Well, he certainly won't be happy.'

'So, what, you'll just do nothing?' Sylvie leaned back, folding her arms across her chest. 'You tried that last year, remember? And Aveline still found you.'

Rose recoiled, her jaw closing with an audible snap. It was a low blow, here of all places. And it tore through her heart like a blade.

Sylvie's eyes softened, her full lips parting in a delicate *o*, as if she wished she could take the words back. 'Sorry, I didn't mean—'

But her apologies were cut off as Ewan swept between them with a trio of drinks. 'So the location could be less gauche, but the bartender is lovely,' they said, completely oblivious to the sharp glance that passed between Rose and Sylvie. With a flick of their wrist, the drinks landed perfectly in front of the pair of them. 'She said these were all the rage in the capital – called the Fellian Fizz, apparently.'

Tearing her gaze away from Sylvie, Rose eyed the garish orange monstrosity. It looked sinfully sweet, bubbling away against the rainbow-coloured glass as balls of ice clinked gently against one another, occasionally sending up puffs of golden glitter. Ewan snorted as they took a sip and one shot dangerously close to their nose.

Rose bit back a grin. It was almost comical how at odds it was with their sleek hair and ink-black coat. Entirely whimsical and irreverent – just the sort of quirky creation Hollis might have once made for her in the quiet of the summer months. The thought sank in her heart like a stone.

It was an odd thing to detest the man for all the vile things he'd done yet still miss the parts of him she'd known for so long. His kindness, his warmth – his friendship. All of it, gone in a single moment. And yet it lingered in her memory, like a ghost all of its own.

But Rose pushed the thought away. It didn't matter now. Instead, she reached for the fizzing drink, lifting it gingerly to her lips. Sylvie, however, hardly seemed impressed by the eccentric cocktail.

She sniffed at the syrupy liquid, raising one eyebrow at Ewan. 'Think I'd prefer a wine or a whiskey.'

'It won't kill you to try something new, Syl.' They rolled their eyes, though a fond smile tugged at their lips.

Grimacing, she took the smallest sip she could manage and wrinkled her nose. 'There, I tried it; it's terrible. Now go get me something that won't make me sick.'

Ewan fixed Sylvie with a hard stare before heaving an exaggerated sigh and slinking back off towards the bar. Following Sylvie's lead, Rose set the drink back down without tasting it. The clink of a glass turned her head as Woodstone cleared his throat from the front of the room.

'Attention! May I have your attention, everyone?'

The room quietened almost instantly. Students who had previously been clogging the paths between the tables suddenly shifted, pressing themselves flat against the walls in neat lines. As if Woodstone had cast some tidying charm upon them.

'Now then, that's better.' He gazed out over the room with a soft sigh. 'Don't worry – I'll keep things brief. I simply wanted to take the chance to announce that you will all be able to attend the first trial tomorrow morning.'

Rose gritted her teeth as a chorus of gasps went up around the room. Even if the champions didn't put on a performance, she could be sure the academies would. Crafting trials and tests meant to torment them, all in the name of 'friendly competition'. And now they would let all of Dunhollow witness it, throwing them all to the wolves the first chance they got if it meant putting on a better show.

'Without spoiling the surprise, you will all find directions to the first trial's location in your dorms when you return tonight.' His eyes flashed with a devious gleam. 'Now, I think I've taken up quite enough of your time. Have a lovely evening, and I look forward to seeing you all tomorrow.'

With a final bow, Woodstone released them to their frivolities, returning to chat with the Maalstrum professor, Mistralus. But Rose's view of the pair was soon lost as the din of excited chatter flooded back, somehow louder now than before. The gentle songs of a lute floated down from the charmed phonograph, but she could barely hear it over the noise.

Rose's fingers tightened around her drink. If she was honest, she'd nearly forgotten the tournament was even happening. In the rush of first-week classes, it had almost been too easy, but now?

Bile stirred at the back of her throat, and she reached for her drink, downing a few generous sips. But that only made it worse. *Gods.* She fought back a gag as the sickly sweet liquid clung to her tongue. Sylvie had been right – the thing was terrible.

Rose's throat burned, eyes watering as bubbles threatened

to shoot straight up her nose. Absently, Sylvie patted her back, but Rose recoiled from her touch.

Sylvie's eyes darkened, almost crestfallen as she dropped her hand. 'Rose, listen—'

A familiar voice cut across her. 'Well, that was a lovely little speech.'

Damn. Rose's brow furrowed before she even turned. He *was* here. But Callum only grinned down at her, his smile somehow darker than his eyes. Her lips twisted in a sneer as she glanced over his rich purple robes and artfully coiffed silver curls. He reminded her of a snake in a way. Beautiful yet venomous, and always an unwelcome surprise when it showed up.

'What are you doing here?'

'We all got the same invitation, dal.' His grin widened. 'Though I must say I wasn't expecting this place to be quite so . . . quaint.'

Sharp words twisted around Rose's tongue but, before she could say anything, Sylvie leaned forward, her mask of casual indifference firmly in place once more. 'Not what you're used to, I take it?'

'Oh no.' Callum took a sip of his drink, some viscous violet cocktail that shimmered within the glass. 'Our student bar is more "pick your poison" than friendly neighbourhood pub.'

Rose raised an eyebrow. She wasn't sure she wanted to know what that meant. Nothing good if he thought this place was friendly by comparison. Perhaps, to the ignorant eye, it was. If one was lulled by the warmth of the fire or the scent of garlic and roasted duck that hung in the air. If one heard only the raucous cries of idle games and not the petty lies her peers traded like coins. Heartbreak and deceit bartered and bandied between them with not a thought for sincerity.

Funny – Rose swallowed a scoff. For all his faults, she hadn't thought Callum would be one to take things at face value. With those keen eyes and that cutting smile, he seemed more the sort to pride himself on peeling back others' secrets. Though she couldn't imagine why he went to such trouble. Surely he could simply delve into the sordid minds of her peers without ever leaving his table and still get all the information his dubious little heart desired.

Rose's eyes slid to the booth where Oliv sat dreamily staring out the window. A few Dunhollow students hung around her, whispering and giggling rather unsubtly. But Oliv hardly seemed to notice, entirely content to stick to herself. Strange, then, that Callum was almost never with her.

Rose forced a thin smile, twirling her glass. 'Maybe you'd feel more at home sitting with your teammate?'

'Hardly.' He set his drink down on their table. 'I reckon we have less camaraderie than even Dunhollow.'

Rose's eyes flicked between him and the drink. He seemed rather comfortable where he was clearly unwanted. 'Really? Oliv seems . . . nice.'

'A mere illusion, I'm afraid.' Callum waved his hand with a wry smirk.

Rose glanced back to Oliv, who no longer stared out the window. Instead, she watched the gathered Dunhollow students with unmasked malice, stabbing her knife into the table beneath her.

Rose frowned. Did she really feel the need to cast illusions to cover something as simple as disdain? She shook her head. Oliv might get along swimmingly with the rest of Dunhollow if she ever deigned to give them a chance.

She turned back to find Callum watching her oddly, as if she were some puzzle he couldn't quite piece together. Rose ducked her head, but not before the soft scents of chestnut and chicory stole over her. Callum's signature, she assumed. But it was far sweeter than she'd have guessed, clashing with his perfume of juniper and pine.

'I wouldn't look to make friends there,' he said after a moment, his voice gentle. Yet something sharper lingered beneath – dark and dangerous.

Rose's head snapped up, locking eyes with him once more. But they had softened somehow. Almost as if his mask had slipped away, just enough to allow her in. Her eyes narrowed. She didn't trust it for a second.

'Except with you, of course.'

All at once, whatever softness lingered in Callum's gaze vanished as his smile widened. 'Of course, dal. And since we're such good friends, I should say, I heard a rather interesting rumour about the two of you.'

'Only the one?' said Sylvie, without missing a beat.

'Mmm, yes, your friend Arden does love to ramble on.' Callum reached for his drink, tapping a finger against his glass. 'He told me that you two were at the centre of a gruesome string of murders last year.'

Sylvie stilled in an instant, any trace of disinterest fleeing her features as her eyes hardened. 'Not really our favourite topic, as you can imagine.'

Her voice was cool and even, but it trembled ever so slightly. Her tawny skin paled, a gasp catching in her throat as her eyes flicked to the door. Beneath the table, she reached for Rose's hand, and the warm touch of it lit a fire in her veins.

Callum spoke of it with no more care than if he were commenting on the weather. Here of all places. Her jaw clenched tight. How *dare* he?

Turning back to Callum, Rose leaned forward, placing herself between him and Sylvie. 'No, please, tell us what else Arden had to say. I'm sure it was riveting.'

He glanced between the two of them. For the first time, he looked the slightest bit unsure. As if he sensed he might be wandering into some sort of trap. Rose's lips twisted in a cruel smile. *Good.*

But then Callum chuckled, smoothing out whatever worry had overcome him. 'I believe his exact words were, "Thenlif loves to play the hero, but she doesn't have the skill to follow through. Everyone close to her just winds up getting burned."'

Rose stiffened as the memory of Sylvie lying in the grass flashed through her mind, her flesh scorched and torn. But she shoved it away. She refused to give Callum any ground – to let him see how deeply the words cut, even as they sliced through old wounds.

She met his stare with an acrid smile. 'Rather rich of Arden to be judging anyone's skills.'

'Oh? He seemed very adamant that you didn't belong in the tournament.' Callum stepped closer, his voice little more than a whisper now. 'That you should just . . . drop out.'

His warm breath brushed Rose's cheek, his words like poisoned honey in her ear. They twisted through her mind all too easily, festering and putrid. For there was a part of her that knew them to be true.

After all, it was painfully obvious that she was outmatched and woefully unprepared for what these trials might throw at her. Rose's throat tightened, concession burning against her lips. Until she caught the scent of chestnut and chicory hanging in the air, so faint as to almost be imperceptible.

Almost.

Her heart lurched and she blinked up at Callum. Was he trying to compel her? All at once, raw heat razed through her veins. Whether it was life or flame she reached for in that moment, she couldn't say – perhaps it didn't matter.

It bolstered her either way, burning beneath her skin as it reached for whatever bindings held her mind.

It was almost too easy to find: a poisonous vine wrapped like a noose around her thoughts. But it was brittle and it snapped all too easily beneath her heat.

'*Vala nan*,' Callum cursed, stumbling back. 'What *was* that?'

Rose's chest heaved. There wasn't an ounce of guilt or shame in his features as he straightened. Only shock, which faded quickly to confusion. And then, finally, amusement. Rose's fists tightened, the audacity of it all kindling that scorching heat in her veins.

In the space of a heartbeat, she latched a hand around Callum's jaw, spinning him around so that his back was pressed against the table. The shattering of glass echoed in her ears, punctuated by sharp gasps as the bar fell silent. But Rose didn't care.

She pulled Callum closer as the heat burst out of her, ravenous flames licking up her skin. 'Stay out of my head.'

Fear flashed through his gaze, just for a moment, and Rose's breath caught in her throat. This close, she could see every bit of him. The faint scar carved across the bridge of his nose, the freckles dusted along his cool brown cheeks – even the flecks of silver scattered through his obsidian eyes. As if he had peered into the depths of the universe and left starlight etched into his gaze. And yet, for all of it, she couldn't help but feel she saw nothing true of him at all. Her stomach twisted. Whatever mask he wore would not shatter so easily, even under threat, and it slipped back into place with a sharp smile.

'Do it, dal.' Callum leaned in closer, tucking a stray curl behind Rose's ear, as if she didn't hold his life in her hands. 'I dare you.'

Rose faltered, searching his gaze. Perhaps he thought she

wouldn't. That she didn't have the gall. *His mistake, then.* The thought stole over her with a strange sort of glee, her flames inching ever closer to the delicate flesh of his throat.

How easy it would be to let them consume him. To watch his flesh blister and burn as his body writhed. How long would it take him to succumb to the agony – for his life to mercifully end and leave him a charred, soulless husk?

'Rose.' Sylvie's voice was low as her fingers curled around Rose's wrist, ice creeping across her skin. 'Enough.'

The shock of cold doused her flames, and Rose stumbled back, releasing Callum with a gasp. Her pulse hammered in her ears, throbbing with a dull ache as she stared up into Sylvie's eyes. Something in them soothed her, extinguishing any trace of flame. The lure of blood, the thrill of brutality, all of it faded in an instant – banished to whatever dark part of Rose's heart it had crept from.

She sucked in a steadying breath, turning back to Callum. But he didn't recoil or flee. Didn't call her a monster. He didn't seem to care at all, simply brushing off his robes and reaching for his drink – the only one lucky enough to survive Rose's assault.

But then his eyes fell upon her, filled only with curiosity and a vile sort of mirth. As if, perhaps, this was what he'd wanted from her all along. Rose swallowed hard.

'For what it's worth, I think Arden has it wrong.' Callum ran a hand through his curls. 'It's not the skill you lack – just the nerve, perhaps. You should work on that.'

Venomous barbs curled around Rose's tongue when Sylvie stepped between them. 'And you should walk away. Now.' Her voice was taut with deadly promise. 'While you still can.'

Rose's breath caught in her throat as the two of them stared each other down, neither willing to give ground. In the thick silence that hung between them, she thought Callum might test his luck. Try to charm his way out of Sylvie's wrath, rather than admit defeat.

But, after a long moment, he downed what little remained of his drink and dropped in a mocking bow. 'Well then, I look forward to seeing you both in the trials.'

Rose's breathing slowed as he sauntered off, leaving them to a fragile peace. But, when she turned back to Sylvie, she almost didn't blame him for conceding so easily. Gone was any trace of fear in her features as she watched Callum's retreating form, like a hunter marking her prey.

She was vibrant, radiant – a fortress all of her own. Rose's pulse skittered. Her magic might have been wild and untamed, but Sylvie's was as solid as her ice. And it never missed. Still, Rose's eyes strayed back across the silent room. She had the sinking feeling that this wouldn't be the last they'd hear from Callum.

8. Nothing Left to Lose

The shroud of slumber clung to Rose in the early hours of the morning, her mind racing from thought to thought as it hung on the cusp of dreaming. Fen's smile flashed behind her eyes – a bright light caught in the cold grip of death. But, when she finally awoke, it was not in her bed.

Rose blinked up at familiar looming shelves and a fern-fettered ceiling, leafy shadows creeping across the crown moulding in the pale light of dawn. Propping herself up on her elbows, she winced as her head throbbed. *The library?* She reached gingerly for the tender flesh just beneath her hairline. How had she gotten here?

A sharp hiss ripped from her lips as her fingers skirted torn skin, and she yanked her hand away. Reddish-brown flakes clung to her fingertips and her stomach sank. Frantically, her eyes darted around from the creaking shelves to the softly snoring books just starting to flutter awake. And, finally, to the table behind her, where jagged lines of crimson stained the wood.

Swallowing hard, she got unsteadily to her feet, gripping the table's ledge as she swayed. The sight that met her in the window's rain-soaked panes wasn't kind. A blurred mess of sunken eyes and pallid skin that pricked at barely healed wounds upon her memory.

Rose jumped as one of the shelves shuddered and groaned, turning aside to reveal violet hair and blue eyes. *Delia.* She stiffened, half expecting a tirade for bleeding all over the floor. But the librarian merely closed the distance between them, setting a bottle of healing tonic on the table.

'Oh good, you're awake,' she signed, before blotting some tonic on to a cloth. 'Hold still.'

The tonic's pungent odour assaulted Rose's nostrils but was nowhere near as bad as its sting when it sank into her wound. She jerked away from Delia, biting back a groan. But the librarian held her tight, her brow drawn in silent consternation as she dabbed away at the wound. Finally, she dropped her hands, eyeing Rose up and down.

'There.' She gave a curt nod. 'Now, care to explain what you're doing bleeding all over my library in the wee hours?'

Rose chewed the inside of her lip. Though Delia's gestures were sharp, a current of concern threaded its way through her eyes. And yet, she had no good answer to soothe it. Ducking her head, Rose eyed the discarded swabs soaked through with her blood. *Head wounds always bleed worst*, Soren had warned her once, her hands sticky with a comfrey poultice as he'd patched her up.

She couldn't have been more than eight or nine then, but she remembered all too vividly climbing to the top of the library shelves. The books hadn't taken kindly to her interrupting their nap and promptly knocked her off. Too embarrassed to tell Delia what she'd done and adamant that her mother not find out, she'd run all the way to Soren's office, blood oozing down her skull.

Rose frowned at the memory. How could that be so clear, yet she had no recollection of last night? She swallowed hard. She remembered the pub, but after that? It was hazy – distant and dulled. Almost as if her body had simply left her mind behind.

No. Her heart thudded dully against her ribs. *He couldn't have.*

Her eyes flicked back to Delia's sharp gaze. If Callum had compelled her, there would be some sort of trace, wouldn't there? A hint of his signature, or some other sign that would betray him. Rose ran her hands frantically over the rest of her body, but there were no other wounds. And there wasn't even the faintest hint of chestnut or chicory.

'Rose?'

'I – erm – fell.' Her fingers trembled over the words. 'I came in for a bit of early reading and wasn't watching where I was going. Sorry.'

The lie coiled around Rose's heart, bitter with shame. Yet how could she give Delia the truth when she was a stranger to it herself? Better not to worry her.

Delia glanced her up and down, her eyes piercing and far too shrewd as she screwed the top back tight on to the vial of tonic. But then they softened. 'Perhaps you should stop by the infirmary ahead of the trial.'

The trial. The thought hit Rose like a jolt of ice water. She'd nearly forgotten about the cursed thing, its threat dim and distant among the shroud of her hazy memories. Swaying slightly, her eyes flew to the window. She couldn't go like this. Yet what other choice did she have? It wasn't as if she could just drop out. Her heart skipped a beat. Maybe *that's* what this was all about.

Some petty revenge of Callum's after she humiliated him in the pub. Get inside her mind and make her injure herself so she couldn't compete. Her jaw tightened. It made a sick sort of sense. It *was* the same thing he'd tried to convince her of last night, after all. A wave of nausea rolled over her. *The bastard.*

Heart hammering, she gave Delia a terse nod. 'Sure, I'll head there now.'

Before Delia could protest, Rose turned and fled unsteadily through the shelves. Her stomach roiled, but still she pushed forward. Afraid, somehow, that the moment she stopped, she would simply collapse beneath the weight of it all. If Callum *was* behind this, then she wouldn't give him the satisfaction of cowing her. Besides, if the trial offered the chance to return the favour, she would be all too happy to take it.

The academy grounds were all but silent at this hour. No bird calls carried on the crisp morning air, and even the ever golden leaves lay flat and quiet. Rose shivered, her pulse skittish and unstable. The pain in her forehead had faded somewhat, though the faint stirrings of a headache still prodded at her skull.

Which was not helped in the least by the fact that she had no idea where she was going. Rose pulled her long woollen coat tighter, glancing down at the harsh lines of the crumpled note in her palm: Woodstone's 'directions', as he'd promised at the pub the night before. Though they were hardly elucidating – little more than a shifting map of the university, with the words 'getting closer' scrawled across the bottom.

The letters brightened as she darted down the path behind the greenhouse to the stretch of rocky shoreline along the still waters of the lake. The only remaining part of Dunhollow's original campus, some six hundred years ago, most of which lingered on as dilapidated ruins dotted along the lakeshore.

Rumours abounded that they were haunted or cursed, which was enough to keep even the most intrepid students away. Rose herself had never paid them much attention until last year, when she'd avoided the area at all costs. She'd had enough ghosts following her around then; she hadn't needed to go chasing after any more.

Still, as she stared out across the dark waters, Rose couldn't shake the feeling that something lurked beneath, watching and ever hungry. A thick mist floated across its glassy surface, reaching out in curling tendrils like ghastly skeletal fingers. Ancient pine-hemmed mountains stood sentinel across its banks, almost entirely shrouded by the same fog that hung over the water.

Rose ducked her head, checking Woodstone's map again. The lines danced and twirled beneath a charm, as if guiding her on some morose scavenger hunt. The glittering letters brightened for a moment as she came to a halt, before, finally, they shifted. *Welcome to the Ashwood Tournament*, the words glared up at her. *Enter at your peril.*

Rose's eyes roved over the lakeshore once more. *Enter where?* As if drawn by her thought, the waters along the shoreline shifted, churning and roiling until they parted over the moss-laden stones of a walkway.

She scoffed. Surely Woodstone couldn't be serious. Only at Dunhollow would it be considered a grand idea to build the tournament grounds *on* the bloody lake. Swallowing a groan, she stretched out one foot tepidly on to the soaking stones. She wasn't even at the first trial yet and already she hated everything about this damn tournament.

Mercifully, handrails sprang forth on either side of her as Rose stepped fully on to the path. Though the slick stones beneath her kept her unsteady all the way, and some small part of her wondered if it would be better to just slip and be done with it. Twist her ankle and sit out the trial altogether.

She wrinkled her nose as the waters lapped greedily at the stones. Likely, Woodstone would have healers on hand to remedy that anyway. Besides, she couldn't bear the humiliation if she overcame Callum's sabotage only to go and disqualify herself.

Finally, the fog lining the path ahead parted, though there was no comfort in its clearing. An enormous stone amphitheatre loomed above Rose, sat upon a verdant isle and crowned by the feeble rays of a dimmed sun. Fog clung to its dark frame like a cloak but faded enough that she could make out the faint lines of several tents.

Had they really built an entire stadium just for this farce of a tournament? Rose's stomach churned. They must have, for no record or chronicle she'd ever read had mentioned anything more than a few rocky outcroppings in the middle of the lake.

Rose stumbled numbly down the last few steps of the walkway, the amphitheatre's shadow falling over her with a damp chill. Before she could wander any further, however, a figure sprang into her path. For a moment, she thought it was Woodstone and recoiled accordingly.

But, when she straightened, she caught just the faintest glimmer of gold around his frame – the smallest trace of magic that betrayed it for what it was: a double. A good one too. *Interesting.* It figured that the chancellor would excel in peddling illusions.

'Good morning!' The double beamed down at Rose. 'Thank you for joining us for the first trial of the thirtieth Ashwood Tournament. If you are one of our distinguished competitors, please follow Path A to find your personal tent.'

Personal tent? Rose raised an eyebrow as the path to her right lit up a brilliant Dunhollow blue.

'If you are a student, spectator or honoured guest, please proceed down Path B.' The figure waved its hand to the path on her left, which now lit up a gleaming silver. 'Please have your invitation available for inspection or purchase tickets from the booth just outside the amphitheatre.'

Gods, now he was selling tickets? Rose's blood boiled at the thought. Clearly, she'd been correct in her assessment that Woodstone's dull appearance concealed cruel guile. He was a showman through and through, and he would have them all dancing on strings to his tune. To whatever end.

With a sigh, Rose shoved past the double as it faded with a soft *pop*. The man was quickly becoming even more insufferable than her mother. Marching down Path A, it didn't take her long to find the competitors' tents neatly arranged in colour-coded trios – emerald for DeVoil, amethyst for Maalstrum and sapphire for Dunhollow.

They all surrounded a larger, pearlescent tent that cowered in the shadow of the amphitheatre, helpfully labelled COMPETITORS' LOUNGE. Rose bit back a groan and ducked into the one sporting her name.

The inside was far more spacious than its exterior suggested, bathed in the warm glow of a dozen floating candles. A full-length mirror stood in the far corner, beside an ebony desk with a few potion bottles and a note. But none of it caught her eye so much as the gaudy uniform hanging on the other side of the desk.

It was a simple enough pairing of blouse and trousers, except the top was cut from a stunning sapphire crushed velvet, while the trousers looked as if they were woven from the finest silver-lined wool. Rose delicately stroked the swirling patterns that crept up the blouse.

Woodstone couldn't really expect them to wear this, surely? She ran her fingers down the shimmering sleeve. If so, the trial must not rely on any form of subterfuge. Dropping the sleeve, Rose reached for the note beside it.

Messere Thenlif, it read.

> Please accept these raiments, custom-made and charmed with resistances to a number of curses and hexes. Oh, and feel free to make use of the tonics. I look forward to seeing you compete.
>
> *Warmly,*
> *Everard Woodstone*

Rose flipped the note over, but there were no further instructions. She shook her head, eyeing the potion bottles arranged neatly on the desk. Two were simple healing draughts, one was labelled a 'quick-and-easy hangover cure', but the fourth was an iridescent vial that bore no marker. *Odd.* She frowned, uncorking it and giving it a sniff. *Ugh.* She wrinkled her nose. *Telka tincture.* Swallowing a gag, she quickly recorked it.

Unlike the sweetly brewed telka students drank each morning to strengthen their casting, the concentrated version was like a shot of pure energy. Bolstering a caster's magic to unfounded new heights, it lasted for only a few hours, luckily. Long-term use was known to cause severe mental decline and sometimes even death. She twirled the iridescent bottle between her fingers. Just the sort of thing Woodstone would deem appropriate to give a group of cut-throat students. Anything for a good show, after all.

Though Rose doubted such a gift had been included in *all* the competitors' tents. Then again, she was sure each school had its own questionable methods of ensuring success. Tossing the potion aside, she grabbed the gaudy uniform from its hanger and quickly shed her clothes.

For some reason, she'd half expected the outfit to hang off her frame like an ill-fitting costume from one of the cheap theatres in the capital. But, as she tugged the blouse into place and buttoned the trousers, they cinched neatly around her waist, stretching and forming around the curves at her hips and shrinking at the ankles. *Of course.* She rolled her eyes. She should've known better. Turning, she examined her reflection in the mirror.

But the figure that blinked back at Rose barely even looked like her. The gash at her forehead was now all but gone, her pale skin pink around the cheeks and flawlessly smooth. Her hazel eyes were bright and keen, and her dark auburn curls were luscious and healthy.

A glamour, she assumed. Courtesy of Woodstone to keep them looking at their best. The only thing it couldn't wipe away entirely were the dark circles that stubbornly hung beneath her eyes. Fainter now but still there. *Hardly surprising.* Who knew how much sleep she'd actually gotten last night?

Her stomach roiled at the thought. Callum could've compelled her to do anything. And, with her mind already mired by murderous impulses, it was no small miracle he hadn't forced her to act upon one of them. Rose's heart twisted. Had he?

No. Besides the gash on her forehead, she hadn't found any other wounds upon her that hinted at anything more insidious. Which meant either he was a shoddy compulsionist or he'd only wanted her injured and unnerved. Either way, she wasn't going to let him get away with it so easily.

Rose jumped as the tent flap opened behind her, her heart leaping. Unless it was Sylvie sneaking in to wish her luck, she had no interest in visitors. But her smile slipped as she turned, for the figure towering before her was decidedly not Sylvie. And yet, it was all too familiar, with a curtain of ink-black hair, alabaster skin and sharp green eyes.

'Mother.'

9. Promises, Promises

A cold, sinking feeling wormed its way through Rose's heart, stealing all the warmth from her veins. What was *she* doing here? Her pulse thrummed in her ears as she backed away, bumping into the desk. Her mother was supposed to be banished – cast away to a fate of insignificance in the Outer Isles.

In an instant, it was as if Rose were a child again, shrinking in on herself against her mother's insidious presence. But she could not so easily escape her notice this time. Not when her emerald eyes were fixed directly on her, piercing and hard.

They stirred something within Rose – some spark of rage she'd buried for far too long. She didn't *need* an escape. Not any more. She straightened her shoulders, meeting her mother's gaze with every ounce of fire she could manage. Whatever venom she might drip into Rose's ear was born only of her own fear. Of irrelevance, powerlessness. Of fading silently into obscurity.

Rose frowned at the dark circles beneath her mother's eyes, at the thin lines etched at their corners. Her pale skin, always a flawless alabaster, was now pallid and dull, as if any trace of life had been leached out of her. Even her long ebony dress hung from her thin frame like a shroud – a far cry from the scarlet gowns of velvet and lace she'd once draped herself in.

She was a hollow echo of the formidable figure she'd once been. A cruel smile twisted at Rose's lips. It was the least she deserved. Still, a serpent was at its most deadly when it had nothing left to lose. She'd be a fool to think her mother harmless, even now.

'Rosera.' Her lips pulled in a thin line, and she leaned heavily on her cane. 'You haven't been answering my letters.'

Rose raised an eyebrow. All this time, and that was the first thing she had to say to her? It shouldn't shock her, of course. They'd never excelled in small talk and pleasantries. In anything, really, save perhaps resentment. It burned within her now, sour upon her tongue.

'Must have slipped my mind.' She folded her arms over her chest. 'What do you want?'

Her mother blinked, something akin to shock flitting across her shrewd features. 'Can't a mother wish her daughter good luck? I brought you a gift.'

With a twist of her wrist, a sparkling crimson box floated through the tent flap, landing in Rose's arms with a dull thud. For a moment, she could only stare at it. She couldn't remember the last time her mother had gotten her a present, but the gesture rang hollow.

It was neither generosity nor kindness that she offered but a noose. A collar she would all too eagerly clasp around Rose's throat given the chance, woven of favours and obligations that she could tug whenever she liked. *No.* Rose's jaw tightened. This chasm between them could not be bridged by something so insignificant, and she would not so foolishly fall into that trap. Not after everything.

Finally, she scoffed, glancing up at her mother as she chucked the box on the desk beside her. It landed with a *thunk*, and she was just the slightest bit surprised it did not explode with some curse.

'Pretences, Mother? I thought we were past that.' She stepped closer. 'What are you really doing here?'

'I may no longer be chancellor, but I am still a ranking

board member.' Her mother sniffed, as if the loss of her title were insignificant, but the twitch of her jaw betrayed her fury. 'We all got invitations to the opening ceremony, and of course I simply had to come and see you compete after all my efforts to get you here.'

'All your—' Rose's stomach dropped, the words numb against her tongue. 'It was you. *You* made sure Woodstone picked my name instead of Ewan's, didn't you?'

Her mother shrugged. 'It wasn't difficult. I knew Imrys would bribe Woodstone into picking Ewan. All it took was a simple switch charm on the name card.'

A simple switch. Rose almost laughed. She didn't even bother to ask how her mother had gained access to the name cards in the first place. It didn't really matter, anyway. She'd always been capable of anything, and the how didn't matter nearly so much as the why.

A play for power, she was sure. Some desperate bid to see herself back in the good graces of her peers. And what had Rose ever been to her besides something to be trampled beneath her feet? A stepping stone that had only now shown its use.

But her mother would not find her so easy to tread upon. A cruel smile twisted at Rose's lips. Her mother was the superior caster by far, but even she would struggle to counter necromancy. A giddy rush bubbled beneath her skin at the mere thought. Even she couldn't stop Rose from simply snipping the tether that held her to life like a loose thread.

No. She gritted her teeth. But it wasn't as easy to shake the thought as it had been with Sylvie; it was rooted in every wound her mother had inflicted upon her, hungry to return the favour.

Swallowing hard, she fixed her mother with an acrid smile.

'All it took?' she bit out. 'And the danger it puts me in? Just another inconvenience for you to sweep away, I suppose.'

Her mother's brow creased. 'Don't be flippant, Rosera.'

'Why, because it's unbecoming? You don't exactly have room to talk on that front. How is banishment treating you, by the way?'

It was a low blow, perhaps, but the very least she deserved. Still, Rose shrank back as her mother straightened. A habit born of years past and etched deep into her very bones, warring against the fire in her veins. A shield she no longer needed to protect herself but could not so easily lay down.

'It suits me about as well as arrogance does you, my dear.' Her mother's emerald eyes flashed, fierce and furious. 'In any case, the danger you so fear won't come from whatever paltry tests Woodstone manages to conjure. It's Imrys you should worry about. He'll not be happy you stole Ewan's spot.'

A scowl furrowed Rose's brow. '*I* didn't steal anything. Surely he knows you had something to do with it?'

'Undoubtedly.' Her mother rested her hands overtop the carved handle of her cane. 'But he'll see us both as complicit. And he's not the type of man to let something like that go. As you well know.'

A shiver crept down Rose's spine as the man's grey eyes flickered through her mind, cold and hard, tracking her through the depths of the Whispering Woods … Her pulse leapt and skittered. Yes, she knew all too well the depths of his wrath, and she wouldn't be shocked at all if it had turned on her in the wake of the downfall of his beloved Order.

A blow for a blow, she supposed. That was always her mother's way, though she'd never needed any particular excuse to cut Rose down. Perhaps this wasn't so much a warning as a promise. Her mother may have hated Imrys, but they were two sides of the same cursed coin. And, whichever side it landed on, either would be all too happy to see her ruin.

Still, Rose fixed her smile back into place. There was not a shred of sincerity in it, and they both knew it, but it mattered little now. 'Well, thank you so much for your concern, Mother. I'll be sure to duly consider your sage advice. Now, I trust you can find your way out?'

Her mother's eyes pierced her a moment longer before she matched her cold smile. 'As you wish, dear.' She turned for the exit but paused just before the threshold. 'Let us hope the casting you've finally managed to scrounge up is enough to see you through the trials unscathed. Though, somehow, I doubt it.'

Her words hung in the air, ringing in Rose's ears as the tent flap closed behind her. She released a slow, shuddering breath, a sob caught in her throat as she steadied herself on the desk. Tears burned at her eyes, her pulse racing.

Her mother shouldn't have been able to hurt her any more. And yet, as hot tears fell down Rose's cheeks, that thought had never seemed more fragile. All it took was a few words and here she was, untethered and unravelling.

Her mother knew exactly which wounds to press – which scabs to pick and which scars to slice open anew – for it had been her hand that had wrought every one of them. Rose wrapped her arms around herself, sinking into the plush chair beside the desk with a choked sob.

Perhaps that, of all things, would never change. No matter how far she ran or how much she grew, that scared, wounded child still lived within her. Buried deep down and clawing for freedom, but Rose would never be free, not truly.

At least, not so long as her mother drew breath.

*

When Rose finally reached the Competitors' Lounge, it was well past nine o'clock. She rubbed at her raw cheeks. They were hidden by her raiment's glamour, at least, though that did nothing to soothe them.

Rose faltered in the doorway, glancing around at the luxurious interior. Like her own tent, it was far more spacious within, dancing tapestries decorating the walls and a plush rug covering the grass beneath. Woodstone stood on the far edge of the tent, a cavernous tunnel looming behind him as he chatted to the professors. Their route to the arena, no doubt.

A shudder rippled over Rose, raising the soft hairs upon her arms as her eyes darted over the rest of the tent. Arden dozed in one of the plush chairs by the crackling fire, adorned in the same gaudy costume as her. Which meant Sylvie must have received one too, though there was no sign of her yet.

Rose's heart sank. A ravenous pit gnawed at the back of her mind, desperate for even one friendly face to chase away the shadow of her mother. She closed her eyes, sucking in a steadying breath, when the grass shifted behind her. She didn't have to turn to know who lurked there, for the sharp scents of juniper and pine wafted over her with a sickening familiarity. *No.* Her heart lurched. Not him – *not now.*

'You can burn through a compulsion.' Callum's low voice rumbled over her shoulder. 'A passive one, but still, it's impressive.'

It was all Rose could do not to curse him. How dare he saunter up to her, teasing her about compulsions as if they were old friends? Now of all times. But her insults fell flat against her tongue as she caught sight of him.

Gone were his luxurious robes and tailored waistcoats, replaced instead by sleek black armour that hugged his lean frame in fitting lines. It was made of some sort of leather, though it bent and moved with him like a second skin. Clearly, Maalstrum valued practicality over Dunhollow's more flamboyant approach.

Callum ran a hand through his silver curls and a fierce heat crept across Rose's cheeks. While he always looked pristine, the black of his armour stood out starkly against his hair as a few strands fell across his sharp cheekbones. His obsidian eyes seemed bright by comparison, though his smile lost none of its edge.

He was beautiful, she had to admit, in the same way that a blade was, perhaps. Delicately carved and perfectly primed to rip through flesh and bone alike. But if Dunhollow had taught Rose anything, it was that the prettiest faces hid the ugliest lies and they were no less deadly.

Her lips curled in a sneer as her eyes drifted back up to Callum's. 'You have a bad habit of sneaking up on people.'

'Don't worry, dal.' He grinned, gesturing vaguely to his attire. 'The armour isn't just for show. It'll keep me safe, even from you.'

Rose raised an eyebrow, her eyes roving over the black leather once more. It was sturdy to be sure, but there were parts it did not cover. Delicate joints around his shoulders and thighs could all too easily be sliced. And his tongue . . .

A sharp smile flickered across her lips. That armour would do nothing to protect him if she ripped it right out of his skull. Her fingers twitched at her side, itching to see just how close she could get before he would even try to counter her. But Rose clenched them tight, breathing out sharply through her nose.

What was it about him that made her so inclined to brutality? From the day he'd arrived, this impulse in her mind seemed unusually fixated on him. Perhaps her unconscious mind simply recognized a threat better than she did.

'We'll see.' She shrugged after a moment. 'But unless you'd like to test its limits, I suggest you go find someone else to annoy.'

Callum's grin only widened. 'Promises, promises.'

'Ugh,' Rose scoffed. 'You *would* enjoy that.'

He leaned in close. Too close. He was so near now that his soft breath whispered against the shell of her ear.

'You have no idea, dal.' A shiver ran down Rose's spine as he pulled away. 'Though probably best to keep your claws to yourself for now. Wouldn't want to ruin that lovely outfit of yours. It does bring out the bloodlust in your eyes so beautifully.'

Her heart pounded against her ribs. Was he *flirting* with her? Truly, his audacity was boundless. Yet if he *had* compelled her last night, he was being awfully coy about it now. Though she had no doubt it was all for show – that it was just another tactic to throw her off ahead of the trial. But why?

Sure, she had humiliated him in the pub, and if he had compelled her, she was sure he saw that as fitting recompense. Trying to prove to her that he wouldn't be easily cowed, perhaps. But even before that, he had been oddly fixated on her. Despite the fact that Sylvie was clearly the superior caster, it was Rose that he'd singled out ever since the welcome party. Her stomach sank. Perhaps, just as she recognized a threat, he knew a weak link when he saw one.

'Anyway, good luck today, dal.' Callum's fingers curled gently around her chin, holding her gaze. 'Oh, and try not to burn the whole place down – I'd hate to see you disqualified so early.'

Rose swatted his hand away. But that only seemed to amuse him, and he sauntered off with a chuckle. A strangled breath caught in her chest as she watched him go. Somehow, she felt no more sure now about what had happened last night than she had when she'd first awoken.

She shook her head, still tracking Callum's retreating form when the tent flap burst open. Sylvie raced through, nearly colliding with him. He stumbled back, glancing down at her with a wry grin.

'Good morning, darling.'

But Sylvie pushed past him without answering, making a beeline for Rose. Her tawny skin was flushed and slightly dewy as she came to a stop by her side, her chest heaving. Late, as always. Yet she looked unfairly stunning, even in Woodstone's ridiculous uniform.

Out of habit, Rose reached up to smooth down a few windswept strands of hair that had fallen loose of her braid. It was rare to see Sylvie with her hair back, but the slightly messy plait suited her well.

'Sorry I'm late.' She pressed a kiss to Rose's forehead. 'You OK? You look . . . tense.'

A dry, humourless laugh tumbled past Rose's lips. 'It's been a long morning.'

Sylvie's eyes flicked across the tent. 'Don't tell me – Callum again?'

'Not just him.' Rose's fingers tightened around Sylvie's, her voice taut against the threat of tears. 'My mother came to see me.'

'Gods.' The flush in Sylvie's cheeks faded. 'What did she want?'

'To wish me good luck, apparently.' Rose ducked her head. 'And to warn me about Imrys.'

'Imrys? Why?'

Rose swallowed hard. 'My mother switched my name with Ewan's at the selection and thinks Imrys will be out for blood.'

'*What?*'

'Are you really that shocked?' Rose forced a weak laugh. 'I should've guessed it was her.'

'By the Nine.' The curse tumbled from Sylvie's lips before her eyes narrowed at Rose's forehead. 'Did she hurt you?'

Of course she could see right through the glamour. It warmed Rose's heart in a strange way. Picking each other apart had been a habit born of anger and pride, though it had lost all its sharp edges now, dulled by fondness and love. Like a jagged stone worn smooth under steady river currents.

It was a small comfort to be reminded that not everything wrought by her mother's hand was broken beyond repair. Rose jumped as Sylvie reached up to examine her wound, but before she could answer, Woodstone's shrill voice rang out. 'Attention! Attention, everyone!'

Rose cleared her throat, turning away from the heat of Sylvie's gaze. All around, quiet chatter faded, and even Arden snorted awake in his chair. Professors and competitors alike ambled over to join the chancellor.

'I'd like to briefly go over some ground rules before we begin.' He tugged at his sapphire bow tie, a matching shade to his long woollen jacket. 'As hosts of the Ashwood Tournament, it's Dunhollow's distinct privilege to craft the first trial.'

Rose folded her arms over her chest. Well, that could only mean that it was designed to torment them. Woodstone could phrase it as prettily as he liked, but engineered adversity was the most enduring tenet of Dunhollow's philosophy and a staple of their curriculum.

'Your goal will be to face off against the trial's perils and be the first to secure the gauntlet.' Woodstone eyed them all sternly. 'To keep things as fair as possible, you will be split into three groups to complete the trial – two groups of two and one of three.'

Fair? As if Woodstone cared for anything more than the appearance of equity. She glanced at the other gathered students, pointedly avoiding Callum's gaze. Competing against them all in one large group was one thing, but going up against one of them on her own? Rose wasn't sure she could bear the humiliation.

'Lastly, I do want to make it clear that, while you're competing against each other, we expect a clean and fair trial.' Woodstone eyed them all sternly. 'Though you may incapacitate your opponents, any serious or malicious injury will cause the Faceless to dock points or disqualify competitors if necessary.'

The Faceless?

'Sorry –' Arden's nasally drawl cut through the air – 'but who are the Faceless?'

'Ah, yes, excellent question.' Woodstone beamed down at them. 'The Faceless are the five distinguished judges of the Ashwood Tournament. To protect both their identities and the integrity of the event, they will remain masked and anonymous at all times, but they will always be watching.'

Rose's stomach flipped. Well, that wasn't ominous at all. Her gaze flicked over the tent, but there was no sign of the Faceless. More likely, Woodstone would make some spectacle of announcing them before the crowd rather than waste such gravitas on this meagre audience.

'Now, as I was saying –' Woodstone cleared his throat – 'our first pairing will be Sylven Belliaris from Dunhollow facing off against Oliv Ivyssen from Maalstrum.'

Rose's fingers tightened reflexively around Sylvie's, suddenly reluctant to let her go. But Sylvie only squeezed back lightly in reassurance. Rose bit her tongue. Sylvie could do this – deep down, she knew that. But this fear was not one she would set aside so easily.

'Following that, we'll showcase the talents of all three schools with Peiren Havillande from DeVoil, Callum Avenhart from Maalstrum and Rosera Thenlif from Dunhollow.'

Rose's stomach dropped, her pulse thudding in her ears so loudly that it drowned out all else. *No.* Anyone but him. Slowly, sourly, her eyes lifted across the circle to find Callum beaming at her, as if Woodstone had played right into his hand.

Wonderful, she thought as his grin widened. Perhaps these trials really would be the death of her. Or, better yet, the death of him.

10. Do Try to Keep Up

The silence of the Competitors' Lounge grated on Rose's nerves. Thick and tense, it was broken only by distant rumbles from the arena. Shouts and cries echoed through the tunnel, tearing at Rose's heart. And, of course, the cloying scent of petrichor hung ever thick upon the air.

She paced a small distance away from the other competitors, who all sat quietly around the cavernous hearth, their eyes fixed on the dancing flames. It was only Rose that couldn't sit still. Only she that seemed to care at all for the outcome of the round. Or maybe the others just hid it better.

Rose sighed. Deep down she knew Sylvie would be fine – that she herself would likely come closer to injury or death in that arena than Sylvie ever would. But that did nothing to still her racing heart.

She glared at Woodstone, who lingered by the tunnel entrance, muttering something to the pen and notebook that hung beside him, preparing his next speech, no doubt. Rose rolled her eyes. Behind him, Soren and Mamsella de Prevath sat at the back of the tent, not too close together but much more familiar than either of them were with Mistralus, who stood alone by the fire.

Suddenly, a horn blared in the distance and a great chorus of cheers went up from the crowd. Rose stilled her pacing, her eyes fixed on the tunnel and her breath wound like a coil in her chest.

One moment passed. Then another.

Until Rose's eyes started to water, and her lungs burned,

begging for air. Finally, two figures darted out of shadow, Sylvie at the head. Her breath burst from her chest as Sylvie slammed right into her, her arms curling around her waist. Rose breathed in the scent of her – orchid and musk mingling in a dizzying array with plum and lilac.

'I won.' Sylvie's voice rumbled in her ear, breathless and ecstatic.

Pride swelled in Rose's heart as she pulled back to find Sylvie beaming. 'Of course you did.'

But Sylvie's smile slipped, her eyes darting to Woodstone before she leaned down to whisper in Rose's ear. 'Lay low, let the others wear themselves out with the source avatars.'

Rose frowned. *Source avatars?* What did that mean? Before she could ask, Woodstone cut between them.

'Round One of the first trial is now complete,' his voice rang out. 'Congratulations to Messere Belliaris on a well-earned victory.'

The rest of the room hardly reacted, save for a burst of applause from Soren. But Rose couldn't take her eyes off Sylvie. Her costume was torn and singed in places, and her hair was mussed, but she was radiant all the same. Cheeks flushed and eyes bright, she looked every inch the victor she was.

'Now,' said Woodstone, 'if our Round Two competitors are prepared, your eager audience awaits.'

Any shred of pride in Rose's heart deflated in an instant, sinking into cold, hard dread as Woodstone herded her towards the tunnel. Peiren and Callum already stood waiting, one slightly dazed and distracted, and the other all too sharp. But Rose couldn't bear to look at either of them. Her mouth was as dry as bone, her heart hammering against her ribs.

Up until this very moment, the tournament had seemed some distant intangible thing, a looming formless dread that was easily avoided if she shoved it to the back of her mind. But now that she was here? Flames burgeoned beneath her skin, her only lifeline against whatever horrors awaited her.

Callum's low voice made her jump. 'First place looks good on her.' Rose turned to find his eyes fixed on Sylvie, whose smile had slipped as she watched the pair of them. 'Let's hope you can keep up, dal.'

The whisper sent a shiver down Rose's spine as they were nudged into the darkness of the tunnel. Her stomach clenched. She couldn't – she knew there was no way. All she could do now was survive. And try not to dig her own grave in the process. Life source swirled within her, as if drawn to the thought, lending strength to her flames.

The end of the tunnel loomed, a bright spot against this creeping darkness. Rose wasn't even certain Callum and Peiren were still beside her, but she inched towards the exit all the same, shielding her eyes as charmed sunshine broke across her skin.

She blinked against it, gazing up at the crowded amphitheatre above. Though she could make out no face or figure, she could feel their eyes upon her, their applause ringing hollow in her ears. Not as loud as for Sylvie's round, she noted. That had echoed back to the Competitors' Lounge.

She wondered if her mother was among them. Whether she'd clapped or cheered at all. Likely not, she guessed, but it didn't matter. Rose gritted her teeth, her eyes shifting to the ring ahead of her, a jagged maze of stone. All she could focus on now was getting through this alive.

As if to punctuate the thought, a shard of ice whizzed past her head and Rose recoiled. For the briefest moment, she thought it was Sylvie, the cold bite of source so familiar across her skin, until a figure drifted out between the rocks, all metallic, icy edges. Rose's heart leapt into her throat.

The strange construct glided towards them, its translucent frame crafted from solid ice, like Sylvie's crystalline cat. It had no legs to speak of; it was merely a hulking chunk of a torso with a smaller sphere sitting atop it for a head. Its eyes were hollow holes cut into the ice, and its arms were little more than swirls of frost. It was as if a child had tried to carve a person out of ice and then covered them in thick plate armour.

A source avatar. It had to be.

Behind her, Rose swore she heard Callum curse under his breath, but she didn't even have time to turn before the avatar raised its frosted arm and a freezing blast cut across the ground.

Rose dived out of its path. *Shit.*

Shards of ice sprayed down upon her hair as she hit the ground, hard. Pain ricocheted through her wrists and knees, but she paid it hardly any notice, her heart racing as she scrambled to her feet. The earth rumbled beneath her and Rose glanced back in time to see thorned roots sprawl out of the ground, wrapping Peiren in a protective embrace.

Damn. Rose leaned back on her heels. She should have guessed that the dazed show he put on was little more than a facade. A few feet away, Callum swayed as he got to his feet. Except another Callum was exiting the tunnel and a third sprinted past the avatar towards the rocks behind it.

Illusions. Rose rolled her eyes. *Of course.* But they seemed to fool the source avatar well enough, for it shot another blast of ice in the direction of the fleeing double. Or perhaps that had been the real Callum. Her head spun. Gods, she didn't know any more.

But then the construct's empty gaze turned back to Rose and any thought of Callum vanished. Turning on her heel, she darted towards the cover of the rocks ahead. Ducking behind the nearest one, Rose struggled to steady her breathing, her ears pricked for any sign of the blasted avatar creeping closer.

The shatter of ice echoed behind her; it was still focused on Callum or Peiren. She didn't particularly care which. Rose's heart thudded dully in her ears and she stared down at her shaking hands, willing some spark of flame to curl around her palms. But they lay empty.

Closing her eyes, she drew desperately on any shred of heat or courage – anything to chase away the sinking fear that ensnared her racing heart. Yet, when she opened her eyes again, it wasn't the orange glow of flame that greeted them, but the cold hollow eyes of the source avatar.

A scream ripped from Rose's throat as the construct's frosted arm clamped down over her own, the cold bite of it burning as surely as any flame. The pain seared at the back of her mind and finally, *finally*, some shred of source broke through, fire curling up her arms in scorching tendrils.

The avatar recoiled. But heat flared through her veins now, and it would not be quelled so easily. Not until the wretched thing's head lay shattered beneath her. A cruel smile spread across Rose's lips as she wrapped a flaming hand around the construct's shard of a head and squeezed.

Ice melted beneath her blazing grip, water dribbling between Rose's fingers and sizzling into steam. The creature shrieked, almost as if in agony, but she didn't stop, pouring every ounce of rage and fear into the heat of her flames. Until they were white-hot, blistering and the avatar fell before her in a melted heap.

Rose's chest heaved, sweat dripping down her brow. But her blood sang in giddy whispers, ever hungry for more. Bile bit at the back of her throat as she straightened, just before another avatar rounded the rock ahead of her.

Her heart dropped. Of course there was more than one. But this one had flames to match her own, writhing in dancing wisps between its molten armour. And hers would be useless against it.

Sucking in a sharp breath, she turned to run when a bolt of lightning arced through the air over her shoulder, shattering the construct's armour in spidery tendrils. The avatar trembled for a moment, caught in the lightning's grip, before its fires faded and it fell to the ground in a crumpled heap of charred metal. Rose blinked as a figure stepped out from behind it, its silver hair gleaming in the sunlight overhead.

'You're welcome.'

A scowl furrowed Rose's brow. She hadn't even known Callum *had* source magic, but she couldn't deny she was grateful for it now. Not that she would ever admit that to him.

'I had it,' she growled instead.

'Sure you did, dal.'

A sly smile pulled at his lips, stoking that fierce heat in Rose's veins. It begged to be fed, fuelled by the delicious stain of Callum's blood. Her pulse throbbed, every fibre of her being crying out for it. Until an icy chill fell over her.

She turned slowly, only to find the avatar she'd just felled once again towering over her. Half its head was melted away but its source had lost none of its potency as it aimed another blast of ice at the pair of them.

Rose dodged at the last second. *Shit.* They couldn't be killed.

Callum wasn't as quick this time, the sheet of ice catching the soles of his boots. Though every bit of Rose's mind begged her not too, she slammed her open palm into the ground, letting her flames fly free. They cracked and barrelled through the plane of ice, encircling the construct behind a wall of fiery tendrils.

Callum stumbled back, blinking at Rose, but she darted past him. He could be shocked all he wanted, but her flames wouldn't hold that thing long, and she didn't plan to stick around for it to free itself.

Yet she'd barely made it more than a few feet before a cry went up ahead of her. Peiren was stumbling out from behind one of the rocky outcroppings, dodging blows from a third avatar, this one with webs of lightning caged between its armour. Rose's eyes darted back the way she came, seeking escape, when lightning arced over her head.

Her fire fled from her without a thought, yet it only glanced the construct's armour, not even slowing its advance as it aimed a sizzling arm at her. Rose ducked, but no impact came as vines sprawled forth, ensnaring the creature. She blinked at Peiren, who flashed her a quick smile before the construct burned away his trap and sent a bolt right through his shoulder.

Rose screamed as he crumpled and the construct turned on her. But a hand curled around her shoulder, yanking her into a hastily drawn barrier. Her pulse hammered in her ears as Callum shoved her behind one of the stones, his arm wrapped firmly around her waist and his warm breath brushing the shell of her ear.

'Don't move, dal,' he whispered. 'I think they respond to motion.'

Rose swallowed hard but nodded slowly. After a moment, she peeked around the edge of the stone, where all three avatars now stood, their hollow eyes scanning the stones. And getting ever closer.

'Source won't take them out.' Rose's gaze darted to the lightning avatar. 'We need a dismantling charm. Or maybe a caging curse.'

Callum flinched as the ice construct crept closer, icicles

clinking beneath its formless feet. 'Curses and charms aren't my specialty, I'm afraid.'

No. Because this trial wasn't designed for him to succeed. Or Peiren. It was an ill-concealed attempt to let a Dunhollow student breeze right through each varied aspect of these tests as the pinnacle of magical learning they were meant to be. But not Rose.

She gritted her teeth. It didn't matter. The constructs would find them any moment – they needed a distraction.

'Cast your familiar.'

'What?' Callum's sharp intake of breath echoed in her ear.

'If they're drawn to its motion, it'll distract them for long enough for us to make a run for it.' She turned to face him. 'Or at least force them to split up.'

Callum's eyes narrowed at her, as if he wasn't quite sure he should trust her. To be fair, Rose wasn't either. But then he nodded, tilting his chin as a blood-red moth crept down his neck, fluttering its iridescent wings. *A nightfire moth.* Rose almost frowned. Somehow, she'd imagined Callum's familiar would be more . . . insidious. But it would have to do.

He cracked his neck as the moth flew away, flitting between the stones and glowing all the way. 'And yours?'

Rose faltered, her eyes darting to her bare forearm. 'I – er – don't have one.'

Shock flickered across Callum's face and Rose braced herself for mockery or disdain, she wasn't sure which. It stung all the same. Yet Callum said nothing. Instead, he ducked his head and shuddered as another figure shifted out of his shadow.

Rose's breath caught in her throat. Another double.

Before she could protest, however, the illusion darted past her, the nightfire moth lingering over its shoulder, as it barrelled into the path of the source avatars. If it wasn't so unnerving, it would have been comical the way their heads all turned in unison at their entrance. Like hounds drawn to the scent of blood, they scattered in a great clamour of metal and source. Criss-crossing and scrambling over each other to chase them both down.

'All right, dal, your brilliant plan worked.' Callum took her by the hand. 'Let's go.'

But Rose didn't move, her feet rooted to the ground as her gaze caught on Peiren's prone form. They couldn't just leave him here. He had helped her, after all. At his own peril too.

'Wait, cast another double.' She turned back to Callum. 'Send for a healer.'

'Why?' His brows shot up his forehead. 'They'll get him once the trial's over.'

Her heart lurched, though she could hardly say why. *No.* It could be too late by then. She didn't even know the boy; there was nothing that tied her to him. Except this pulsing urge within her. Not brutal or murderous this time but born of an old thought. Of another face – one she'd failed to save in her apathy. Aveline's blue eyes pierced her mind, her body prone and lifeless on the river's edge. She couldn't do nothing. Not again.

Rose's fingers tightened around Callum, furious flames inching up her free hand as she pulled him in close. 'Do it, unless you want to end up just like him.'

Callum fixed her with a hard stare and Rose thought he might refuse her. That he might wrench himself from her grasp and leave her alone with the twisted feeling that ensnared her. But he didn't. And something in that dark gaze softened just for a moment.

'Fine.' He sighed. 'But your bleeding heart will be the death of us.'

Rose almost laughed. For, in the horrid hollows of her

chest, it was not caring or compassion that stirred to life; it was anger – bitterness even. That apathy was the expectation in this wretched place and complacency was labelled a virtue. But she wanted none of it.

She would not be Dunhollow's gilded instrument, ever dancing to their tune. She would be what she'd always been: the thorn in their side. And she would make them bleed. If they wanted cruelty, she would give them only kindness, even if it bore claws.

Shaking his head, Callum stretched as another double stepped out of his shadow, no less potent than the first. Even with his familiar boosting his casting, it must have been an incredible strain, but he showed no sign of it. Rose blinked at the double before it winked at her and darted off towards the tunnel.

'Happy now?' Callum raised an eyebrow as Rose nodded numbly. 'Then let's go.'

She didn't stop him as he took her hand again, dragging her forward. The stones twisted and protruded at odd angles ahead of them, just waiting to trip them up and deliver them into the hands of the source avatars. Their metallic clanging echoed across the arena, a warning as much as a threat.

Callum's barrier held steady as they ran, yet Rose couldn't fathom why he shielded her. If he'd wanted to sabotage her last night, why help her now? And, perhaps more importantly, why didn't she let go of him? But the thought fled her head as they stumbled out of the maze of rocks, Callum drawing her sharply to a halt. Before them, the ground was ruptured and writhing beneath a serpentine mass of ropes that brushed their boots eagerly.

'Looks like it could be an imitation charm.' Rose bent down to examine them more closely. 'Or maybe a coiling curse?'

'It's an illusion is what it is. And a poor one at that.' With a flick of Callum's wrist, the slithering ropes disappeared and he recaptured Rose's hand. 'Come on.'

'Wait!' she cried as he dragged her forward, but it was too late.

A soft click echoed beneath them and the ropes sprang back to life. They grasped at their ankles with a startling hunger, twisting up their bodies, ensnaring the pair of them in a choking grip and pressing them ever closer, until they were chest to chest – heart to racing heart.

Rose glanced down at the ropes as they stilled their ascent just below her throat, and then pointedly back up to Callum. He at least had the decency to look sheepish as he squirmed against their bonds.

'Do you care what they are now?'

He pursed his lips. 'I'd prefer it if you had a clever solution to get us out of them.'

Rose flinched as he shifted against her, his thigh caught between her own, and his lean torso pressed flush against her breasts. Thankfully, with him standing a head taller than her, it was easy to duck away from his gaze. To hide the hot flush that crept across her cheeks as her eyes caught on the throbbing veins of his throat.

Yet the heat that bloomed within her now did not pull at the urge to tear tender flesh, but to brush her lips across it. To press herself closer and see if the stiffness that held his spine so rigidly echoed lower too. But then she blinked, shaking away the thought with a shudder.

Instead, she glanced back down at the ropes. She had no talent for counterspells, yet even a curse might fall to flame. Stretching her fingers out as far as she could, Rose let the warmth burgeoning beneath her skin flood into her palms until the acrid stench of burnt twine filled her nostrils and the binds started to loosen.

It was a delicate dance, allowing enough fire to slice through the slithering ropes without engulfing them both. Especially with Callum twisting and turning against them. Rose winced as one of her flames cut too close, searing her skin. But, finally, they loosened, falling away with a sizzle.

Callum stumbled as they scattered across the ground but caught himself quickly. 'Glad I didn't leave you behind, after all.'

'Don't be.' Rose's eyes flicked to the scorched ropes still slinking hungrily towards them and she shoved him back. Callum gaped at her as the bindings once again crept up his ankles, and Rose saluted him with a sly smirk. 'Oh, but do try to keep up, *dal.*'

Leaving Callum struggling, Rose dashed away before he could even call out her name. Served him right, anyway. A pang of guilt pulled at her heart, but she buried it. He'd been ready to leave Peiren to die, and he may well have compelled her the night before. Besides, he'd only saved her now because he'd thought she'd be useful to him. He didn't deserve her pity.

Her feet pounded against the stone, the scent of petrichor clinging to her nose, but Rose didn't slow. Twisting and turning through the maze, she didn't check if Callum was behind her – didn't stop to map her way through the stones. It was all she could do to keep running.

Until the rocks ahead of her opened into a fog-laden clearing and she drew to a sharp halt. All three source avatars loomed within, circling the mist like predators seeking prey. Callum's familiar was nowhere to be seen, nor was his double. Meaning either his spell had faded or he'd called them back. *Bastard.* Though, in truth, she could hardly blame him.

Rose stood rigidly, hardly even daring to look behind her

for an escape route. Going through wasn't an option either. There was no cover; the rocks entirely encircled them like the jagged teeth of a ravenous jaw with only empty fog between them. The avatars would have a clean line of sight on her all the way through.

Her stomach sank. *There was no way out.*

Even life source would not save her now, not that she could use it. All she had at her disposal were fading flames and a head full of knowledge that was little use against metal and source. Briefly, desperately, she wished Sylvie were here. She'd taken these things out with barely more than a breath, Rose was sure. *Lay low*, her voice whispered through her memory, *let the others wear themselves out.*

Rose blinked down at the fog as it ebbed against her chest, a spark of an idea catching at the back of her mind. What if Sylvie had meant it *literally*? Before she could think better of it, she dropped to the ground, the damp earth seeping through the crushed velvet of her costume.

But Rose paid it no mind, a giddy laugh almost bubbling to her lips. Because, at last, she could finally see. The fog hung suspended about a foot in the air, but the grass beneath her was green and clear, as were the stony bases of the rocks encircling her.

And there, pulsing in the centre of it all, was a small box. Metallic and nondescript, it would have passed her notice entirely if it weren't for the three twines of source curling around it. Gritting her teeth, Rose crawled forth, avoiding the gliding figures of the avatars, if only marginally.

When the box was right before her nose, she stilled, her heart racing in her ears. There was no time to try to decipher its inner workings or dismantle it carefully. Instead, she slammed her palm into it, crying out as the entwined sources bit through her flesh. But she didn't let go.

Pain flooded every inch of her – every vein and synapse – until all that remained was a hollow hunger aching between her bones and a heat all too eager to swallow her whole. But something within Rose held fast, the smallest shred of power. Of life itself. And it would not suffer defeat.

It flared out of her, bolstering what remained of her flames, turning them a sinewy silver, hotter than they'd ever been. Yet they did not burn Rose, only the metal beneath her palm. It cracked and caved, melting away until it was little more than a charred heap in her hands.

All at once, the fog faded and plates of armour clanged all around her as the source avatars collapsed, leaving the field in utter silence. Rose blinked, counting her heartbeats. Once. Twice.

And then the stands erupted into cheers: uproarious applause as they whooped and whistled. Rose let the scorched metal box fall from her fingers with a dull thud, glancing up at the crowds above with a frown.

Yet they did not calm or quiet as she got unsteadily to her feet. It was strange, she thought. Such a display would once have soothed her haggard soul. Praise and adulation that she'd lacked for so long, she'd have once greedily gathered them up to patch those empty holes within her. But now?

Now it rang hollow in her ears. They did not cheer for her, not really. Not for her cleverness or tenacity – not for anything that made her who she was. No, they cheered only for their own entertainment and the show she had provided. Bile bit at the back of her throat, and it was all she could do not to choke on it.

Behind her, something cracked loudly and Rose stumbled as the earth shook. Her eyes flew back to the centre of the field, where an obelisk rose amid the remnants of the fallen source avatars, scattering stones as it cracked open. And there, staring back at her, was the gauntlet she needed. Her breath caught in her throat. She'd done it. *She'd won.*

The thought set her heart racing as she reached for the gauntlet. But something seized her – a cold, hard grip right around her heart, rooting her to the spot. Around her, the arena faded to utter darkness, not a breath of sound echoing in her ears. Except one.

A warm voice greeted her. 'Rose?'

A familiar voice, one that brought tears to her eyes.

'Fen?'

His face crept out of the shadows slowly, like some sort of sick dream. Rose's eyes traced the sharp lines of his jaw, his russet skin sun-kissed and glowing even in the darkness. But it was his smile that pierced her most, soft and sorrowful. And all too fleeting.

It vanished in an instant, his skin turning ashen as his eyes rolled back, leaving behind the hollow holes of his skull as his skin sloughed from the bone. *No.* She staggered back. Hot flames licked at her wrists, feeding on her fear.

She squeezed her eyes shut. It couldn't be him.

Applause crashed over her – thunderous against the sickening silence of this cruel vision. Rose's eyes flashed open but Fen was gone, as was any trace of shadow and smoke. All that stood before her now was Callum, his silver hair gleaming and his eyes bright as he lifted the gauntlet over his head.

11. Fair is Fair

Flames still licked at Rose's skin as she stormed out of the tunnel. They were no longer searing but ever ready, like embers clinging to the last dregs of life, starved of fuel, yet easily revived. She didn't even slow as she entered the tent, her eyes focused solely on the exit. On freedom or whatever counted for it now.

Until a solid form stepped into her path. 'Rose?' Sylvie caught her arm. 'How'd it go?'

Rose blinked up at her, the flames faltering and her words failing. She wasn't even sure she had any to explain what had happened. None that would soothe her anyway. Or Sylvie, for that matter.

But Woodstone's voice rang out behind them. 'Round Two of the trial is now complete. Congratulations to Messere Avenhart.'

'Thenlif lost?' Arden's nasally whine cut across the tent. 'Figures.'

Rose stilled, rounding on him with slow purpose. He leaned against the tunnel entrance, a sneer on his pinched lips and his pale eyes ever sharp. But he only reminded her of a spoilt child, primped, preened and mewling for attention. Before Rose could say anything, however, a crisp voice crept over her shoulder.

'I think if anyone cared to hear your opinion that they would ask, no?' Azalaïs sauntered towards them, idly pinning her sleeve back at the seam of her vinewood forearm as if she had all the time in the world. 'I'd be more worried about your own impending loss.'

Arden's eyes narrowed, but then he scoffed, muttering quietly as he skulked over to Woodstone. He might have been a fool, but he was a coward at heart, and he knew when he was outmatched. Grinning smugly, Azalaïs gave Rose a sly wink before brushing past her. But Rose only released a shaky breath, her hands trembling as she watched them go.

Sylvie pulled Rose aside, rubbing her arm. 'Ignore him. What happened in there?'

The words still tangled around Rose's tongue, burning with shame. The cloying feeling crept beneath her skin, ever lurking – waiting. Whether compulsion or the vile frailty of her own mind, she couldn't say. Perhaps it truly didn't matter. She hated it all the same, just as she hated herself for falling to it.

But then Sylvie reached for her arm, stroking it gently. And it was that simple action that almost broke her. The softness of her touch, the way Sylvie didn't even seem to realize she was doing it. As if caring for her was just second nature now.

Rose's throat tightened, the truth finally spilling from her lips. 'I almost won, but something forced me to stop.' Her eyes slid to where Callum leaned against a tent pole, fiddling with the gauntlet in his hands. 'Or someone.'

Sylvie followed her gaze, her eyes darkening. 'What, you think he compelled you?'

'I-I don't know.' She wrapped her arms around her middle, her flames finally flaring out with a soft hiss. 'But it might not be the first time.'

'What do you mean?'

'This morning, I—' Her throat tightened. 'I woke up on the floor of the library with a gash on my head and no memory past leaving the pub. It's like my mind wasn't my own and now . . . I don't know.'

Sylvie's eyes widened, her lips parting in a gasp when a

throat cleared behind them. Rose and Sylvie both stared at Woodstone, but he seemed utterly unfettered by the heat of their gazes.

'Pardon the interruption.' He sniffed, clearly not caring one bit. 'Messere Belliaris, might I steal you for a moment?'

Sylvie hesitated, her eyes flicking between Rose and the chancellor. More than likely, he wanted to discuss how best to celebrate her victory, how to show her off to her adoring fans. Rose's heart twisted. The thought made her skin crawl, but Sylvie deserved every inch of praise and adulation for the marvel that she was. And Rose wouldn't be the one to keep her from that.

'Go on.' She squeezed Sylvie's hand. 'I'll get some air while you're gone.'

Sylvie's brow furrowed but, finally, she nodded. 'Just be careful.'

Rose forced a wan smile as Sylvie took Woodstone's outstretched arm and let him drag her away. She watched them go, the space Sylvie had left behind now cold and empty beside her. But the air of the tent was heavy, tiresome given the weight hanging over her mind.

Turning on her heel, she darted out the exit. She needed to get to her tent. To steal a moment alone, away from all this madness. But she barely made it halfway there when a familiar voice lilted over her shoulder.

'Beautiful and ruthless.' She could almost hear Callum's lips curl in a smirk. 'You are full of surprises, aren't you, dal?'

Of course he was lying in wait for her. What else had she been expecting really? He was always over her shoulder, after all. Always the venomous voice in her ear – lurking, watching. Waiting.

She almost didn't stop, but something held her back. Not a compulsion; this time it was her own will. Some restless, fervent energy that longed for the delicious friction of barbed words and heated lies. A fight to match the fire in her veins.

'Leave me alone,' she snarled.

'No need to be a sore loser.' Callum caught her wrist, pulling her around to face him. 'Fair is fair. Though I *am* curious why you didn't take the chance when you had it. The gauntlet was right there and you just froze.'

It was galling how saccharine his voice was. Like syrup spun into a smooth, delectable confection that might poison anyone foolish enough to eat it. But Rose was no fool. And neither, she thought, was Callum.

His eyes were too sharp, glinting in the grey light like honed blades. He knew exactly what he'd done, just as he knew precisely how to pare away her defences and wheedle his way beneath her skin.

'Please.' Rose yanked her arm out of his grasp. 'You know why. Now get out of my way, or you'll find out just how ruthless I can be.'

Without another word, she shoved past him. She didn't stop to check if he followed – didn't care to. Her feet pounded against damp earth, carrying her past the maze of tents, desperately seeking solitude. Her breath burned in her lungs, ragged and fierce against the cloying scent of petrichor. She could never flee from it – not truly. Just as she would never be free of this wretched place. Of its cruel smiles and cutthroat lies.

Tears pricked at Rose's eyes, as she stumbled into her tent. Something of Dunhollow's rotten core had carved itself into her bones – seared itself into the deepest folds of her mind. It was as if every step she took was weighted by chains she could never unshackle. Every breath bound by memories that would never fade.

Flames burgeoned at her fingertips once more as Fen's smile flickered through her mind. But she didn't shove it aside this time, didn't cull or conceal her source. The pain cut too deep, burned too bright. But it was all she had left. And she was drunk on it.

Gods, how she wanted to let it consume her. Consume the world. To watch as this wretched facade crumbled to ash beneath her power and all that was left was smouldering ruins. And how easy it would be to let go . . .

No. Rose tried to force the craving away. Head spinning, it was all she could do to hold herself upright. To not collapse beneath the weight of it all. She stumbled as her vision blurred and she gripped the edge of the desk, desperate to steady herself.

But it was no use. A shiver ran down her spine, an aching hunger stretching through her veins. She barely even heard the flap of her tent sweep open, nor the dull thud of a cane as darkness welcomed her into its cold embrace.

The acrid stench of smoke burned at Rose's nostrils, jarring her awake. She blinked, her cheek pressed flush against the damp earth and her head throbbing. *Not again.* The thought flickered through her muddled mind.

The gems of her ridiculous costume bit into her skin as she rolled, slowly pushing herself up. Beyond her tent, the muffled cries and shouts of the trial carried on the air. Yet her mind was utterly dark, devoid of any recollection or reason. Anything to explain how she'd gotten here.

Callum. Rose's heart sank – had he followed her? A shiver skittered across her skin and her eyes flicked to the full-length mirror. But there was no mark of any injury upon her. The glamour of her costume hung by a thread over mussed curls and grass clinging to her skin. She seemed perfectly fine.

Until her eyes skirted left, landing upon the curved hood of an all too familiar cane. Leaping to her feet, Rose whirled around, only to nearly collapse once more. For there, stretched upon the verdant grass before her was her mother.

Prone, listless and very much dead.

12. Sorry to Disappoint

Hollow eyes stared up at Rose, no longer a piercing emerald. Instead, they were scorched and blackened – any flesh within the sockets burned away. Her mother's mouth was twisted in a silent scream, but no poison spilled from her sharp tongue now. Only smoke. Rose's heart thudded dully as her eyes traced the blistered edges of her mother's wounds. It was as if some flame had gripped her from within and seared away her life from her rotten soul.

No, not some flame – *her* flame. Bile crept up Rose's throat, sour upon her tongue. This macabre tableau could only have been wrought by her hand. But why?

Rose stared down at her palms, still red and pulsing with heat she could not recall casting. All at once, it was too much. The acrid stench, the smoking wounds. The sinking feeling of something dark and restless deep within her falling dormant once more.

It was all she could do to stay upright as she fled. But the air beyond her tent did little to soothe her, and she tumbled to her knees, retching into the grass. What had she *done*? The thought twisted around her heart as she choked on ragged breaths.

But she couldn't shake the images from her mind. Couldn't stop it from reeling – grasping at visions of her mother writhing beneath a fiery grip. Not a memory. *No*. Just the broken, brittle workings of her own mind as it tried to piece itself back together, forcing her to conjure up vile imaginings to fill in the holes.

Rose's head spun and she curled in on herself. What would happen to her now? How could she ever explain this to Sylvie? To Soren? They would hate her – spurn her. Call her a monster. And maybe they were right.

'Rose?' A familiar voice tore through her thoughts.

Callum. Her chest tightened as his footsteps grew closer. Of course he would find her. But he did not tease or toy with her. Didn't laugh or ridicule her for the mess that she was. He only dropped to his knees beside her, pulling her hair away from her face.

'What happened?'

Rose flinched at his touch, blinking up at him. Something of her almost wished for that keen edge to his gaze. For his sharp tongue to slice through her defences and lay her bare. It was the least she deserved now.

But his eyes were drawn only in concern. When she didn't answer, however, he got to his feet, pulling aside the flap of her tent. And there he fell utterly still.

Rose turned away, gritting her teeth. She couldn't bear to see the gruesome truth of it again. So she simply stared at the grass beneath her, waiting for the moment Callum's kindness soured to judgement with bitter anticipation.

'*Vala nan,*' he swore finally.

Rose's head snapped up. 'You don't understand. I-I didn't—'

He cut across her, not even turning away from the tent. 'We should hide the body. Before the others see.'

She froze. Surely she hadn't heard correctly. 'Hide it?'

'Yes, dal.' He sighed, letting the tent flap drop as he turned back to her. 'I don't suppose you know any good places?'

Good places? Rose's pulse throbbed against her skull. To hide a corpse? *Her mother*, she corrected herself with a twinge. Not just a body to be buried – not a thing to be cast away.

Her own flesh and blood. Whatever that meant now. Still, her mind whirled around Callum's offer.

She couldn't fathom how he would manage such a thing while the grounds were crawling with spectators. Or why he was even helping her, for that matter. He should have been fleeing or crowing about her crimes for all to hear. *Something.* But he seemed utterly unfazed, only his eyes betraying any sense of urgency as they flitted back and forth between the tents.

A cold, hard dread twisted around her heart with an iron grip. Perhaps it was all some ploy. Perhaps *he'd* gotten in her head and made her cast the fatal spell. It would explain his lack of surprise. And the aching chasm in place of her memory too.

'You're not even going to ask what happened?' Rose got unsteadily to her feet, wiping away the last stains of tears and snot.

'I think it's fairly clear what happened.' He glanced pointedly back at her tent. 'And frankly, I don't care.'

Rose folded her arms over her chest. 'Then why help me?'

'Because my heart bleeds for your tragic plight. Does it matter?'

'A bit, yeah.' Even if he hadn't compelled her, he was far too calm about stumbling upon a scorched corpse. 'You happen upon a gruesome crime and you have nothing at all to say about it?'

'And what would you prefer?' His lips twisted in a grimace. 'That I lecture you? Judge you? Call the capital inquisitors down upon you? Sorry to disappoint, dal, but I've done far worse, so if you want self-righteous admonishment, you'll have to look elsewhere.'

Rose recoiled. For, in the space between his words, something had shifted. The facade crumbled, the mask slipped away and all that remained in those dark eyes was anger. Frustration. Fear. Not of her but *for* her. And it cut straight through Rose's heart.

'I—'

'Gods, you're stubborn.' He closed the distance between them, the scent of juniper and pine falling over her. 'We only have a few minutes before they call us back over to announce the winners, so let's move.'

His fingers wrapped around her wrist, cool and firm, but they struck her like a blow. Something stirred deep within her, burning hot as it latched on to him, pulling at his mind, peeling back her own. Emerald eyes stared up at her, blood pouring from a thousand slices in sallow flesh. And then only screams. Piercing, shrill and all too familiar.

Her mother.

With a gasp, Rose wrenched her arm from his grasp. 'Get away from me!'

Callum stumbled back, cradling his hand as if she'd burned him. 'What *was* that?'

Rose's breath caught in her throat. A vision, maybe, like those Aveline had given her last year? Or perhaps a sliver of memory? Though it almost felt as rooted in the foul depths of Callum's mind as it was in her own.

'Rose?'

She glanced up to find Sylvie gliding towards them. Like a burning star on this dim field, her eyes were full of fire as they slid to Callum. 'What did you do to her?'

'*Vala nan.*' He sighed. 'We really do not have time for this.'

Rose's breath faltered. For a moment, she wanted to let Sylvie's wrath burn right through him. Let Callum play the villain and Sylvie her avenging hero, but she couldn't keep the truth from her. Not even if it turned her from Rose's side for ever.

'Sylvie ...' Her throat tightened, but she tugged her towards the tent and pushed the flap aside.

'Shit.' The whisper slipped between Sylvie's lips, her tawny skin turning ashen. For several long moments, she didn't move. Finally, she shook her head, her jaw set as she turned back to Rose. 'We need to get you out of here. Now.'

Rose's heart leapt. Even after seeing the wretched truth charred into her mother's flesh, she still wanted to *protect* her. It was enough to make her head spin.

'Aren't you forgetting something?' Callum jerked his head towards her mother's body. 'Can't just leave that lying around, can we?'

Sylvie's eyes narrowed. 'I don't recall asking your opinion.'

'Forgive me for trying to be helpful,' he scoffed, 'but unless you want your girlfriend to rot in prison for the rest of her life, we should take care of the body first. Trust me.'

'Trust you?' Sylvie drew herself up to full height, stepping closer to him. 'Why should we? What are you even doing here?'

It was a fair question. One Rose was all too eager to hear the answer to herself. But a restless, skittish urge sent her eyes flying back to the Competitors' Lounge. Her heart fluttered in her chest. Loath as she was to admit it, Callum was right. They had to get her mother's body out of here. And soon.

'As it happens, I—'

The words died on Callum's lips as the air around them popped. Rose recoiled, jumping back as a familiar figure with brown hair and dull eyes stepped between them.

Shit.

'Messeres, what is all the ruckus?' Woodstone hissed. 'This is meant to be a civil tournament, not a—'

Both Sylvie and Callum scrambled to pull the tent flap shut, but it was too late. Woodstone's skin went utterly pale, his mouth falling agape as his eyes flicked between the three of them.

'This isn't what it looks like, Chancellor,' Sylvie said hurriedly.

But Woodstone's eyes didn't focus on her. On anything really. As if the scene before him had sent him reeling somewhere else altogether. Finally, he blinked, resignation falling over his features with a sickening lurch.

'I'm sorry, Messere Belliaris.' He shook his head. 'But I'm afraid this is quite out of my hands now.'

13. Secrecy and Death

The Competitors' Lounge sat in utter silence. Unease held on the air like a taut thread, the other competitors eyeing Rose as if she were a caged serpent while Sylvie glared at all of them in turn. Rose tugged at the ends of her stained sleeves, avoiding all their gazes as if they might burn her.

Callum had rejoined the Maalstrum cohort as soon as they'd been ushered into the tent by Woodstone. Eager to wash his hands of this whole mess, Rose assumed. The chancellor hadn't stayed long either, frantically corralling the professors to debrief them and then rushing off. A small mercy, in the end. She didn't think she could bear his prying gaze now. Or Soren's.

Rose swallowed hard, staring down at her hands. The redness left by her flames had long faded but they still pricked at her mind. Dark shadows, screams wrenched from a scorched throat. She clenched her fists tight, her eyes skirting to the enshrouded figure lying prone in the corner of the room.

Someone had taken the time to cover her mother's corpse, though Rose couldn't say who. Woodstone, probably. Yet she doubted it was out of reverence, more likely to keep them all comfortable. Though if that were the case, she couldn't imagine why they hadn't just left her where she'd fallen in her tent.

Rose's throat tightened and she stared at the cream linen, willing herself to feel *something*. Regret. Shame. Even grief. Yet there was only a strange numbness that had taken root in her heart, swallowing all else.

She wondered briefly, darkly, what her mother would feel if their roles were reversed. Relief probably. Joy at finally being rid of a daughter who lacked all semblance of talent and grace. Who had never been anything beyond a burden and an ungrateful one at that.

No. Her mother would not mourn her. Not, at least, beyond what was required to keep up appearances. Anything for that.

Yet her mother hadn't simply died – Rose had *killed* her. She'd stolen her life without even a memory to mark it. Or something within her had, anyway. Something that craved violence. Something that finally sat sated and silent. For now.

But still *her* in the eyes of the law. There was no proof of her guilt but none of her innocence either. Her stomach twisted. Her only defence, perhaps, was her questionable power. Burning someone from the inside out without leaving a charred husk was no small feat, and not one she alone was strong enough to cast.

A bitter scoff burned against Rose's lips. Not enough to possess any real skill and not enough to stop herself either. Not enough, no matter what she did.

Rose jumped as the tent flap flew open, but it wasn't Woodstone or any capital inquisitor sent to arrest her. Instead, Soren swept through, Ewan close on his heels. In spite of everything, her heart leapt.

'Rose!' Soren wrapped her in a choking hug. 'Are you all right?'

'I'm fine.'

And, for the first time all day, she actually felt it. Cradled by his strong embrace, the cold grip of her mother's death could not reach her, nor could the searing heat of her own flames. It didn't matter now what unspoken words lay between them. What wrongs and worries had soured their bond in the last weeks. She felt like a child again, seeking refuge from some nightmare within his arms.

Rose wished she could stay there, safely tucked away from the accusing stares that surrounded her and enveloped in warm scents of spiced whiskey and cigar smoke. But she couldn't. She was a child no longer and this nightmare would not simply fade with the dawn of a new day.

'Soren,' she said finally, pulling away. 'My mother—'

He cut across her. 'I know. And I'm sorry to ask you, but we'll need to get your facts straight. The Faceless are on their way.'

'The Faceless?' Rose recoiled. 'Not the inquisitors?'

Soren shook his head. 'Woodstone would rather keep things quiet for now.'

'Not quiet enough,' said Ewan. 'Soren and I caught my father sniffing about your tent. No doubt Woodstone saw fit to fill *him* in. And I'm sure he's now gone to "brief" the Faceless.'

Wonderful. Her mother's warning floated through Rose's mind and her stomach sank. Could Imrys be behind this? Some petty scheme to have her disqualified and take her mother out in one fell swoop? It seemed a bit extreme but that didn't mean he wasn't involved.

In matters of secrecy and death it seemed he always was.

'He always manages to worm his way in, doesn't he?' Sylvie muttered, as if reading Rose's mind.

'Well, he was obsessed with your mother, Rose.' Ewan lowered their voice. 'Now that you've taken that away, I wouldn't be surprised if he turns his ire on you.'

'*Ewan.*' Sylvie jabbed an elbow into their ribs.

'Oh, right, sorry.' Their golden-brown cheeks flushed as they rubbed their side gingerly. 'I mean, now that she's gone.'

Rose shook her head. 'It's fine.'

It was strange how easily they and Sylvie dismissed her guilt. Or accepted it, perhaps. Honestly, Rose wasn't sure any more, but something flickered within her all the same. Desperate for their understanding, yet grateful for their nonchalance.

'Right, well, just give them as little information as possible.' Ewan tugged at the collar of their long black robes. 'From what I understand, they don't have much actual evidence, so don't volunteer anything they don't ask for.'

Rose nodded numbly. If Imrys *was* set against her, she was quite sure that whatever she said wouldn't matter; he would twist it to his purpose all too easily. Though, for all she'd learned of the man last year, she couldn't really say what lengths he'd be willing to go to. But she trusted Ewan knew them well enough. And Soren too, for that matter.

'What do you think, Soren?' Rose glanced over to find his gaze lingering on her mother's shrouded corpse. 'Soren?'

He almost jumped, frowning as he cleared his throat. 'Sorry, just hard to imagine she's really gone.'

Before Rose could respond, the tent flap opened once more, this time producing Woodstone and five cloaked figures. They towered over everyone in the room, peering down at them out of gilded delicately carved masks that betrayed neither thought nor feeling. *The Faceless.* Her heart fluttered.

The hollows of their eyes were shadowed, the lines of their veiled visages etched into the shape of various beasts. A wolf, a raven – even a viper. Their identities were utterly hidden; there was nothing to even mark them as mortal.

But it was the figure looming behind them that truly sent Rose's pulse racing. *Imrys Elaegius.* Tall and broad, Ewan's father swathed himself in shimmering robes of onyx and ruby, his pale eyes flicking over the tent as if it were beneath him, somehow.

Once, Rose would have called his face, if not conventionally attractive, at least intriguing, all sharp angles and thin features. Now it only seemed hollow and shrewd – no more genuine than the masks the Faceless wore. Yet there was something frayed about the taut line of his thin lips, as if he was barely keeping his fury at bay. *Strange*.

'Here we are.' Woodstone strode forward into the tent. 'As you can see, I've cast a preservation charm on both the scene and the body, but, out of respect, we did enshroud it.'

'That will certainly make our job easier; thank you, Chancellor.' The viper-masked figure nodded grimly, their voice a low rasping wheeze. Glamoured like the rest of them, Rose was sure. 'Now, Imrys said the daughter found the body?'

Rose flinched. Well, he certainly hadn't wasted time sinking his claws in. Yet Imrys didn't even meet her gaze now; his grey eyes were fixed on Woodstone as he stared down his nose at him. Though Woodstone's smile held no warmth for Imrys either. *Interesting*. Rose's eyes narrowed at the pair of them. Perhaps it was another prerequisite of any chancellor that they be detested by Imrys Elaegius. Or vice versa.

Woodstone's lips pulled in a tight smile before he nodded. 'Yes, she's just over there.'

Rose's pulse skittered as the Faceless all turned almost in unison. Somehow, she'd not expected Woodstone to throw her to the wolves so easily. For their part, Sylvie, Ewan and Soren formed a protective cage around Rose. As if they could hold the judges' questions at bay through will alone. Imrys glowered at Ewan, but he said nothing as the first of the Faceless approached them.

'Messere Thenlif.' They gave a curt jerk of their head. 'My condolences on your loss. You may call me the Aratis, the first of the Faceless, for whom I shall be speaking. Is it true you found the body?'

Their voice was so low it almost reverberated in her bones, more like a growl or a death rattle than anything belonging to a person. Almost as if there was nothing beneath that mask but bones.

Rose glanced at Soren before nodding slowly. It was hardly something they didn't already know, but she was hesitant all the same, reluctant to let either the Faceless or Imrys lure her into any trap. It would have been all too easy for her words to stick, what with Imrys filling the judges' ears with honeyed poison, she was sure.

'Yes.'

'That must have been a rather gruesome shock.' They gave a soft *tsk*, as if they pitied her. 'What time would you say it was that you entered your tent?'

'I'm not sure.'

It was true enough, though Rose fought to keep her face even all the same. She had no idea how long the first two rounds of the trial had taken and her mind had been notably elsewhere after Callum's win.

'Her trial finished at around eleven o'clock,' Woodstone supplied, stepping forward. 'She left the Competitors' Lounge shortly after, while the third round of the trial was ongoing, and I sent Messere Belliaris here to locate Messere Avenhart for the announcement of the victors.'

Woodstone waved a hand vaguely over Rose's shoulder. Her eyes followed the motion, catching on Callum's shock of silver curls as he leaned idly against the stone fireplace. But whatever his posture implied, his eyes tracked them keenly, as if he were waiting for the right moment to strike. Rose's pulse quickened, and she forced her gaze away.

'At which point you discovered all three of them together?'

'Yes.'

'I see.' The golden mask barely moved as the Aratis turned

slowly back to Rose, almost as if it were fused with their skin. 'And where were you prior to discovering your mother's body, Messere Thenlif?'

Rose's mouth went dry. She couldn't very well say her tent, nor could she plead a loss of memory without incurring suspicion. Yet it wouldn't do to get caught spinning a full falsehood either. Not when the Faceless could still prise the truth from Callum's lips. Though he hadn't said anything yet...

'I was, erm—'

Imrys cut across her. 'I'm sorry, but to be frank, you must see how this looks. You found your estranged mother burned to death in your own dressing tent and you can't even give a simple answer as to your whereabouts?'

Soren stepped forward, his normally warm gaze now as cold and hard as steel. 'Are you accusing her of something?'

The Aratis cleared their throat, not the least bit fazed. 'I'm sure he was just making an observation, isn't that right, Imrys?'

Rose resisted the urge to roll her eyes but only barely. That the Faceless allowed Imrys to be present at all during their questioning spoke volumes. It was almost laughable to try to dismiss his involvement now.

'If I may,' said Ewan, 'those observations seem oddly targeted. Araminta Thenlif wasn't exactly a beloved figure by any stretch of the imagination, as my father himself can confirm. But I'm sure he told you as much when he was filling you in?'

The Aratis faltered. *No.* Rose didn't imagine Imrys would have mentioned his long-standing feud with her mother.

'And anyone here might want to frame Rose for the crime,' Ewan continued, entirely undeterred by the rather puce hue of their father's skin. 'Get her disqualified from the tournament, perhaps? Though I can't imagine who would have wanted that.'

'Indeed.' The Aratis did not raise their voice, but it echoed with a clipped finality all the same. 'However, that does not change the fact that Messere Thenlif was the one to find the body, had personal ties to the victim and is yet unaccounted for in the time leading up to the murder.'

'As are quite a few others, no doubt?' said Soren.

Rose bit her tongue. They could talk in circles all they liked, but it didn't change the fact that she'd done it. Broken, snapped, compelled – it didn't truly matter. It had been her flames and her hands that had cast them. Her mind that was mired by murder. And even they couldn't protect her from that.

'Honestly, all this hemming and hawing is rather dull, don't you think?' Callum's bored drawl crept over her shoulder. 'Just tell them where you really were, dal.'

Rose's eyes snapped up as he ambled over, looking just as calm as he had upon finding her mother's body. The dull pace of her heart picked up as Callum came to a stop beside them. Was this what he'd been waiting for? The moment when he could draw the most blood?

The Aratis cocked their head. 'Did you have something to add, Messere . . . ?'

'Avenhart.' He stuck out a hand. 'And, yes. I can confirm that after the trial, Rose and I were *quite* occupied in my tent. We only found her mother when we stopped by her tent so she could freshen up.'

'Is that so?'

Rose blanched, her eyes flicking from Callum to Sylvie, and back to the Aratis. What was he *doing*? She'd known he was bold, but outright lying in an inquest? If they found him out, he'd face prison, the same as her. Or worse.

Though Callum hardly seemed perturbed as he fixed Rose with a particularly lascivious grin. She fought the urge to recoil, glancing instead at Sylvie, who looked crestfallen. Surely she didn't *believe* him?

But the Aratis's gaze drew Rose back, still awaiting an answer. 'I – er – yes.'

'And why did you not simply say so sooner?'

Rose bit her tongue, swallowing the urge to admit that she'd rather go to prison for slaughtering her mother than be caught in bed with Callum of all people. Then again, that was a truth the Faceless might actually accept.

'It's not a mistake I would want widely known.' She met Callum's gaze pointedly, who smirked.

'I see.' There was a long beat of silence before the Aratis sighed. 'Well, thank you all for your candour. That will suffice for now, though we shall return if we have any further questions.'

Rose's breath fled from her chest as they jerked their head towards the other Faceless, who all swept out of the tent as one. Imrys stared at her a moment longer before sneering at Ewan and ducking through the exit. But a nagging, restless worry refused to settle in Rose's chest. This wouldn't be the end of it. Imrys wasn't the type to let this go, and neither, she suspected, were the Faceless.

More questions would come, of that she was sure. And she had to discover the truth before they did. Whatever that might be now.

14. A Favour Owed

Rose stared at the tent flap, her heart hammering against her ribs as it fluttered. Even surrounded by warmth as she was, wedged in between Soren and Sylvie, she couldn't help the cold shiver that stole over her. It was as if a silencing spell held over the tent – every eye fixed on her.

'Well –' Woodstone's voice jarred her – 'thank you, everyone, for your cooperation; you're now free to go. But bear in mind that this is an open inquest. If any of you have any further information, it should be shared directly with me or the Faceless.'

His gaze lingered on Rose for a moment before he turned with a swish of his cloak. Swallowing hard, she glanced back at Sylvie and Soren, and then, finally, Callum. But he was no longer at Rose's shoulder. Instead, he'd already crossed the tent, whispering something in his professor's ear before darting out the exit.

She almost made to follow him when Ewan sighed deeply.

'So that went about as well as can be expected.' They ran a hand through their gold-streaked hair. 'Can't say I'd normally suggest lying in an inquest, but your new friend came in handy. For now, at least.'

Soren's eyes widened at this. 'He was lying?'

'Of course.' Rose raised an eyebrow. 'You can't really think I was sleeping with him? He found me only a few minutes before Sylvie did.'

Sylvie's shoulders visibly loosened, a soft sigh slipping past her lips, almost inaudible. But Rose frowned. Surely she couldn't really think that Rose would betray her so easily, with Callum of all people?

'Then where were you, Rose?' Soren whispered, snapping Rose's attention away from Sylvie. 'And why would Callum lie for you?'

Rose's eyes flew back to the exit. That was the question, wasn't it? And it was well past time that Callum owed her some answers.

'That's what I intend to find out.'

Before Soren could protest, Rose pushed past him and out of the tent. She was vaguely aware of Sylvie following close on her heels, but Rose's gaze was caught by the silver-haired figure stepping on to the stone pathway across the lake. If Callum heard her coming, he made no show of it, letting out a surprised huff as Rose grabbed his shoulder and shoved him into the metal railing.

His eyes widened, just for a moment, as the dark waters of the lake lapped hungrily behind him. But he smoothed out his features quickly, a wry smirk creeping on to his lips.

'Steady on, dal.' He chuckled, grabbing Rose's hand as her fist curled around the collar of his armour. 'You wouldn't want people to think we were having a lovers' spat.'

'Why did you lie to the Faceless?' She flinched as his thumb brushed her wrist, but she didn't loosen her grip.

Callum's grin widened as his eyes flitted to Sylvie, who had stilled at the water's edge. 'Is she always this violent?'

'Only when it's warranted.' Sylvie folded her arms over her chest. 'Now answer the question.'

A soft warmth burgeoned around Rose's heart as she met Sylvie's eyes. She made no move to stop her this time – didn't try to rein Rose in at all. As if she were all too happy to let Callum meet whatever fate he'd earned at her hands.

'Fine,' he said finally, shifting against Rose's grip. 'It seemed the best thing to do at the time. And it worked, didn't it?'

'That's not the point.'

'Come now, it's not the worst thing in the world to be accused of, is it?' He sighed. 'Besides, having two powerful casters indebted to me seemed a fair trade.'

So that's what this was about. A favour done, a favour owed. And Callum would dangle it over their heads until it suited his cruel whim. Rose swallowed a scoff. Did he want to win the damned tournament so badly that he would resort to coercion and extortion?

Behind Callum, a school of colourful mummer fish inched closer to the shallows around the rocky path. Their song floated softly above the inky waters, sweet and alluring, hiding sharp teeth and ravenous appetites. Rose shook her head against the lure of their lullaby, her eyes narrowing at Callum. Perhaps the mummers had been drawn in by him, recognizing like for like – a beauty that lay only skin deep, ever covering a more insidious nature.

'Indebted?' Sylvie spat out the word. 'You can't be serious.'

Callum shrugged, turning back to Rose. 'Well, if you don't want the alibi, I'm happy to retract it.'

'Are you threatening me?'

'I wouldn't dare, dal.' He fixed Rose with a saccharine smile. 'I've seen what happens to people on your bad side. I simply think we'd all benefit from working together rather than fighting one another.'

Working together? Rose shot a glance at Sylvie, whose lip had curled as if she'd smelled something foul. And yet there was a spark of . . . something in her eyes. Something Rose couldn't quite place.

Gritting her teeth, she turned back to Callum. 'Can't say I agree.'

'Pity.' He stroked one finger across her forearm, sending a shiver down Rose's spine. Until his hand curled around her wrist and wrenched it away as if it were nothing. 'If you change your mind, you know where to find me.'

Shoving Rose back, he turned and strode off down the walkway. For a moment, all she could do was stare after him as he disappeared into a haze of fog and the faintly glimmering lights from the campus above. But then Sylvie brushed past her, and Rose instinctively reached for her.

'No, let him go.' She tugged Sylvie back. 'He clearly isn't going to tell us anything more.'

Sylvie's shoulders slumped as she sighed, her eyes straying back to the tents behind them. 'Maybe we should go back. Talk to Sylverfir.'

Rose followed her gaze, but the very thought of speaking to Soren made exhaustion sink deeper into her bones. Facing those kind eyes and admitting it was she who had ripped her mother's life away? That she had gone behind his back to cast the Spell of True Revival and unwittingly dragged him in to this whole mess? *No.* He deserved answers from her as much as she had from Callum, but she couldn't bear the thought of giving them now.

'Not now.' Her throat tightened. 'Not yet. I-I just need some time, please.'

'Sure.' Sylvie nodded numbly. 'Whatever you need.'

The stillness of Rose's dorm held her in a soothing embrace. Candlelight danced against her walls, chasing away cold shadows but its light was warm and gentle. She counted Sylvie's steady breaths, her chest rising and falling beneath Rose's ear.

Here she could pretend it was a day like any other. Just another lazy weekend spent wrapped in Sylvie's arms, hiding away from the world. But it wasn't. Rose's stomach sank.

And there was too much that lay between them to leave it unspoken now. It was Sylvie who broke the silence first, her voice soft, even as her words crashed over Rose.

'Are you ready to tell me what happened?'

Rose stiffened. 'Are you sure you want to hear it?'

Sylvie nudged her arm, pushing Rose back so she could sit up. 'I've already guessed that I won't like the truth, Thenlif. But I'd still rather hear it from your lips.'

Rose faltered, dropping Sylvie's gaze. What was the truth any more? Nothing that she could give easily. She gritted her teeth as her mother's scorched eyes flashed through her mind, her charred lips frozen in an eternal scream. Her fingers tightened around her bedsheets, and she drew in a steadying breath.

When Rose finally found her voice, it was feeble. 'Even if I did it?'

Sylvie's eyes widened and then danced away from her, but she didn't recoil or rebuke her. She didn't move at all for several long moments, silence binding the air between them. Finally, she sat up with a deep sigh, her gaze fixed on her painted ebony nails.

'*You* did?'

'I-I'm not sure.' Rose leaned towards her slowly – as if Sylvie was some skittish creature that might flee at the first sign of movement. 'I remember talking to Callum, and then going back to my tent, and that's when everything went dark. When I woke up, I was standing over my mother's corpse. I fled, and that's where Callum found me.'

Sylvie pulled a knee up to her chest, locking her fingers around it. 'You think he made you do it, then?'

'You don't?'

'I don't know – maybe.' Her eyes fixed on the duvet beneath her. 'I mean, I could see him sabotaging you last night, but what reason did he have to kill your mother? Seems a bit extreme if his goal is just to get you out of the tournament.'

'Maybe.'

'Besides —' Sylvie tucked a strand of gossamer hair behind her ear — 'you said you were having brutal thoughts *before* Callum arrived. What if they just got the better of you? I wouldn't blame you, after everything your mother's done.'

Rose chewed the inside of her lip. Sylvie was right, though the realization didn't soothe her. These impulses *had* lurked in her mind since she'd cast the Spell of True Revival, that much she couldn't deny.

Perhaps even before that. Her stomach flipped. Whatever had led her to that spell in the first place was a hunger that had lived within her longer than she cared to admit. It had been fuelled by Fen's death, perhaps, but it was a pyre that had been built piece by broken piece over years of ridicule and doubt. And now she had perhaps sacrificed her own sanity upon it.

Rose leaned back on her hands, picking at the edges of her duvet. It couldn't be that alone that led her, though. Her mother had been the architect of that pyre and Rose had constructed it dutifully under her watchful gaze. But something else had lit the spark that now engulfed her. *Someone* else.

'What if they're connected somehow?'

Sylvie raised an eyebrow. 'What?'

'If Callum compelled me, maybe it weakened my mind, made me more susceptible to acting on these urges.' Rose tugged at the stained ends of her sleeves. 'Or maybe the other way around, and the backlash from the spell made it easier for him to slip in.'

'Maybe.' Sylvie heaved a great sigh, leaning back against the pillows. 'But talking ourselves into circles over it isn't going to fix anything.'

'I know.' Rose ducked her head. 'And I will talk to Soren – first thing tomorrow.'

She jumped as Sylvie leaned forward, linking her fingers through Rose's. 'I'll hold you to that, Thenlif.'

Rose's eyes met hers, slowly. It felt unreal that she was still here. Even when it might risk her own safety.

'Maybe—' Rose's voice cracked. 'Maybe you shouldn't stay here tonight.'

'What? Why not?'

A shocked, scathing laugh slipped past her lips. 'Because, in the last day, I've blacked out twice and murdered my own mother, Sylvie. Perhaps sleeping next to me isn't the safest plan.'

'Did you ever consider it might not be safe for you either?' Sylvie straightened. 'At least if I'm here I can make sure no one else gets hurt – you included. Besides, I can protect myself.'

Gods, she was beautiful when she was stubborn. Even singed and tattered, her eyes still blazed, her tangled hair making her look feral. Rose had no doubt she would be utterly ferocious in the face of death. But to be the one who brought her to that brink? *No.* She couldn't bear it.

'I know you can, Sylvie, but I don't want you to have to.'

At this, Sylvie leaned in, cupping Rose's face between her hands. 'I told you we'd figure this out together, and I meant it. I trust you, Thenlif.'

Rose's throat tightened. Where Sylvie found such grace for her, she might never know, but it was more than she deserved. Still, she clung to it, unwilling to let it go.

15. What's Done is Done

Soren's door towered over Rose with a worn sense of familiarity. The grooves in the dark wood, the little vines carved into the golden knob. Patterns and shapes she knew all too well, yet they filled her only with a twisted sense of unease now. Her eyes flicked to Sylvie beside her. It hadn't been so long ago that they'd come here to snoop through Soren's things, believing him responsible for heinous crimes. He'd been innocent, of course. But Rose no longer was.

Her heart fluttered like some erratic caged bird. What would she even say to him? How could she look him in the eye and admit she'd fallen for the same folly he had? *No.* Not fallen – *chosen*. She gritted her teeth. And now that choice might have led her to depths far worse than he'd ever delved.

Would he grieve her mother? Her nails bit into the flesh of her palm. Their relationship had soured in the months he and Rose had been away, but still. They'd been friends once and she'd ripped her mother's life away without a shred of remorse or purpose.

The weight of it hung cold and hollow in her chest, but it wasn't grief or guilt, just numbness. As if the truth of her crime hadn't quite sunk in. Still, she wouldn't blame him if he hated her.

Yet, somewhere deep down, she knew he wouldn't. And somehow, that made it so much worse. That those soft brown eyes would never turn away, that his kind smile might falter but would never fade. Not even if she broke his heart.

'You can do this.' Sylvie squeezed her hand, making Rose jump.

Glancing up, her heart twisted. Not for the first time, she wondered how Sylvie could still bear to stand here with her. Why she hadn't simply walked away, though it would have been easier – safer. What mercy lived in that fierce heart of hers that let her remain at Rose's side, unscathed and undeterred?

The same that kept Soren bound to her, she supposed. The same that tied Rose to them in turn. Even when she'd thought Soren was at the heart of last year's brutality, it had never occurred to her to hate him. And Sylvie? She'd detested her enough for one lifetime, and loving Sylvie was far easier than loathing her had ever been. There was nothing that could now keep Rose from her side – save perhaps herself.

'I know.' She sighed. 'You're right.'

Sylvie gave her a wry grin. 'Well, if you can bring yourself to admit that, then telling Soren the truth should be a piece of cake.'

In spite of herself, Rose almost smiled. 'You're insufferable.'

A soft warmth curled around her heart as Sylvie planted a kiss on her forehead, bolstering her resolve. Straightening, she raised her fist to knock. But her knuckles barely brushed the door before it swung open, producing Mamsella de Prevath.

They stared at each other for a long moment, neither having expected the other, it seemed. Rose's mouth went dry, any lucid thought fleeing her head as her eyes roved over the woman's figure.

Even at this hour she was stunning. A satin turquoise gown hung loosely off her shoulders, her golden braids twisted into a thick topknot, though a few hung free, artfully framing her high cheekbones and sculpted brows. Her warm brown skin bore neither wrinkle nor blemish, yet sun-kissed freckles dotted the broad bridge of her nose.

Mamsella de Prevath raised one brow, a wry smile tugging at her lips before she turned and called over her shoulder. 'Soren, *tai filha ese'aici.*'

Rose blinked as the Arbelian words rolled smoothly off the woman's tongue. *Your daughter is here.* Despite everything, it warmed her heart. The flicker of nostalgia for hearing Soren's mother tongue, the ease with which the Mamsella named their bond. It took her back to simpler days of Soren reading her stories from his homeland or muttering curses over failed potions in words he thought she couldn't grasp. But Rose shoved the memory down. They were far from that now.

With a little hum, Mamsella de Prevath flashed Rose and Sylvie a smile and swept past them, a cloud of lavender and oakmoss hanging in her wake. Only a second later, Soren stumbled out of the washroom, his hair still wrapped up in his satinette sleeping cap and wearing nothing but a pair of loose linen trousers.

'*Ques*— Oh.' The words died on his lips as he took in Rose and Sylvie, his eyes widening. 'Good morning. Er – give me one moment.'

Rose averted her gaze, though she caught Soren darting back towards the washroom out of the corner of her eye. A fierce heat crept across her cheeks. Suddenly, she regretted turning up unannounced.

'We can come back later,' she called out as the washroom door clicked shut.

'No, no.' Soren's voice was muffled through the door. 'I'll just be a minute.'

Beside her, Sylvie snorted, and Rose turned to glare at her. 'Not one word.'

'I wouldn't dare,' she said, though she hid her laughter poorly behind her hand.

Rolling her eyes, Rose dragged Sylvie into the room and shut the door behind them. The quarters were small but no longer the drab, untidy room that Rose remembered from years past. The four-poster bed was freshly made with crimson gold-threaded sheets, and Soren's mahogany bookshelves were stacked in neat, colour-coded rows. He'd also added a small fireplace and a kitchenette since she'd last been here, Rose noted, her eyes roving over the small stove.

Truly, it looked like an entirely different room, and yet so much like *him* now. A small smile tugged at her lips as she glanced at the desk by the window. A jacket was draped over his chair, and the desk itself was littered with knick-knacks Soren had picked up on their travels. At least that hadn't changed.

Rose was jarred from her thoughts as the washroom door swung open once more and Soren fixed her with a sheepish grin. He'd slipped a cream linen blouse and an ochre cardigan over his sleep trousers, his hair loosened from its cap. Smiling softly, he launched forward and wrapped Rose in a tight embrace.

Something stirred deep in her chest as the wool of his cardigan tickled her nose, and she burrowed into his shoulder. It was safe there, in the warmth of his arms, like sinking into a plush leather chair with a glass of spiced whiskey and a cigar. And a part of her never wanted to leave. To stay shielded from the truth just a little longer.

'Sorry about that,' Soren said as he pulled away, moving to embrace Sylvie. 'I was just—'

Rose cut across him. 'It's fine.'

She had a guess what he and Mamsella de Prevath had been up to, and she was quite sure Soren didn't need to fill her in on the details. Rose shuddered inwardly. It was good to see him moving on, no longer stuck in the past and pining for her aunt, and she was happy for him – really, she was – but she hadn't needed to hear about every one of his trysts on their travels, and that hadn't changed.

'Isn't she a bit young for you?' Sylvie teased, apparently not at all gripped by the flushed shame that crept across Rose's cheeks.

Soren's eyes widened slightly before he laughed. 'Not that it's any of your business, but she's actually older than me. The waters of Arbelis are a powerful tonic.'

Sylvie looked him up and down. 'If you say so.'

Soren rubbed the back of his neck, his brow furrowing as he glanced over at Rose. 'Right, well, I'm guessing you didn't come here to discuss my romantic life?'

Sylvie nudged Rose forward. 'Not quite. Rose has something she needs to tell you.'

Soren's grin slipped, and Rose resisted the urge to glare at Sylvie. It was fair, she supposed, trapping her into a confession. She'd been running from it long enough, after all. But it still rankled.

'Of course. Please, sit.' He gestured to the tiny table in the corner by the stove. 'Telka?'

'Sure.'

The three of them squeezed in around the tea table, silence falling between them as Soren pottered about. He set three clay mugs before them and a jar of sweet cream, and reached for the porcelain pot. Muttering a warming charm under his breath, he poured the steaming dark liquid neatly into their cups, its rich sweet scent swirling between them. Rose and Sylvie both nodded their thanks as Soren finally settled into the wicker chair with a creak, steam curling up to fog his glasses.

'How are you doing?' He tapped his fingers against the side of his carved mug with a grimace. 'Yesterday, you just disappeared after the inquest, and I, well, I know this must be . . . complicated for you.'

Rose dropped his gaze, staring down at her mug as Sylvie added a little sweetened cream for her. She could lie. Pretend she'd hidden herself away over some sense of grief for her mother's death. But what would be the point? Sylvie was right; she couldn't run from this or bury the truth behind the weight of another lie. Not any more.

'I think I did it.' Rose swallowed hard. 'I think I killed my mother.'

'Well, I would have led up to it a bit more than *that*,' Sylvie muttered as Soren sputtered into his telka.

'*Dia vhal.*' Soren's throat bobbed as he leaned back in his chair, his umber skin going a shade paler. 'I don't—I mean, *why* would you do that?'

That was the question, wasn't it? Rose's throat tightened. Curse or compulsion, neither amounted to much against the gravity of what she'd done.

Rose chewed the inside of her lip. 'It's – er – complicated.'

'Good gods, Thenlif,' Sylvie scoffed before turning to Soren. 'Rose cast a revival spell for Fen, then started having the urge to murder people. She thinks the spell weakened her and that Callum is taking advantage of that to compel her, and that he provided her with an alibi to cover up that he's the one that compelled her to kill her mother in the first place.'

Soren's eyes widened and his cup clattered on to the table, some of the telka splashing the smooth surface. A rather choked sound escaped him, as if any words he might've had had gotten stuck. Rose watched him with bated breath, the seconds ticking by on the clock behind him with grating surety. Finally, he sank his head into his hands with a soft groan.

'Soren?' she ventured cautiously.

He shook his head, as if trying to fend off her concern. 'Just give me a moment.'

Rubbing his hands over his face, he exhaled deeply into his palms. After a few minutes of staring blankly at the table, he got to his feet, crossed to the cupboard beneath his wine rack and pulled out a half-empty bottle of whiskey. Rose raised an eyebrow as he added a splash to his telka but elected to say nothing as he took a long sip.

Instead, she glowered at Sylvie. 'I was going to tell him.'

'You were going to give him a heart attack dancing around the truth.' She shrugged, lifting her mug to her lips.

'And this is better?'

'Than thinking you murdered your mother for no reason?' Sylvie hissed. 'Yeah, I'd say so.'

Rose bit her tongue. She couldn't say she entirely agreed, but there was little to be done now. The truth lay bare between them, and all that remained was Soren's judgement. But he didn't even look at her; his eyes were fixed on his mug.

'Soren?' she tried again after a moment. 'I understand if you're angry with me.'

'I'm not angry, Rose.' He still didn't look up, his voice soft and brittle. 'I'm heartbroken. That you would do that to yourself – to Fen.'

Rose ducked her head. Tears burned at her eyes, but she forced them back. They wouldn't save her from his judgement and she didn't want them to. She didn't want him to bury the truth of his fury behind love or pity. He deserved to be angry with her. To scream, shout – tell her she'd been a fool. Somehow, that would have been easier to stomach than the bitter disappointment etched deep into his features.

'I was trying to *save* Fen.' The words tumbled from her lips. A paltry excuse and it carried little weight now.

'No, you weren't.' Finally, his eyes met hers. 'You were trying to assuage your own pain. *Your* guilt. I know, because I did the same.'

Rose's throat tightened. 'That's different.'

But it wasn't. Both of them had been bound to their pride, their grief – reaching out for the love lost to them, even against all reason. And the truth of the matter was that she had tried to save Fen for her. Not for him. As much as she wanted to pretend otherwise.

'You're right; it is.' Soren nodded, though somehow the concession didn't comfort her. 'You knew better. You knew the risks of crossing that line. You knew that Fen had made his choice.'

Rose clenched her hands beneath the table, her voice hoarse when she finally spoke. 'It's a choice he never should've had to make.'

'Maybe, but he *did* make it.' He leaned back in his chair. 'And you had no right to take that from him.'

'I know.' The whisper held between them, so quiet even Rose could barely hear it.

It was something she could no longer deny. That she'd been selfish – foolhardy. Her jaw tightened. If only reason had been her teacher instead of failure.

'What's done is done.' Sylvie broke the silence between them. 'How do we fix it?'

Soren stilled for a moment before he sighed, pulling his glasses off to rub wearily at the bridge of his nose. 'First, we need to understand exactly what's happening. You said you were having murderous thoughts – what else?'

'Memory loss, mainly.' Rose lifted her hands on to the table, her throat tightening against the strain of tears. 'I keep losing time, like the night before the trial. Or right before I . . . found my mother.'

Hot tears rolled down her cheeks, spilling on to the back of her hands as Soren reached for her. Rose flinched. His touch was nothing but gentle, but the shadows in his eyes pierced straight through to her soul. And she didn't deserve his mercy.

'And why do you think Callum is compelling you?'

She squirmed away from him. 'He was the last person I spoke to in both cases where I've lost time.'

'And he has seemed oddly focused on her since he got here,' said Sylvie.

'Hmm.' Soren stroked his neatly groomed beard. 'In my experience with compulsion magic, it's rare that the victim loses their memory altogether. More often, they're fully aware of their actions and believe them to be of their own volition until the compulsion wears off.'

'But it's possible?'

'It's not *impossible*.' Soren got to his feet, pacing as if his thoughts wouldn't allow him to be still. 'The compulsion techniques they teach at Maalstrum are highly specialized, so it could be a form we've never seen. Or compulsion could react differently to your necromancy. Or it could be interacting with a side effect of your revival spell.'

Rose's skin prickled as he paced. His eyes skirted past her and Sylvie like they weren't even there. As if he'd disappeared into some world all of his own. She tugged at her collar. Somehow, she felt like one of his alchemical experiments – volatile and vile, missing some ingredient he couldn't quite place.

'So what do we do?' Sylvie leaned forward on her elbows.

Soren stopped in his tracks and rubbed at his temple. 'Normally, I'd say she should go to the infirmary, but that may be more of a hindrance than a help in this case.' He sighed. 'I do know a diagnostic formula, but it's a bit complicated to brew up, so it may take some time. And I'll need to stock up on a few things first.'

Rose nodded slowly. It was the best option they had, yet some small shred of hesitation pulled at her heart. A whisper of doubt, a splinter of fear. What if the diagnostic told them there was nothing wrong with her at all? That every brutal thought and foul deed came neither from Callum's compulsion nor a complication of her spell but rather from her own mind? That the blame lay solely at her own feet?

Her jaw clenched tight, almost painfully. It didn't matter. Whatever the truth, she needed to know – one way or the other.

Straightening, she met Soren's gaze with a steely resolve. 'What do you need?'

16. What Friends Are For

The sun beamed down upon Rose's shoulders through the greenhouse's glass roof, its heat seeping through her linen blouse. The dirt floor warmed her toes through the thin soles of her leather loafers, and the air was light with the earthy scents of herbs and flowers. It should have been a comfort, but she felt more like a thief in the night.

Or in the middle of the day, as it were. Rose glared down at her dirt-stained hands. The rosemary had been easy enough to find, but the *Astera parthenis* was proving far more difficult. Of course Soren's formula required rare herbs. She hoped Sylvie was having an easier time gathering the minerals they'd need from the alchemy wing.

Brushing away a stray curl from her brow, Rose scanned the room for any sign of telltale white petals. Bees buzzed past her, filling her ears with their gentle song as they darted between the planters lining the edges of the space, all alphabetically sorted and meticulously cared for. It should have been right beside the camomile. She bit the inside of her lip. Perhaps Briony had some in her dried stores?

Sneaking across the room, Rose ducked into the storage closet hidden away behind the sprawling branches of the oak tree in the centre of the room. It was somewhat odd not to see Briony pottering about here, even on a weekend, but she wasn't about to spurn a turn of good luck. Easier if she could get in and out without the professor ever being the wiser.

Rose's stomach twisted. Would Soren's diagnostic even

work? What if it failed or, worse yet, found nothing at all? Her jaw tightened as the door clicked shut behind her. There was no use in what ifs now. She had no other option except to trust that it would work. That Soren could help her before she hurt anyone else.

Rose swallowed hard, eyes flicking up to the full-length herb cabinets. Dozens of drawers were built into the walls on three sides, labelled in Briony's jumbled, sprawling script. She stepped closer to the left side, quickly scanning through the 'A's. ASTERA AMELLUS, ASTERA CYANUS – there. ASTERA PARTHENIS. The wooden drawer creaked as she opened it and she pulled out a small cloth satchel. *Perfect.*

Rose tucked the bag into the pocket of her trousers and gently shut the drawer. She would have to replenish Briony's stocks later. Turning on her heel, she darted back out of the storage closet, only to nearly trample over Briony herself. Her heart leapt into her throat, pounding in her ears with a grating echo.

'Oh, Rose, darling!' The professor's throat bobbed and her eyes widened. 'You startled me.'

'Sorry, Briony,' Rose bit out rather breathlessly. 'I just popped in for some ingredients for one of Soren's formulas.'

She jerked her head towards the rosemary poking out of the cloth bag at her shoulder. Hopefully that would fend off any further questions, though a pang of guilt ran through her for the lie.

But Briony's brow only furrowed. 'Soren shouldn't have you out running errands, not after—' She cut herself off with a short breath. 'Well, I heard what happened in the trial. I'm sorry; it must have been awful.'

Tears welled in her large brown eyes in a way that made Rose squirm. She was sure Briony expected her to mourn – to feel *something* at her mother's passing. Perhaps the weight of it all would sink in soon and the tears would come. But, for now, it only rankled somehow.

Years of cruelty and apathy indignantly keeping her from true grief, she supposed. After all, why should she uphold some pristine image of her mother in death when she'd barely shown an ounce of decency in life? Just as age did not always grant wisdom, neither did death always grant grace. At least, none that Rose was willing to give.

Finally, she managed a small smile. 'It was, yes.'

'And I heard they questioned you over it?' Briony clucked her tongue. 'Honestly, the nerve of those Faceless. You couldn't hurt a fly.'

Rose's eyes darted to the doorway. If only she knew how wrong she was. And how easy it would be to prove her so – show her just how much pain she could cause. Her breath caught in her throat, and she stepped away from Briony.

'Yes, hopefully they'll get to the bottom of it soon.' She tried to edge past the woman, but Briony didn't budge.

Instead, she snorted, shifting the basket full of dandelions she carried at her hip. 'With Imrys Elaegius whispering in their ear? The man couldn't find the truth if it slapped him across the face.'

In spite of everything, Rose almost laughed at Briony's candour. But she was wrong; Imrys *could* find the truth easily enough, if only to cover it up. Not that he would, in her case. *No.* Rose gritted her teeth. He saved such corruption for his own crimes.

'Sorry, Rose.' Briony flashed her a sheepish smile. 'That was uncalled for, and I'm sure you don't want to dwell on it. Keep your chin up, eh?'

Rose ducked her head. 'Sure, Briony.'

Seemingly content, she stepped aside to let Rose pass. The cool air beyond the greenhouse hit her like a balm as she slipped out the door, a light mist of rain drizzling down on to her face. The lake loomed like a dark stain to her left as Rose darted back up the path towards the main courtyard.

The walls of the assembly hall and the School of Magical Theory boxed her in on either side, rain trickling over well-worn divots in the ancient stones. A chill skittered across her skin, caught by some unseen gaze. Out of instinct, she stilled, half expecting gaunt eyes and a pale visage to flicker upon the windowpanes. But when she turned, there was no one there.

'You cannot be serious.' A voice shattered the quiet, making Rose jump.

'The Faceless do not believe there's enough evidence to disqualify her,' came a sharp reply.

Rose's heart sank into her stomach. She knew those voices. Pressing herself up against the slick stone wall of the School of Magical Theory, she peered around the corner. Sure enough, there was Woodstone, a translucent shield cast over his dull brown locks to protect him from the rain. And, towering over him, was none other than Imrys.

He cast no shield to guard him from the rain, almost as if daring it to impede him. But his thin features were pinched in a sneer that even the grey skies couldn't dim, his black hair hanging in severe straight lines down to his shoulders. And his eyes were sharpest of all.

'She's volatile and dangerous, Everard,' he snarled. 'Remove her before she becomes a liability.'

'And replace her with whom . . . your heir?' Rose couldn't see Woodstone's face, but his voice sounded strained, as if this were a conversation they'd had many times prior. 'They declined once already. And anyway, it's out of my hands now.'

Rose shook her head. She'd known Imrys was ruthless, but

she'd thought he'd wait more than a few days to capitalize on her mother's death, if only for the sake of appearances. Still, would he have killed her to get what he wanted?

Rose's fists curled at her sides. He certainly didn't lack the gall, though she doubted he would've done it directly. Perhaps it had been his hand behind it, though, pulling her strings to carry out his dirty work. But it seemed too easy, somehow. To lay the blame at Imrys's feet and wash her hands of it. *No.* In this, he was a mere carrion picking over a corpse, but the kill had been hers.

'Spare me the diplomacy,' he hissed, leaning closer to Woodstone. 'You could remove her if you wanted to.'

The chancellor didn't budge, despite the fact that Imrys had at least half a foot on him. 'Yes, but doing so now would make Dunhollow look weak, disorganized.'

'And how will it look when she goes after one of the other competitors next?'

When. The word burned at the back of Rose's mind. Not *if.* He was so sure she would. Just like her mother, never doubting his conclusions for a moment.

But was he right? Her heart skipped a beat. *No.* She wouldn't allow it, if for no other reason than to spare her pride the blow of proving him correct. And yet, there were so many pleasant ways she could dance around that. Taking *his* head instead, for example.

Perhaps she could leave it on the altar of his vile lodge – a gruesome lesson in hubris. And one he all too richly deserved. Heat bubbled beneath her skin, licking at the thought with a delicious thrill.

'You're just making friends all over the place, aren't you?' Callum's whisper crept over her shoulder.

A scream caught in Rose's throat as she whirled to face him. But, before she could blink, he grabbed her wrist, pushing her up against the wall, and sliding a firm hand over her mouth. A muffled cry burst from her lips as she met his gaze, though it did nothing to loosen his grip. Instead, he leaned in closer, scents of juniper and pine clinging to his skin.

'Careful, dal.' His voice was little more than a whisper in her ear. 'We wouldn't want to be overheard.'

Rose's heart pounded against her ribs as a shiver crawled down her spine. She squirmed beneath Callum, but he only held her tighter. His chest pressed flush against hers, his damp silver curls brushing her throat with tantalizing tenderness. Just like in the arena.

Her pulse raced at the memory. He was so close now that it was all she could do to tear her eyes away from the soft curve of his lower lip. But then Woodstone's sharp voice inched closer, and Rose stiffened, pressing herself even further into the wall.

'No, until the Faceless find proof enough to charge her, Rosera will stay on in the tournament.'

She couldn't hear Imrys's response but seconds later he tore past them. Callum pressed an arm against the wall beside her head, shielding Rose from view and blocking her line of sight. Her eyes darted up to meet his gaze but it was utterly unreadable. Caught somewhere between curiosity and amusement, perhaps? Either way, she rankled beneath it.

Waiting a moment to ensure Woodstone didn't follow Imrys, Rose snaked her hands up against the taut muscles of Callum's chest and shoved him away. 'Get off me.'

He released her but didn't move away. Not that she should've expected anything else at this point. Instead, he leaned casually against the stone wall, as if they were old friends catching up on gossip. Casting a shimmering shield over both their heads, he flashed a self-sure grin. 'So what was all that about?'

'None of your business.' She brushed off her coat. 'What are you even doing here?'

'I could ask you the same.'

'Right.' She rolled her eyes. 'Forget it.'

'Oh, come now, dal, I'm only trying to help.' Callum caught her arm as she turned away. 'Isn't that what friends are for?'

Rose stiffened. *Friends?* She couldn't imagine what gave him that idea – perhaps they counted their friends differently at Maalstrum. But the very thought of it seethed beneath the racing beat of her heart.

'We are *not* friends.'

He raised an eyebrow. 'Aren't we?'

She blanched, unable to do anything but blink at him. 'Friends don't lie to each other, and they certainly don't compel each other.'

'You're still mad about the pub?' He had the audacity to look amused. 'I told you, that was a passive compulsion; it wasn't intentional.'

Rose scoffed. He couldn't really think she still cared about the pub, after everything. No, he was far too clever for that, and playing the fool was not a role that suited him. She stepped closer, heat lacing every word as they seared her tongue.

'And what about my mother?' she snapped. 'Does that count?'

Finally, he had the decency to look something other than smug. But it wasn't guilt that furrowed his brow or lingered in the way his lips pursed. It was shock – fast and fleeting across his gaze.

'You think *I* compelled you to kill her?'

'Didn't you?' Rose folded her arms over her chest. 'I can't see why else you'd provide me with an alibi.'

'I see.' His voice was soft, almost pitifully so. But then he straightened, his eyes hard as they slid back to hers. 'Well then, I guess you were right – we're not friends.'

Before Rose could say another word, he pushed past her. Vanishing into the fog and rain, and leaving her alone with a strange weight taking root in her heart.

17. In Spirit

The dark walls of Soren's office held in a dull silence in the early hours of the morning. The only thing that dared break it was the cauldron bubbling away beside Rose, and Sylvie's quiet muttering to Ewan at the dining table across the room. Catching them up on recent events, if Rose had to guess by the way Ewan's blue eyes steadily widened. Little else could scandalize them so.

Though Rose wasn't completely sure why they were even here. It'd been nearly a week and a half since the trial, and neither she nor Sylvie had seen much of Ewan since. Until this morning, when they'd shown up unannounced at Rose's dorm at nearly the exact same moment that Soren's little dragon familiar, Nora, had arrived with a summons, and they'd insisted on tagging along.

Rose flinched as Soren added some of the powdered *Astera parthenis* to his cauldron, the bubbling liquid within turning bright blue. He worked quietly at the makeshift alchemy table he'd set up behind his couches, peppering in dashes of ingredients now and then and stirring almost religiously. But the furrow of his brow betrayed his unease, his lips pressed thin in a grim line.

Rose's stomach roiled beneath the weight of his silence, her eyes darting about the room. While his quarters were almost entirely changed, nothing of his office had in the last nine months from the vast fireplace to the desk at the far wall made of beautifully carved ironwood. Teetering stacks of papers, books and journals still gathered dust upon its surface, dotted between antique inkwells, a quill pen and even a well-worn pipe.

Mahogany shelves still towered over them on all sides, filled with ancient tomes and old spellbooks, and the walls were still adorned with the same swirling tapestries. Without a fire crackling in the hearth, however, they were somewhat diminished, their charmed threads rather plain in the pale light of day. Though the plush rug tucked between the couches and fireplace still snored softly, no matter the hour.

'So, let me get this straight –' Ewan's lilting voice made Rose jump – 'you actually *did* kill your mother then?'

Rose's eyes widened, darting between Ewan and Sylvie, who looked somewhat sheepish. She didn't think she'd just outright *tell* Ewan. Rose bit back a groan as she glanced at Soren, but his attention pointedly didn't stray from his formula. Whatever thoughts he had on the matter, he still didn't see fit to comment. Which was strange. He and her mother had been such good friends until last year – she would've expected a flicker of something from him. If only regret.

Finally, Rose turned her gaze back to Ewan. 'So it would seem.'

'Huh.' They kicked their feet up on the table. 'I'll admit, Thenlif, I'm almost impressed.'

'Ewan . . .' Sylvie fixed them with a warning glare.

'Except you did prove my father right, which is vexing,' they continued, entirely unfazed by Sylvie. 'Unless you want to kill him next?'

'*Ewan!*' Sylvie shoved their feet off the table.

'What?'

'You're not helping!'

'I wasn't trying to!'

It should have pricked at Rose, their blithe acceptance

of her crime. But it didn't somehow. Sylvie was so sure this problem was beyond Rose's own heart and soul while Soren seemed steadfastly determined to treat this as little more than a formula to be properly measured and calculated. Ewan's nonchalance, by contrast, was somewhat refreshing.

'Actually.' Rose sucked a breath in between her teeth. 'I almost did the other day.'

Ewan snorted. 'Almost? Next time follow through.'

Sylvie pushed away from the table, shaking her head. 'Gods, you two are as bad as each other.'

'Sylvie is right,' Soren chided them, though there was little heat in it. 'As your professor, I'll ask you not to plot murder in my presence. At least not one that uses Rose as the vehicle of the crime. Otherwise, you'll get no objections from me over your father's untimely demise, Ewan.'

He barely even looked up from his formula as a small smile twitched at the corners of his lips. Of all the people to want Imrys dead, Soren certainly had enough reason. Still, Sylvie rolled her eyes, letting out an exaggerated groan.

A pang of guilt ran through Rose. It *was* a little gauche to jest about it when they still didn't know why she'd done it, she supposed. Or if she'd do it again. Her stomach sank, a wave of nausea rolling over her.

Yet she couldn't deny that it felt good to not be treated like a box of tinder set to spark or a monster to be bound and chained. To not be burdened by the expectation of grief for her mother. Rose ducked her head. She'd seen it all too keenly in Briony's eyes the other day in the greenhouse, and she was sure polite society would judge her for her lack of mourning.

But it felt hollow all the same. Empty and useless. It wasn't the first time she'd killed, yet she rather thought she'd feel . . . more for her mother's death. Memories of Hollis's charred corpse flashed through her mind; so little of his flesh had been left that it'd been hard to see the man he'd once been.

Yet even in the wake of all his crimes, Rose had still felt *something* for his demise. Shock and anger for all the gruesome things he'd done. Grief at the burden of having killed someone she'd once called a friend. Regret that he'd driven her to it. Even pity for the sorrow that had led him to such vicious desperation.

But for her mother? There was simply nothing. Not directly tied to her, anyway. Fear avidly burrowed its way into Rose's chest, but that was for whatever had driven her to it. For the loss of her own body in those moments, and for what punishment may come as a result.

She tugged at the end of her sleeve. Perhaps it was because her mother had died a long time ago in her eyes. Or, at least, the idea of motherhood had. The beacon of parental warmth, the guiding hand that could have been – Rose had given up on that years before she'd even had the words to explain why. There was simply nothing of a mother to mourn, only the cruelty she'd wrought into Rose's heart. And that was hardly worth shedding tears over.

'Are you almost finished then, *Professor*?' Sylvie's voice jarred Rose from her thoughts as her gaze slid pointedly over to Soren.

He sighed, wiping his hands on his apron. 'Just about, *Messere Belliaris.*'

In spite of everything, Rose's heart swelled. It was rather sweet to see how easily Soren and Sylvie had taken to one another. Though it had been Soren who had brought her to Dunhollow in the first place, they had rarely had the chance to interact once she was here. With Sylvie being a source prodigy and Soren comfortably tucked away with his books in the School of Magical Theory, their paths hadn't crossed much until last year.

But it was almost instant the way they'd clicked after Fen's death. Before Rose and Soren had fled to the far corners of the world, it had just been the three of them bound together in the wake of their grief, bantering and trading barbed wit over weekly suppers and lazy weekend mornings. Even during their travels, Soren had always been pestering Rose for news of Sylvie or sending her letters of his own.

A little family forged by broken hearts and shattered memories that no other could understand. Not that Rose had expected Soren to be anything less than welcoming to Sylvie, but she was glad of it all the same. It was more than her mother would have given her if she'd ever been bothered to care.

Ewan got to their feet, gliding over to peer into the cauldron. 'And what exactly is this formula of yours meant to do?'

Soren pushed them back gently. 'It'll work similarly to a diagnostic charm, except I've modified it to identify traces of magic instead of illness or injury.'

Sylvie perked up as she settled on to the couch beside Rose. 'Can it detect whose magic was used?'

Rose snorted. 'He's not *that* talented.'

'Thank you for that vote of confidence, Rose.' Soren's eyes fell flat as he pursed his full lips. 'But she's right. No one has quite figured that out yet.'

An apology burned at her tongue, but Rose bit it back. It was odd that such magic had never been studied. While there were formulas for testing traces of magic, or to match someone's blood, there was no spell or potion that she knew of which could determine a strain of magic as belonging to a particular caster. And yet, people had their own scents to mark their magic – she was inundated by them almost daily, as was Soren. Not entirely unique to them, of course, but distinct enough to differentiate them, so it stood to reason that they should also leave an individual trace. Then again, in the empire, Rose suspected such a spell might lead to more scandals than good.

'So Syl and I are here for what then, moral support?' Ewan perched upon the back of the couch.

Sylvie rolled her eyes. 'Don't pretend you have anything better to do.'

As they sneered at one another, Soren gave his formula a final stir, muttering under his breath. The concoction pulsed brighter for a moment before settling. He leaned in to sniff at it lightly before ladling most of it into a silver goblet.

'Here.' He pushed the cup towards Rose. 'Drink up.'

Rose eyed the swirling indigo liquid uncertainly. 'Are you sure about this?'

Soren's eyes softened as he reached for her hand. 'I'll be right here, Rose. The whole time.'

'And so will I.' Sylvie leaned over to kiss her forehead.

'I will be in spirit,' said Ewan, already moving back to the table. 'From all the way over here.'

Sylvie and Rose fixed them with matching glares, but they seemed utterly undeterred. And really, she couldn't blame them. Breathing in deeply, Rose stared at the contents of the goblet before downing them in a single sip.

The formula burned against her tongue with a rancid sort of sweetness, and she gagged as she swallowed. But Soren seemed unperturbed, and his golden dragon familiar, Nora, wrapped herself around his shoulders as he reached out to steady Rose.

'*Aelvide intes ealorpus,*' he whispered.

The warmth in Rose's veins grew, singing beneath Soren's

call. Her tongue felt heavy, her mind muddled, as Soren opened his eyes, now glowing a brilliant gold. Her head spun as he ran his hands over her, pulling at an odd thrumming that had taken up in her pulse. It pounded within her like a heartbeat, but it was broken – distant. And not altogether her own.

He hummed. 'There's definitely something there. Some kind of binding component, and a powerful one at that. Hmm . . .'

'A binding?' she heard Sylvie ask.

Her voice sounded so far away suddenly, as if reaching for Rose over a vast ocean. And whatever answer Soren gave, she couldn't hear it. The thrumming in her veins grew louder, drowning out all else as inky tendrils snapped over her eyes, plunging the room into darkness. Somehow, she didn't fear them, though. She was weightless, buoyant in the shadow's grasp.

She was *free*.

'Rose?' A familiar voice crashed over her.

It couldn't be. A gasp ripped from her lungs as she whirled around. And yet it was.

'Fen?'

18. It Wasn't You

For a moment, all Rose could do was stare. Fen wore exactly what he had on the night he was taken, the dark robes of the Order, and he was missing his telltale glasses. But he stood there with the softest gaze, warm and inviting, like a solitary flame chasing away all shadows. And it set her shattered heart racing.

A smile split his lips as he chuckled. '*Dia vhal*, you're a sight for sore eyes.'

Before Rose could think better of it, she launched herself into his arms, breathing in the scent of him. Cedarwood and caraway mixed with a heady blend of red wine and worn leather. Gods, she had missed him. Fen staggered back with a laugh, but his arms curled fiercely around her, and Rose sank desperately into his embrace.

'It's really you.' The whisper fell from her lips as she squeezed him tight, half expecting him to disappear.

But he only held her closer, another chuckle rumbling through his chest. 'It's really me, Rose.'

Finally, she pulled back, her eyes tracing the soft waves of sable hair that framed his striking features. His eyes welled with tears, ever bright and kind. Though his russet skin was a tinge ashen, his cheeks a bit sallow. Her stomach flipped. Still, he was here – *alive*.

'How is this possible?' She ran a hand gently over Fen's cheek, wiping away his tears. 'Did my spell work?'

His smile slipped. 'What spell?'

'The Spell of True Revival.'

He shook his head, stepping away from her. Rose stumbled forward in his absence. As if he were a piece of her heart she couldn't bear to let go, drawn back to him no matter the cost.

'Rose, tell me you didn't . . .'

'I'm sorry, I know I shouldn't have —' her voice cracked — 'but I had to try.'

His eyes darkened, his brow furrowing into a thick knot. It pulled at something deep within her. Some shred of shame was held taut, waiting for Fen's response. When he finally spoke again, his voice was little more than a whisper.

'No, Rose, you don't understand.' He reached for her hand once more. 'I'm not the only one you revived.'

Rose blanched. 'What?'

He opened his mouth, but before he could say anything at all, claws reached out of the darkness, snatching him away.

'Fen!' Rose's scream tore through the empty space around them, ringing in her ears.

Her fingers tightened around his, but they slipped all too easily from her grasp. His eyes widened, her name falling from his lips like a prayer as he was dragged away, disappearing like nothing more than smoke.

No, no, no.

Rose's chest heaved with shuddering gasps, and she squeezed her eyes shut. She couldn't lose him — *not again*. Yet, when she opened her eyes, it was not empty shadow she found, but the snoring furs of Soren's rug.

Rose blinked as the rest of the office filtered back into view. *What? No.* Her stomach lurched. Where was Fen?

She struggled to push herself on to her knees, something cutting into her wrists like tiny stinging needles. A tall figure loomed over her, blue eyes bright, even through the haze of her muddled mind.

'Ah, welcome back.' Ewan's voice drifted over her. 'Try not to move too much. Those bindings will bite.'

Rose stared at them blankly. They sat rather primly upon the back of Soren's couch, watching her as if she were some feral creature. Rose bristled. Had they tied her up?

'Ewan, why—'

But the words died on her tongue as her gaze drifted past them to two figures upon the floor. *No.* Soren lay supine and listless, his sepia-coloured cardigan and cream blouse covered in a thick layer of blood, seeping out from an athame wedged roughly between his ribs.

Sylvie sat beside him, blood pooling down her arms from deep gashes etched in her skin. Yet she paid no notice to her own wounds, cradling Soren's head and whispering softly in his ear before she wrenched the blade from his chest. But he didn't stir.

'No,' Rose whimpered.

Had she done all this? Her stomach roiled at the thought. Who else could've? Sylvie's eyes slid towards her, meeting Rose's in a strangled silence. Words were held tangled upon their tongues, marred by bated breaths. Finally, Soren groaned, shifting slightly as Rose's heart leapt into her throat. He was all right.

Sylvie jumped, running a hand over his frame. 'Soren! Can you hear me?'

'Yes.' He sat up with a gasp, cradling his head in his hands as Sylvie sank back on her heels beside him. 'Ooh, that never gets any easier.'

He rubbed wearily at his brow, examining the stain of blood seeping across his chest. His nose wrinkled and he tutted gently, but he hardly seemed concerned. Until, finally, his gaze met Rose's, and he stilled.

Fresh tears spilled down Rose's cheeks. 'Soren, I'm so sorry.'

'It's all right — it wasn't you, Rose.' He scrambled to his feet. 'It wasn't you.'

But what if it was? That shadowed monster may have guided her hand, but it was still her flesh that wrought such wounds. *Her* spell that had trapped Fen. *Her* hubris that had awoken the beast in the first place. Whatever darkness lived within her may not have been born of her, but it had taken root all the same.

Tears splashed on to her trousers as she twisted against Ewan's bindings. Bile burned at her throat, her breath catching like a loose thread over a jagged edge. She couldn't do this — couldn't be here. It wasn't safe.

She wasn't safe.

The thought stilled her, the fire within stoked by its heat as Rose slowly lifted her eyes. Ewan watched her like a cat ready to pounce. Soren's gaze was caught somewhere between sorrow and concern. And Sylvie . . .

Oh, Sylvie.

Her amber eyes blazed, so full of life and love. But even she couldn't hold Rose in them any longer. And when she looked away, something deep within Rose shattered. A choked sob ripped through her chest as flames coiled against her skin, searing through Ewan's bonds. Staggering to her feet, she pushed past them, heading straight for the door.

Sylvie's voice carried after her. 'Rose, wait!'

But she didn't stop. *Couldn't.* She stumbled into the corridor, not even bothering to check if any of them followed. Whatever apologies she owed, whatever promises she'd made, she couldn't let them be sealed in blood.

19. As You Wish

The next morning dawned far too early. Cold grey light seeped through the tiny windows above Rose's head, but it found her long awoken. Pacing between the clutter of forgotten magical artefacts that littered the third-floor storage closet and fighting back another yawn.

A repository for discarded things, she'd once called this place. Filled with abandoned curios of spellcasters past and tucked far away from prying eyes, it had always been her favourite hideaway. A safe haven and a home. For her and Fen.

Fen. Her heart lurched as his smile kindled at the back of her mind. Wrenched away by that wretched creature – lost to its cruel shadows. Perhaps it would have been kinder to leave him to the emptiness of death.

Rose shook her head, her gaze drifting to the cauldron tucked away in the corner of the room, surrounded by empty carafes of wine and pillows. Remnants of late nights and long talks, now covered in a thick layer of dust. Untouched in the months since his death, and any warmth fled from their memory. Rose swallowed hard. *No.* Whatever this place was now, it could no longer be called home.

But it was still safe. More so than her dorm, at least, and far from where Sylvie or Soren would ever look for her. For now. The tap-dancing clock in the corner ticked away ceaselessly, echoing her footsteps as she paced. Until it hit nine o'clock and let out a truly bone-shattering shriek.

Yet Rose barely even jumped. It was only thanks to those screams and an unholy amount of telka that she'd managed to keep herself awake all night, though it weighed heavily on her now. Her eyes ached from reading, her muscles sore and stiff from sitting up, and a dull throb already pulsed against her temples. She couldn't keep it up for ever.

But what else *could* she do? She couldn't allow herself to sleep – couldn't trust her body would remain her own. She couldn't go to the infirmary, and she wouldn't put Soren or Sylvie in danger again. Nowhere was safe, neither for her nor from her. Not so long as this . . . thing had hold of her.

Rose ceased her pacing. Perhaps it was safer for everyone if she never left. Yet the idea of being trapped within these walls, caged with only that strange entity in her mind, sent a shiver of dread down her spine. How long until it broke free from her, enraged and seeking vengeance?

No. Cooping herself up would not slow it, not when she couldn't trust her own body not to set it free. Besides, she couldn't skip her classes indefinitely, and she had no doubt Woodstone would track her down before the second trial this weekend, no matter where she hid. For now, she just needed to stay awake a little longer. Until she thought of a better solution.

But a yawn cut through her thoughts, her weary mind begging for rest. She looked from her empty pot of telka to the dancing clock. She couldn't very well go for a refill now. Her peers would be buzzing around campus already, snatching breakfast and hurrying to their morning classes.

As she should be. Rose bit back a grimace. Soren would be preparing for Spellcrafting Symbiosis right now. Would he be recovered enough to attend? Would he expect *her* to? *No.* She couldn't bear the thought of even meeting his gaze, let alone haunting his lecture.

And Briony? She couldn't put her at risk just for the sake of her marks in Advanced Botanical Studies. Unless . . .

Of all the places that might have a potion to keep her awake, the greenhouse would be it. Or maybe a paralytic tonic to ensure that, even if she did sleep, her body would not wander. And campus would be quieter that late in the afternoon. Rose chewed the inside of her lip. It was risky, but she could always feign some illness or excuse to leave class early.

Straightening, she drew in a steadying breath. It wasn't perfect, but it was the only choice she had. All she had to do was make it through one class unscathed. She would do that much, even if it killed her.

The charmed sun of the greenhouse beat down on Rose like a flame illuminating her horrid decisions. A handful of her peers were dotted around the tables and cauldrons lined in neat rows around the great oak tree. Their chatter bounced and buzzed against the glass roof as surely as the bees darting between them.

Rose groaned, glaring at the hand-painted bug homes and compost floating overhead as it sorted itself into well-coded piles. She should never have come here. The dancing flowers were far too cheerful this morning and her peers too grating. Even the air was cloying, heavy with the heady perfume of strange blooms and the subtle hum of arcane energies.

Her stomach sank as she caught the eye of Professor Burroak. Soft lines crinkled around the professor's eyes as she beamed at her, her sage hair bouncing as she trotted over. Reluctantly, Rose plastered a smile on her face.

'Oh, Rose, you're here!' Briony caught her arm. 'I was afraid you wouldn't be in today with – er – everything, but I think you'll find the lesson fascinating.'

Rose squirmed in her grasp. 'I'm sure, Professor.'

'We're working on a glypholiate potion ahead of the trial this weekend.' She lowered her voice to a whisper. 'It was the only clue that Mamsella de Prevath would give me.'

Rose raised an eyebrow at her. Was Briony trying to *cheat*? She hadn't thought she had it in her.

'Erm – fascinating.'

'I knew you'd think so.' Briony's smile widened as she guided Rose over to a half-empty bench. 'Ah, here, you can sit with Messere Avenhart.'

Rose's eyes flew to the head of silver curls at the low table and her stomach sank. *Gods*. Couldn't Callum give her a single moment of peace? He'd already bested her in the first trial, surely his time was better spent unravelling the defences of the DeVoil students. Or the other half of his own cohort if he was that desperate for enmity.

But he only met her gaze with a slow smirk, as if they shared some salacious secret. Whatever beast lived within her reared its ugly head simply at the sight of him, curling barbed words around her tongue, sharpening her gaze as she looked him up and down.

Yet no murderous thoughts filled her head. Her blood didn't sing with the desire to tear flesh from sinew. Rose shifted, her eyes narrowing as Callum's smile widened. Today, it seemed, this revulsion was entirely her own.

'He decided to "observe" our class today. Don't let him touch anything,' Briony whispered in Rose's ear before swiftly departing.

Callum's eyes traced the professor's retreating figure before sliding back to Rose. 'Good morning, dal.'

'You're still here.' She slung her satchel on to the floor and sank onto the stool beside him. 'Pity.'

Callum chuckled, fidgeting with the carbona salt that sat beside Rose's cauldron. 'Where else would I be?'

'Far from me if luck were kind,' she muttered, nudging her ingredients out of his reach.

He may have been able to attend whatever classes he liked, but clearly Briony wasn't foolish enough to let him experiment. Or perhaps she just didn't want to give him any advantage in the next trial. A surprising turn of competitiveness from the woman, Rose had to admit.

Either way, Callum's side of the table sat empty, lacking the cauldron, powders and vials that littered Rose's bench. The thought almost made her smile. That he would be forced to sit there idly throughout the class, like a child with their toys taken away. Of course, that would only leave him more time to pester her. Rose's lips pursed. And she would never be able to sneak into the storeroom with his sharp eyes on her.

'Ah, well, I hear she's a fickle mistress,' said Callum. 'Rather like yourself, actually.'

Rose rolled her eyes. If he wanted to waste his time, let him. She turned back to the front of the room, where Briony was reviewing the differences between potions and alchemical formulas. Alchemy was usually the more volatile of the two. Whereas botanical potions were often limited to healing tonics and sleeping draughts, alchemy comprised anything from explosives to transmutation. Or diagnostics.

A cold shiver lingered on the edge of Rose's spine as Soren's listless corpse flashed through her mind, but she sucked in a steadying breath. Callum's eyes were fixed on her too keenly – watching for any hint of a weakness, she was sure.

Her jaw tightened, forcing her attention back to Briony as she went over the glypholiate potion they would be making today. Rose paused, eyeing the ingredients before her once more. She hadn't really been paying attention when Briony had mentioned it earlier, but that was a weedkiller. She raised an eyebrow, a scoff nearly slipping past her lips. *That* was the great clue for the second trial? Honestly, she'd rather thought DeVoil's trial might involve a different weed altogether.

Rose sorted through the ingredients. It was an easy enough potion if one followed instructions. Though it had to be watched constantly, and she certainly didn't trust Callum to mind it while she slipped off to the storeroom.

Besides, with white-powdered vials of glyphol ichor, kaolin and carbona salt right next to each other and a burner waiting to be lit beneath the cauldron, Briony had certainly set the stage for simple mistakes to overcome the ignorant and unaware. No wonder she didn't want Callum touching anything. Rose gritted her teeth as she added a vinegar base into her cauldron, intentionally not lighting the burner.

Beside her, Callum shifted, and Rose made the mistake of glancing up to meet his sharp gaze. 'Your mind is like a storm, you know.'

Rose flinched, her fingers tightening around her spurtle as she stirred in some selea soap. 'Stay out of my head.'

'Relax, dal.' He sighed. 'I wouldn't dare. Your mental energy is just a bit of a tempest this morning.'

He couldn't really expect her to just take his word for it, surely? Yet no notes of chicory and chestnut lingered in the air. Rose scowled. He was just toying with her then.

'And stop calling me dal,' she snapped. 'I'm not your sweetheart or your darling.'

'Everything all right, Rose?'

She glanced up at Briony, her cheeks burning as the woman's gaze flicked between her and Callum. 'Yes, sorry, Professor.'

Rose ducked her head, fixing her eyes back on the potion before her. But Callum leaned in, until his lips were mere inches from the shell of her ear.

'As you wish –' his voice lowered to a whisper – '*dal*.'

Rose refused to meet his gaze, stirring her potion rather aggressively. He really was incorrigible. And insufferable.

Setting her spurtle aside, Rose sprinkled sea salt in her potion as she eyed Callum. 'What is it exactly that you want?'

He fidgeted with her vial of glyphol ichor, not meeting her gaze. 'Who says I want anything?'

'Every time I turn around, you're there, whispering in my ear.' She stirred her potion thrice counterclockwise. 'So if it's not to compel me into doing your dirty work, what is it? What do you want from me?'

Callum stared at her, as if he were shocked by her directness. Fair, she supposed. The cat rarely liked it when the mouse bit back. Finally, he cocked his head, a smile tugging at the corner of his lips. 'You're a puzzle.' He shrugged, running a hand through his silver curls. 'And I like puzzles.'

Rose recoiled. She'd been called a lot of things in her life, but that wasn't one of them. 'A puzzle?'

To her surprise, he laughed. A soft sound so unlike the sharpness that lingered in his dark gaze. It sent a shiver down her spine.

'From what I've heard, until last year, you didn't have a lick of magic in you.' His eyes roved over her. 'Now you're a casting prodigy. You play the demure schoolgirl, but I reckon your temper could take out this whole academy if you'd let it. You burn through my compulsion with ease and then turn around and accuse me of compelling you. Which means something has hold of you – something more powerful than me. So, yes, you're a puzzle.'

Something stirred at the back of her mind at the thought, and Rose's jaw clenched hard. Flashes of that shadowed visage curling its claws around Fen crept into her mind, leaching away any warmth in her veins. Rose shuddered. Whatever entity lurked within her, it did not want to be known.

Her mouth went dry as she chanced a glance at Callum. 'You think something has hold of me?'

'I could find out for you.' He leaned in, his voice low and all too alluring. Until he straightened with a bored sigh. 'But, unfortunately for you, I only help my friends.'

Bastard. Though she probably deserved that. She had accused him of murdering her mother, after all. Then again, the presence of this entity guarding Fen didn't necessarily preclude him from also compelling her. The doubt that pricked at her now could all too easily be leading her right into his trap. And between the visitor lurking in her mind and her lack of sleep, she trusted herself least of all.

Wrinkling her nose, she tore the vial of powdered glyphol ichor from Callum's hand and sprinkled some into her mixture. It landed on the viscous surface with a sizzle that made Rose's stomach sink. *Carbona salt.* The thought flickered through her mind a moment too late as thick bubbles burst over the rim of her cauldron. It hadn't been glyphol ichor that Callum had been holding, but carbona salt.

Shit.

The potion exploded with a soft *pop*, and Rose threw an arm over her face to shield herself as the concoction splattered all over her. Her stool tipped at the sudden motion, and she hit the ground with a thud, though it barely registered. Her sleeve sizzled as the potion ate through the fabric, searing her skin.

Rose tore frantically at her blouse as white-hot pain ripped up her arm, her pulse pounding in her ears. Bile bit at the back of her throat, twisting in her gut as dark tendrils swirled around the edges of her vision. Claws that tore all too eagerly at the folds of her mind, peeling them back.

She could almost sense the shadowed creature now – its hunger. The way it smiled as it slipped into her skin. *No.*

Rose tried to shove it away, but the sunny roof of the greenhouse faded all too quickly into darkness.

Until a hand curled around the back of her neck, cradling her as Callum's voice cut through the haze. 'Let her go.'

At once, the creature's grip loosened, but it didn't release her. Like a fox in the henhouse who'd gotten a taste of blood, it would not so easily let its prey slip away. Scents of chicory and chestnut fell softly over Rose, pulling her back to the warmth of the greenhouse. She clung to them desperately, dragging herself away from the ravenous maw that held her, even as its fangs sank deeper.

Until she met Callum's gaze – not full of wry wit, but hard and piercing all the same. Yet, there, beneath roiling obsidian and that sharp ring of silver, something new awoke. Concern. And it struck Rose like lightning to a pyre.

Heat razed through her veins in trembling waves. Her mind sang beneath its own strength, pulsing against the tendrils that held her, cutting them away. The creature recoiled with a muted shriek, its claws loosening ever so slightly. But it was all the purchase Callum needed.

Rose could feel the cool grip of his magic, so unlike the heat of her own. Yet it didn't seek to strangle her under his yoke but rather to shield her. With one final push, the creature released her, settling uneasily at the back of her mind. Rose blinked at Callum, words tangling around her tongue.

'There you are.' He let loose a shuddering breath, stroking a stained matted curl away from her cheek. 'Hang on, dal.'

Rose swallowed hard as he lowered a hand over her wounded arm. She trembled beneath his touch, the pain almost sinking deeper now that the shadowed entity had been sated. Her skin itched and burned as he healed her, until he got to the tender flesh of her hand and a new wave of pain engulfed her.

Images flashed through her mind, dark and fleeting. A woman with ink-black hair towering over her, pain wracking through every fibre of her being as laughter bounced off cold stones, and her own blood dripping from a gleaming blade. *No.* Not her blood – *his.*

Rose sat up with a gasp as Callum stumbled back, his eyes wide. Had that been his memory? How? She blinked down at her forearm, almost entirely healed, save for a little redness. Had his spell connected them somehow? But, when she glanced back up at Callum, his cool brown skin had gone ashen, and he scrambled to his feet.

Rose's heart leapt into her throat. 'Callum?'

He didn't extend a hand to her, nor a word. Not even a sly smile. Instead, tears pooled in his eyes as he stared at her a moment longer before turning on his heel and fleeing from the greenhouse.

'Callum!' Rose's cry carried after him.

'Rose, darling, are you all right?' Briony's voice made her jump.

Rose's eyes flicked to the professor, who'd hurried over to her station as the rest of the class watched her avidly. Some snickered behind their cauldrons while others simply stared. Only Briony looked the least bit concerned, her chest heaving and throat bobbing as her eyes roved over Rose.

'Yes, Professor.' She cleared her throat, staring at the empty space Callum had left in his wake. 'Just fine.'

20. For a Moment

The darkness of the storage closet did little to still Rose's mind when she finally returned to its solitude. In the chaos of the explosion, she'd forgotten entirely about any potion or tonic, and returned to her hideout empty-handed. Sleep nipped all too eagerly at her mind, but no shadowed visage took root in her thoughts now.

Instead, it was flashes of Callum's memories that lingered there. Dark hair and a twisted smile. Blood inching down scarred arms. Her stomach roiled. He'd had every chance to take over her mind. To let that entity make prey of her and reap whatever chaos ensued. But he hadn't.

Not only that, he'd *helped* her.

Rose shuddered. Somehow that unnerved her far more.

Was it some ploy to gain her trust, perhaps? A sour taste lingered faintly at the back of her tongue. He could have planned it all: mixing up her ingredients and then swooping in to play the hero. But sharing his memory?

She'd glimpsed something of the same after he'd found her with her mother's body, and she was quite sure he hadn't meant to share it then, so surely he wouldn't now. Rose shook her head. It didn't matter.

It was clear enough that she couldn't be trusted to control herself. And if Callum was her only hope of containing whatever claimed her mind, then perhaps she was better off letting it consume her.

The thought hung heavy as she sank against Fen's old cushions, her eyes fluttering shut. But as soon as they did,

Soren's bloodstained shirt flashed behind her eyelids, Sylvie's gaze dancing with fear. And Callum's, dripping with such concern that it turned her stomach.

With a scoff, her eyes flew open – anything to chase the wretched thoughts away. But it wasn't the cold shadows of the storage closet that met them. It was sapphire bedsheets, dark hair and kind eyes she knew all too well.

'Gah!'

Rose scrambled back, tumbling over the edge of the bed and landing on the floor with a hard thud. Pain rocketed up through her spine, but fled her mind as Fen peered over the side of the mattress.

'Rose, it's all right.' He gave a throaty chuckle, completely unfazed.

No. Rose shook her head numbly. It couldn't be him – that creature had stolen him away. She squeezed her eyes shut, her breath hitching in her chest as she counted one heartbeat. Then another. Until her lungs burned and her head spun. But, when her eyes flickered open, Fen was still there, head cocked and a wry smile on his lips.

'How are you here?' Her voice came out choked. 'That thing took you.'

His smile slipped. 'And it'll be back soon enough. Faster if we speak of it.'

'But I don't—'

'Please, Rose.' He extended a hand to her. 'We're safe enough here. For now.'

Still, Rose recoiled, her eyes flicking about the room. *His* room. She sucked in a sharp breath, nearly choking on the heady incense that filled the air with a rich haze.

Bright, cosy and opulently decorated, it was exactly as she remembered it. A phonograph played soft piano music in the corner, spinning under some charm. The notes bounced playfully off the teak dresser cluttered with ornate decorations, lending warmth and life to the luxury of the sapphire satinette bedsheets upon which Fen sat. A small sanctuary rebuilt upon the bones of everything they'd lost.

Rose glanced back to meet Fen's gaze as he shifted. His hand still outstretched, he beamed down at her, patiently waiting for her to break the silence, to join him in this sliver of peace. Clenching her jaw, she finally took his hand, letting him pull her back on to the bed.

She ran her fingers over the sapphire sheets, tracing their gold-threaded designs. Familiar grooves that had etched patterns into her skin many times over the years as they'd hidden away within this canopy, pretending the rest of the world didn't exist. As if they were the only two souls alive, bound together in eternity.

But they weren't – not any more.

Rose's stomach sank and she met his soft gaze with a grimace. 'This isn't real.'

Fen's smile faltered but he covered it easily, leaning back on the plush pillows with a sigh. 'For now, it is.'

Still, something in his visage flickered, some broken piece slipping through the cracks in the facade. Dark circles hung beneath his eyes, the fine fabrics of his burgundy night shirt fading to the ebony of Order robes. Just for a moment – there and gone. But it prodded at Rose's raw and aching heart with a restless worry. He'd always worn glamours, but never for her. It was her gaze alone that he'd always trusted with the truth of himself. So why not now?

'Fen, what really happened to you?' Her voice cracked under the threat of tears. 'What did *I* do to you?'

'Don't.' He sat up, cupping her face gently in his palms. 'You didn't mean to.'

'Does it matter?' Tears burned at her eyes as his thumb stroked over her cheek. 'I still did it.'

'Rose...'

'Please, I just need to see.'

Fen's hands slipped away, his shoulders slumping as his eyes fell to his lap. As if her request had sucked the life from him, deflating him in an instant. Rose flinched as he waved his hand, shattering the illusion.

Her stomach heaved, a shudder crawling across her flesh as the painted walls and vibrant tapestries faded into a melancholic grey. Dull and unending in every direction – profound only in its unyielding monotony. The floor too was a worn and weathered charcoal. Made of stone perhaps, though in the dim light it was near impossible for Rose to say.

There was one lonely window carved into the wall, but not even a sliver of Dunhollow's pallid skies filtered through its clouded panes. There was sheer nothingness beyond – a dismal, dense abyss that almost mocked those trapped within. The only light that flickered through such darkness was a wan silver glow. Coming from somewhere beyond Rose's reckoning, it held them in its dim embrace, like the pale light of a waning moon. Yet still she could see every inch of the bent figure sitting upon the cold floor beside her – a gaunt echo of the friend she'd loved.

Without his glamour, Fen's hair fell flat against his forehead, his sharp features hollowed out by sallow cheeks and dark circles clinging like stains beneath his eyes. The onyx robes of the Order draped off his thin frame as if he were little more than bone beneath.

But it was his eyes that haunted her most. Glazed and clouded, as if every spark had been snuffed out by the desolate halls of this place. Rose's mouth went dry, her throat tightening as she reached for him. 'Fen, I'm so sorry.'

'No, it wasn't your fault.' He got shakily to his feet, as if it took all the strength in the world.

But it was. Rose pushed herself to stand with him. Whether to steady Fen or hold him, she couldn't really say. But it was as if a tether held between them, binding her to this fragile mockery of a life she'd cursed him with.

Her voice was barely more than a whisper when she spoke. 'Wasn't it?'

'Please, it's all right.' He pulled her close, stroking her curls.

Rose blinked up at Fen as the air quivered and shifted around her. Dull grey was replaced by bright sapphire once more, the warmth in Fen's arms returning as he held her tighter. Despite everything, she settled easily against his chest, her cheek at his heart and his arms wrapped snugly around her shoulders. Like the threads of a torn cloth stitched up and rewoven. Not quite the same but still made whole.

Yet something nagged at the back of her mind. Some small shard of reason that shattered the fantasy. They couldn't stay like this – not for ever. And she couldn't simply leave him to this cruel fate. Not when it was her hand that had wrought it.

'I'll find a way to fix this,' she whispered into the stillness.

Fen stiffened. 'No. You can't.'

'Why not?' Rose pulled back to peer up at him. 'I can't just leave you here.'

'Because you . . .' His throat bobbed. 'You'd unleash that *thing* too.'

'Then tell me what it is.' She frowned, stroking a stray hair away from his face. 'Help me fight it, and then we can free you.'

'Gods, I wish you could.' A shuddered sigh burst from his lips, almost a sob. 'But it would destroy everything. It's not worth it.'

But *he* was. Tears pooled in her eyes. Life without him was like a sky absent of the sun. The stars missing their moon. A heart without a beat. There was nothing Rose wouldn't give to have him back.

She reached out to cup his cheek in her palm, stroking a thumb gently over the wet tracks she found there. 'Yes, you are.'

Fen stilled, his lips trembling as he met her gaze. He was so close now, his brown eyes gentle and his breath warm as it softly brushed her skin. Rose's heart faltered, but neither of them moved, either to close the distance between them or to break apart. They simply stared at one another, held in the glow of each other's gazes, with the threat of words unspoken.

Finally, Fen pulled away slightly. 'Rose, I—'

But the words died on his lips as dark talons curled around his chest, wrenching him back with a shriek. Rose lurched forward as the illusion shattered around her, a scream wound in her throat.

'Fen!'

But he was already gone – swallowed up once more by shadow and smoke and leaving her alone in this desolate prison. The silver light faded, as if woven by Fen's presence alone. Only darkness swirled before her eyes now, cold and cruel. And so very empty.

Until it wasn't.

The air shifted suddenly, and Rose blinked down at the glimmering pane of ink-black water skimming across her toes. It rippled and folded beneath her, moonbeams dancing across its surface. But shadows lingered beneath, beckoning her ever closer, as if the very waters were spun from the threads of forgotten nightmares. Rose's heart hammered in her ears, her eyes straining for something – anything beyond the murky depths.

There, behind a thick haze of fog, a rocky shoreline lay

shrouded in darkness, yet still faintly familiar. *The lakeshore.* A silent witness to her torment, ever beyond her reach. Rose whimpered as ink-black tendrils of water crept up her ankles, ensnaring her in the lake's grasp. Whispers echoed in her ears – lamentations of lost souls still lingering within the water's memory.

And then, with a lurch, they wrenched her away and into its depths.

A scream burst from Rose's throat, dying as she plunged into the water's icy embrace. The chill seeped through the thin fabric of her night clothes and into her very bones, a stark contrast to the heat of her racing heart. She kicked wildly against the tendrils but they held fast, biting further into her flesh as they dragged her ever deeper into the abyss.

Rose's lungs tensed as she sank into inky blackness, her breath held like a coil within her chest. Her eyes flicked to the surface. To the twisted silhouette of the pale moon she'd left behind, dancing merrily through the water as if mocking her.

The grip on her leg tightened, and Rose's eyes flashed down, burning against the cloudy water. Yet it was not tendrils that greeted her but bones. Bubbles skimmed past her skin as a sharp breath escaped her. *Hundreds* of them, covering the lakebed like a skeletal tapestry. Corpses upon corpses – lives buried away in the shadows of this cursed lake to rot in obscurity.

Bile bit at the back of her throat as they twitched and shivered to life. Clamouring over one another, reaching out to her through the water's haze. Pleading, begging, beckoning to the one soul that could still see them. Who might yet save them. Rose's lungs burned, clawing at her chest as if they might break free. But something stilled her.

Some strange serenity settled over her like a cloak – a fleeting moment of peace. Perhaps this was where she belonged, amid the dead and disregarded. Perhaps she should stay. The thought thrummed through her, her head spinning pleasantly. For there was a certain poetry in fading softly to bittersweet sorrow.

Yet her heart stirred, pulled beneath a melancholy hymn that sang gently at the back of her mind. A haunting melody that cradled her in its soothing embrace, almost an entity all of itself. Not bound in shadow or cruelty.

No. This was Death. Beautiful, terrifying and – in this moment – her only saving grace. The firm hand upon Rose's shoulder, the fading thrum in her chest. That steady, inevitable presence ever holding the threads of life and tenderly whispering 'not yet'.

It held her there, afloat and adrift in the water's depths. Until, all at once, everything faded. The bones, the lake, the aching burn in her lungs. It was just Rose and this strange song, bound together in a haphazard harmony. Two heartbeats strung to the same rhythm, the same sad fate.

And then . . . air. It burst through Rose's chest, water slicking away from her face as she broke the surface. She sucked in frantic breaths, choking and spluttering as her knees hit steady stone, sandy pebbles curling under her grasping fingers.

The shore. She dragged herself on to it, rocks biting into her bare flesh as she collapsed. For a moment, all she could do was lie there, heaving breath after shattered breath. The air hung heavy with the scent of damp earth and mossy stones, mingling with the faint perfume of nightweeds blooming along the water's edge. But, when Rose finally urged her aching muscles to sit up, the lake was utterly still.

No ripple or wave to mark her frenzied descent. No sign of any bone or soul lurking beneath its depths. Nothing. Just silent waters staring back at her like liquid ebony and the raging beat of her own fearful heart.

21. The Whispering Woods

The skies held in the grey silence of early morning as Rose made her way down the dirt path. The air, heavy with the scent of damp earth and decaying leaves, hung like a funeral shroud over the looming treeline, and Rose bit back a shiver. It shouldn't have come as a surprise that DeVoil wanted to host their trial in the Whispering Woods, but still, it prodded at a restless dread lingering at the back of her mind.

Twisted roots reached out like gnarled bony fingers from the earth. Rose's throat tightened, her breath quickening as flashes of skeletal hands echoed in her mind. She faltered, fists curling at her sides. It wasn't real – it had just been some horrid dream.

Though if those hollow corpses had been nothing more than nightmare, then why had she woken on that cragged shore, soaking wet and her lungs aching? And it didn't explain a whole day passing without her notice. A fact she'd discovered upon fleeing back to campus, only to run across some of her peers stumbling back from week's-end drinks at the cantina. Her heart skipped a beat. It was like the library all over again – hours lost with only wounds and empty memories to mark them.

And yet, Rose couldn't deny that she felt more rested than she had in days. Sated, somehow. As if the shadowed creature within had granted her that small mercy while it masqueraded about in her form. *No.* The thought did little more to soothe her than her long bath or the sobering effect of Woodstone's summons when they'd arrived earlier this morning.

Rose stumbled over one of the moss-covered stones littering the ground before the forest's edge. Straightening, she breathed out slowly. All she needed to do was get through the trial. She could spend the entire time cowering behind a tree for all that it mattered whether she won or lost. It might even be a boon, should the Whispering Woods swallow her up in their wrath before she could hurt anyone else.

Shrieks tore through the damp morning air, making Rose's pulse skitter. They were faint at this hour, but still, they pierced her memory. Thundering footsteps over unsteady ground, screams hanging on the wind like the lingering heartbeats of a thousand lost souls. Suddenly, her velvet collar felt too snug around her neck.

Fidgeting with her sleeves, Rose glanced down at the scrawled map in her hand. Like the last trial, Woodstone had it sent to her dormitory sometime last night, though she'd only found it when she'd dragged herself back there in the early hours – sopping wet and exhausted.

Rose scanned the empty field before the treeline. She glanced between the flashing 'welcome' message scrawled on the parchment and the barren stretch of trees before her. This was definitely the right place, but no one else was here. *Strange.*

She jumped as a twig snapped behind her, whirling to find the two DeVoil students approaching. Rose sucked in a sharp breath, willing her racing heart to calm as Azalaïs's eyes roved over her, though she said nothing. There wasn't even a hint of judgement in her gaze.

Behind her, Peiren looked rather dazed, as usual. Though they both wore the same carved wood and leaf-laden armour, he looked rather plain beside Azalaïs. Her raven hair had lost its flowers, braided instead in a loose plait that curled around her head like a crown, and her copper skin glowed, even in this pallid light. She looked like some deity of the woodlands – so at one with the forest as to be a part of it.

'Morning,' Rose said finally, clearing her throat.

Azalaïs nodded, but Peiren stared up at the towering trees. 'Your forests are . . . very loud.'

Rose winced as a shriek ripped out of the treeline. 'Yes, we don't usually spend much time in them if we can help it.'

'It's in pain.' He kneeled down to stroke the exposed root of one tree, humming. 'Sewn up over old scars and left to rot and fester for so long that nothing can grow there.'

Not so unlike Dunhollow. Rose grimaced. Or the students it produced. But under Peiren's palm, the root shuddered. And there, from darkened bark, sprouted a solitary leaf. A feeble, fragile thing, but verdant, nonetheless. Rose gasped, glancing over to Azalaïs, but she only rolled her eyes, as if such a display were a rather common occurrence.

'Don't mind him.' She chuckled. 'Root magic is Peiren's specialty. He's a bit overly fond of all things green and growing.'

'So am I,' Rose muttered.

'Really? I thought your specialty was fire source.'

Rose opened her mouth to respond when Peiren straightened, peering deep into her eyes. His were hazel, the same as hers, soft against his pale skin. But where Rose's were a whiskey hue of brown ringed by emerald, Peiren's were like the forest incarnate – leaf green encircling rich brown, dappled through with flecks of gold and blue.

'There's life in you,' he breathed. 'A spark of it that you hide away.'

Rose recoiled. Could he *sense* her necromancy? Call to it like he had to that sprout? Perhaps he saw her as little more than another rotted root needing new life drawn from its withered bark. She took a step back.

'Right, well, be careful with that spark,' Azalaïs said. 'Flames in a forest that thick are likely to swallow us all, and I'd prefer not to end up as another of your pretty corpses.'

Rose blinked as she turned and glided off towards Mamsella de Prevath, who was just cresting the hill alongside the other professors. Though Azalaïs's words were sharp, they didn't feel like a barb, just a simple warning. Fire was dangerous, after all, and a blaze untamed was nothing but destruction.

But Peiren eyed Rose for a moment longer before a slow smile spread across his lips. 'Sometimes a forest needs a good fire to grow.'

She stared after him blankly as he caught up with Azalaïs. Well, that was ... something. Honestly, she couldn't quite decide what to make of the DeVoil students. Though Callum's motives were questionable, Maalstrum in general seemed like the sort of place that cared for winning and little else, just like Dunhollow. Or, at least, that was the impression Oliv and Mistralus gave. But DeVoil, by contrast, seemed to simply *be*. Unfazed by her and nonplussed by the competition, Rose couldn't fathom why they'd bothered to turn up at all.

Shaking herself from her thoughts, she moved away from the growing crowd of competitors and professors. Soren already eyed her from his place beside the Mamsella, and it was only a matter of time before Sylvie showed up. In this damned costume subterfuge wasn't an option, but she could still keep her distance. But fate seemed turned against her at that juncture, for all too soon, a familiar voice floated over her shoulder.

'Rose?'

Her heart sank into her stomach as, reluctantly, she met Sylvie's piercing gaze. She shouldn't *be* here. But Sylvie's eyes burned bright as she stepped closer, Soren hovering a few feet behind her. Neither of them should. Hadn't they learned by now that she couldn't be trusted?

'Don't come any closer.'

Soren's brow furrowed. 'We're not going to hurt you, Rose.'

'It's not you I'm worried about.' She inched away from them, stumbling over loose stones and tangled roots until she was pressed at the very edge of the forest.

Sylvie didn't relent, closing the distance between them with a scowl. 'Is that why you've been avoiding us, because you think you'll hurt us?'

Rose blanched. Was that a joke? It wasn't a matter of what she thought but what she knew. Even now, something within her stirred as Soren's blood-soaked listless form prodded at her memory. Those shadowed talons waited in the wings of her mind, twitching to life at the slightest provocation.

'I *did* hurt you, Sylvie,' Rose managed hoarsely. 'Would you really give me the chance to do it again?'

'Gods, you really haven't learned anything, have you?' Whatever patience Sylvie had for her tore like an errant thread. 'Just like last year, you'd rather bury yourself away than ask for the help you so clearly need.'

'Sylvie, please.' Soren held a hand up.

But Rose's throat tightened. What other choice did she have? Her own life she could barter in the balance, but theirs? It was a lonely fate to bear on her own, certainly, but kinder. Still, some foul shred of doubt whispered at the back of her mind. Was it really concern that held her, or simply fear? A well-worn noose that kept her in strangled solitude.

'And what if you can't help me?' she snapped. 'I *killed* you, Soren. I rammed a knife into your ribs, and I can't even remember why. If Ewan hadn't stopped me, I might've killed you too, Sylvie. Maybe you two can live with that, but I can't.'

And there, in the space between her words, something shifted in their eyes. The same fear that ensnared her was echoed in their gazes. But it was the way they flinched as she stepped closer that tore her heart in two. As if their bodies understood what their minds wouldn't allow them to admit.

Rose's lips trembled, her eyes pricking with tears. Before they could utter another word, she turned on her heel and fled. Yet she had only made a few steps when Woodstone cleared his throat behind her. Rose stilled, her eyes sliding towards him in a piercing glare. The man truly had a knack for inserting himself into matters at the most inconvenient moments.

'Messere Thenlif, might I have a word?'

Rose's gaze darted from Woodstone to Soren and Sylvie, who lingered where she'd left them, and then to a figure ambling over the hill with slow purpose, his silver curls bright amid the fog. She swallowed a groan. This was going to be a long trial.

'Of course, Chancellor,' she said.

She let him lead her a short distance away – far enough from prying eyes and ears, though Rose could still feel them upon her. Finally, Woodstone came to a sharp halt, wringing his hands as his eyes darted back across the field.

'Messere Thenlif. Rosera, if I may. There have been some – er – concerns as to your eligibility to compete, given the recent inquest into your mother's death.'

Concerns. Rose almost snorted. She didn't have to guess who those had been expressed by.

'From Imrys Elaegius, I presume?'

Woodstone's eyes widened, flicking back to the other competitors before he cleared his throat. 'The source of the concern is not the issue; it's the fact it exists at all.'

Rose raised an eyebrow. 'Because it threatens Dunhollow's reputation?'

'Precisely, my dear.' A beaming smile split the chancellor's lips, but it didn't reach his eyes. 'I'm so glad you understand.'

'All too well, Chancellor.'

Appearances were everything, after all. Even to a man who hid his guile behind a dull facade. Any brutality could be excused so long as it remained in the shadows of discretion. But imprudence was a crime that could not be forgiven.

Woodstone fixed her with a thin smile. 'Wonderful. Then let's try for no further incidents today, shall we?'

Without waiting for her response, he ushered Rose back towards the other competitors. But her heart hammered numbly in her ears. Even without proof of her guilt, the impression of it, were any other 'incidents' to occur, would be enough to damn her in Woodstone's eyes, she was sure.

She suppressed a shudder as the chancellor left her side, almost jumping out of her skin when a solid form stepped into her path. Arden's red hair practically shone against the grey skies – the only shock of colour in the dim light. But the sneer curling at his sharp features curdled Rose's stomach.

'You're still here?' he scoffed. 'I thought Woodstone would disqualify you.'

Rose faltered, sinking back on her heels. If Woodstone had a knack for finding inopportune moments, then Arden had a talent for it. Like a persistent terrier, always sniffing out where he was least wanted. Fitting, she thought. He was probably Imrys's favoured pet now that he'd lost control of Ewan's leash, sent to keep an eye on Rose for little more than a pat on the head in reward.

'Why? Were you hoping for an easy win?'

'More hoping not to be slaughtered by you.' He stepped

closer to Rose. 'I'd have thought being charged with murder might be enough to get rid of you.'

Rose bristled. She hadn't been charged. A technicality, perhaps, but if Arden was going to waste her time being an audacious prick, he could at least be a well-informed one. It prodded at her – the mere annoyance of it enough to revive that shadowed sleeping beast from the depths of her mind.

How easy it would be to wipe that smug sneer from his lips. Or perhaps it was so ingrained upon his features that it would rest there in eternity, even if she stole the very life from his veins. *No.* That was far too kind.

'Such camaraderie from Dunhollow.' Callum's voice shattered her thoughts, reeling in the sickening impulse that ensnared her. 'Though, I must say, if you're hoping to avoid a gruesome death, mouthing off to an accused murderer seems like a strange strategy.'

He slung his arm over Arden's shoulders as if they were old friends, his leather armour squeaking as his smile widened. Though there was no warmth in Callum's eyes as he tightened his grip. Rose almost laughed at the shock that ricocheted over Arden's thin face, but he covered it quickly.

'Don't tell me you've fallen for her helpless ploy too?' He shrugged Callum off, his gaze sliding back to Rose. 'Fen, Sylvie, Callum – you always find someone more powerful to hide behind, don't you, Thenlif?'

'Bit rich, coming from you.' A smirk curled at the corners of Rose's lips. 'How is Imrys doing these days, by the way?'

He almost looked stricken. But then he leaned in, making Rose's skin crawl as his lean frame pressed against hers. 'One of these days, they'll see you for what you really are. I just hope I'm there when your luck runs out.'

Rose pulled back with a jolt, forcing an acrid smile across her lips. 'Don't hold your breath.'

They stared at each other for a long moment, neither willing to be the first to back down. Until, finally, Arden turned on his heel and marched back towards Woodstone. But the sickly feeling lingering in Rose's chest didn't retreat so easily.

Beside her, Callum sighed. 'Well, that was fun.'

Rose's eyes slid up to him, still sharp after Arden. 'I didn't need your help.'

He grinned, as if her foul mood only brightened his. 'I'll take that as a thank you.'

'Attention, all participants.' Woodstone's voice rang out between them, calling Rose's gaze back to him. 'Today will mark the second trial of the Ashwood Tournament, which Savoissanta DeVoil will graciously be hosting within the Whispering Woods, as you can see.

'Since we'd rather not put our audience in any harm, they will be watching in the assembly hall through a series of broadcasts from the eyes of some of the challenges you might encounter in this trial, like so.'

With a wave of his hand, several shimmering screens appeared behind Woodstone, each showing a different view of the forest. They darted to and fro, almost dizzying in the way they scanned the gnarled trees. Rose couldn't help but note that each vantage point seemed to stand nearly half as tall as the trees themselves, and she could swear rumbling growls echoed from some of the screens. She shivered. What *exactly* would be watching them?

'To outmanoeuvre them successfully, participants will have to – er – listen to the forest?' Woodstone glanced down at a piece of parchment in his hands, and then back up to Mamsella de Prevath, who nodded. 'All right then. Best of luck, everyone, and I look forward to celebrating with our lucky winner.'

Listen to the forest? Rose frowned. What kind of instruction was that? The DeVoil sort, she was starting to suspect, from the way its students nodded sagely as Woodstone stepped away. Before she could ponder it further, Callum turned towards her, his lips turned in a coy smile and his eyes ever sharp.

'Well, this should be fun.' His smile slipped as he leaned in, reaching a hand up to cradle the back of Rose's neck. 'Do be careful out there, dal.'

The air of the forest hung over Rose like a shroud as she stepped into it. Dense and thick, it carried a stale chill upon it that bit down to her very bones. Even so, a cool sheen of sweat crept along her brow as she tore away from the other competitors almost immediately.

Which wasn't terribly difficult, in the end. Woodstone had had them enter at different points, and the foliage was so thick here Rose could barely see her own feet, let alone any other form or figure. She swallowed hard as she picked her way over another twisted root.

Above, trees loomed in a tapestry of tangled leaves and bristling twigs, though it was strange to see them in the light of day. Once, it might even have been peaceful, the oppressive quiet that hung beneath it not so haunting, but, whatever it once had been, it was only a horror now.

Rose shivered, her memory dancing over fractured moonlight and gnarled branches reaching out like skeletal fingers. Of thundering footsteps and the metallic tang of blood. Of death.

Clenching her jaw tight, she shoved the thought away. She just needed to find a safe spot to hide. To wait out the trial far from Callum's prying eyes and Sylvie's piercing gaze. Somewhere that the memories etched into this cursed wood couldn't reach her.

She could hardly say how long she ended up trekking

through the wretched woods, in the end. Between avoiding the other competitors and the many pitfalls DeVoil had designed, Rose hadn't much mind for counting minutes. How they were meant to 'listen to the forest' when every other step was littered with venomous vines and muddling spores was beyond her. Though, in fairness, it was hard to say whether that was DeVoil's doing or just the nature of the Whispering Woods.

She stumbled as her foot caught on a root, and she gripped a nearby tree to steady herself. Moss clung to its trunk, covering it in a mottled green that squished beneath her fingers, sliding away all too easily. And then the tree groaned, shuddering as if she'd drawn it from a great nap.

Rose scrambled back but the tree latched on to her, its bark inching up her wrist, fusing with her flesh. Devouring her. A scream wound at the back of her throat as she struggled against its grip, but it was no use. Pain ricocheted up her arm as her fingers were bent at odd angles, nearly cracking.

But it lit a fire within her, pulling at the magic coiled at the back of her mind. Whether it was life or flame she reached for, she didn't know, but it seared through her all the same, flying from her with a caustic surety as it sank deep into the tree's flesh with a flash of silvery light.

There was a great creak – almost a squeal – before the tree recoiled, bark receding and branches shivering as it curled in on itself. Rose released a haggard breath. The tree's trunk shifted, revealing a familiar shock of red hair. *Arden.*

Rose's heart leapt and she reached instinctively for the boy's hand, pulling him from the tree's grasp. His skin was cold and clammy, but it warmed as her grip tightened. As if her very touch brought life back to his veins. With a final yank, the tree gave way and Arden tumbled free of its grasp, sending them both sprawling on to the twisted forest floor.

Pain jolted up Rose's shoulder as a twig snapped beneath her, its jagged edge cutting deep into her flesh. She cursed, shoving Arden off her as she sat up. He groaned, his pale eyes fluttering open before they fixed fiercely on her.

'Thenlif?' He spat out her name like an insult, his freckled nose wrinkling as he pushed himself slowly on to his knees. 'Have to say, I wasn't expecting a rescue from you, of all people.'

'Don't mention it.' She cradled her shoulder, wincing as her fingers found tender flesh beneath torn fabric.

He scoffed and muttered something under his breath, but Rose didn't catch it. Her eyes were fixed instead on the crimson stain soaking her skin as she pulled her hand away. So bright and so deliciously fresh. Her stomach churned, her vision swimming at the edges. It would be so easy to drown this forest in it, slicing through root and tendon alike. Perhaps that's what this rotted soil craved – to be bathed in warm rivulets of innocent blood and bask in the shadow of death. And she could be the perfect tool for such a demise.

'Thenlif!' Arden's voice crashed over her as he reached for her arm.

Rose recoiled, but she wasn't fast enough. His fingers curled around her shoulder in a bruising grip and the world pitched. Her vision narrowed, the forest spinning as white-hot pain razed through her.

She cried out, trying to wrench away from him, but her movements were slow and sluggish. Her name fell from his lips, but it sounded miles away, and any response lay heavy against her tongue. It was all she could do to blink up at him as her vision blurred, and the world went utterly dark.

22. The Edge of Death

Shadows hung at the back of Rose's mind, stretching out in every direction. Thick and ravenous, they licked at her flesh, beckoning her further into their cruel grasp. And she fell to them all too easily, sinking eagerly into their embrace. There was no love here, no light. Only loss, and the warm sensation of slipping away.

But one thing still clung to her. A sharp truth that pierced the shadows' grasp all too keenly. *Pain.*

It arced across her skin, searing down her spine in cracked, spidery fissures. The shadows buckled beneath it and then shattered like little more than glass. All at once, every sight returned to Rose. Every sound.

The gnarled tapestry of dense branches and mottled leaves hanging overhead. The scent of damp earth and rot that lingered in the air, and the faint shrieks tearing through its brittle stillness. And, finally, the shock of red hair before her, held upon the threads of her own magic.

Arden.

His pale frame was warped and bent, his limbs caught beneath silver tendrils and twisted into a grotesque display. Veins bulged beneath his milky skin, his eyes rolled back in his head, and bones cracked beneath her strength. Rose's stomach turned, but she couldn't tear her gaze away. For a heady rush of pure power razed through her veins, euphoric in its vigour: his life source – drawn by her own and feeding this fire that burgeoned within her. Yet even it could not drown out the pain that splintered across her flesh. With a cry, Rose wrenched her hand away, cutting off her source as she tumbled to her knees.

Arden landed in a crumpled heap beside her, unmoving, but she couldn't bring herself to care; every nerve in her body was alight with agony – a throbbing pulse that held the shadow of her mind at bay, but only just.

She pitched forward, writhing as the pain twisted beneath her trembling limbs, spurring desperate pleas from her lips. A choked sob wracked Rose's chest and she dug her fingers into the pine-laden soil, begging for the kind grip of death to reach her once more and end this suffering. But her only answer was a dull thudding in her ears. Soft at first, and then louder. Until they were close enough that she could recognize them for what they were. Footsteps.

They came to a sharp halt beside her, then faltered. Rose's breath caught in her throat, tears leaking down her cheeks. But then knees dropped into the dirt beside her, cool hands pressing against her burning flesh.

'I've got you.' Callum's voice crashed over her through the haze of pain, gentle and so earnest as he cradled her against his chest. 'Come back to me, dal.'

Rose whimpered against him, clutching at any part of him she could reach, nearly biting through her own tongue as she held back another scream. He pulled her closer, muttering softly in her ear, though she couldn't quite make out the words. Warm notes of chestnut and chicory wafted over her, delicate and serene, as the pain in her neck slowly dulled.

Drawn out of her like poison from a wound, pain lingered in her quivering limbs a moment longer, until finally Rose lay still, her breath heaving in her chest and her tears raw against her cheeks. But Callum didn't release her; he held her steady against his chest, while his free hand gently stroked her tangled curls.

His voice rumbled through his chest as he muttered softly, though the words came out in broken rhythms that fell empty upon Rose's ears. Tarilian, she realized. His mother tongue. Though it held little meaning to her, it lulled her somehow.

Rose stared up into the canopy above them, carved by ancient boughs, gnarled and twisted like the hands of time. Dark trunks stood sentinel around them like silent spectres, their bark hewn and weathered. Through the thickets of thorns and tangled roots, the grey skies above cast their feeble light, painting the forest floor in ghostly hues.

She shifted with a soft sigh, but her pulse refused to settle. Not with Callum's heartbeat racing in her ear and his touch lingering softly on her skin. It was almost cloying, his kindness, like the stale air of the forest that surrounded them. And yet, Rose craved it so deeply in that moment that it nearly broke her. Some jagged shard of her wretched heart that longed for mercy even when she deserved it least.

But she couldn't trust it – not from *him*.

Mustering what little strength she had left, Rose pushed away from Callum, staggering to her feet. 'W-what was that? What did you do to me?'

All at once, every ounce of concern in Callum's eyes fell flat, like a spell snuffed out. 'What did *I* do?' he scoffed. 'I saved you. Which, you're welcome, by the way.'

Rose rubbed the back of her neck, dread settling into the pit of her stomach – as cold and heavy as lead. 'Saved me from what?'

'That is the question, isn't it, dal?' A sly smile quirked at his lips as he stood.

But the moment he shifted, Rose's gaze flew down to the prone form behind him. Her blood ran cold. *Arden*. Before she could think better of it, she rushed forth, tumbling to her knees and running her hands gently over him.

Callum peered over her shoulder. 'What are you doing?'

'Trying to heal him,' she snapped. 'What does it look like?'

She wasn't sure why. Likely, he wouldn't even want such care or pity – not from Rose, at least. But it was hers to give all the same, and something within her would not allow her to leave him there. Not like this.

His flesh was bruised by the grip of her magic, his bones broken by its strain. Against all rhyme or reason, she reached out with her source, searching for the faintest trace of life left within him. It flickered feebly beneath his skin: a fragile heartbeat quickly fading.

No.

Rose sank back on her heels, but snapping twigs and rustling branches turned her head towards a familiar form as it stumbled into the clearing. *Sylvie.* She crashed towards them through the thick undergrowth, her eyes flicking between Rose and Callum and magic burgeoning in her hand.

'Get away from her,' she growled, a blast of ice fleeing from her fingers.

Callum dodged at the last second, the icicle tousling his silver curls and shattering into a tree behind him. '*Vala nan.*' He sighed, as if bored. 'Not you too.'

'Sylvie, wait!'

Rose lunged forward to still her hand, and it was only then that Sylvie's eyes slid to Arden's form. 'What did you *do*?'

Words tangled around Rose's tongue. Explanations and excuses that sounded far too hollow to her ears now. But the forest floor quaked beneath her before she could speak, staggering them all.

Rose straightened shakily, her eyes darting between Sylvie and Callum. But they wore matching expressions, as still as statues as the ground rumbled again. It was stronger this time, almost knocking them over as the trees shook. Whatever it was had to be enormous – and was getting closer.

Rose launched herself towards Sylvie, grabbing hold of her hand and pulling her away from the clearing. But they'd barely made it a few steps before the trees around them splintered. Shards of wood and pine scattered through the air, raining down upon them.

Rose screamed, her fingers loosening their grip on Sylvie's. She reached to reclaim her hand, but Sylvie stood frozen, staring up at a massive beast born of the very essence of the forest itself. *A bahalan*, she marvelled. It towered over them, half as tall as the trees surrounding it and built of thick vines and plates of darkened wood. Horns curled out of its skull like thick branches, and it prowled with a sinuous grace, its talons carving the dirt beneath. Rose's heart lurched as its eyes of gleaming gold fixed upon her, a bright reflection of Dunhollow's unchanging leaves. Its fur, a cloak of earthy hues, rippled like the pine coating of the forest floor that quivered beneath it.

But it didn't pounce. Didn't charge forth and devour them.

It simply watched them for a long moment, as if assessing them. Perhaps it was. Rose's stomach sank. This had to be what was broadcasting them back to the audience, but Woodstone had shown them several screens... Rose's blood ran cold. How many of them were out here? But the thought fled as the beast threw back its massive head and roared.

Shit.

Before Rose could stop her, Sylvie tore from her side, ice already at her fingertips as she summoned her crystalline cat. It charged at the bahalan's corded ankles, icy teeth sinking deep into its flesh. The creature snarled, a massive paw lashing out to shatter Sylvie's cat with little resistance. But Sylvie didn't falter, slamming her palms into the ground, turning the pine-laden earth into a sheet of ice.

Rose's mouth went dry as the beast stumbled and slipped. But Sylvie's ice barely slowed it, its claws digging in and cracking its glimmering surface. Snarling, the bahalan turned and charged.

Until a bolt of lightning arced down through the treeline, catching the beast in its grasp and splintering across its frame in spidery tendrils. The creature groaned, buckling beneath its heat, and it pitched forward just enough to reveal the shock of silver hair behind it.

Callum. Rose's heart leapt. He'd stayed. Somehow, she'd half expected him to have abandoned them as soon as the bahalan's attention was turned, but there he was. Windswept and his eyes sparking in the glow of his lightning.

After a moment, his source faded, the beast twitching on the ground before him. A slow breath fled from Rose's chest as a sly smile danced over Callum's lips, and he stepped towards them. But it slipped as the creature groaned and shuddered, shaking off the shock of his source with a terrible roar.

Before Rose could blink, its tail swung around, slamming into Sylvie's stomach and tossing her into a nearby tree like she was little more than a doll. Her back hit the gnarled bark with a sickening thud and she crumpled to the ground. *No.* Tears burned at Rose's eyes when she didn't stir. She had to get up – she *had* to.

But she remained listless and broken upon the damp earth, even as the bahalan stalked towards her. Finally, whatever fear rooted Rose shattered, heat surging through her veins in rhythm with her pounding heart.

'Sylvie!' The scream wrenched from her lips as she darted forward, ravenous flames licking up her arms.

But Callum got there first, throwing himself over Sylvie's prostrate form just as the beast's massive paw slammed down on them both. Rose's heart shot into her throat, but the creature's claws shattered against the green shell of a barrier. It was raggedy and waning but holding strong. For now.

Callum cradled Sylvie beneath him, pulling her head protectively against his chest as the bahalan snarled, its claws slashing out once more. They sliced through the fragile shield, catching Callum's armour at his back and tearing it away. He cried out but didn't waver, resealing his barrier as his eyes turned furiously upon Rose.

'What are you waiting for, dal – an invitation?'

His words pricked at Rose's heart, her flames flaring as she turned back to the beast. They flew freely from her outstretched palms – a torrent of fire aimed straight for its heart. But flame didn't engulf its wooden frame, instead glancing off the plates of its chest like sparks on wet stone.

They didn't even slow the creature, whose barbed tail lashed out overhead and splintered the tree behind her. Rose ducked out of its path, her breath coiling in her chest as she hit the ground. She cried out, pain lancing up her side, but the beast didn't falter. It shrugged off lightning like mere shocks, and flames as if they bore no more heat than sunlit rays. Even ice was no use against the great shell of its body. None of them could defeat it – not alone.

Rose's heart leapt. But she wasn't alone. Not truly. And if that cruel shadow within her craved death so dearly, perhaps it could grant them their lives in exchange. Pushing herself on to her elbows, she reached into the very depths of her mind as the bahalan prowled ever closer. She could feel the shadowed talons reaching between the folds of her thoughts, but they found no purchase, as if something still held it at bay.

No. Rose glanced back at the bahalan, but it paid her no notice. Ambling over her as if she were little more than an afterthought, its attention was solely on Callum and Sylvie. Yet the sight only spurred her, a spiteful heat kindling beneath Rose's skin.

Not them.

All at once, it was as if every ounce of fear and doubt vanished from her body. The melancholy song from the water's depths now flooded her mind. Strings of a melody pulled at her veins, drawing at the very earth beneath her as she got to her feet. Fuelling every raging beat of her murderous heart. But she didn't swallow it back now.

Because this anger was a part of her – perhaps it always had been. And Rose was tired of shoving it away into the deepest recesses of her mind. Telling it that it had no place at her table, no room in her heart, and all the while letting it grow and fester into things far worse. Resentment. Fear. Hatred. So afraid that if she let it take root, it would strangle her.

Rose's jaw clenched. Once, she'd thought it a noose, but now she saw it for what it truly was, a wick – meant to kindle to life within her, a lone beacon against all darkness. Meant to burn. And she'd only ever snuffed it out.

But not any more.

With a cry, magic tore out of her in searing waves, flames roiling off her flesh – silver-white and sweltering. But they met no resistance now, razing the forest floor, cutting through root and stone alike before they slammed into the beast's side. And this time no armour could save it. Her magic latched on to it, wrenching it back as it leached away every shred of its life. Rose's head split beneath the strain of it, tears streaming freely down her face. But she didn't let go.

Until, finally, the creature went rigid and the forest fell silent. With one last great shudder it crumpled upon the damp earth with a dull thud. Smoke curled off its ruined body, the acrid stench burning Rose's nostrils.

But she didn't care. Releasing a shuddering breath, she raced to Sylvie's side. Callum shifted off her, his barrier dissipating as Rose fell to her knees beside them.

'Sylvie?' Her voice was barely more than a whisper as she gathered her into her arms. 'Please. Wake up.'

The veins in Sylvie's throat throbbed, betraying the life still bound within them. Still, it felt like an eternity before her eyes fluttered open, amber meeting hazel in a strained silence. A breath held between them, as fragile as cracked glass. And then Sylvie surged forward, capturing Rose's lips in a searing kiss.

It nearly stole her breath away as Sylvie's fingers coiled through her curls, rooting her to the spot. Her tongue teased Rose's lips, and she leaned in, deepening the kiss with a broken gasp. But the moment shattered as Callum softly whistled.

Rose pulled away from Sylvie dazedly, turning to find him standing over the remains of the bahalan. Ever so slowly, his gaze drifted back up to Rose, a singularly vacant expression veiling his eyes. 'You're a necromancer.'

Shit.

'Please.' Her voice sounded so small and pitiful. 'Don't tell anyone.'

For a moment, she thought he might laugh in her face. Might flee from this muddled mess of bristling branches and rally the Faceless. But he only stared, his eyes sliding from Rose to the beast and back again. And then he stepped closer.

'On my honour, dal.' He extended a hand to her, pulling her up so they stood on level ground. 'Now let's get out of this godsforsaken place.'

23. Odd Reflections

The edge of the forest loomed like a lone light at the end of a long tunnel. Rose's feet pounded beneath her, her heart hammering in her chest as she raced forth. Sylvie ran just ahead, her long legs carrying her gracefully over roots and thorns. Callum was somewhere behind, Rose figured, though she had no will left to check.

They were so close now. To escape, to freedom – to consequences. Her heart skipped a beat. She'd insisted they take Arden with them, tied up in the charmed ropes of Sylvie's portability spell and growing ever paler. Rose's stomach flipped. Vile as he was, even he didn't deserve to be left like that.

Still, there was a part of her that raged against the idea. Admitting it was her hand behind his fate would cost her everything, even if her mind hadn't been her own. And the thought of losing everything for a spoiled prat like Arden dug deep at some cruel corner of her heart.

It would be so much easier to turn away, to pretend she'd seen nothing. To *do* nothing. It would hardly be out of place here. Her jaw tightened. Apathy was a cruel master, but compassion without discernment was no less dangerous, and it all too quickly rotted to complacency. After all, Arden had never once in his life been burdened by kindness or caring. Even so, the thought twisted within her, refusing to settle as they burst through the treeline.

The field on the other side of the trees lay in almost absolute silence, and Rose came to a sharp halt, letting the stale air of the forest fade away like a bad dream. But the stillness did little to soothe her. Like the quiet before a storm, she knew it wouldn't last.

There was no audience – no deafening cheers this time. Nothing to mark the end of this wretched trial. Just a lone tent hastily set up at the edge of the treeline, where she was sure Woodstone and the Faceless lay in wait to condemn her.

Her pulse trembled beneath her skin, aching and raw as her eyes flashed between Sylvie and Callum – and finally to Arden as Sylvie released him from her spell.

'We need to get him to a healer.'

Callum winced, clutching his side. '*You* shouldn't be anywhere near him, dal.'

Rose opened her mouth to protest when Sylvie's soft voice cut across her. 'What happened out there?'

Rose shuddered, the back of her neck pricking beneath a phantom pain. It had all but faded now, though some faint hint of it lingered on her skin. Yet it did nothing to chase away the images of Arden's bent and broken form as her magic had drained the life from him. She sucked in a sharp breath as a wave of nausea roiled over her.

'I-I don't know,' she managed finally, glancing back at the wall of trees, their branches outstretched like gnarled fingers. 'One minute, I was arguing with Arden, and then everything went dark. When I woke up, I was standing over him, and this pain ripped through me – like it was burning away whatever held me.'

'Ah,' said Callum. 'It did its job then.'

Rose turned on him, her eyes narrowing. 'What?'

He approached her slowly, his hands held up in peace as if she were a wild animal. 'Turn around.'

Despite everything, Rose did as she was told. As if her

body trusted him where her mind did not. Slowly, delicately, Callum lifted her hair, brushing the back of her neck with a whisper-soft touch. She shivered, heat blooming across her cheeks.

Sylvie stepped closer. 'What is that?'

'An anti-compulsion sigil.' Callum released Rose's hair, tucking it gently over her shoulder. 'I figured your little friend might make another appearance in the trial, so I marked you while we were talking.'

'*Marked* me?' Rose whirled around. 'This thing almost killed me!'

'It wouldn't have killed you,' Callum scoffed, though his eyes shifted guiltily away from her. 'I didn't even think it would sting that much. Whatever had hold of you must not have wanted to let go.'

Rose blanched. The pain still razed through her thoughts, every fibre of her being tingling with the memory of it. Yet she couldn't deny that it had brought her back, snapped her out of the shadow's grip. Her heart lurched. Could it really be so simple?

This festering rot that had rooted itself in her mind had fallen so easily to his magic. To a spell he'd cast in mere moments. Which meant either he held the key to stopping it or he had been behind it all along. But the thought held little heat now.

Before Rose could respond, however, a furious voice cut between them. 'Messeres, what is the meaning of—'

She turned as Woodstone came to a sharp halt, his dull eyes flicking from Rose to Sylvie and Callum, and, finally, to Arden. Even in the dim light, all the colour faded from his skin, his throat bobbing as he stumbled back.

'Oh dear.'

*

The main hall lay rigidly still. Dim candlelight held them all in a glum silence, only the dull thud of Woodstone's footsteps daring to break it as he paced before the professors. Waiting for the Faceless to join them, no doubt.

After sending Arden off to the infirmary, he'd wasted no time in corralling them all up here to be questioned. Though she could hardly fathom why – it wasn't like Woodstone suspected anyone but her. She dug her nail into the bed of her thumb, forcing her eyes away from the chancellor.

The DeVoil competitors had commandeered the end of one of the long tables. Mamsella de Prevath sat perched at the bench, absently rubbing Peiren's shoulder as Soren towered over her. But his eyes were fixed solely on Rose, so intense she couldn't meet them. What must he think of her now?

Jaw tightening, her eyes darted to Oliv and Professor Mistralus at the other end of the table, whispering heatedly as they glared at Callum. Rose leaned against the stone wall behind her as her gaze followed theirs. Honestly, she couldn't really blame them. The way he had glued himself to her side, she wouldn't trust it either.

She faltered, clenching her jaw. *Didn't* trust it. Her eyes narrowed as he leaned beside Sylvie at the window, sipping on a healing tonic. The pair of them stood so close now. Almost like odd reflections of each other, shadow and light mirroring one another until they were all but indistinguishable.

Rose's pulse leapt. How easily Callum had come to Sylvie's aid in the forest. Leaping before the claws of that beast, shielding her with his own body. It sent a shiver down her spine – eager and almost feverish in the way it curled beneath her skin. Yet the feeling fled her as the great doors creaked open, shattering the silence around them. Rose jumped, expecting the masked visages of the Faceless, but it was

Ewan who sauntered into the room, as if they had all the time in the world.

'Messere, what are you doing here?' Woodstone hissed. 'This is an—'

'Open inquest?' A thin smile spread across Ewan's lips but did not reach their eyes. 'Yes, I know. Don't worry, Chancellor; I was invited.'

Woodstone opened his mouth, presumably to protest, when the Faceless swept into the room, and Ewan darted to Sylvie's side. A knowing look passed between them and Rose frowned. What *was* Ewan doing here? But she had little time to ponder it as Woodstone's voice drew her back to the front of the room.

'Ah.' He swept forward to shake the Aratis's hand. 'I trust you saw the whole sordid affair for yourself?'

'Of course.' The Aratis's voice crept out of their mask in a wheezing rasp. 'We've spoken to the healers already and Messere Osiander has been stabilized, but they aren't certain he'll pull through. As to what put him in that state, the footage from the tournament was . . . inconclusive.'

The footage? Rose's heart lurched. Of course – the audience. She'd all but forgotten about them. Woodstone had said they'd be watching the whole thing from the bahalan's eyes. But then . . .

Her stomach roiled beneath the prick of unease. Could they have seen how she killed it? *No.* She'd hit the beast from the side – outside its line of sight. She must have. After all, if the Faceless had proof of her necromancy, they'd have dragged her off in chains rather than going to all this trouble.

'How terrible.' Woodstone wrung his hands. 'I've gathered the others for questioning whenever you're ready.'

With a nod, the Aratis stepped towards Rose immediately, making no pretence of speaking to anyone else first. Yet, this time, she didn't cower, holding their hollow gaze as they approached. The rest of the Faceless hung back, seemingly once again content to merely observe.

'Messere Thenlif, let's begin with you.'

Rose jutted her chin up defiantly. 'I'd expect nothing less.'

'Quite.' Their gaze flicked over her shoulder. 'Though perhaps we could speak without your posse?'

Rose glanced over to find that Sylvie and Ewan had stepped closer. Callum, for his part, watched on intently, one hunter eyeing another as they circled prey it had claimed. Somehow, it soothed her. Whatever blades the Aratis sharpened behind their mask, they would not reach her so easily now.

'Surely whatever questions you have can be asked in front of my *friends*.'

Rose didn't miss the smirk that tugged at Callum's lips, and she gritted her teeth. She could recant the concession later, but she couldn't afford to spurn him now. Friend or foe, the Aratis was a far greater threat.

'Very well.' The Aratis sighed deeply. 'I suppose I'll need to speak to Messeres Avenhart and Belliaris regardless. Though would you care to explain your presence, Messere Elaegius?'

Woodstone's brow furrowed. 'They said they were invited.'

'Perhaps I overstated things.' Ewan shrugged. 'But you'll find that I'm very well informed on the matter at hand. For example, I've been made aware that the Faceless are staying in town on my father's coin, isn't that right?'

Even the mask couldn't hide the Aratis's shocked scoff. 'Well, I—'

'Anyway,' Ewan drawled over their spluttering, 'I figured you'd have more questions, and Rose here is entitled to legal representation, so here I am.'

It was so nonchalant the way they made themself so at home where they clearly weren't wanted. An audacity they'd inherited from their father, Rose was sure, though she could hardly begrudge it now. She'd almost forgotten what it was like to be on the receiving end of their condescending superiority, but the Faceless were clearly unprepared for it.

After a moment, the Aratis took a deep breath, as if steadying themself. 'Very well. What footage we were able to recover from the summonings showed you standing over Messere Osiander's unconscious body. Could you confirm your whereabouts during the time of his attack?'

Before Rose could answer, however, Ewan shook their head, as if dealing with an unruly pet. 'Come now, without the medical report, we can't definitively call Arden's misfortune an attack.'

'He was inches away from death.'

'Pity,' Ewan muttered, though it sounded like they regretted Arden's survival more than his near demise.

'The footage came from the bahalan, right?' Sylvie piped up. 'If that's true, then you would have seen both Callum and me standing over Arden's body as well – not just Rose.'

Rose's heart leapt. It was foolish, she supposed, to ever think that Sylvie might abandon her, but she could at least not throw herself so freely into the Aratis's jaws. Not for her.

'That's true,' said Callum. 'Interesting how you left that out.'

Rose whipped around to face him, not missing the way he winced as he stood. The beast's claws had dug deep, the marks still raw and reddened along his back as he moved to shield her. Yet the sight only set her pulse racing. How was he even still standing?

The Aratis leaned back on their heels, tapping their pen against their notebook. 'Yes, how lucky for Messere Thenlif that she should once again find herself in the presence of you two.'

'Isn't it just?' Ewan agreed with a dry smile. 'Did you have any other questions, or are you just in the business of making baseless suppositions?'

Rose could almost feel the Aratis's frustration burning through the hollow holes of their mask. 'At what time did you two see Messere Thenlif in the forest?'

Callum scratched his chin, as if thinking hard. 'Maybe about half an hour into the trial?'

'And you, Messere Belliaris?'

'I ran into them shortly after.' Sylvie cleared her throat. 'I thought Callum might have been trying to sabotage Rose, but then one of those beasts attacked and he helped us. Which I'm sure you saw.'

The Aratis scribbled another note. 'Yes, that all lines up nicely with the footage. However, none of it accounts for what happened in the first half an hour of the trial, or how Messere Osiander wound up one breath away from death.'

'It seems rather clear to me what happened' came a tired voice from behind them.

They all turned to face Azalaïs, who stared right back. Her armour creaked as she folded her arms over her chest, barely even tarnished by the trial. Yet her expression was nothing but distasteful, her brow furrowed and her lips thinned as she stared at the Aratis down the bridge of her aquiline nose.

'You have something to add, Messere L'Espina?'

Azalaïs shrugged. 'Clearly, Arden was no match for the dangers of the trial – he would have been easy prey for the bahalan if these three hadn't come along.'

Rose blinked at her. Azalaïs spun this tale of heroism so easily that even she almost believed it. Wanted to, even. It was far prettier than the truth, after all.

'It's a fair point.' Soren's voice startled Rose as his eyes flashed between her and the Mamsella. 'Fiorella laid the course out herself. She could tell you there were countless dangers.'

Mamsella de Prevath nodded sagely. 'The *sumar mimsoia* could've had such an effect. I'm told he was rather foolish – perhaps he wandered into it unwittingly.'

Sumar mimsoia? Rose's heart leapt. It was a type of ivy native to Arbelis that was known to put its victims into a coma before consuming them. Gods, had the Mamsella been *trying* to kill them all?

'You see, Aratis, it may have been nothing more than a tragic accident.' Soren got to his feet. 'Surely until you've confirmed the nature of Arden's injuries, you can allow the other competitors a moment of respite after such a trying day?'

The Aratis sighed deeply, a tremor of impatience that held them taut – a small crack in their mask, so to speak. Yet, for once, Rose couldn't begrudge them for it. After all, she couldn't fathom why Azalaïs or the Mamsella would intercede on her behalf. A small coil of dread tugged at her stomach. What would this display of camaraderie cost her, in the end?

'Well, I would still like to confirm the whereabouts of the remaining competitors.' Their voice was muffled as they turned rigidly to Woodstone. 'But I suppose I can speak with them in the morning.'

'Of course.' Woodstone nodded. 'Thank you for your time.'

Without another word, the Aratis nodded tersely at the other Faceless before sweeping out of the room. The hall held in silence in their wake, like a tense cord threaded between them, and none dared to snap it.

Finally, Woodstone cleared his throat. 'Well, now that's settled, if all the professors could stay behind a moment? I'd like a quick word.'

'Of course,' Soren muttered, though his scowl suggested he was less than amenable to the idea.

'The rest of you may head back to your dorms,' Woodstone

continued. 'Though those of you not yet questioned please report back here at nine o'clock tomorrow for a formal statement. And, Messere Avenhart, I'd like you to visit the infirmary to ensure that healing potion did the trick.'

An uneasy feeling stirred within Rose's heart. It was where he should have been all along. Not blithely handed a tonic and made to suffer in silence. Sylvie too. That beast could easily have cracked her ribs, and it had most certainly concussed her. Yet here they both sat, defending Rose from the Faceless's questions with not a thought for themselves. It turned her stomach.

'Sylvie should go too,' she blurted out.

Woodstone cocked his head. 'Pardon?'

Sylvie's eyes turned upon her with startling severity, but Rose ignored her. She couldn't stop Sylvie from lying to protect her, but she wouldn't let her ignore her own well-being so profoundly.

'She was knocked out by one of the bahalan.' Rose cleared her throat. 'She could have a head injury.'

'I'm fine.'

'No, Messere Thenlif is right.' Woodstone nodded grimly, beckoning to Sylvie. 'Better to be safe than sorry.'

Sylvie threw Rose one last glance before she turned to follow Woodstone, but she didn't meet it. She could be angry with her later – could hate her even. Perhaps that would make this all easier, in the end. When Sylvie finally realized Rose was not a lifeline to cling to but a noose to be cut loose.

24. Not Any More

A rather tense silence hung over Rose's dorm, broken only by a rumble of thunder outside her window. She'd rarely seen it storm in Dunhollow. Rain was a near constant, but thunder and lightning that arced across the bloated grey sky? Almost never.

Raindrops slanted against the windowpane, their pearlescent shapes caught in the orange glow of the dozen flickering candles behind her. Swallowing a yawn, Rose lifted her wine glass to her lips, but even its heady taste didn't soothe her.

Though her body ached under the weight of exhaustion, her thoughts raced too fiercely now for anything to calm them. Even the hot water of her bath had had little effect. Instead, her mind caught on Callum's screams as he'd thrown himself between Sylvie and that beast. On Sylvie's broken eyes as Rose had sent her away.

The wine soured on her tongue, and her fingers tightened around her glass. It had been for her own good, that much was true, but Rose could have easily gone with her. Could have stayed by her side instead of fleeing like a coward.

Gods. She should never have kissed her in the woods. She should have made a clean break of it instead of stoking the fires of hope. But she'd been desperate, selfish. *Weak.* And how could she face Sylvie now?

In the end, it didn't truly matter – she doubted Sylvie would give her much choice. She was not the type to let things slip away quietly or turn and run at the first sign of trouble. As with that beast in the forest, she would plant roots and fight, even unto her death.

As if summoned by the thought, a knock rapped against the door and Rose stilled. She didn't need to call out or ask who it was. Who else could it be? Rose gritted her teeth, sucking down the last of her wine to bolster herself before she slipped from her window seat.

There was no point in delaying the inevitable now. No point in hiding away at the bottom of a bottle. Sylvie's sharp tongue and ever bright eyes would find her some way, and she would have to snuff out their light eventually. Rose's throat tightened as she set her glass aside, crossed the room and threw open the door.

But Sylvie didn't rush in. She didn't tear into the room in a fury or chew Rose out. She merely leaned against the doorframe, her arms crossed and staring down at Rose as rain dripped through the soaked tangles of her dark hair. The crushed velvet of her tournament costume was equally drenched, and droplets of water etched gentle paths down her tawny skin, dripping into the low-cut curve of her breasts. Yet her amber gaze still burned like two embers in the dim light, setting Rose's nerves alight.

Even like this, she was beautiful – almost breathtakingly so. Whatever mark or blemish the beast had left upon her had faded under the healers' care. The only thing that marred her lovely face now was the scowl that furrowed her brow as she looked Rose up and down.

'I'm surprised you answered,' she said finally, shoving herself away from the doorframe.

Rose retreated, curling in on herself. 'Sylvie . . .'

'Don't,' she snapped, pushing past Rose.

But Rose caught her arm. 'You shouldn't be here.'

'Gods. Aren't you tired of it?' Sylvie shook her off, her

eyes burning as she rounded on Rose. 'Binding yourself with shoulds and should-nots – constantly wrapping the rest of us up in that same trap because your pride can't bear to ask for help.'

Rose let the door slip from her grasp with a soft click, her heart thrumming against her ribs. *There* was the fire she'd expected. The heat and anger that had been simmering beneath Sylvie's skin for weeks now, just waiting to break the surface. All richly deserved, though it would do Sylvie little good now.

It didn't matter how sharp her tongue or how deep her words cut. The vile brutality that lurked at the back of Rose's mind would do so much worse. It was silent now – sated, perhaps, after what had happened with Arden. Or maybe still cowed by Callum's spell. But how long would that last?

A day? A week? Rose's throat tightened. *No.* She couldn't hold that in the balance, counting the seconds until she snapped again. Pushing Sylvie away might break both their hearts, but they would heal. Sylvie would *live*. And that was the best Rose could hope for.

'It's not safe for you.' Rose's voice was thin, unsteady against the threat of tears. 'You should leave.'

'I don't care, Rose!' Sylvie threw her hands up, an exasperated groan falling from her lips. 'What part of that don't you get? Besides, how can I leave when you've never let me in to begin with?'

'That's not fair.' The words came out choked and mangled.

'Isn't it?' Sylvie stilled before the foot of the bed. 'Ever since you got back, you've shut me out because you think that by pushing the rest of us away, you'll only hurt yourself. But you're wrong.'

Rose recoiled. Would a blade carved into her heart not hurt her just as surely? And it would come. Perhaps not a blade, perhaps a hand around her throat to choke her life away, or a flame to tear flesh from bone. Perhaps Rose would awaken in the middle of the night to her magic slowly draining Sylvie to little more than a husk of herself, as she had with Arden. *No.* She couldn't let that happen.

'There's blood on my hands, Sylvie.' She stared down at them now, wringing them as if she could somehow wipe the stain of carnage away. 'My mother's, Arden's – I can't let yours be next.'

'And you think mine are spotless?' Sylvie scoffed, and then her eyes softened. 'Nobody's are, Rose.'

Rose turned away, unable to face the fierce spark in Sylvie's eyes any longer. She was so sure, so bright against this shadow that threatened to swallow Rose that she almost couldn't bear it. But whatever sins Sylvie held in the darkest corners of her past, they were still hers.

Unlike Rose's. Hers were beyond the boundaries of both her mind and body. Yet it was her heart alone that would bear the weight of them.

'You don't understand.'

'Don't I?' Sylvie stepped closer. 'I know you're terrified. That you'll hurt me – that you aren't worth the risk. But you are. And burying yourself beneath the weight of that fear will only suffocate you.'

As if it didn't already. Tears burned at Rose's eyes. As if she hadn't buckled under that burden a thousand times before, slowly stripping away every inconvenient part of herself until she could no longer recognize what remained. And yet, Sylvie turned it all upon her like a mirror. Forcing her to gaze upon a hollow reflection of herself and grasp desperately at a sense of surety that slipped away all too easily.

When Rose finally spoke again, her voice was unsteady, barely more than a cracked whisper. 'I can't even trust myself.'

'Well, *I* do.' Sylvie refused to relent, closing the distance that remained between them as she took Rose's hand. 'I don't know what has hold of you, but I know *you*, even when you don't. When you've forgotten your mind, your mercy – every last scrap of your sanity – I will fight for you. I will bring you back to yourself. And I won't stand by and let you suffer on your own. I love you, Rose.'

Rose stumbled back, tears spilling down her cheeks before she could stop them. For there, in the space between her words, something far too fragile took root. Beyond fear, beyond anger, it tangled in the passion lacing Sylvie's promise and left Rose trembling beneath it. *Hope.* And that was perhaps the most dangerous thing to a broken soul like hers.

Yet she reached for it all the same. Greedily and with abandon, she wrenched open her own heart and let hope take bloom.

'I love you too.'

For a moment, the admission held between them in stunned silence, as if the truth were some skittish thing that might flee at the first sign of motion. But then Sylvie pulled her close, and any fear that still lingered in Rose's heart burned away in the heat of her embrace.

Sylvie kissed her as if she were something precious and pure. Despite the blood that stained Rose's mind and the shadows in her heart, Sylvie's hands cupped her face as if she held the very waters of life between her palms and she drank of them eagerly. Catching Rose's lower lip between her teeth, her fingers tangled in her curls as if they were a tether. As if this moment might be all they had left, and Sylvie was desperate to hold it tight before it slipped away.

Rose stumbled back, her heart thudding in her chest as Sylvie broke their kiss, just for a second. But uncertainty passed sharply over her eyes, seeking something within Rose's. *Permission*, she realized with a jolt.

It was foolish, perhaps, to take this any further. A horrible risk against what they both knew in their hearts to be true. Yet it was a flame they toyed with all too eagerly, even if it left them both singed. And Rose had never been able to deny Sylvie anything.

She couldn't say which of them cast the die first. Who stepped forward across this chasm between them and tossed away the last shred of reason and sanity. But when they crashed together again it was like a spark to kindling, and they laid themselves upon a pyre of their own making.

Their lips caught each other's in broken kisses, trailing away hungrily to jaw and throat – to any patch of skin they could grasp. Rose's breath hitched as Sylvie's arms curled around her, hands gripping tightly at her thighs before lifting her up. She let out a small gasp, her legs wrapping instinctually around Sylvie's waist as heat pooled low into her core.

Rose moaned as Sylvie laid her upon the mattress, aching to close what little distance remained between them. But Sylvie revelled in her torment, her eyes bright as she took a step back from the foot of the bed. Rose frowned, propping herself on her elbows. Slowly, Sylvie's fingers snaked under Rose's satin night dress, hooking around her lace panties and pulling them away, inch by slow inch.

She leaned back as Sylvie's nails trailed gently over her skin, sending a shiver down her spine. It wasn't the first time they'd lain together. Not even close. But each time before had been almost shy and intrepid – tinged by the grief of Fen's death or the fear of Rose's inevitable departure. But now their touches were fervent and fierce, drawn by a ravenous desire that threatened to swallow them both.

'This is hardly fair.' Rose panted as Sylvie bunched the

fabric of her nightclothes over her bare hips, still fully clothed herself.

She paused, raising an eyebrow. 'Seems to me there's a simple solution, Thenlif.'

Rose didn't even take the time to frown at her teasing tone before she rose up to meet her, pulling at any scrap of Sylvie's clothes she could reach. She tore first at the crushed velvet of that ridiculous blouse – soft to the touch, even when soaked, but nothing compared to the dulcet feel of Sylvie pressed against her.

Candlelight flickered across the dampness still clinging to Sylvie's skin as Rose fumbled with the straps of her bra, licking away droplets of rain from her collarbone. Finally, the fabric dropped to the floor, and Rose's lips fell upon the supple curves of Sylvie's breasts. With a groan, Sylvie sank a kiss into the hollow of her throat before pulling Rose's nightgown over her head in one swift motion.

A shiver crawled across Rose's flesh at the brush of cool air. But her eyes were fixed on Sylvie as she quickly toed off her boots, stumbling back into Rose for a hungry kiss. Their lips never broke apart as Rose tugged at the laces of her trousers, shoving them down over the curve of Sylvie's full hips. Finally, with a breathy giggle, Sylvie took over shimmying out of them and kicked them across the floor.

Standing bare in the quiet of ragged breaths and racing hearts, she paused, her eyes sparking in the soft glow. Fear coiled around Rose's heart for the briefest moment. Had she changed her mind? But then Sylvie smiled, pushing Rose back against the bed and parting her legs gently. A hot flush crept across Rose's cheeks, her need so blatantly evident, until she met Sylvie's darkened gaze again, and any thought of embarrassment fled her mind, buckling beneath blazing desire.

'Do you trust me?'

'Always.' The answer fell from Rose's lips easily, simpler than drawing breath into her lungs.

With a small grin, Sylvie stole another kiss, only to pull back once Rose leaned in. Lightly, she traced her hands over the curves of Rose's breasts and down her stomach, coming to a stop just above the auburn curls that crowned the juncture of her thighs.

'*Miral neris*,' she whispered almost reverently, her hands pulsing with a golden glow.

Rose shuddered as a gentle warmth fell over her. 'What was that?'

'A mirror charm.' Sylvie's grin widened. 'I want to feel what you feel.'

Her hands ghosted over Rose's body – mere echoes of the sure grip she truly craved. But then Sylvie's touch vanished, and Rose blinked up at her with a soft whine. She held her gaze for a moment, her thumb hovering over Rose's soaked core while Sylvie's other hand stilled just inches above her own nipple.

Rose squirmed beneath her, hungry, greedy, begging for any grace she might grant her. But then Sylvie's fingers found her again, and she had to stifle a cry as her touch met Rose's skin like fire, her pleasure mirrored as it rippled through her.

'Every kiss – every touch.' Sylvie's teeth grazed the inside of her knee as she whispered against Rose's skin. 'Everything.'

And she would feel the same.

Rose groaned, biting her lip. Sylvie knew her pleasure well – a practised hand that easily found where she longed for her touch most. Yet she also knew her torment in equal measure, edging her ever closer to her finish, only to steal it away with softened strokes just before Rose reached it.

She whimpered as, with one final flick of her thumb,

Sylvie disappeared from between her legs altogether. Rose blinked away the haze of desire, only to be met with a peal of gentle laughter as Sylvie nudged her towards the centre of the bed. She shuffled over as Sylvie settled beside her so that her knees bumped against Rose's shoulder while her head came to rest by her thigh. Sylvie propped herself up on one elbow, her teeth grazing Rose's skin playfully.

'Don't worry, Thenlif; I'm not going anywhere. I just want to taste you.'

The soft whisper sent a bolt of heat straight to her core, and she nearly came from the thought alone. Her stomach coiled in anticipation as Sylvie lifted Rose's leg, resting her calf over her shoulder. Long nails bit into Rose's thigh to hold her in place as Sylvie pressed torrid kisses ever lower across the sensitive flesh there. She squeezed her eyes shut, a burst of colours exploding behind them as Sylvie's lips kindled the restless heat in her body to a wild blaze. Yet Rose could do nothing beneath her grip, moaning and writhing against every faint touch, frustration fuelling her growing need.

'Please, Sylvie,' she begged. 'I—'

Rose choked on a broken groan as Sylvie cut her off with a slow lick across her centre. She could almost feel Sylvie smirking against her, but she didn't care. She could torture her with her smugness all she wanted in the morning so long as she didn't *stop*.

And mercifully, she didn't. Perhaps she could sense Rose's need. Or perhaps Sylvie had simply built up her own enough with her agonizing touches that she'd lost the patience to tease her. She bit the back of her hand to stifle another cry, Sylvie's clever tongue unravelling her faster than she would have liked. If only she'd known what it had been capable of all these years – known that it could be turned against her like this, and not just in sharp antagonism.

'Gods,' Rose said, half whisper and half curse.

Her fingers twitched as Sylvie's tongue quickened, laving against her at a ravenous pace. One hand wrapped tight around the bedsheets, Rose reached out with the other, stroking the soft skin of Sylvie's inner thigh.

Sylvie flinched at her touch, clearly not expecting it. But then Rose's hand inched lower, to the dark curls tangled delicately between her thighs and the slick heat that glistened there. Sylvie's tongue faltered just for a moment, the smallest breath hitching in her throat.

But then Rose sank a finger into her, and Sylvie moaned against her, nearly sending her over the edge. She could feel every inch of it beneath the mirror charm. Every stroke of her fingers against that spot deep within Sylvie struck as if it were her own, Rose's pleasure coiling tighter and tighter as she brought them both closer to the edge.

Every heartbeat, every breath shared between them, as if they were indeed only one being now, their pleasure matched and reflected. Until, all at once, it swelled up to meet her, and Rose dissolved into soft cries. It seemed an eternity before her pulse slowed, stars dancing at the edges of her vision as she struggled to catch her breath.

With a chuckle, Sylvie finally unhooked Rose's thigh from around her shoulder with a playful slap to her bare flesh. Rose yelped, but then Sylvie surged upwards to catch her lower lip, and any protest she might have made faded beneath a contented moan.

Then, without warning, she shifted, pinning Sylvie back against the mattress. Chest still heaving with strangled breath, Rose gave her barely a moment to rest before she inched lower, ghosting kisses over the ample swell of her breasts. Sylvie panted against her, keening as Rose caught her nipple gently between her teeth.

A small smirk played at her lips as she met Sylvie's gaze, her dark hair splayed across the pillows in a messy crown. Like a goddess of old – a vision of lustful beauty before an eager acolyte. And, oh, how Rose would pray.

'My turn,' she whispered, and then sank lower still.

25. Monsters

Dawn crept almost shyly through the window, casting delicate tendrils of grey light across the room. Rose stirred beneath them, her skin flushed and warm against the figure beside her. *Sylvie.* She blinked awake in a moment, her heart leaping in her chest.

Sylvie lay utterly still, her dark gossamer hair falling over her face like a shield against the encroaching dawn. But her chest rose and fell with gentle breath, so at peace in the lull of slumber that Rose didn't dare to wake her. Instead, she merely brushed away a stray hair that threatened to tickle Sylvie's nose.

But Rose's fingers stilled just above her cheek, longing to trace tender patterns upon the canvas of Sylvie's skin, mapping out the contours of her visage with a reverence of a supplicant bowing before an altar. The heat of Sylvie's touch lingered on her own flesh, sending a flush of desire pooling between her thighs.

Rose shuddered against it, pulling her hand away. She would not be the one to ruin Sylvie's peace. Not after everything. But she needn't have worried, for Sylvie stirred restlessly anyway. Amber eyes fluttering open, they landed on Rose with such warmth that it quickly sapped away any chill brought by the pale light outside.

A small smile broke across Sylvie's lips. 'Good morning.'

'Morning.'

Sylvie's smile dropped, her eyes deadly serious as she traced a thumb over Rose's cheek. 'You look like shit, Thenlif. Didn't you get enough sleep?'

Smug bastard. Rose bit back a laugh, shoving Sylvie away before she rolled on top of her and captured her lips in a bruising kiss. 'If I didn't, it's your fault.'

A laugh rumbled through Sylvie's chest as Rose laid her head atop it. The heat of her bare skin sent a shiver down Rose's spine as she curled closer. She ran her fingers through Sylvie's hair, utterly sated and unwilling to move as the dim light of day grew brighter through the window.

She wasn't sure how long they lay there like that, counting each other's breaths, listening as their hearts melded into one steady beat. But Rose's mind stirred restlessly, caught on the edge of shadow as she mulled over the fight that had led them here.

Sylvie shifted slightly. 'What's wrong?'

Rose chewed the inside of her lip, words sticking to her tongue. Surely it would be easier to tell her she was fine – a simple lie to let it all slip away unspoken. The peace between them seemed so fragile, after all, and she was loath to be the one to break it. But Sylvie deserved better than that. After everything, honesty was the least Rose owed her.

'Last night, you said your hands weren't spotless either.' She glanced up, her voice barely more than a whisper now. 'What did you mean?'

Sylvie stiffened. For a moment, Rose thought she might refuse to answer. Evade the question, or perhaps even leave the room altogether. But then she sighed, leaning back against the pillow.

'It was a long time ago.'

Rose nodded, rolling off her. Giving her the space to escape, if she needed. 'You don't have to talk about it if you don't want to.'

And it was true, even if the thought pained her. That Sylvie did not trust her with her secrets. But it was her right to keep them, and Rose couldn't be a hypocrite and demand she part with them, as much as the thought burned at her mind.

'No, it's not that. I—' Sylvie sat up, pulling her knees up to her chest. 'Last year, I told you I was a scholarship orphan, but I never told you why.'

Rose blinked, easing herself forward. Sylvie looked so small then, the bedsheets tangled around her as she cradled her knees. As if shielding herself from the rest of the world – from Rose. The thought made her heart lurch, and she reached for Sylvie out of instinct.

'Sylvie . . .'

She shook her head, swallowing hard before she exhaled sharply through her nose. 'Fire was my first specialty.'

Rose recoiled. 'What?'

That didn't make any sense. She'd always thought of Sylvie as a blazing star, she supposed, but one whose cold light cut brilliantly through an endless night. Undimmed even upon the edge of darkness and mesmerizing in its beauty. Ice had always carved beneath her will as if she'd breathed its very creation into the world. Sharp, insidious and kept tightly under her control. Rose couldn't imagine her wielding something so untamed as flame.

Sylvie's eyes darkened. 'You're not the only monster in attendance here, Thenlif.'

'You're not a monster.'

The words fell from Rose's lips without thought – a truth she had no need to question. No matter what Sylvie had done in the past, there was nothing that could turn Rose from her side now, even if she'd burned the world to little more than ash and smoke. But she faltered. Had Sylvie not said much the same to her? So why had that rung hollow in her ears?

'When I was eight, a plague swept through Tol Qilius,' Sylvie said, startling Rose from her thoughts. 'The Crimson Death.'

'I remember,' Rose muttered.

The sickness had never reached Dunhollow, but it had still thrown it into turmoil. Some parents frantically calling their heirs back to their estates, while others had used the university's remote surroundings to quarantine their children. It had been the only time that Rose had ever left Dunhollow, sequestered away with Soren at his villa in Arbelis after classes had been cancelled for the term. Those had been some of the most pleasant, unfettered days of her childhood, until she learned the carnage the plague had caused. And, clearly, Sylvie had not gotten clear of it so unscathed.

'My parents were imperial financiers, but not high-ranking enough to be secluded with the other courtiers.' She tugged at the edges of the sheets. 'They died choking on their own blood while I was left untouched. Even then, my magic was strong, and the healers thought maybe it burned the plague right out of my system.'

Rose frowned. 'You survived – that doesn't make you a monster.'

'Don't worry, I'm getting there.' A wry smile pulled at the corners of Sylvie's mouth, but it didn't reach her eyes. 'After they died, I was sent to live with my aunt and uncle. But they were strict – cruel. My magic was a volatility they couldn't abide. They tried to train me at first, but it was too much. *I* was too much. Any time I got upset or excited, flames would pour out of me. I set countless little fires, anytime and anywhere.

'Finally, they'd had enough.' Sylvie sucked in a breath. 'When their training failed, they hid me away in their manor, safely away from their high-society friends and any embarrassment I might cause. Any outburst, any sign of trouble at all, and they would lock me in the basement. Alone in the dark with a dampening collar to temper my magic until I'd "learned my lesson".'

'Oh, Sylvie.'

Rose's heart twisted around the thought of her, young, alone and forced to hide the magic she so loved. But then her stomach sank. Had she not been the same? Almost as if they were two sides of the same coin – one always too much and the other never enough. But both taught to fear themselves. Silently, she reached for Sylvie's hand, squeezing lightly.

'But there was one night, when I was fourteen.' Sylvie's voice was taut as she dabbed at her tears with the bedsheets. 'I don't remember how it started or what I did, but they locked me away, as usual. Except they forgot. They kept me down there in the dark, trapped and powerless, for what felt like days. Until the hunger and fear got to be too much and my magic broke through. There was fire everywhere, but not a flame touched me. And when it was over – when there was finally light again – I remember their charred bodies. Their jaws wrenched open in silent screams, their flesh little more than dust.'

Rose's jaw clenched tight. She hoped they suffered – that they felt every inch of the flames creeping across their flesh. Her fists curled tight around her duvet, but the brutality didn't scare her now. For Sylvie, she'd have done so much worse.

'It was the least they deserved,' she managed finally.

'Maybe.' Sylvie shrugged, her gaze fixed on the sheets beneath her. 'But they weren't the only ones in the house that night. Servants, guests – anyone unlucky enough to be in their presence. They all got caught in the blaze, and I killed every last one of them.'

Rose's shoulders loosened, every ounce of anger fleeing her body for the sorrow in Sylvie's eyes. It wasn't fury or vengeance she needed now, but comfort – *love*. Her heart ached as she pulled Sylvie close.

Sylvie only stilled, holding herself rigidly. Until something within her snapped and a ragged sob tore from her lips. Bitterly, she wept into Rose's shoulder, clinging to her as if she were her only lifeline. Tears of her own welled in Rose's eyes, but she held them back, smoothing down Sylvie's hair with tangled strokes. How she longed to keep her there – safe and warm in her arms. But the world would never grant them such peace.

'It wasn't your fault,' she offered instead, a paltry comfort drawn from her lips in a hushed whisper. 'You didn't mean to.'

'Neither did you,' said Sylvie, pulling away after a long moment. 'But we both still did it.'

Drying her eyes, Sylvie sank back on to the mattress. Rose felt cold without her – an aching chasm left in her wake that could not be soothed by words alone. Sylvie tried to pull her hand away, but Rose refused to release it, pressing soft kisses along her knuckles. Sylvie flashed her a smile before ducking her head almost shyly.

'After, there was an inquest, but it was quickly shut down.' She sniffled. 'Had to protect the family name, after all. My records were sealed, and I was made a ward of the court. They sent me to a temple of The Nine to live with the clerics, hoping they might teach me some discipline. But it didn't matter – I never touched fire again. When Soren found me, I jumped at the chance to get away. To come to Dunhollow and write a new story for myself. I should have known it wouldn't be so easy.'

Of course not, Rose thought bitterly. Dunhollow would never have offered her such grace. Instead, it treated her like nothing more than a blade – a tool to be sharpened and cared for as long as it had use but ultimately discarded. And Rose had been the stone they'd whetted Sylvie against.

The star student and the resident casting defect, pitched

against each other until they both bled. But they were more than what others had moulded them into – more than tools to be used by another's hand. They were two lone flames desperately flickering against the same darkness, but together they could be a blaze.

Leaning forward, she pressed a gentle kiss to Sylvie's forehead, her words heavy against her tongue. 'It's our hands stained by the blood, but their hearts at the core of the crime. It's not a weight either of us should have to carry – not any more.'

Sylvie sagged against her, a hollow snort fleeing from her lips. 'When you learn how to be free of it, let me know.'

'With you, I feel like I could be.'

The whisper was barely loud enough for Rose to even hear, but a smile ghosted across Sylvie's lips before she leaned closer. They sat like that for a long moment, two broken souls bound in silence. Two monsters whose claws and teeth had been filed down, no fire left in their fight.

Rose shivered, her memory racing to the beast they'd faced in the forest. And to the other monster that had protected them. Though the thought hardly seemed fair now.

Sylvie leaned back. 'What is it?'

Rose shook her head. 'Just thinking about monsters.'

'Rose . . .'

'Fine.' She sighed. 'I was thinking about Callum – when he found me outside my tent after the first trial. He said he didn't care if I was innocent because he'd done far worse.'

'You think he meant he'd killed before?'

'Maybe?' Rose shrugged. 'I don't know what to think any more.'

Sylvie fell silent for a moment. But then she turned, her brow furrowed pensively, even as a smirk tugged at her lips. 'Do you want to hear what *I* think?'

'Probably not.'

'You should talk to him.'

Rose snorted, leaning back against her pillows. 'Definitely not.'

'Don't be stubborn, Thenlif.'

Rose folded her arms over her chest as Sylvie stared down at her, looking all too much like she was scolding a petulant child. But it wasn't stubbornness that kept her from speaking to Callum. At least, not *only* that. A creeping feeling of dread coiled around her heart. How many secrets did he now hold against her? They were poised like blades to destroy her with one sure strike.

'And say what?' she scoffed finally. 'Best case, he now has my false alibi and knowledge of my necromancy to hold over me. Worst case, he's already told Woodstone and the Faceless everything.'

'Please, if that were true, they'd be tearing down the door, not letting us have a lie-in.' Sylvie trailed a finger gently over Rose's bare arm. 'Besides, I don't think he wants to hurt you.'

Rose frowned at the softness in her voice. 'How do you figure that?'

'Because I think he likes you.'

She stilled, but she couldn't deny the way her heart flipped at Sylvie's words. Though she would die before she ever admitted it. 'Pardon?'

'Or us, really.' Sylvie's tawny cheeks flushed a shade darker. 'He and I – er – talked in the infirmary, and the way he spoke . . . it was almost tender.'

'Oh.'

'I mean, think about it.' She flopped back on to the mattress with a dramatic sigh. 'He lied to the Faceless for you and, despite saying he did it for a favour, he's asked for nothing. Instead, he had the foresight to hit you with a counter charm, then shielded me from the bahalan with his own body. How else would you explain all of that?'

A fierce heat crept across Rose's cheeks for the way the light glowed over Sylvie's skin, illuminating the supple curves of her breasts and the generous arc of her hips. Rose's pulse skittered beneath her skin, her mouth going dry. Surely Sylvie couldn't expect her to think of Callum *now*.

'Fine, let's say you're right, which you're not.'

'I am.'

'Even *if* you are,' said Rose through gritted teeth as Sylvie's grin widened, 'why are you so calm about it?'

Sylvie frowned, her fingers halting in the map they drew across Rose's chest. 'What else should I be?'

'I don't know?' Rose squirmed beneath her gaze. 'Angry, jealous?'

Shouldn't she be? The briefest tremor of insecurity raced through her heart. Perhaps she simply didn't care enough – perhaps this was little more than a dalliance to be collected and cast away.

No. Rose scowled, shoving the thought away. Sylvie loved her; she'd proven that in more ways than Rose could ever count. But, still, doubt pricked at her.

Sylvie, however, only looked thoughtful. 'Do you love Fen?'

Rose startled, the name lancing through her heart like a blade. 'What?'

'It's not a trick question,' Sylvie said calmly. 'Do you love him?'

Of course. The thought came to Rose unbidden, as natural as breath to her lungs. She had; she *did*. And perhaps she always would. For all the good her love had ever done him.

'Yes.' She nodded, her throat tightening.

'And do you love me?'

'You know I do.'

'That's why I'm not jealous.' Sylvie nuzzled her nose against Rose's jawline. 'As much as you like to bury your heart, Thenlif, I don't think it was built to love only one person. And neither was mine. Doesn't mean we love each other any less. I'm not jealous, because even when I was pining silently for you, I always thought Fen would be a part of anything we had.'

Rose almost laughed at the idea that Sylvie had ever pined for anything. Honestly, their years of trading banter and sharp wit had practically been foreplay for Sylvie, she was sure. Still, Rose's heart clenched around the thought of the bond that could have been between the three of them.

But could it truly be so simple? She chewed the inside of her lip. She had loved Fen, body and soul – had known him inside and out, just as she now did with Sylvie. But was that a love they could have shared between the three of them had he lived? She swallowed back tears. It didn't matter now. Fen was lost to her, and Callum would never replace him.

'Sorry.' Sylvie cleared her throat. 'I shouldn't have brought up Fen like that.'

Rose shook her head. 'No, it's fine. But Callum isn't Fen, and I certainly don't love him.'

'No.' Sylvie grinned, running her fingers tantalizingly over Rose's skin. 'But he's attractive, clever, and you're determined to hate him for something he may not have actually done. Can't say you don't have a type.'

At that, the hunger lurking low in the pit of Rose's stomach vanished, replaced by indignant revulsion as she shoved Sylvie's shoulder. Firstly, comparing their relationship to whatever strange bond linked Rose and Callum was a low blow. Secondly, it was precisely because they didn't know what Callum was capable of that Rose was loath to even dignify Sylvie's suppositions with a response.

'Ugh.' She swatted her hand away. 'You're insufferable, you know that? And also very wrong.'

'Whatever, Thenlif.' Sylvie leaned in for another kiss. 'You can lie to yourself, but not to me.'

26. Caster's Intuition

When Sylvie finally left, it had taken every ounce of Rose's strength not to flop back into bed and sleep for the entire afternoon. A part of her wished she had done now. Instead, she stared down the quiet paths of Dunhollow's campus, pulling her coat tighter as the late-afternoon chill pierced her.

Biting back a shiver, Rose's mind wandered all too easily to the warmth of her bed. To Sylvie's loving embrace and the turn of her talented tongue. A shiver ran down her spine, but the memory rang rather hollow now as her parting words echoed through her memory.

Talk to Callum, she'd said before fleeing the safety of their bed to seek out an update on Arden. An easy enough task, really, but not one Rose was keen to carry out. She tugged at the edges of her sleeves. She would have to speak with him eventually, but something still held her on the edge of indecision as she stared at the looming oaken doors of the stone building before her.

Sylvie would call her a coward for retreating to the comfort of the library instead of facing her problems. And perhaps she'd be right. She'd already spent most of the day holed up in her room, catching up on coursework ahead of midterms. She'd only left now because she feared Sylvie's reaction if she'd found her in the exact same spot. Rose glared up at the ashen skies, held on the edge of dusk.

Can't say you don't have a type. She chewed the inside of her lip. She wasn't too proud to admit that Callum was attractive, of course, but in the same way she found poisonous flowers beautiful – lovely to look at but dangerous to touch. Rose stilled, her traitorous heart fluttering. Had she not said much the same of Sylvie once?

But Callum wasn't Sylvie. There were no sweet kisses to cover the stain of deceit. No bonds of trust forged between the edges of life and death to fall back upon. He was utterly unknown to her, a rogue actor who now held her fate in his cruel hands.

Something she could only remedy by talking to him, she knew, though it felt all too much like walking willingly into a round of Dead Man's Bluff with a losing hand. With a sigh, she shoved through the library doors. She could worry about Callum later.

An earthy scent of ancient stones and aged books curled around her as she stepped through, covering the faintest hint of must as the whispers of eager tomes echoed above her. Despite everything, a smile flitted across her lips. A shred of peace held within this place still curled around her heart with such ease.

But, it seemed, the universe was not content to treat her to any such reprieve. For, between the whizzing books and shifting shelves that greeted her as she marched up the steps, a telltale head of silver curls caught her gaze at the far end of the room. Rose stumbled to a halt. What was *he* doing here?

Callum sat by himself at one of the long tables by the window, a book held idly between his fingers. He looked like a work of art with the grey light from the window flickering over his dark robes, catching his curls in luscious waves. Rose pursed her lips, shaking away the thought. An illusion, she was sure – designed to lure in the innocent and unwary.

Not that there were many around to fall for it. The library was quiet at this hour, though midterms lurked only a week away. A few other students dotted the tables near the grand windows, hunched over parchment and notebooks, while Delia busied herself at the counter with some overeager first-years.

Chewing the inside of her lip, Rose's eyes flicked from her peers to Callum. There was hardly anyone to overhear them, even if he did bring up her necromancy, but the thought still made her pulse skitter. She shook her head. He clearly hadn't told anyone about it yet, or she doubted the Faceless would have still bothered with their questioning this morning. But that didn't mean he couldn't still, and she had to know what game he was playing. Crossing the room before she could think better of it, she sank into the chair beside him.

'What are *you* doing here?'

Callum jumped, his eyes widening as he took her in. But he recovered quickly, closing his book with a sly smirk. 'Well, hello to you too, dal. I was trying to study, but if you were looking to chat, I could be amenable.'

Study? Rose couldn't help wrinkling her nose. What did he have to study for? He wouldn't even be required to participate in exams as a visiting student. *No.* Her gaze roved over the books and papers sprawled before him. Little more than random news articles and some scribbled notes. Like almost everything else about him, she doubted his reasons for being here were genuine.

'I'm not here for a social visit,' she snapped, slinging her bag over the back of the chair. 'We need to talk.'

'Sounds like a social visit to me, dal.' He lifted a glass of amber liquid to his lips.

Spiced rum by the sweet smell that wafted off it. How he'd snuck that in without Delia noticing, she couldn't fathom. Illusion, probably. Though it seemed odd to go to such trouble when there were plenty of places in the village he could've gone. Perhaps he preferred to drink alone.

'This isn't the pub.' She jutted her chin at his drink. 'Spill that and Delia will have your head.'

'Yes, I'd gathered.' His eyes flashed to the violet-haired librarian, who paid them no notice as she wrangled a few misbehaving books. 'Though I should be fine, provided you can keep your hands to yourself this time.'

Rose shifted in her seat. That rather depended on whether he kept that sharp tongue in check, she supposed. Though she could think of far better ways that he could put it to use, anyway. The thought made her pause, a hot flush creeping up her neck.

Where had *that* come from?

Sylvie, probably. Putting such ideas into her head that they came to her now unbidden and unwanted. Still, it was better than longing to rip his tongue out, if only just.

'I'll do my best,' she choked out, brushing her hair away from her burning cheeks. 'Provided you don't compel me.'

If Callum noticed her discomfort, he said nothing, instead leaning forward to prop his elbows on the table. '*Vala nan*. I told you, it was passive. I don't deal in true compulsion any more.'

Rose almost laughed at that. He was a top student at Maalstrum – what else would he deal in but compulsion, illusions and petty lies? But something in those dark eyes of his stilled her, some shred of truth that she could not deny. He actually *meant* it.

Her stomach flipped. If that were true, then ... *No*. She shook her head. It was humiliating how easily her heart wavered. How, at the merest suggestion of his innocence, it longed to dismiss any hint of menace or malice and get lost in the depths of those obsidian eyes. But Rose quelled it in an instant. He was dangerous beyond just the bounds of his magic, and she would be a fool to forget it.

Gritting her teeth, Rose straightened. 'At the first trial you said that I could burn through a passive compulsion.'

'Is there a question in there?'

Rose glared at him. '*Passive* suggests that you can hold a compulsion without trying, which seems like it would take an impressive amount of skill and energy to cast.'

'It's true, I am pretty impressive.'

'And incapable of giving a straight answer, apparently.'

Callum sighed, setting his drink on the table. 'Fine. Yes and no. The most powerful compulsionists can cast passive spells, but it doesn't take a great amount of energy. It's simpler, but far more dangerous.'

'How so?'

'Passive compulsion slips out as easily as breathing, laced into a word or a look. You'd get wrapped up in it before you even knew what hit you.' He frowned, pulling back slightly. 'Well, maybe not you, specifically. Though I still can't figure out how you broke through it, even with your newfound . . . talents.'

Rose scowled, her eyes darting around at the other students, though no one seemed to be paying them any attention. Even Delia was too busy swatting away a particularly indignant tome to so much as glance in their direction. It was only Rose, caught in the heat of Callum's gaze and whatever tangled web he was weaving between them. But no notes of chestnut and chicory fell over her. Just his perfume of juniper and pine, and the sweet scent of spiced rum on his breath. Even so, she shivered. Clearly, he didn't need the strength of his magic to be compelling all on his own.

Rose sighed, leaning back in her chair. 'Your signature gave you away.'

'My what?'

'Your casting signature.' She folded her arms over her chest. 'The scent of your magic?'

This, at least, seemed to earn a flicker of genuine shock from Callum. 'You can *smell* people's casting?'

'Some better than others.' She shifted under his gaze. 'Why?'

'I've just never met anyone who could.' He thumbed the rim of his glass. 'You think that has to do with your necromancy?'

Rose stilled, her spine rigid as her gaze flicked wildly over the other tables.

'Relax.' Callum took her hand. 'I cast a silencing spell the minute you walked in.'

Rose blinked, pulling her hand away sharply, though the flush in her cheeks refused to fade. 'Oh.'

'So is it?' Callum prompted after a moment.

'What?'

'Part of your necromancy?'

Rose frowned. She'd never really thought much of it, honestly – always accounting her keen nose to her robust knowledge of plants. Yet it was true that she didn't hear many other people talk about it besides herself and Soren. And he didn't have a knack for necromancy, unless one counted his failed spell and his unending life, Rose supposed.

'I – er – I don't know.'

'Hmm.' Callum's eyes narrowed. 'What does mine smell like then?'

'Chestnut and chicory,' Rose said automatically, for the scent had lingered at the back of her mind for weeks now, like a bur caught on the hem of a cloak. 'It's sweeter than I imagined.'

His brow quirked as he watched Rose over the rim of his glass. 'You don't think I can be sweet?'

'If there's something in it for you.' She snorted. But a shy grin crept over her lips before she could stop it. 'Maybe.'

To her great surprise, Callum's eyes didn't spark with insidious intent, and his lips didn't turn in his usual smirk. Instead, he laughed – a rich, throaty sound that cut a shiver straight down Rose's spine. 'How well you've come to know me, dal.'

Rose's stomach flipped and she ducked her head. It was all too easy to be taken in by him, somehow. But she couldn't allow herself to be. She needed answers from him – needed to . . . what? Make sure he kept his mouth shut? And yet, here she was, bantering with him as if they were old friends. As if he didn't hold the strings of her fate within his hand, ready to snip them on the slightest whim. Still, deep down, she had to admit there was a part of her that no longer believed he would. That *trusted* him. And perhaps that made her more a fool than anything.

'You'd be quite popular in the imperial court with that talent.' Callum's drawl jarred Rose from her thoughts.

She snorted, reaching for his glass and downing the last sip before he could protest. 'Trust me, I have no interest in the imperial court.'

'No, I don't imagine you would enjoy it there.' He took the glass from her, his fingers brushing hers as his eyes flicked over her shoulder. 'You have enough people trying to ensnare you already.'

Rose followed his gaze to the arched windows beside her and froze. For there, striding down the path towards the village, was the Aratis. Instinctively, she recoiled, but their masked gaze remained fixed ahead. They didn't even slow, marching past with such purpose that it made Rose's skin crawl.

Had they found something out? Were they going to report

it to Imrys, perhaps? Rose frowned, a restless energy curling around her mind. She could stay here, safe and hidden away in the library with only Callum's coy conversation for company. Or she could stop running away from her problems and face them head on for once. Her jaw clenched, for she could almost hear Sylvie's voice weighing the options in her head with wry witticism.

Finally, with a scoff, Rose shoved away from the table. 'Stay here.'

She barely even looked at Callum as she darted out the door and into the cool air of the courtyard beyond. Like the library, the rest of campus was quiet at this hour. A few students ambled around the colonnade, and some loitered on the green, casting shimmering shields above their heads to protect them from the rain. But Rose paid them little notice, darting around the corner of the library. It wasn't difficult to spot the Aratis – the gilded curves of their wretched mask stood out like a sore thumb. Still, Rose kept her distance. With no one else on the cobblestoned path into the village, the Aratis would spot her in an instant, but they never so much as glanced behind them. Finally, they stalled at the front gates, peering left and right before vanishing around the corner.

Rose frowned, sneaking closer. And there, as she rounded the corner, she let out a sharp gasp and ducked behind the stone wall of the gate. Her pulse leapt as she steadied her breath and peered back around the corner. Imrys and the Aratis stood tucked amid the silent pines at the edge of the river, heads bent together in the flickering light of the oil lamps dotting the bridge.

Rose frowned. What was so urgent that they had to meet about it *here* of all places? She was quite sure Imrys had no shortage of more private spots to have such meetings. The

Order Guildhall came to mind rather bitterly, though she couldn't say if it was even still in use.

Even so, he had manor houses, villas and chambers all over the empire to fall back on. Though, with his finely woven robes and air of disdainful superiority, this *was* the last place anyone would think to look for him.

Rose leaned closer, but still their words didn't meet her ears; they were shrouded in some cloak of secrecy. Or a spell. Her pulse faltered as Imrys's eyes lifted, sharp and cruel as they scanned the path, like pools of darkness in the fading light.

She gasped, slipping back behind the safety of the wall. Resting her head against the cool stone, she counted the seconds as they slipped by, her breath coiled in her chest. Yet no curse lashed out to meet her, nor Imrys himself. Slowly, she moved to peer past the wall once more when a hand curled around her shoulder.

'You know, dal –' Callum's hushed voice crashed over her with a jolt – 'this is all starting to feel a bit familiar.'

Rose stifled a scream as she jumped, turning instead to glower up at him. Did he always have to follow her like some fickle shadow? Perhaps he just enjoyed the opportunity to startle her – or to linger so closely. To push her up against the wall and press his body flush against hers as he had that day outside the greenhouse . . . Rose swallowed a curse as the memory sent a fierce heat across her cheeks.

'I thought I told you to stay put?' she hissed.

'I'm not a dog.' The corner of his mouth quirked in sly amusement. 'You'll find I don't sit or heel on command.'

'Right.' Rose tilted her chin to hold his gaze defiantly. 'Next you'll tell me you don't bite either.'

At this, Callum's grin widened, lips flashing over pearly

white teeth in a way that made him look all too much like the fox that caught the hen. 'Only if you ask, dal.'

In spite of herself, a shiver crept down Rose's spine, pooling into a simmering heat at her core. Her body was betraying her against any shred of reason – so eager to toss away her dignity and give in to mindless desire. But, for once, she was all too glad for the sharp sting of pride that chased the thought away like a nightmare caught on the edge of dawn. Alluring as he was, she couldn't bear the idea of giving him the satisfaction of her submission.

'Do you mind?' she snapped, jerking her head towards the bridge. 'I'm trying to listen.'

'Not much use in that.' He followed her gaze. 'They've cast a silencing spell. Or can't you smell it?'

Swallowing a scathing retort, Rose peered around the wall just in time to see Imrys hand the Aratis a sizeable coin purse. Yet whatever words passed between them still didn't meet her ears. *Damn* – he was right.

As was Ewan, she noted. Clearly, the Faceless were on their father's payroll, though to what end? Before she could ponder it further, however, Imrys cast a glowing portal at the end of the bridge, muttering some final words to the Aratis before the judge stepped through. And then, in a heartbeat, Imrys turned and swept towards them.

Shit. Rose's blood ran cold.

Until she heard Callum's coarse murmur at her ear. 'May I?'

'Yes.' The breathy whisper fell from Rose's lips before she could stop it.

She didn't even know what he asked – what sin he sought permission for. Yet she gave it all the same, without thought or reason. Her breath fled from her lungs as his long fingers curled at her hips, flipping her around. Something flashed behind Callum's eyes at her gasp, but it was gone too quickly for Rose to catch before he shoved her against the wall, bracing himself with one arm.

A low chuckle reverberated through his chest, breath quivering against the shell of Rose's ear. Desire snaked through her veins like a blaze, pulling her towards him like a moth to flame. It hung on the air between them like the scents of his casting as Callum lowered his head, his lips only a hair's breadth from hers.

She didn't dare to meet his eyes – to see what dark promises might linger there, waiting to lure her into his trap. Though perhaps he already had. Her stomach flipped. Every glance, every whisper, every breath. It felt all too much like dancing on the edge of a knife just waiting to be plunged into her chest. And yet, at the moment, all she wanted to do was drive it home herself.

But then a towering form swept through the gate, and any thought of pleasure fled Rose's mind, replaced by cold, hard dread. Whatever illusion Callum spun, it caught Imrys's gaze only for a second before he looked away sharply, a sneer curling at his lips. Callum's grip tightened around her for just a second, until Imrys finally turned and swept off up the path.

A beat of silence held between Rose and Callum before his grip loosened. It was gone as quickly as it had appeared and left her hollow in its wake.

'Sorry about that.' Callum stepped back. 'Quick illusions are easier to cast when they're close to the truth, and no one likes walking in on what they weren't meant to see.'

Rose's breath coiled in her chest, her pulse thudding dully in her ears. He spoke of it so easily, as if it hadn't affected him at all. And perhaps it hadn't.

But then she peeled herself unsteadily away from the wall,

nearly stumbling into Callum when he failed to step back in time. And there, as he reached out to gently catch her arm, she heard the smallest hitch of his breath, the sliver of silver disappearing from his eyes as they darkened to the colour of a moonless night.

They stood there, caught in each other's gaze, neither quite daring to move. Perhaps neither wanting to. But Rose shook herself away from the thrall of his closeness, swallowing hard.

Clearing her throat, Rose tucked a stray curl behind her ear. 'What *did* he see?'

'Just a kiss.' Callum's sly smile returned in an instant, covering whatever glimpse of the truth had lingered in his gaze. 'Unless you wanted something more?'

Rose's breath caught in her throat. 'I . . .'

'Relax, dal. I was teasing.' He pushed away from the wall with a shrug. 'I just wanted him uncomfortable enough that he wouldn't stick around. Besides, it worked, didn't it?'

Rose glowered at him. That wasn't the point. 'Only at the cost of our dignity.'

'Your dignity, maybe.' He grinned, running his thumb over his lips as if he truly did have the taste of her upon them. 'Now, if it's all the same to you, I think it'd be best if we found somewhere private to carry on with—'

'I'm not going to sleep with you,' Rose bit out before he could finish, her cheeks painfully hot.

'Our conversation, was all I was going to say.' His eyes danced beneath a wry chuckle. 'But if you've got other ideas . . .'

'Absolutely not.'

'Pity.' Callum's voice didn't hold an ounce of sincerity as he straightened his robes. 'So, my dorm or yours?'

Before she could answer, he turned on his heel and glided

up the path, so sure she would follow. Rose's jaw clenched so tight it was almost painful, but she took a steadying breath. Grudgingly, she trailed after him, bitter ire biting at her thoughts. Though, for once, the murderous impulses that simmered beneath her racing heart were every bit her own.

27. Behind Your Back

It was nearly dark by the time Rose and Callum reached her dorm. Her hands trembled as she fumbled with her keys, fully expecting some sly remark from Callum for not simply casting an unlocking charm. Yet he remained uncharacteristically quiet, looming over her shoulder like a shadow.

Rose didn't meet his gaze as she finally pushed the door open and stepped into the darkened room. Reaching for the matches on her dresser, she went about lighting her candles. It felt odd to have him here somehow.

She'd thought it might steady her for what was to come – standing on familiar ground as they waged whatever battle of wits he had planned. And she was quite sure he wouldn't easily give the answers she sought. Yet there was something that excited her about the prospect. To win without difficulty would be a disappointment, even if there was a part of her that was loath to recognize that truth.

Finally, she turned to face Callum, only to find him eyeing her dorm curiously. Out of habit, Rose bristled. She hadn't changed it much since she'd returned from her travels, save some trinkets now added to her desk, and a few of Sylvie's sketches adorning the walls. But it was still a mundane room by the standards of Dunhollow.

The hanging plants that covered every spare inch of the walls and ceiling did not sing with magic. They did not chatter or dance in their baskets – useful only for teas, tonics or simply for decoration. The books tucked neatly into the shelves at the back wall did not snore or snap as Callum's eyes roved over them, and no charm lay upon the furniture to keep it tidy. Yet he didn't taunt or tease her.

Instead, he merely cocked his head, not bothering to bury the shock as it flickered over his features. 'I must say, it's not quite what I was expecting.'

Rose folded her arms over her chest. 'Sorry to disappoint.'

'More surprise than disappointment.' He shrugged. 'I had you pegged as more of a "volatile sorcerer" than "lonely botanist".'

Sorcerer, not necromancer. Rose faltered. It was almost strange the fear that fled her heart, in that moment, for she hadn't even realized she'd held it there. A gnawing worry that was so common to her as to evade her notice entirely. That the stain of her true magic would overshadow all else that she might have been in his eyes. And yet, judgement was perhaps the only thing she sensed she never truly had to fear from him.

Rose forced a wan smirk. 'What can I say? I'm versatile.'

'Clearly.'

With a sigh, Callum sank on to her bed, making Rose scowl. He was awfully keen to make himself comfortable, though she hardly should've been surprised by that. Still, her mind burned beneath the weight of her thoughts, teetering upon that knife's edge he always held between them. And she had allowed him to delay long enough.

She perched uneasily upon her window seat, scowling at Callum all the while. 'You wanted to talk, so talk.'

He raised an eyebrow, seemingly unfazed by her tone. 'Not a very warm host, are you? Not even a drink on offer?'

'I'm not hosting you – I'm tolerating you.' Rose followed his gaze as it flicked to the half-full bottle of wine at her feet, forgotten from the previous evening. 'And barely at that. So, if you have nothing useful to tell me, you can see yourself out.' Though, even as the words left her mouth, her fingers twitched to uncork the bottle. Perhaps a glass of wine *would* help make this dance between them more bearable.

'Fine, dal.' He grinned, as if sensing her thoughts. 'But fair's fair. I'll tell you whatever you want to know, but you have to return the favour. Deal?'

Rose blanched. It was a dangerous gamble. Already he held the winning hand, hoarding her worst secrets while she still knew so little of him. His mind, his motivations. His weaknesses. And yet, perhaps this was the surest way to find out. If she could trust that he would meet her with any form of the truth.

Holding his gaze, she heaved a great sigh and got to her feet. Callum watched her almost warily as she crossed to her bedside table, throwing open the cupboard beneath to retrieve two clean glasses. Settling back into the window seat, Rose uncorked the bottle, filled both nearly to the brim, and reluctantly handed one to Callum with a silent prayer that he made this worth her while.

She held her glass up expectantly. 'Deal.'

Callum eyed her for a moment before chuckling softly and clinking his to hers. 'I knew you'd come around, dal.'

Ignoring him, Rose took a long sip of wine, letting its warmth bolster her. 'So why did you protect me in the trial?'

'Which one?' He leaned back on one hand, balancing his glass in the other as he stretched his long legs out leisurely between them. 'You'll have to be more specific.'

Gods, not even a minute in and she was already tempted to throttle him. Yet the thought didn't bubble beneath her with sickening brutality. In fact, her mind was almost blissfully free of any shadowed influence, whatever lurked within her falling silent in Callum's presence. As if it feared how he could counter it.

'Take your pick,' she said finally.

'Well, the first one was sheer pragmatism.' Callum fiddled with her bedsheets. 'I could tell something had hold of you and thought it prudent not to end up on your bad side.'

He had sensed it even then? Rose shifted beneath his gaze. If he could feel its influence upon her, what else did he know of it? And why did he care at all?

'Then why help me in the second trial?'

'Firstly, I never help anyone but myself.' He clicked his tongue in a soft *tsk*. 'And, secondly, it's not your turn, dal.'

Rose pursed her lips, reluctant to concede the point. 'Fine. Ask away.'

'You're a necromancer.'

In spite of herself, she smiled wryly. 'Is there a question in there?'

Callum scowled at the echo of his own words, but there was little heat to his gaze. 'That's powerful magic for a woman who couldn't cast a year ago. How'd that come about?'

Rose paused, measuring her next words carefully. It was a natural question, she supposed, but she was reluctant to get into the specifics with him. What little she actually knew of them. She sipped at her wine before she answered.

'Dunhollow had a spate of murders last year. Somehow, only I could see the ghosts, which led to me unlocking life source.'

Callum leaned forward, his brow furrowing. 'I suspect there's more to that story.'

'Suspect all you like.' Rose forced a nonchalant shrug, or as close to one as she could manage. 'Why did you protect me in the second trial? Why cast the anti-compulsion sigil?'

Callum shook his head. 'Well, technically that's two questions, but the answer is the same, so I'll grant it to you.' But then his eyes softened, something fleeting and unfathomable dancing through them for the briefest moment. 'I know what it's like to have your mind stolen and your body turned against you, and I can tell that whatever's latched on to you is hungry for blood. We had enough monsters to deal with in those woods – I didn't want you becoming one of them.'

Rose's heart lurched. As Callum had done with her, she suspected there was more of a story behind his empathy than he was saying, but she didn't dare ask. His past was his own and, in that, at least, she was content to let him keep his secrets. Though his answer didn't explain why he'd protected Sylvie . . .

'Satisfied?' Callum asked wryly once the silence had stretched too long between them.

Rose lifted her gaze, shaking away any cloying thoughts. 'For now.'

'All right then: you can only cast life source?' He twirled his wine glass between his slender fingers. 'And how does flame fit in?'

She sucked a breath between her teeth. Of course he wasn't willing to grant her the same courtesy with her past – prising apart deep beneath wounds she wasn't eager to reopen. Not with him, at least.

Memories flickered unbidden through her mind. Of Hollis's basement and the orb crackling to life beneath her palm. Of Fen's broken pleas and tearful goodbye. Rose's throat tightened beneath the threat of tears but she forced them back. She wouldn't be the first to break – to show her hand and let Callum gather up the victory.

'Life source and a various few other spells,' she managed after a moment. 'As for flame, it wasn't mine. Not to begin with anyway. My friend was one of the victims in those murders I mentioned. I tried to save him with necromancy and our magic intertwined somehow.'

Her glass was almost half empty now as she stared down into the crimson liquid, tears welling in her eyes. It was as close to the truth as she was willing to give. Anything more burned too brightly at the back of her mind to speak of it.

'So you're more a half necromancer then.' Callum's tone was soft, almost musing. As if he were considering nothing more concerning than the weather. 'Interesting.'

Rose's gaze snapped up. 'Why?'

'Is that your official question, dal?' The sharp edge to his voice returned all too easily.

'No.' The word fell from her tongue with such force that it made her grimace at her own eagerness. Clearing her throat, Rose straightened. 'This thing that has hold of me, can you tell what it is?'

'Maybe.' He tapped a finger against his glass thoughtfully. 'But I'll need more information.'

Rose scoffed. 'I'm not letting you out of an answer that easily.'

'Then how about we speak plainly?'

She eyed him warily, doubting very much that he truly meant it. But there was an earnestness in his dark gaze as he searched her face. For what, she could hardly say. Perhaps the wine was simply loosening his tongue, making his mask slip away to reveal the want he buried so neatly beneath. But if this was nothing more than some new strategy of his, she would not fold easily.

'You first.'

'Very well.' He shrugged, his eyes flicking out the window behind Rose. 'I told you before that you're a puzzle, dal, and a deadly one at that. I could figure out who or what is pulling your strings, but you'll have to let me in.'

Rose's pulse skittered. 'Let you in?'

'To your mind,' he clarified with a dry chuckle. 'But going

in without all the pertinent information could be lethal for us both. So I'll need to know everything you can tell me about your ... condition. Who you've pissed off, what magic you dabbled in – everything. Agreed?'

He brushed away a drop of wine from the corner of his mouth, the picture of casual ease as he lounged upon her bed. As if he weren't discussing delving deep into the sanctuary of her mind. But the thought made Rose falter. Her mind was no haven – it wasn't even entirely hers any longer. What was the worst Callum could do?

With a sigh, Rose crossed her legs, the hem of her chequered skirt skimming her knee. 'Well, besides you, my only enemy is Imrys Elaegius, as you know. And now his pet Aratis too.'

'I'm hurt, dal – I thought we were friends.' Callum's eyes filled with such pain that she almost believed him. Until his pout was wiped clean with a hollow smile. 'But yes, those two seem singularly focused on your guilt. Anything else?'

'The Spell of True Revival.'

The truth slipped out before she could stop it. Rose's breath coiled in her chest as she waited for him to laugh or chide her. But he did neither, simply watching her instead as he twirled his glass between his fingers.

'You cast it for your friend, didn't you?'

Rose nodded, a fresh wave of tears threatening to overcome her.

'Could he be the one compelling you?'

'No,' she choked out. 'He would never. But I saw him in a ... vision of sorts. He said he wasn't the only one I revived.'

'Well, they say necromancers attract restless spirits – malicious ones most especially.'

Rose shuddered, her mind flying back to Aveline's gaunt features and piercing shrieks. 'Trust me, I'm aware.'

Callum frowned. 'And what happened after you cast this spell?'

'I started having these thoughts,' Rose admitted with a heavy sigh. There was little point in hiding them now, she supposed. 'Brutal, ravenous things that craved only blood and death. And then you arrived and, after the night in the pub, I started losing time.'

'And you thought I was compelling you?' His voice was so soft now that it almost stilled Rose.

'I – Yes.' She ducked her head. 'I thought you wanted me out of the trial.'

She glanced up as Callum scoffed, but his eyes were fixed on the contents of his glass. 'I would never compel you. Certainly not for that.'

'I know.'

And she did. Without rhyme or reason, she believed him. Not because she trusted him, but she'd seen enough of him now to understand that he wore his mask all too easily when he wanted something from her. When he wanted to curry her favour or control her perception. Yet now it had fallen, leaving only the truth to shield him. And Rose was not fool enough to deny it any longer. Callum seemed just as shocked by this as she was, his eyes widening before he nodded slowly.

'Good.' He drained the last of his wine and got to his feet. 'Then let's see if we can identify your little stowaway so we can all sleep better.'

Rose shifted back on the window seat as he towered over her. At this angle, her head only reached his navel, and she wondered briefly what he would do if she were to take hold of his hips and tug him a little closer. A hot flush crept up her neck at the thought, not helped in the least as Callum nudged her knees apart, pressing himself against her torso as he reached out to cup her face.

'Close your eyes.'

Rose did as she was told, her eyes fluttering shut as Callum's fingers pressed gently against her temple. The warmth of his magic fell over her with the familiar scents of chestnut and chicory, and she had to stop herself from breathing them in. The last thing she needed was Callum stumbling on to this strange desire that had taken hold of her while combing through her thoughts.

'Your magic – it's knotted.' His voice made Rose jump, his breath softly brushing her forehead.

'What?'

'It's like someone has tied it off.' She could almost hear him frown. 'A binding curse maybe – and a powerful one at that.'

A binding curse? Wait, hadn't Soren mentioned sensing something similar in his diagnostic, before she'd – well. Rose grimaced. She hadn't given it much thought in the aftermath, but what if it was the same thing? Yet the thought only gave her pause.

'I don't understand.' Her grip around Callum's wrist tightened. 'If my magic is bound, then how can I cast at all?'

'I suspect it's why you couldn't for so long.' He hummed. 'But the binding feels . . . frayed somehow. Curses like that can last a lifetime, but perhaps it was torn when you unleashed it last year? And your power has been leaking through ever since, like a dam ready to burst.'

Rose's heart leapt. That didn't make any sense – who would've bound her? Soren, perhaps? *No*, she dismissed the thought almost as soon as it came to her. He would never have done something like that without telling her, even if it was to keep her safe.

Her mother then? A faint bitterness lingered on Rose's tongue as her stomach sank. She'd certainly not lacked either the power or the cruelty to weave a curse like that, but why bother? If she'd known that Rose hid such power within her, surely, she would have snipped through such a barrier with little hesitation – consequences be damned.

Rose's eyes flew open, seeking any kind of answer within Callum's, though his remained closed. 'So my life source – my flames – they're only a fraction of my power?'

'And a small one at that.' He nodded, his throat bobbing. 'You've slipped that noose from around your throat, but your hands are still tied behind your back. I could cut those binds, if you want.'

Rose's breath hitched as he opened his eyes, burning with such intensity that it stilled her. When he looked at her like that, she almost didn't hear his words – didn't heed any plea for reason or caution from her wary mind. But she couldn't allow herself to be drawn in. Not now. 'At what cost?'

'Who could say?' His throat bobbed, his eyes darting away from hers. 'A greater well of magic could let you fight this thing, but it might make it stronger too. The risk is yours to take, dal.'

Rose clenched her jaw tight. Her whole life, she'd buried herself under the weight of shame and fear, buckling beneath others' expectations. How could she look into the well of her own power and deny it now? Even if it did pitch her over the edge of a precarious precipice, the abyss below all too eager to welcome her into its shadowed embrace.

'Do it.'

Callum pulled her closer, his thumbs grazing her cheekbones. But then they dropped, nearly brushing her lips as his gaze lowered. He was so still for a moment that Rose almost thought he hadn't heard her. Until his eyes lifted, and any doubt she'd had fled from her mind as his whisper broke the stillness between them.

'As you wish.'

Rose's breath caught in her throat as, without warning, his grip tightened around the back of her neck. His fingers wound against the soft hairs there, pulling lightly as a warm pulse flashed through his fingertips. A gasp slipped from her lips as the room around her faded, the walls of her dorm lost to the beige canvas of a tent. Her dressing tent.

'What were you thinking, Rosera?' Her mother's voice crashed over her with a shock. 'You were so close to victory, and you let that wretch from Maalstrum get the better of you.'

Rose's heart hammered in her chest. This was her memory – from the day of the first trial. From the day she'd *killed* her mother. And yet she couldn't turn to face her. To see what venom was etched into her pale face that had led to her cruel fate. As if her body was not even hers to command.

Because it wasn't, an insidious voice hissed at the back of her mind.

'And for what?' her mother continued, ignoring her silence. 'Gods, even with all that power at your fingertips, you still haven't learned how to use it. Perhaps you never will.'

Still, Rose did not answer her. *Could* not.

'Rosera?' A firm hand gripped her shoulder. 'Are you even listening?'

Finally, a voice answered – cold, cruel and not entirely her own. 'Rosera isn't here any more, Mother.'

Bile crept up Rose's throat as the memory went dark, the echoes of her mother's scream ringing in her ears. She longed to drown it out – to rip herself out of this horrid spell. But her tongue lay heavy and silent against her lips.

Instead, only one word lingered in her thoughts. *Mother.* Over and over, both a plea and a curse. But it wasn't her voice that had uttered it, nor was it her memory that took shape in the edges of her vision.

Rose frowned up at the form that now towered over her, but her gaze felt distant somehow. As if she were peering through the hazy panes of someone else's eyes. Even so, the figure filled her with such an overwhelming sense of dread that it felt as if she'd always harboured it, even if she didn't recognize them. Although, that wasn't quite true. Their golden-brown skin and dark hair were unfamiliar, but their obsidian eyes she knew all too well.

'Mother.' Rose's voice caught on a sob. No – Callum's voice. This was *his* memory. 'Please.'

Rose's chest tightened as her eyes flicked down, a blade held in the trembling hands before her, crimson stains catching the waning light. A wave of nausea washed over her as blood seeped between her fingers – *his* fingers. Enough to make her head spin.

The woman's lips thinned, her eyes unmoved against Callum's plea. 'Again.'

Rose stifled another sob as, ever so slowly, Callum's body obeyed, turning the blade back against the torn flesh of his arms. But the pain faded in an instant, the memory waning and flitting to another image. The same woman again, but no insidious words slipped from her lips this time.

No. She lay with a dull finality upon the ground now, her flesh carved beneath a thousand wounds. Blood pooled in crimson rivulets beneath her, splayed around her dark hair like some macabre crown. But, as Rose stared down into those lifeless eyes, she couldn't help but feel the strangest stirring of joy. And that was perhaps the most frightening thing of all.

Suddenly, the image shifted again. Only this time there were no grim memories – no painful truths wrenched from the depths of the past. Instead, it was only darkness. Writhing shadows gnawed hungrily at her skin, seeping down to her very bones with an icy chill.

Rose tried to scream, but no sound came out, and her body fell limp beneath any shred of will. She was formless in the dark – nameless and shattered, without even her mind to call her own. Until some sharp shard of magic twisted around her and pulled.

All at once, the illusion buckled, wisping away as the warmth of her dormitory faded back into view. Rose shuddered, her knees sore against the cold floor. She and Callum sat tangled upon it – a mess of ragged breaths and raging hearts.

'Thank you,' Rose whispered after a long moment.

But Callum said nothing. He didn't even look at her – slumped against the floor as if the spell had sucked every ounce of energy out of him. Rose reached out, but he shied away from her touch, wordlessly shaking his head before he stumbled to his feet and darted out the door.

Rose's heart sank, wavering over the keen sting of pity, but she had no strength left to follow after him. Yet, as he fled from her room, something else took root at the back of her mind. A presence she recognized with sickening familiarity as it wrapped her in its cruel grip.

Hello, Rosera, it whispered between her thoughts. *I've been waiting for you.*

Her mouth went dry, her heart hammering in her chest. 'W-who are you?'

I've held many titles over the years, the voice purred at the edges of her mind. *But you may call me Ionas.*

'What do you want from me?'

There was a long pause. An aching beat of silence in which Rose was almost certain this Ionas had disappeared once more. But then he stirred, his voice like shards of ice burying into her very veins.

Everything.

28. Every Poisonous Root

The cloying, acidic scent of potions and tonics hung on the air, burning Rose's nostrils. The vaulted ceilings of the infirmary stared down at her, charmed to echo the soothing whir of a forest at dawn. But it did little to calm her now.

Instead, her eyes remained fixed on Arden's shock of red hair lying flat and listless against the pillows of his cot. His skin was sweat-slicked and pallid, almost grey in the dim light that filtered through the latticed windows. The shadow of sickened veins carved their way up his throat, as if they were draining the life from him rather than keeping him alive. Because of her.

Rose's heart flipped. She shouldn't even be here. Not only was she missing Strategy and Summoning against her better judgement, if the Aratis or Imrys ever found out she'd gone anywhere near Arden, they would arrest her in a heartbeat. And yet, some strange sense of need had drawn her here. Some shred of desperation she'd kept buried, even from herself.

But the gentle surge of magic now simmered beneath her skin, bolstering her with ... hope, she supposed. That she didn't always need to be bound to volatile flame or the fickle threads of life. That she could do some *good* with this power. The thought made her stomach sink. Or what if it made her far more dangerous?

That insidious voice from last night still hung at the back of her mind. Ionas, it had called itself. It was hardly anything to go on, she knew, but after weeks of silence and shadowed intent, it was *something*. It'd since gone dormant again, but at least the creature now had a voice, if not a face. And an ever more voracious hunger that lurked beneath each beat of her heart.

But Rose forced it back, her gaze darting left and right. Glowing vials, bottles and jars filled with powerful elixirs and potions pulsed in the silence. But otherwise the infirmary was lonely and abandoned. No healers pottered about yet, and no one else had been condemned to lie in these cots. None save the boy before her. A broken, half-dead shell of what he'd once been.

It was strange, perhaps, the guilt that coiled around her heart for the thought of Arden's plight. Were circumstances different, she might have been overjoyed at the prospect of never again having to meet his smug sneer. Even now, a caustic part of her was glad that, of all the people in those woods, it was Arden that Ionas chose to wield Rose's necromancy against.

But it *was* her power that put him there. Bent and moulded into a weapon not of her own making, perhaps, but hers all the same. Though maybe, with its newfound strength, that needn't be true.

No, she corrected herself – *not newfound*. This power had been within her all along, after all, simply caged. Wilfully withheld.

Rose gritted her teeth, the bitter taste of resentment souring on her tongue. For, as Callum's spell had broken last night and he'd fled from her room, she'd caught the most familiar scent. Balsam and gardenia. So subtle as to almost go unnoticed. Yet in the light of dawn it had stung her with bitter recognition.

Her mother's signature. Though she hadn't smelled it in months, she would know its cloying scent anywhere. Which could only mean that she'd been the one to cast the binding curse.

Bile crept up Rose's throat. She couldn't even say it truly surprised her; there was little about the depths of her mother's cruelty that would. And curses like that were designed to never be unbound by the bearer – one last 'gift' from her mother that could reach Rose even from beyond the grave. The only thing she couldn't fathom was why.

After all, her mother had never cared about protecting her, even though she'd long hidden her secrecy behind that guise. But casting was the only demand she'd ever made of Rose that she'd been unable to fulfil. So why would she knowingly cut off the one thing that would have given her the daughter she longed for?

'I have to say –' Sylvie's voice crashed over her, making her jump – 'I expected you to skip class, but this isn't where I thought I'd find you.'

Rose whirled around, her heart hammering in her ears. Even in the cool light filtering through the windows, Sylvie was a sight for sore eyes. Though she could hardly bear to look at her now, her gaze sliding back to Arden.

'I thought I could . . . I don't know. Save him?'

'Is that a good idea?'

Rose's head snapped up as Sylvie took a seat in the chair beside her. 'You think I should just *let* him die?'

'No, but –' Sylvie reached across the table to squeeze her hand – 'he's stable, according to the healers I spoke to yesterday and, without his account, the Faceless can't link anything to you. If you wake him up, how long do you think it'll take for him to turn against you?'

Rose's stomach sank. Did that really matter? From what she'd witnessed last night, she doubted it. With the Aratis on Imrys's payroll, she was sure they wouldn't even need to prove her guilt to ruin her with it.

'I wouldn't be so sure.' She sighed. 'Callum and I saw Imrys and the Aratis meeting last night. Imrys gave them a bribe and sent them off through a portal — I'm sure a technicality like proof won't inconvenience the pair of them too much.'

'Bastards,' Sylvie cursed. But then her eyebrow quirked. 'You and Callum, huh?'

Rose blanched as the memory of Callum's warmth skittered across her skin. Of course that would be what Sylvie took away from this whole mess. It had been her who'd put such lurid ideas in Rose's head in the first place.

'It wasn't like that.' She frowned. 'We just talked.'

'Sure.' Sylvie nodded, barely containing her smugness. 'And how did your little chat go?'

'Not how you'd expect, I'm sure.' Rose ducked her head. 'He discovered that my mother put a binding curse on me and — er — broke it.'

'What?!'

'The minute he did, I could . . . sense the presence that has hold of me.' Her tongue felt heavy under the weight of the truth. 'It told me its name was Ionas.'

'*What?*'

Sylvie sank back in her chair. Yet her silence stunned Rose. She'd expected something . . . more, she supposed. Some kind of shock, at least, or questions. But Sylvie's gaze strayed out the window, tinged by something Rose couldn't quite place.

'All this time,' she muttered finally.

Rose cocked her head. 'Are you all right?'

'Are *you*?' Sylvie turned back to fix her with the full intensity of her gaze. 'Your mother knew all along why you couldn't cast, and she still—'

Before she even finished the thought, Sylvie was on her feet. Rose blinked as her chair screeched over the stones in protest, but it didn't slow Sylvie in the slightest. Jaw clenched tight, she made to brush right past Rose when she caught her hand.

'Wait. Where are you going?'

Sylvie shook her off, her eyes almost molten beneath her rage. 'To get some damned answers.'

Rose's breath caught in her throat as she struggled to keep up with Sylvie's pace. She hadn't said a word since they'd left the infirmary, marching down the path beside the lake with singular purpose. Rose didn't try to stop her, didn't slow her at all, even when she nearly mowed over some first-years that didn't dodge out of the way fast enough.

It was clear enough where she was going now, for they'd walked almost the exact same path a year ago, albeit for very different reasons. Or perhaps not that different. Soren's office was just ahead, and Sylvie didn't slow at all as she reached the doors to the professors' hall, barrelling right through them.

Rose flinched as the door nearly swung back into her. She couldn't fathom where Sylvie's fury stemmed from – she'd already told her that it was her mother who cast the spell, not Soren. But she also knew Sylvie well enough to know that little she said would dissuade her.

And maybe a part of Rose didn't want to.

Her stomach twisted as they reached his office door. They still hadn't spoken since the second trial, and something within her loathed the idea of breaking that silence now. What would she even say to him? Rose tugged at the hem of her blouse, lagging behind Sylvie as she rapped her knuckles sharply against the door.

Soren must have been right beside it, for the door opened only a few seconds later, just as Sylvie was poised to knock again. His eyes widened as he peered at her over the rim of his glasses.

'Oh, Sylvie, I was just on my way to class. Can—' He faltered as his eyes slid from Sylvie to where Rose lingered behind her. 'Rose.'

Her heart twisted at the softness in his voice and she ducked her head. She didn't want to see what unspoken truths lay buried in his dark gaze – what questions or pity he still held there. Sylvie, however, seemed to have no such qualms.

'Did you know?' Her tone was as sharp and brittle as glass.

'Good morning to you too.'

Rose glanced up at Soren's wry chuckle.

'Don't give me that.' Sylvie folded her arms over her chest. 'Did you know about Rose?'

When Soren didn't answer immediately, Sylvie pushed past him into the office. He frowned after her before looking back at Rose. Yet she remained silent and, after a moment, Soren sighed and followed Sylvie through the door.

'Know *what* about her?'

Sylvie rounded on him, her eyes flicking to Rose. 'Do you want to tell him? Or shall I?'

Rose shrank in on herself almost instinctively. Why should she? It was Sylvie who'd led them here. And yet, she knew this truth, of all things, should come from her, no matter how it pained her. But, gods, she hoped that she was right and that Soren knew nothing of her mother's spell. She didn't think she could stand it if he did.

Finally, Rose sighed, her shoulders sagging in defeat. 'My mother bound me.'

Soren frowned. 'What?'

'My magic, I mean.' Rose swallowed hard. 'Callum said it was knotted somehow, like there was a binding curse in place. When he cut it, I – I could smell her signature on it.'

In an instant, Soren's umber skin went ashen, and he

staggered back on to his couch. He stared at her for a long moment, as if he hadn't quite understood her. But then his eyes flicked back to Sylvie, who nodded, and he released a long, slow breath. One hand gripped the back of his couch as if it alone held him steady now, and he pulled off his glasses, rubbing at his brow. Rose reached for him but hesitated. Would he even welcome her touch as a comfort now?

'No, I didn't know,' he said finally. 'Gods, if I had, I would've—'

'What, killed her yourself?'

Soren's eyes darkened, brow furrowed as he took a step towards her. 'No, Rose. I would have gotten you away from her — away from here. From all of this. Maybe I still should have.'

Rose blinked at him. It wasn't the response she'd expected, yet she couldn't help her mind reaching for the thought with piercing longing. What would her life have been like if he had? If he'd stolen her away from her mother and raised her far from here on the shores of Arbelis?

He'd always been her one constant in this place. Before Fen and Sylvie, before she'd even had the words to describe the wounds her mother left upon her, Soren had always been there. Sneaking her treats, consoling her after her mother's cruelty — always a bright light amid these hollow halls. And how much brighter would he have burned away from her mother's reach? But Rose's stomach turned, for she knew it was a useless fantasy. Her mother never would've let either of them escape her shadow easily.

'It's not your fault.' She shook her head. 'She wouldn't have let you take me.'

'I still should have tried.'

Rose's heart buckled beneath the weight of his words. Because, when all was said and done, he was the only one who ever had. Who'd ever stood up to her mother's wrath, who'd encouraged Rose to grow despite her lack of casting. He did everything her mother should have – he'd *loved* her. Just as she was. And there wasn't anything more she could've asked from him.

Before she could think better of it, she launched forward, wrapping her arms around his waist with such force that they both nearly toppled over the back of the couch.

'You did,' she whispered into his shoulder. 'You were more a parent to me than she ever was.'

Soren was so still that Rose thought he might push her away. But then his arms tightened around her, his warmth holding her steady against the raging beat of her heart. And there was something in his embrace that felt more like home than any place she'd ever known.

In his arms, it didn't matter what her mother had done or whose blood ran through Rose's veins. She was tired of begging for scraps of affection from those who never had any love in their hearts to begin with, or who'd left her behind all too easily. Soren was the only father she needed – the family she chose. Him and Sylvie.

It seemed an eternity before they broke apart, but when they did, Soren's eyes were glassy and a lopsided smile pulled at his lips. Rose squeezed his hand, tears of her own welling in her eyes. Turning to Sylvie, she reached out to her, linking their fingers gently together as Soren dried his eyes.

'So,' he managed after a moment, 'you have access to your full magic now?'

'For all the good it will do me,' Rose scoffed. 'I can cast a few more spells, but I have no practice with it.'

Even as the words left her mouth, she could almost taste the bitter irony. How long had she wished for this very thing, only to spurn it now? Yet it was never the power of such magic she craved – it was the safety she saw that it was tied to. Another of her mother's lessons she'd never fully let go of, she supposed.

And why should she be bound to them now? To that empty, useless cruelty she'd turned against Rose like a knife. Constantly slicing away at each thread of her will or want, knotting them around the keen sting of fear. And all the while, she'd known Rose could never give her what she wanted. Holding her always at the base of a mountain whose summit she could never reach and forcing her to walk every painful step anyway.

Rose gritted her teeth. If her mother's legacy had been a blade, then she would use it to cut away every poisonous root she'd planted.

'My power wasn't the only thing I unlocked.'

Soren stilled as he pushed his glasses back into place. 'What?'

'I know what's possessing me now.' Rose's fingers tightened around Sylvie's. 'Or who.'

'He's called Ionas,' said Sylvie. 'Rose "met" him after Callum unbound her.'

'Ionas?' Something sharp flickered through Soren's eyes. 'Did he tell you anything more than his name?'

Rose felt Ionas bristle beneath her skin before his presence stilled. But it was enough for her to almost taste his anger. His unmitigated thirst for freedom. And she knew, in that moment, that he would bleed them all dry to see it through.

'No.' She shook her head. 'But whoever – or whatever – he is, I don't think it's death he wants. It's freedom.'

29. My Hero

The gambling den beneath the florist's shop was not a quiet place at this time of night. A haze of smoke filled the air, cut through by the clink of coin on wood, the folding of paper cards and raucous shouts of laughter. Only a few low-hanging lanterns were dotted haphazardly around the room, barely casting enough light to see by. Though Rose guessed that was rather the point.

Most of Dunhollow had wordlessly agreed that this was the better locale to shake away the cares of the week with a stiff drink than the brightly lit decor of the cantina. It wasn't too crowded for a weekend, though. Most of her peers gathered by the crooked bar, charmed to hand out a rather limited array of wine, whiskey and tepid ale. The rest were grouped around the small rickety tables littering the space, though there was a larger game of Dead Man's Bluff taking place at the central table.

Rose frowned as she sipped her wine. She couldn't say it was her favourite place, but not having to set foot in the overly cheerful remains of the pub was never a bad thing. Yet the sting of fear hardly even pierced her now as she sat beside Sylvie and Ewan, the dull din of chatter floating around them. She would have liked to think it was a good sign – that perhaps the place was starting to lose its hold on her memory. But she knew it wasn't true.

It was simply that her heart didn't have the strength any more. Ensnared by Ionas's insidious presence and all the horror he held, it was difficult to fear anything else now. For all his crimes, Hollis was dead and gone, his body buried with little aplomb in the local cemetery with few left to mourn him. He couldn't do anything to her any longer except linger in her thoughts. Nor could the pub. Ionas, though . . . Her stomach twisted. Despite over a week of near silence from him, she couldn't shake the feeling he was just getting started.

'So, let me get this straight —' Ewan's voice drew her from her thoughts — 'your pet monster finally has a name, he's holding Fen prisoner and you're actually an incredibly powerful caster, your mother just cut off your magic for most of your life?'

'Gods, Ewan,' Sylvie scolded. 'Have a little decorum.'

Rose almost grinned at the outrage in Sylvie's eyes. Protective, as always. But Ewan's bluntness didn't bother her, not really. And it was the truth, after all, even if she could do without the smug tilt of their lips.

'Pretty much, yeah,' Rose said finally.

They shook their head. 'And I thought my father was bad.'

For some reason she couldn't fathom, Rose bristled. What her mother had done was awful, but it was their father who threatened her now. Her mind flicked back to Imrys's meeting. No, they were as bad as each other — a match made in some rotten heaven. It was almost ironic, considering they'd detested each other right up to the bitter end.

'He is.' Rose twirled her glass between her fingers. 'I caught him passing the Aratis some sort of bribe before sending him off through a portal last week.'

'Not exactly a surprise.' Ewan leaned back in their chair, bringing their sweet white wine to their lips. 'They were probably on their way back to the capital to fabricate evidence against you. I'd be careful at the next trial if I were you.'

'If they hold it.' Sylvie shrugged. 'Arden still hadn't woken up, last I'd heard.'

Rose flinched, her eyes dropping to the faded wood of their table. Woodstone and the Faceless he hid behind wouldn't care one bit about the danger. If anything, to them, the threat of blood spilt probably only made the Ashwood better sport.

'They'll hold it. The show must go on, after all.'

Ewan's eyes flicked between Rose and Sylvie, their lips tightening. 'If they do, what are you going to do about your plus-one?'

Rose faltered. What *could* she do? She didn't know enough of this Ionas to counter him – she didn't even know when he would strike next. And she doubted Woodstone would simply let her sit it out.

Her stomach sank as her eyes caught on a familiar head of silver curls at the far end of the room. Callum didn't meet her gaze; his eyes were fixed glumly on the drink in front of him. The two students at the table beside him cast longing glances in his direction, tittering into their drinks, even as Callum ignored them. But there was a part of Rose that rankled at their lust – some bitter sting of jealousy she had no right to possess.

She gritted her teeth. She was being ridiculous. If Callum wanted to talk to her, he could've found her at any time in the last week. Still, her heart softened under the stirrings of pity. Perhaps he couldn't find the words. After what she'd seen of his memories, she wasn't sure she'd be able to either.

Finally, she sighed. 'I don't know.'

Sylvie frowned. 'Maybe you could ask Callum for another anti-compulsion charm?'

Rose's skin prickled beneath a phantom pain, and she rubbed the back of her neck. Her eyes flicked back to Callum, who still steadfastly ignored her presence as his teammate Oliv joined him at his table. He wouldn't even look at her — she doubted he'd be willing to come close to her with his magic again anytime soon.

'I'm not sure he's feeling particularly inclined to do me any favours at the moment.'

Ewan and Sylvie exchanged a glance at this, but before they could ask anything further of her, a bright pink cocktail floated over to the table, landing at Ewan's elbow. All three of them simply blinked at it before Rose's gaze slid back to the bar, where Azalaïs sat.

She flashed them a coy smile, a vision in an emerald dress that nearly made her copper skin glow in the low light. But her eyes fixed on them in a way that made Rose feel all too much like prey about to be ensnared in some trap.

Sylvie snorted into her whiskey. 'Looks like you've got an admirer.'

Ewan coughed, their golden-brown cheeks flushing a shade darker. 'Where did she even get this?'

'More importantly, why'd she send it?' asked Sylvie, clearly enjoying their embarrassment.

'I – er—' Ewan tugged at the collar of their ebony shirt. 'I went by the Faceless's questioning the other day to gauge what they were playing at, and Azalaïs and I got to chatting. She's rather . . . impressive.'

'I'm sure she is.' Sylvie's grin widened. 'So, just chatting then?'

'Oh, I really don't think you're in a place to be asking prying questions, Syl,' Ewan scoffed, any humiliation left in their features vanishing under playful disdain.

'Fine, but you certainly have a type.'

Rose almost grinned. That seemed to be Sylvie's favourite line these days. Or perhaps she and Ewan both really were just that predictable. Still, at this rate, she may have missed her calling as a matchmaker.

'Do I?' Ewan quirked a brow. 'Please, enlighten me.'

'Raven-haired women with sharp smiles and even sharper tongues?'

They cocked their head as if confused. 'So, Azalaïs, and who else?'

Sylvie smacked their arm, but Rose only laughed. She had walked herself right into that one.

'I hope I'm not interrupting?' drawled a voice behind them.

Whirling around, Rose choked on a gasp. Up close, Azalaïs was even more stunning, her jet-black hair tossed over her shoulder in luscious waves and brown eyes burning in the warm light. Rich scents of honeysuckle and wild rose wafted off her in a tantalizing aroma, and Rose had to stop herself from breathing it in. It was fitting for her, she thought: as pretty as a flower but with thorns hiding beneath.

'Not at all,' said Ewan, smoothly summoning an empty stool from the table behind them and motioning for Azalaïs to sit.

'Thank you.' She flashed them a winning smile as she hopped on to the stool, her shimmering sage-green drink remaining remarkably steady between her vined fingers.

'So,' said Sylvie, 'what can we do for you?'

'Oh.' Azalaïs tossed her long hair over her shoulder, grinning mischievously as it brushed Ewan's skin. 'I couldn't help but overhear you talking about the trial. You really think it'll still go ahead?'

The three of them shared a glance, and Rose swallowed hard. If she'd picked that up, what else might she have overheard?

She cleared her throat. 'Er – yeah.'

'Even with your teammate dead?'

Rose's heart leapt into her throat. 'Dead?'

'You didn't hear?' Azalaïs quirked one sculpted brow. 'The Mamsella said they declared Arden's death this morning.'

Ewan's gaze darted to Sylvie and then to Rose, their golden-brown skin going ashen. '*What?*'

But their voice was so soft that Rose barely even heard it over the pounding in her ears. Arden was dead. She'd *killed* him. She sucked in a breath, waiting for some shred of grief to take root in her heart. But her thoughts rejected the notion, racing through a thousand reasons it couldn't be true.

'No, I – *we* saw him just last week.' She swallowed around the corded lump in her throat. 'He was on the mend.'

Azalaïs shrugged. 'Not sure what to tell you – they didn't give the Mamsella much information either.'

Sylvie reached for her shoulder. 'Rose . . .'

But she shook her off. 'I'm fine.' Whatever else, she couldn't afford to fall apart in front of Azalaïs.

After a moment, the woman sighed. 'Look, we may as well not skirt around the issue – I might have covered for you with the Faceless but I'm no fool.'

Sylvie leaned forward, her gaze suddenly sharp. 'What are you saying?'

'That whatever happened to Arden wasn't some accident.' Azalaïs rubbed at the twisted vines of her wrist as her eyes slid to Rose. '*Someone* did him in.'

'I don't—'

'Relax.' Azalaïs cut across Rose's protest. 'I don't care what you did or why. From what I gleaned of the boy, he probably deserved it. I just want to make sure it doesn't happen to any of us.'

Rose recoiled. Was she really so disinterested? Or was it a ploy to make her let her guard down? She chewed the inside of her lip, measuring her next words, when Ewan leaned forward.

'So, whatever happens to the Dunhollow competitors is fair game – you just don't want it affecting DeVoil?'

'Exactly.' Azalaïs raised her glass to theirs with a soft clink. 'I'm so glad you understand.'

Rose took a long sip of her wine, eyeing Azalaïs with a frown. Surely it couldn't be so simple. Yet she smiled at Ewan as if all was forgotten already, Arden's death and Rose's guilt little more than inconveniences to be swept away. Her eyes narrowed. Like Callum, the woman was proving increasingly difficult to read.

As if summoned by the thought, a familiar scent tingled against Rose's nose – chestnut and chicory. Her pulse leapt and she turned suddenly, searching for his dark eyes over her shoulder. But he wasn't there. Instead, Callum still sat with Oliv, sipping his rum and chatting away.

Sylvie followed her gaze. 'What is it?'

'Callum,' Rose muttered. 'I can smell his casting.'

Sylvie frowned but said nothing as Rose's eyes slid to Callum's table. It was odd to see him enjoying his teammate's company – he'd said himself that they didn't care much for each other. And yet, the pair were all smiles now, looking like nothing less than a perfect picture of camaraderie. *Too perfect.*

'It's an illusion.' Her stomach sank. 'I think he wants me to break it.'

'Why? You think he's in trouble?'

She bit her lip. 'Maybe.'

'Rose . . .'

'Whatever it is, he got himself into it, he can get himself out.'

It was true enough – Callum was certainly more powerful than Oliv. But it sounded hollow, even to her ears. He wouldn't have cast to get her attention unless he absolutely had to. Which meant that, whatever illusion Oliv had spun, he couldn't break it himself. He *needed* her. And the thought set her pulse racing.

Sylvie sighed deeply, throwing back the last of her drink before fixing Rose with a particularly hard stare. 'Sometimes you're just as bad as him.'

Pursing her lips, Rose reached out with her magic. It was almost too easy now to find that delicate cord of compulsion – a gentle ripple in an otherwise steady stream. But it pulsed around her and Sylvie's minds like a tightening noose, and it cut away just as easily beneath the sharp edge of Rose's source.

Yet the truth brought her no comfort.

For Oliv and Callum didn't sit casually at all. Instead, she stood over Callum's broken and bloodied form as he knelt upon the ground. Strands of pale blonde hair fell like a curtain across Oliv's face, but it couldn't hide the sneer that twisted the girl's lips, nor the piece of shattered glass she held against Callum's cheek. Rose's stomach sank. How had she overpowered him? And why?

'Do you want to help now?'

Rose was on her feet before the words were even out of Sylvie's mouth, her blood pulsing furiously in her ears as she crossed the room. She didn't need to hear her smug 'I told you so' – not now. No, the only thing she longed for was blood. To take that shard of glass and shove it down Oliv's wretched throat. But she stilled as she got closer, the girl's hushed words finally meeting her ears.

'Perhaps like just recognizes like,' Oliv was saying. 'One mad killer drawn to another.'

Bile bit at Rose's throat. Was she talking about *her*?

'They should have left you to rot in the sanatorium.' Oliv yanked Callum's head back by a fistful of his silver hair. 'And she should be right there with you.'

And it was only then that Rose saw just how badly she'd wounded him. Cuts and bruises littered his face, his eyes and lips were swelling and his nose gushing blood. Her heart lurched. How long had she beaten him before he'd swallowed his pride and asked Rose for help?

It didn't matter. Rose's jaw snapped shut with an audible click, her blood singing with the thought of mapping sweet agony into Oliv's flesh. It should have scared her, perhaps, yet no shadowed figure lingered at the back of her mind now. *No.* Whatever brutality she craved was hers alone.

'You know, I never thought Maalstrum cared much for solidarity –' Sylvie's voice made Rose jump – 'but I can't say I care much for your tone.'

Oliv recoiled, her eyes darting up as if checking that Sylvie was, in fact, speaking to her. Rose stepped forward to Sylvie's side as Oliv's grasp around Callum's throat loosened. Clearly, she hadn't been expecting an audience.

'How did you—'

'Break your compulsion?' Rose flashed her a cruel smile. 'Magic.'

In spite of his wounds, a weak grin split Callum's lips. But Oliv's gaze only darkened.

'This is Maalstrum business.' She sneered. 'Do yourselves a favour and walk away.'

Before Rose or Sylvie could respond, a throaty chuckle broke between them. She jumped as Ewan slung an arm over each of their shoulders, their eyes flying back to their table, where Azalaïs still sat, watching avidly. Rose frowned. Had she broken the compulsion for all of them? Or had it perhaps slipped in Oliv's shock? Though the rest of the den's denizens paid them no attention.

'Now, that sounded curiously like a threat,' Ewan drawled – their blue eyes far too bright. Like a spider eagerly inching towards its prey. 'Which, I must say, I wouldn't advise.'

Oliv blanched, but her thin face lost none of its malice. 'And why's that?'

'Well, for one, because you really don't want to go toe to toe with these two.' They squeezed Rose and Sylvie tighter. 'Secondly, and honestly more importantly, because you'd find all of Dunhollow would become rather . . . inhospitable.'

It was impressive how utterly bored Ewan could sound while issuing threats. As if the very act of speaking to Oliv was as inconsequential as her implied demise. Rose blinked. She almost couldn't blame Azalaïs for enjoying the show.

'Please, as if any of you care,' Oliv scoffed. 'You simper over insipid lies and stab each other in the back like it's a game.'

'Oh, I'll grant you that.' Ewan nodded with a hollow laugh. 'But playing such games is a privilege we extend only to each other, not our guests. So come after one of us and you'll discover exactly how cut-throat Dunhollow can be.'

A slow smile crept across Ewan's lips as Oliv's eyes narrowed. Rose shuddered. It was rare to see Ewan smile at all, but the emptiness of the expression nearly turned her stomach. And Oliv didn't seem to disagree, finally releasing Callum and retreating with a sneer.

Yet there was a part of Rose that was disappointed at her departure. At the fact that she was given grace to leave with her flesh still intact. She seethed silently at the thought. Until Sylvie darted over to Callum, gathering him up in her arms. Rose's heart faltered for the way he groaned softly, his eyes fluttering open as he weakly stroked Sylvie's cheek.

'Thanks, darling,' he slurred. 'My hero.'

'Ugh, he's drunk,' Sylvie groaned.

Ewan sniffed at the lone glass left upon Callum's table.

'Not just drunk – drugged. You think she was trying to keep him out of the next trial?'

Rose didn't answer, her eyes tracking Oliv as she swept out the doors. Her fists tightened at her sides, vengeful fury biting at her thoughts. But they fled her head as Sylvie slung Callum's arm over her shoulder and hauled him to his feet.

'Come on then. Let's get him to the infirmary.'

'*No.*' Callum's gaze sharpened and then he winced. 'No healers.'

Rose's heart ached under the fear etched into his broken gaze, her mind flicking back to the memory of his mother towering over him. How many wounds had he been forced to bear over the years? How many times had he been allowed to truly heal them? Never, if she had to guess.

'Let's take him back to my dorm,' she said finally, taking hold of Callum's other arm. 'We can patch him up there.'

He leaned heavily against Rose, resting his head atop hers. 'Aww, dal – you do have a heart.'

Sylvie peered at her around Callum. 'Are you sure?'

'Not really.'

'Do you want help?' asked Ewan.

Rose paused, nearly stumbling as Callum swayed. *No.* Whatever this was – whatever unspoken truths lay between the three of them – she was quite sure they would not come any easier with Ewan around.

'No. We'll handle this.' Rose shook her head. 'I'm fairly certain it was about us anyway.'

30. The Death of Me

By the time they'd reached Crannaigh Hall, Callum was an aching weight on Rose's shoulder. She flung open the door to her room with great effort, stumbling through the dark as she tried to stay even with Sylvie, and heaving Callum on to the foot of the bed. He landed with a grunt, and Rose let out a breath, steadying herself before she turned to light her considerable collection of candles.

She could've used magic, she supposed, but there was something comforting about digging through her drawers for matches. Something calming in the well-timed strike against the box as the flame caught between her fingers. Something so soothing in the mundane, even as Rose's hands shook and her pulse trembled beneath her skin.

But the flickering light provided little relief as Rose turned back to Callum. A wave of nausea rolled over her for the way his cool brown skin was swollen and bruised around his face, his lip split and nose bloodied. He could barely even open his eyes to look at Sylvie as she bent over him, though Rose could hardly say whether that was due to the drink or his wounds. She frowned as Sylvie ran a hand over his face, muttering something as a soft green glow took hold of her palm.

'What are you doing?'

'Sobering charm.' Sylvie shrugged, moving her hands along Callum's frame as if she could leach away the drink from his blood. 'Should help get whatever Oliv used out of his system.'

Rose nodded numbly but said nothing, a lump cording in

her throat. Instead, she ducked into her washroom, grabbing a glass of water and every healing tincture and tonic in her cabinet. But then she paused, her fingers idling on the vials.

Such effort for so little, an insidious whisper hissed at the back of her mind. Merely a week ago, she'd have chided herself to see how she coddled him. Yet Rose shook the nagging voice away. Her kindness may have borne claws, but there was a part of her that knew she would not allow them to reach Callum. Not any more.

Straightening, she gathered the vials tight in her arms and trod carefully back into her room. But there, she stilled, for Sylvie no longer sat beside Callum. Instead, he was now supine upon the mattress, and she leaned over him, standing between his legs, which were sprawled over the edge of the bed. Rose's heart leapt at the way Sylvie balanced herself with one hand at Callum's waist, the other still running over his skin as she muttered healing incantations.

Rose's pulse thrummed in her ears, but the sound only soured at the back of her mind. She should have been envious, if anything, burning under the heat of jealous fury for the way Sylvie's fingers skimmed oh so gently over Callum's face. But an altogether different sort of fire had pooled low into her core, as she was struck merely by the thought of how *close* they were.

How easy it would be for Sylvie to close that distance between them. To breathe those healing charms into his wounded flesh with a brush of her lips. To lave kindness into the hollow of his lovely throat with her clever tongue as Callum's long fingers twisted through her dark hair, pulling her closer still . . .

Rose stumbled a bit, a gasp catching in her throat as a fierce heat crept across her cheeks. But Sylvie only glanced up at her innocently, her eyes darting to the vials in her arms.

'Oh, good, we'll need those.'

'Er – yeah.'

Rose nodded, handing Sylvie one of the vials and a linen cloth before turning to examine Callum herself. Beneath the swelling, his brown skin was almost ashen, a sheen of sweat creeping across his brow in the flickering candlelight. Her stomach turned. Gods, what had Oliv *done* to him?

For a moment, rage twisted in searing coils around her heart, desperate to rain fury down upon Oliv, to carve the true depths of her ire into her very flesh. She tried to shake the thought away, but her anger did not recede so easily now.

Clearing her throat, she reached for his shoulder. 'Let's get him up, at least.'

Sylvie nodded and stepped back, grabbing Callum's other arm with her free hand as they heaved him into an upright position. He wasn't terribly heavy, but he had gone limp, swaying back. Sylvie caught the back of his head, tilting it up towards Rose as Callum's eyes fluttered.

'By the Nine,' Sylvie muttered.

Rose gripped Callum's chin gently. 'I thought you cast a sobering charm?'

'It could only do so much.' She grunted as Callum leaned against her shoulder.

Rose pursed her lips. 'Well, hold him there and I can at least patch him up.'

'I thought you didn't want to help.' Sylvie's voice inched up in a mocking pitch.

Rose flashed her a glare, taking the tonic and cloth from Sylvie's hands a little more harshly than was necessary. 'Bit late for that now, isn't it?'

Sylvie said nothing, but her smirk made Rose roll her eyes. This didn't prove a damn thing, but she already knew Sylvie would never let her hear the end of it. Gritting her teeth, she turned back to Callum, tilting his head towards the light.

The swelling around his eyes and brow had lessened after Sylvie's spell, but his split lip glistened with barely dried blood, and the bruises mapped horrid lines beneath his skin. Wetting the linen cloth with the tonic, Rose set about gingerly tracing over them.

Callum winced as she did, and it stirred something within Rose's heart. Some unspoken, mangled thing buried deeper than her mistrust and anger. Something that, were she to give it a name, she was quite sure would no longer content itself to be hidden away. Yet she was tired of shoving it to the back of her mind – tired of the pretence that kept it ensnared by nothing more than her pride. For it was no longer disgust that met her when she looked upon him. Not annoyance or even fear. It was a softly blossoming warmth that echoed all the way from the racing beat of her heart to the flush creeping across her cheeks.

It was the sweetest flicker of caring. For the pain etched into his flesh, for the broken, bloodied boy sat within her arms. For *him*. And, as his eyes slowly opened and obsidian met hazel in the silence between them, Rose wondered if she'd ever be able to look away again.

'Hello, dal,' Callum muttered, one hand stroking lightly down her arm. With a shiver, Rose moved to pull away, but his fingers tightened around her wrist. 'No – stay.'

The whisper curled around her ear like a promise, pulling her in ever closer. To the spark dancing in those dark eyes and the heat of those lips now only a hair's breadth from hers.

But then the gentle scents of chestnut and chicory stole over her, and Rose reeled back. Burning through the compulsion with such ease, she blinked the haze away, though the heat between them didn't recede at all. Nor did Sylvie retreat.

She practically clung to Callum now, her lips nearly brushing the shell of his ear in a way that sent Rose's stomach fluttering. Shaking her head, she pushed the feeling away and nudged Sylvie's arm.

'Sylvie.'

'Hmm?' Sylvie blinked and then frowned, pulling away from Callum. 'Oh.'

'No.' He caught her hand too, his eyes flicking between her and Rose. 'I'm sorry. I didn't mean to – please don't go.'

Rose and Sylvie exchanged a glance, but Sylvie didn't pull away from his grasp, instead settling back at Callum's side, albeit slightly further away. Intrepidly, Rose reached for the folds of Sylvie's mind, searching for any tether that might still bind her to Callum. But there was nothing, save Sylvie's own want. Oh. Rose's cheeks flushed. *Oh.*

Ducking her head, Rose went back to brushing the tonic over Callum's face. He didn't protest, the torn skin around his lip already knitting itself together as she turned her attention to his nose. After a moment, Sylvie reached out her hand, and Rose wordlessly passed her the second cloth, avoiding her gaze as Sylvie took to cleaning Callum's brow.

He remained silent through it all, his gaze fixed dazedly on some stray point between them. Wiping away some dried blood at his chin, Rose pushed aside his collar and faltered. For, staring back at her was not just dried blood and bruising, but scars.

Dozens of them. Horrible jagged lines flayed his skin by some cruel hand. His mother's – if she had to guess. Rose's stomach lurched and, for one wild moment, all she wanted to do was pull him close. To tear away the fabric that separated them and brush soft kisses across his flesh until every trace of pain and torment was nothing more than a distant memory. Rose stroked her finger over one scar that carved its way up the side of his throat, but Callum hissed softly, catching her hand.

'Don't.' His voice was barely more than a whisper. 'Please.'

And there was such agony in his eyes that it nearly broke her beneath its weight. Beside him, Sylvie frowned, leaning forward to peer at his collar. A small gasp slipped past her lips, but Callum didn't look at her. Didn't move at all.

Slowly, Rose pulled her hand away, but she didn't drop it, or his gaze. For something rose to meet the heat that flared in her veins as she lifted her hand back to his chin, cupping it gently. Some shred of mercy – of life itself. Desperate to fix what had been broken, even if her magic could only reach his flesh.

Silver flames flared from Rose's hand, dancing across Callum's face, but they did not burn him. Instead, they stitched his skin together, smoothing out every wound and easing each bruise. Reaching even for his blood and chasing away the last vestiges of poison they found there. Callum released a shuddering breath, leaning into Rose's hand before ever so slowly lifting his head. And, when he met her gaze again, his eyes were clear and bright, if no less pained.

Still, he tried to bury it with a sly smile, leaning back on his hands. 'That's a rather neat trick, dal.'

Rose almost scoffed, but didn't step away. 'I'll take that as a thank you.'

Sylvie's gaze flicked between them, but she said nothing for a long moment. Finally, she leaned closer to Callum, tugging his collar back into place. He jumped at her touch, as if he'd forgotten she was there, and a deep flush stole across his cheeks.

'Why were you fighting with Oliv?' Sylvie tucked a silver curl behind his ear, wiping away some blood that still lingered there.

Callum didn't push her away, but a dry chuckle fell from his lips. 'You don't beat around the bush, do you, darling?'

'And you never give a straight answer.' Sylvie's hand traced a gentle path down his arm. 'Why were you fighting?'

Finally, Callum looked up at her. 'Over you, if you must know.'

'Me?'

Callum's eyes slid to Rose, his throat bobbing as he dropped her gaze. 'Both of you.'

'Oh.'

Rose and Sylvie both fell silent, the look they shared as guilt-laden as it was fleeting. Oliv had nearly beaten him to a pulp and left him to bleed on the bar floor – how could she and Sylvie be worth that?

'What about us?'

'Does it matter?'

'When Oliv nearly killed you over it?' Rose's words were sharp, yet they fell upon him with so little heat. 'I'd say so, yeah.'

Callum let silence hang between them a moment before he finally sighed. 'She thinks I'm losing the tournament for you two.'

'What?' Sylvie frowned. 'But you're doing just as well as Rose and me – better than Oliv too.'

'And therein lies the real problem.' Callum leaned back on his hands. 'In her mind, I should've let Rose take the fall for murdering her mother. I should've let that beast crush you in the forest.'

Rose blanched. It was nothing she hadn't thought before, after all. Because, for all that she was determined to paint him as a foe, she couldn't deny that he kept coming back to help her – protect her. Them both, really. *One mad killer drawn to another.* Oliv's words flickered through her memory. Was that all it truly was? Some vanity that compelled Callum to see himself in her, like mirrors reflecting the same shadows back at each other.

Rose's stomach roiled as she straightened. 'So why didn't you?'

'Rose!'

'What?' She shrugged off Sylvie's protest, stepping closer still, until her hips were nearly pressed flush against Callum's chest. 'You said before that you only help yourself, so why even bother?'

Without warning, Callum caught her by the waist and pulled himself to his feet. Rose stumbled back, but he didn't release her, instead holding her steady as he towered over her. For a moment, she thought he might kiss her – close the distance and break this unbearable heat that had built between them. But all he did was stare, locked into her gaze for what felt like an agonizing eternity.

Then, finally, he leaned in, the smell of rum clinging to him. Warm and spiced, it sparked something deep within Rose. Dangerous yet familiar – and all too alluring. But his eyes promised only regret.

'Because when it comes to the two of you, I think I care far too much.' Callum's fingers tightened around Rose's jaw. 'And it'll be the death of me.'

He held her there, lost in the depths of her gaze. Or maybe in the truth as it hung between them. And then, without another word, he brushed past Rose and swept out of the room, leaving them both behind in stone-cold silence.

31. Whatever the Cost

Sleep did not come easily to Rose that night. It rarely did any more. Caught on dancing shadows and the restless churning of her own thoughts, it lingered tantalizingly at the back of her mind, ever out of reach.

Instead, she tossed and turned, fluffing her pillows and pulling her bedsheets up to her chin. Behind her, Sylvie stirred at the motion, pressing herself tighter against Rose's back, but her heat didn't warm her. The weight in her chest sat, cold and heavy, refusing to be chased away, even by Sylvie's soft touch.

Her fingers traced gentle paths over Rose's shoulders, slowed by the haze of slumber, but still sending a shiver down her spine as they sank lower. The strap of her nightclothes slipped down her arm as Sylvie's lips ghosted over her skin, fervent and featherlight

Sylvie moaned against her, pulling Rose closer with a hunger that echoed her own. But something shifted. The curve of Sylvie's lips, the strength of her arms wrapped around Rose's waist — the floral scents of orchid and musk sharpening to pine and juniper. Rose pulled back, but it wasn't Sylvie's amber eyes that stared down at her. It was cool obsidian, creased by a sly smirk that crept across Callum's lips.

Rose's heart leapt, and she recoiled, shoving away from Callum. Her eyes squeezed shut, willing this strange nightmare to fade. She sucked in a sharp breath, but when she opened her eyes, it wasn't the darkness of her dorm that greeted her. It was the sapphire shadows of Fen's room. *His prison*, she corrected herself, her throat tightening as she turned.

But Fen didn't watch her with those broken eyes of his. He didn't even stir, his lean chest bare and soft bedsheets tangled around his body as he sprawled out on top of his cushions in an almost serene slumber. Rose faltered. His warmth beckoned her, a soothing solace to her racing heart, but she hesitated.

She knew none of it was real. The plush mattress, the opulent trappings. The peace that hung over him like a shroud. Did he even need to sleep in this place – or had he spun the lie so deeply that he now believed it himself?

Fen groaned softly in his sleep, catching her hand and pulling her closer. Rose landed as gently as she could, careful not to wake him. But, finally, she let herself ease into his embrace, moulding herself along his side as she had so many times before.

They could have stayed there in the silence for an eternity, caught in each other's arms, but something tugged at her heart. An ugly, restless worry at the back of her mind that refused to settle. Finally, she lifted her chin, laying it against his bare chest.

Fen's eyes fluttered open, something sparking behind them as they took her in, and a slow smile spread across his lips. But then it faltered, and he pulled away. After a moment, his features shifted – his skin returning to russet and the dark circles fading beneath his eyes. Scents of red wine and worn leather fell uneasily over her and Rose recoiled. Once, it had been a balm to her soul; now, it stung like poison.

A sigh brushed past her lips. 'Why do you show me what isn't real, Fen?'

His eyes dropped as he caught her hand, pressing it against

his cheek. He didn't speak for a while, as if silence could keep her from seeing the truth. But, when he lifted his gaze again, they welled with tears.

'Hope, I suppose.' Fen let her hand fall away. 'That it could be someday.'

Rose's heart twisted, flaring beneath the spark his words carried. 'Could it really?' she all but whispered.

Fen sighed. 'I don't know.'

'Yes, you do.' She reached for him once more. 'Please, don't give me hope where there is none.'

'There's always hope.' He stroked a strand of hair away from her face. 'But it won't come without a cost.'

Rose almost scoffed. What in this damned world didn't cost something? They only sat here because his life had been the cost of hers. Even in this small shred of reprieve, what did it cost them to hope? Yet she couldn't deny the soft bloom that took hold in her chest. If setting Ionas loose was the price of freeing Fen, then she would do it in an instant.

'Whatever the cost, I'll pay it.'

'No, Rose.' He shook his head. 'I died so you wouldn't have to. I won't change my mind now.'

'Do you know that I would?' Her voice was strained, almost reedy in her desperation. 'I have more magic now. I could try again and—'

'And what if you're not strong enough?'

The words were held between them as Rose recoiled. It shouldn't have stung. After everything she'd learned – the powers she'd unlocked – it should have slipped away from her, entirely unheeded. Yet, still, it lanced her heart like a blade. A little tear in her chest, wrenched open so many times that it refused to heal. But never by him.

And somehow, that only cut deeper.

Or perhaps it was because she'd always known it was the

truth, and now Fen finally saw it too. And why wouldn't he? She hadn't been strong enough to save him when he'd needed her. She hadn't been strong enough to bring him back. Now she lacked the strength to save him from this fate she'd doomed him to by her own foolish hand.

Why *should* he trust her when all she'd ever offered was the bitter sting of failure, dulled by this paltry love that still ached in her ever weakening heart? It pounded against her ribs, almost in protest, but there was no heat in it. Spurned and turned brittle over the years, her useless heart finally shattered beneath the weight of it all.

'Well,' she said, her voice taut against the threat of tears, 'then I guess we'll find out.'

Before Fen could utter another word, Rose tore herself away. From his warmth, from this illusion – from all of it. But she couldn't escape this aching chasm in her chest, tearing her open inch by painful inch. Her eyes fluttered open to the darkness of her dorm. To the earthy scents of her plants and the soft embrace of Sylvie's arms, who still slumbered peacefully beside her. But none of it comforted her now. Pulling her knees up to her chest, Rose released that final shred of hope she'd been clinging to for so long and simply wept.

32. Best of Luck

Rose stared down the dark lengths of the corridor, her footsteps echoing softly against the stone floor. Somehow, it felt as if she were walking towards her own grave. Her fingers tightened around the parchment in her hand, and she glared down at Woodstone's trial summons. It had arrived a few days ago in the haze left behind by her dream of Fen.

A grim reminder that whatever hope she clung to was a flimsy, fragile thing. Rose glanced up at Sylvie, who walked quietly beside her, her brow etched in a scowl. She still hadn't told her of her dream – hadn't had the heart to really. Or perhaps the courage.

Rose chewed the inside of her lip, her eyes roving over Sylvie. Even dressed in that ridiculous sapphire uniform, she was the picture of grace and raw beauty. A flush crept up Rose's neck and she ducked her head, nearly running into Sylvie as she came to an abrupt halt.

'The third trial is in the infirmary?' Sylvie's voice held a rather brittle edge as she scoffed. 'Isn't that a little . . . on the nose?'

Rose's eyes darted up to the oaken doors above them and then down to the summons in her hand. *Welcome*, it blinked back at her, and her stomach sank. Was Woodstone trying to unnerve her? Remind her of the cost of her crimes? Arden's pallid visage flickered through her mind with a twinge of regret.

'Perhaps they're just anticipating the inevitable.'

Sylvie faltered at this. 'Do you – I mean, is Ionas . . . ?'

'He's quiet,' Rose assured her, though the thought comforted her little. 'Almost too quiet.'

Sylvie's gaze lifted slowly. 'You think he'll try something in this trial?'

Rose fell silent for a moment. It seemed likely, given the last two trials. Yet she'd barely had a murderous impulse or cruel thought that wasn't born from her own heart since Callum had awoken Ionas. Perhaps the full brunt of her magic made it harder for him to take over. She hoped, at least.

'Honestly? I don't know.'

Sylvie nodded slowly. 'Perhaps you should sit this one out.'

'You think Woodstone would let me?' She grimaced. 'He doesn't care what happens to any of us, as long as Dunhollow gets the win.'

'I know.' Sylvie sucked in a sharp breath. 'Gods, they should have just cancelled this damned thing after the first trial.'

Rose paused. Maybe Sylvie was right — maybe she should just run and never look back. What was the worst they could do? Yet, deep down, she knew it wasn't about what could happen to her, it was what she could unleash on the rest of them that truly scared her. And there was nowhere far enough that she could run where she wouldn't be a threat.

'Sylvie, if I—' Rose's mouth went dry as her voice cracked. 'If Ionas does take over in there, promise me you'll stop me. Whatever it takes.'

Sylvie's eyes darkened beneath the shadow of her brow as it furrowed in a scowl. 'Rose, no.'

'Please.' Rose reached for her hand. 'Callum stopped him last time, but who knows if he can again. Or will. And if it comes down to me or you, I know who I would pick every time.'

Sylvie pulled her closer, tilting her chin up to face her. 'So do I.'

Rose blinked against the sting of tears. Ionas would use

that against Sylvie in a heartbeat. He would wear the guise of Rose's face to make her drop her defences, to make her feel safe just before he struck the mortal blow.

'But it wouldn't be me.'

'Maybe not.' Sylvie lifted Rose's hands to press gentle kisses against her knuckles. 'But I told you that I'd fight for you, and I intend to hold to that.'

No, Rose wanted to say, *just let me go*. But the words echoed in her mind – haunting and hollow. Fen had asked the same of her once. With his last words, he'd begged her to save herself, and she still hadn't listened. How could she fault Sylvie for doing the same? Squeezing her hand, Rose turned and shoved open the doors.

Yet whatever strength she'd gathered fled the moment they stepped into the infirmary. A dozen pairs of eyes fixed on them as the room fell silent. Her heart skipped a beat as her gaze roved over the gathered figures – it seemed they were the last to arrive.

After a few seconds, Woodstone plastered a wide smile on his face. 'Ah, Messeres, welcome. We were just about to get started.'

He gestured for them to join the others with a vague wave of his hand. Rose flashed a look at Sylvie, who shrugged before settling in awkwardly beside the others. Azalaïs acknowledged them with a brief nod, while Peiren smiled and waved. Oliv, however, steadfastly ignored them, which was no great shock. But so did Callum. Rose frowned. She'd thought he might at least grant them the courtesy of a glance, but his eyes remained on his boots.

Biting her tongue, Rose took her place in front of Soren, who squeezed her shoulder lightly. Yet even that didn't do much to ease the dread that had coiled around her heart as her eyes flicked over the tidy rows of beds. Utterly empty now. Her jaw clenched tight. Had they sent Arden's body off to the embalming halls or simply swept him away for the sake of this blasted trial?

'Now that we're all here, before we begin, I must acknowledge the violent endings of the last two trials.' Woodstone jarred Rose from her thoughts as his eyes slid directly to her. 'As such, we've decided on a more . . . intimate setting, and the Faceless will be taking a more active role in today's proceedings.'

Rose's heart sank as five figures swept into the hall. The Aratis gave a small nod at Woodstone's introduction, but Rose could feel the heat of their gaze upon her, even as she avoided it. Clearly, they'd made it back from whatever errand Imrys had sent them on.

'Additionally, to avoid any further incidents, this trial has been graciously designed by our Maalstrum cohorts, so you will face no greater a threat than your own minds.'

Woodstone waved a hand at the cots before them, and Rose blanched. A mindscape? She'd read about them in her rather limited studies of mental magics but, from what little she knew, they were incredibly powerful and near impossible to navigate for those not studied in compulsion or illusion. Exactly the type of trial Maalstrum would set up, then.

'We will place you under a simple sleep charm, and you will have to make your way through the course created by Professor Mistralus. As with the last trial, the mindscape will be broadcasted to our eager audience in the assembly hall.'

Rose gritted her teeth as Mistralus stepped forward, his dark hair slicked back and lips pinched in a thin smile. Though not ideal, it might be safer, in the end. For everyone else, at least. Her own mind already betrayed her – she doubted there would be any mercy for her in a course designed by Maalstrum's malice.

'As the winner of the last trial, Messere L'Espina will be given a time advantage of five minutes.'

Woodstone beckoned to Azalaïs, who faltered, her eyes flashing to Mamsella de Prevath. Something unspoken seemed to pass between the two before Azalaïs stepped forward. But she paused in front of Rose, leaning in close. 'Do be careful in there.'

Rose pulled back, searching her gaze. Was it kindness that caught in her tone or something more sinister? 'You too.'

Azalaïs's eyes narrowed, but she finally nodded and joined Woodstone at the cot where he stood waiting. Rose's pulse pounded in her ears as Azalaïs lay down upon the bed. What if she couldn't control herself? She couldn't bear to wake up holding someone's life beneath her grasp again.

But it was too late to turn back now. Rose wrapped her fingers tighter around Sylvie's as Mistralus approached Azalaïs and held his hands just inches above her face. With a few muttered words, her eyes fluttered closed and she slumped against the mattress.

'Lovely.' Woodstone clapped his hands together. 'Now, if the rest of you would please make yourselves comfortable, once her five minutes are up, we will put you under as well.'

Oliv was the first to move, marching proudly to the cot nearest her. After whispering something to the Mamsella, Peiren followed suit, leaving only Rose, Sylvie and Callum without a bed.

She and Sylvie shared a glance, but Callum still didn't meet their gaze. *Fine*, Rose thought. If he wanted to be petty, two could play at that game. Giving Sylvie's hand a final squeeze and flashing what she hoped was a reassuring smile at Soren, she made her way over to the nearest cot.

Sylvie settled into the one beside her with a soft sigh. The cot on her left creaked beneath Callum's weight as he sank into it, still not even looking at her. She frowned but said nothing as Mistralus stepped towards them.

She felt the effects of his spell almost immediately, her eyelids drooping as Woodstone approached her bedside. Unease stirred within her beneath his sharp gaze, but her limbs were too heavy to move, her tongue lying silent as he held up what looked like a collar. Her heart sank. *A dampening collar.*

'To ensure nothing goes wrong this time . . .' Cool metal curled around Rose's throat, silencing her with a gentle clink. 'Best of luck, Messere Thenlif.'

33. A Vain Fantasy

It was a gentle warmth that woke Rose. Soft and subtle, it flickered across her skin in a featherlight caress that made her eyes flutter open slowly. *Sunlight.* Rose frowned. She couldn't remember the last time she'd seen such a thing at Dunhollow.

She sat up with a start, but it was not her own bedsheets that fell away from her chest. These were woven of crimson and gold, and they covered a truly staggering number of pillows. Where *was* she?

Instinctively, she reached for her throat but found it bare. *Strange.* She'd had the oddest sensation of something being there – choking her. She shuddered. Must have been a bad dream.

Swallowing hard, Rose glanced at the rest of the room, blinking as the familiarity of it dawned on her. Though lacking its usual clutter, it was still unmistakable. *Sylvie's dorm.* The thought filled her with quiet fondness, eyes roving over the charcoal drawings upon the wall. But when her gaze fell to a pile of forgotten clothes upon the floor, her memory flickered.

Of Sylvie's eyes fixed upon her in the low light, slowly pulling down her blouse. Mapping kisses across Rose's flesh . . . She leaned back into the pillows, her skin growing flush from the thought alone. But her reverie was shattered as the door flew open, revealing Sylvie.

'We did it!' She took a running leap on to the bed, landing beside Rose with a soft 'oof'. 'We're free.'

Rose frowned at the crinkled pages Sylvie held in her hands. 'What?'

'Gods, you're still half asleep.' She gave a breathy laugh, leaning over to press a kiss to Rose's cheek. 'It's nearly ten o'clock, Rose.'

Rose's unease slowly melted away beneath her touch. There was a spark of something that lingered at the back of her mind – something she was sure she should remember. But it slipped away all too easily in Sylvie's embrace, like the last dregs of a nightmare upon the breaking of dawn.

Her lips quirked as Sylvie's kisses dipped lower down her neck. 'It's not my fault someone kept me up late last night.'

'I don't remember you complaining then.'

'Mmm, no, I wasn't.' Sylvie's breath against her collarbone made Rose shudder, but she finally pushed her away, sitting up. 'Now what are you on about?'

'These!' Sylvie shoved the papers excitedly under her nose.

Rose frowned at the parchment, her eyes scanning them quickly before she gasped. 'Our results are in?'

'And we passed with exception.' Sylvie pulled her closer. 'We did it.'

Rose set the papers aside with a small smile, leaning into Sylvie's embrace. 'We still have graduation to get through, though.'

'Yes, but after that we're free.'

Her heart skipped a beat. For so long, freedom had felt like a mere dream. A bright star on an otherwise bleak horizon, ever out of reach. But with Sylvie? Anything seemed possible.

'And Fen dropped off our tickets this morning.' Sylvie patted her pocket fondly. 'Two first-class tickets on the earliest cavalcade to Ashurd the morning after graduation.'

'Fen?' Rose's heart lurched, the thought stoking something at the back of her mind. Something she couldn't quite place.

'Yes?' Sylvie eyed her oddly. 'He said to tell you that he and

Hollis have a surprise for us at the end-of-term party tonight, by the way.'

'But Hollis is—'

The words died on Rose's lips, any protest faltering on her tongue. There was a wisp of a memory there, lingering about Hollis, about Fen – all of it. Had they mentioned this surprise to her and she'd simply forgotten? *No.* Something told her it was far worse than that.

Sylvie nudged her shoulder with a small frown. 'Hollis is what?'

'Nothing.' Rose shook her head. 'Er – never mind.'

'Are you all right?'

The concern in Sylvie's eyes made her chest squeeze, and Rose reached over to soothe the furrow in her brow. 'Yeah, just strange dreams, I guess.'

'Hmm.' Sylvie's lips quirked. 'Well, then I guess we'll have to find some way to wake you up. Callum will be here any minute, and we can't have you half asleep.'

Callum? Rose's pulse skittered and thrummed beneath her skin. *Of course.* Maalstrum's graduation had been last week, and he'd promised to attend Dunhollow's before the three of them headed down to Ashurd together. How could she have forgotten?

As if summoned by the thought, a knock rang out through the room. With a grin, Sylvie waved a hand, and the door clicked open, producing Callum.

Rose's mouth went dry at the sight of him. Windswept and flushed, a jolt of heady want coiled around her heart as his eyes fixed on her. He slammed the door behind him, sloughing off his coat and tossing his bags aside before eagerly sinking on to the bed beside them.

'Well, isn't this a nice surprise?' he murmured, catching Sylvie in a searing kiss before reaching for Rose.

She shivered as he pressed his lips softly against her bare shoulders, inching ever higher up the delicate flesh of her throat. But just as his lips brushed hers, the sweet scents of chestnut and chicory fell over her. *Was he casting?* Rose's heart flipped as a warm hand suddenly gripped her arm and spun her around to face Callum's dark gaze.

'Hello, dal.'

All at once, the scene faded. Sylvie no longer trailed her fingers down Rose's forearm, and Callum didn't cradle her to him. There was no bed, no dorm at all – just darkness and a raw, aching chasm gnawing at Rose's chest. She stumbled back, her breath coiled in her lungs as Callum grinned down at her.

'I thought you'd be embroiled in some vile nightmare, but this?' He waved a hand vaguely as the last trappings of her dream vanished. 'I'm almost sorry I interrupted.'

A fierce heat crept up Rose's cheeks as her memory came flooding back – the mindscape, the trial. *None of it had been real.* A wave of nausea rolled over her, and she staggered back. Away from Callum's sharp gaze and the warmth of his touch. From all of it.

But, oh, how she'd craved it. The taste of freedom, the heat of passion. The peace of knowing Fen and Hollis were still alive. Tears burned at Rose's eyes. It was only a vain fantasy but, in that moment, she longed for nothing more.

And that Callum had been there to witness it . . . Her jaw clenched tight. Whatever unspoken words remained between them from their last meeting, she was quite sure she'd only added fuel to that fire.

'How much did you see?' she managed finally, unable to meet Callum's eyes.

'More than our dear audience.' His voice was softer than she'd thought it would be. 'I blocked their view on the way in. Though I am curious why you didn't break yourself out of the compulsion in the first place?'

Rose's memory flickered, her fingers reaching for the cool metal resting against her throat. *The dampening collar.* A curse brushed her lips.

'I couldn't,' she said finally. 'I can barely cast.'

For several long moments, all Callum did was stare at her throat. As if he hadn't heard her or perhaps wasn't real at all. Just another illusion that would wisp away as soon as she reached for him.

Until whatever spell held him shattered, and he stepped towards her. His touch was almost gentle as his fingers curled around her collar, but his eyes were filled with fire – raw flames fit to raze the very world to ash.

'*Vincaris rima,*' he whispered.

Rose staggered back as the collar shattered beneath his spell, and metal shards fell away into the cold shadows pooling at their feet. Yet her blood sang in the echo of their ruin, fire racing through her veins as her casting returned to her. Like life breathed back into hollow lungs.

'I—' She faltered, steadying herself. 'Thank you.'

Callum eyed her curiously. 'I suppose this makes us even.'

'What, for rescuing you from Oliv?' Rose scoffed. 'I wasn't aware we were keeping score, but I wouldn't say this qualifies.'

An easy smile ghosted over his lips. 'So difficult to please.'

Rose frowned, searching his gaze. How easily he hid such blazing intensity behind the mask of his wit. As if he feared that as soon as he dared show any truth to the depths of his heart, Rose might drive a blade straight through it. And so the mask remained.

Though could she really say she was so dissimilar? Burying everything true beneath the more familiar weights of anger and shame, never letting him see anything more. Perhaps it was time they both let their masks fall.

'Are you coming, dal?'

Rose blinked as Callum's voice jarred her from her thoughts; his hand stretched to her. 'Where to?'

'Well, I had assumed you'd want to save your girlfriend, but if you'd rather stay . . .'

Rose's breath caught in her throat. 'You know where Sylvie is?'

'Not yet, but we'll find her.'

We. The thought warmed Rose more than it should have. For a moment, she didn't move. Until, wordlessly, she took Callum's hand, not missing the way a small smile quirked at his lips. With his free hand, he reached out through the shadows, a shimmering portal appearing in the wake of his touch.

'Ready?'

'As I'll ever be.' Rose squeezed his hand tighter and, together, they stepped through.

34. Ever So Alone

Rose wasn't quite sure what she'd expected when stepping out of the portal, but it wasn't this. An achingly long stretch of corridor spread out before them, swirling with a darkness so deep she could barely see the glass floor beneath her. Shadowed mists curled around her ankles, soft and cool. Yet there were sparks of light between them, glowing orbs that seemed to reach towards Rose.

She came to a stumbling halt, releasing Callum's hand as the air flooded with the heavy scents of red wine and worn leather. *Fen.* Her heart skipped a beat, her feet almost moving of their own accord towards the nearest ball of light. Rose shivered as its tendrils gently stroked her skin, but Callum caught her hand.

'Don't.' His voice was low – a warning.

Rose's stomach sank as the scent soured. 'What is this place?'

'It's where Mistralus trapped us all.' Callum's eyes darkened. 'Each is a portal.'

Rose nodded, a thick cord knotting in her throat as she glanced back at the lights. One echoed with Sylvie's laughter, while another rang out with a lullaby Soren used to sing to her as a child. Her jaw clenched tight, and she forced her gaze back to Callum, who watched her oddly.

'Problem, dal?'

'They're . . . singing to me.'

At this, he laughed. 'Yes. I suspect they'll try to draw you in with things you long for only to trap you again. Mistralus is cruel, but not particularly creative.'

Callum prodded gently at one of the lights, which pulsed at his touch. Rose's heart fluttered. What did he want? It hadn't occurred to her to ask earlier when he'd broken through the throes of her desires, but the thought burned at her now. Was his own longing buried so deep that even he couldn't find it any longer?

'What about you?' Rose all but whispered.

Callum flinched, as if shocked by the sound of her voice. 'Pardon?'

'How do they draw you in?' She took a step closer to him. 'What do *you* want, Callum?'

He fell silent, his head bowed as his fists tightened at his sides. As if gazing into that thread of desire was suddenly too much. Rose's heart flipped, stinging beneath the pangs of pity as she took another slow step towards him. But then he looked up, his eyes blazing so bright that they stopped her in her tracks.

'Nothing I can have.'

Rose faltered. She wasn't sure she wanted to know what that meant. As if she'd somehow dug too deep and unearthed a truth she did not want to face.

'Callum—'

He cut across her. 'Come on. We should find Sylvie.'

Rose fell silent as he turned on his heel and marched down the shadowed corridor. Yet her pulse thrummed in her ears as she followed him, unspoken words hanging on the air between them. She frowned as they passed light after glowing light, their shimmering edges catching in his curls.

Was his desire really so shameful that he couldn't even share it? Clearly, it couldn't have sunk its claws that deep if he'd broken out of its hold so easily and come to track her down. But then, why not simply say what it was? For that matter, why come to rescue her at all? Or Sylvie? He could have woken up ages ago and won the trial, but he hadn't. So why risk it?

Because when it comes to the two of you, I think I care far too much. His words from the other night echoed through her memory, making her heart flip. And perhaps it really would be the death of him.

The thought hit her so keenly that she wasn't prepared for Callum's sharp halt, nearly stumbling right into him. But he didn't step back as she gripped his arm to steady herself, something dark and dangerous dancing within his eyes.

'Here we are.'

Rose cleared her throat, straightening as Callum muttered something under his breath and the light blazed a little brighter. Shielding her eyes, she peered through her fingers as a doorway appeared, glowing slightly at the edges. She dropped her hand, frowning at the flowered field before her.

'You're sure Sylvie's in there?'

'Do you doubt me, dal?'

No. The thought came to her mind unbidden. But not entirely unwanted. For all he kept from her, in this, at least, she trusted him. With a small nod, she made to step towards the portal when Callum caught her.

'Wait.' His fingers tightened around her arm.

'Why?'

'It's just—' He released her with a soft sigh, running a hand through his silver curls. 'She'll be stuck in there with her greatest desires. You may not like what you find, and she may not appreciate you prying.'

'Didn't seem to concern you when you came crashing into mine,' she muttered darkly.

'Yes, well, I never considered that *I* would be a part of yours.'

Rose blanched. He said it so simply, yet she couldn't deny

the weight behind it, and it made her chest seize almost painfully. Perhaps it was never that his desires didn't match hers, but rather that he could not fathom that hers might echo his. That *she* could want *him*.

And somehow, that only made her want him more.

Shaking her head, she turned back to Sylvie's portal. 'Whatever I see in there can't be worse than leaving her.'

'If you say so, dal.'

He looked so unsure then, so weary of it all that Rose took his hand without thinking. He flinched at her touch but didn't let go. And, together, they leapt through the portal.

A soft breath huffed from Rose's lungs as she landed upon sandy soil. Blinking, she squinted against the evening sun, which dipped ever lower across the pale line of a glittering sea. She frowned as she straightened, eyeing the cosy cottage that stood beside them, a haphazard array of mossy stones, creeping ivy and flowering vines.

She traced her fingers along the wall. It was oddly peaceful for Sylvie. Almost mundane compared to the accolades and illustrious halls of some capital office Rose had been expecting. But the thought made her pause.

Sylvie cared for power, sure, but as a shield — Rose couldn't honestly say she'd ever seen her crave it. So why had she assumed it was something she would desire? She squirmed beneath the realization. How long had she been holding up Sylvie's mask as a reflection of the truth, ignoring what lay beneath?

Because what Sylvie desired wasn't power; it was safety. The freedom to truly be herself. And whatever idyllic reflection of that she'd built here, Rose would now have to be the one to break it.

As if to punctuate that point, a peal of laughter echoed

through the air. Jolting with a start, Rose peered around the corner of the cottage, to the garden where Sylvie sat before a small bonfire, watching the sun disappear over the burnt horizon. But she wasn't alone.

No. She lay sprawled across Rose and Callum's laps, sipping wine as Callum ran his fingers through her gossamer hair. And, leaning against Rose's legs, was Fen, his eyes sparking with mirth as he gestured wildly over whatever tale he spun.

The sight alone made tears well in Rose's eyes. Not with pain or sorrow, but with a craving so intense that it stole her breath away. Even without Fen, could they ever have something like this? Away from Dunhollow and all the poison it held for them, far from the depths of death and grief – could they truly be happy?

A pang of guilt lanced her heart, and she glanced back at Callum, as his grip on her hand loosened. His eyes were glassy, fixed on the charming scene with such startling longing that it stilled her. Did he recognize something of his own desire in it? Rose's heart sank. If he did, would he ever join them in such a future?

Finally, he caught her gaze, looking away sharply as he cleared his throat. 'We'll have to wake her eventually.'

Rose nodded, gritting her teeth. 'Do it.'

'It might be kinder if you do.' His gaze flicked back to the fire. 'Less jarring that way.'

She frowned. Was he not a part of this vision as much as her? Did he think that Sylvie would welcome him any less? Or perhaps he simply didn't want to be the one to shatter such a lovely illusion.

'We should wake her together.' Rose turned back to where Sylvie lay. 'I'll try to get through to her and you break the compulsion – that way we can ease her back.'

'If you think that's what she'd want.'

Rose gestured to the peaceful little reverie of the four of them. 'I think Sylvie has already answered that herself.'

This seemed to silence Callum, but Rose didn't wait around for him to find his voice again, stepping towards Sylvie. None of the others looked up as she approached – nothing more than beautiful fantasies of light and laughter in this tapestry Sylvie had woven. But cutting those threads would never get easier, no matter how long she waited. Sucking in a sharp breath, Rose reached out.

'Sylvie?' she said softly. 'Can you hear me?'

Sylvie's brow furrowed, but she didn't turn. The scent of chestnut and chicory wafted over Rose as Callum's spell took hold, the edges of their imagined figures fading slightly. Sylvie gasped, sitting up as her eyes darted about wildly. Finally, they landed on Rose with hazy recognition.

'Rose?' She shook her head. 'I-I don't understand.'

'This isn't real, Sylvie.' Rose's voice cracked over the truth. 'I'm so sorry, but we have to get out of here.'

Sylvie's eyes darted back to the illusion of Rose, now little more than smoke. 'No, I—But you were . . . just here.'

'I know – it's all part of the trial. They're just toying with you.'

Sylvie's eyes slid back to her, utterly crestfallen as they welled with tears. 'I don't want to leave.'

Rose's jaw clenched tight. And what a cruelty it was that they had to. To return to a world that cared so little for them it would ensnare them in their greatest desires for its sick games.

'You have to, darling.' Rose jumped as Callum stepped closer, dropping to his knees before Sylvie and taking her hands gently in his own. 'I know you think it's better in here, but I promise it's not. It'll all just fade away, until everything real you've ever loved is gone, and all that's left of you is a hollow husk feeding on empty promises. And you deserve better.'

Tears spilled down Sylvie's cheeks, and Callum brushed them away with a gentle stroke of his thumb. Rose's heart stirred, restlessly thrumming against the cage of her chest. He was so tender with her – so soft against the edges of Sylvie's grief. Finally, Sylvie nodded, reaching for Rose's hand too as she stood shakily.

'OK.' Her voice was hoarse. 'Let's go.'

Rose squeezed her hand tighter before nodding to Callum, who dispelled the creeping shadows with another portal. Holding firm to each other, they all walked back into the silence of the corridor. But its stillness fractured with a shuddering groan. Rose's stomach dropped as the mists around them hissed and lurched, the tendrils of light popping and shattering one by one.

'Bastard,' Callum cursed.

'What's happening?' Sylvie moved closer to him, her eyes fixed on the encroaching darkness.

'Mistralus is punishing us.'

'For what?' Rose snapped.

'If I had to guess?' His eyes darted left and right down the corridor, now closing in on both sides. 'For helping each other. This is a Maalstrum trial, after all – camaraderie isn't encouraged.'

'Then how do we get out?'

'I think I have an idea.' His gaze hardened with steely resolve. 'This way.'

Rose didn't protest as he dragged them down the shrinking hall, the shadows creeping ever closer. The soft *pop* of shattering glass echoed behind them, pushing them ever faster down the corridor. Until, with a great clatter, the floor pitched beneath them.

Rose screamed as it vanished, hurtling them all into the eager shadows beneath. Her breath coiled in her chest, wrenched from her lungs when she slammed into solid ground. Pain ricocheted up through her legs as she fought to steady herself. But it was no longer shadow that surrounded them now. The floor beneath them was made of cracked glass, as tenuous as it was bright, reflecting corridor after corridor – an endless sea of glass in all directions, shifting and shattering in a fractured array. It was enough to make Rose's head spin, her stomach turning as she swayed.

'Hang in there, dal.' Callum held her steady. 'Trust your feet, not your mind – remember, it's all illusion.'

'Can't you break it?' Sylvie sounded as if she were going to be sick.

His voice clipped on the edge of a sigh. 'I'm doing the best I can, darling, but it's me against the man who trained me. He knows all my tricks.'

'Rose, can you help?'

Rose's mouth went dry as she forced herself to focus on the sound of Sylvie's voice – on the desperate plea that hung there. Squeezing her eyes shut, she tried to locate that tendril of compulsion snaking through her mind. But this was nothing like Callum's subtle threads. Instead, it felt all too much like being trapped inside some crystal orb, unable to see beyond her glass prison, even as she banged her fists futilely against it.

'I-I can't – it's too complex.'

A sharp shattering sound punctuated her words as the ceiling cracked, raining glass down upon them. Sylvie quickly cast a barrier, the flimsy green light shielding them as Callum wove his spell. Rose gritted her teeth. There had to be *something* she could do. But, even with all this power unlocked, she simply stood there, as useless as she'd ever been.

'Just a little longer,' said Callum. 'I'm almost through.'

Rose's heart flipped. What would happen if they died here? Would it be like a dream and they'd be jolted awake upon impact? Or would their fate be a slow torture – trapped forever in the recesses of their minds as their bodies slowly wasted away?

A chill crept beneath Rose's skin as, from the very depths of her fearful broken thoughts, came a low chuckle. *Oh, my dear, what a mess you've gotten yourself into.* Rose could almost feel Ionas smile as he clucked his tongue. *Shall I help?*

'No!' she cried.

But it was too late. All at once, shadows swarmed around them, licking eagerly against their flesh. Ever hungry and oh so dark, with every ounce of Ionas's greed and cruelty etched into them.

'What's happening?' Sylvie swatted at the shadows curling around her, her barrier wavering.

'Ionas – he's here.'

'Shit,' Sylvie cursed. 'Callum?'

'Working on it.' His voice was strained and thin. But then he let out a triumphant cry. 'There!'

Rose squinted as a glimmering outline took shape in the darkness. *A doorway.* Her heart leapt. *Their way out.*

Callum yanked them towards it, dragging them through the darkness as Sylvie fought to keep the shadows at bay. Their swirling edges clung to their frames as the three of them raced down the corridor. It seemed an eternity before they reached the arching door, its light pulsing as Callum's hand curled around its knob.

He didn't hesitate before he threw it open, jumping through first, and then steadying Sylvie as she leapt through after him. But, as he turned back to Rose, the shadows shifted. Curling around her waist, they wrenched her away, smothering her scream as the door slammed shut with a dull finality.

Rose's heart raged against her ribs as the darkness swallowed her up in a cruel embrace, stealing every shred of light, every sound, every smell. Everything except the furious beat of her pulse and the insidious voice at the back of her mind.

Always running. Ionas chuckled through the void. *Always scared. And ever so alone now.*

'She's not alone.' A familiar voice crashed through the stillness.

'Fen?'

Rose turned desperately to find him standing in a doorway of flame, his hand reaching out to her like a beacon in the darkness. And his eyes, so bright and sure, stilled her racing heart in an instant. A soothing balm to her haggard soul, even after everything.

'Come with me,' he begged.

And it was all the promise she needed. With one final glance at the fathomless depths of cruel shadow, Rose took Fen's hand, holding him tight as she leapt into his prison with him.

35. Yours to Lose

Rose hit the ground with a dull thud, Fen's arms shielding her from the worst of the pain. Her chest was sore with a strangled breath as her eyes fluttered open. The dank walls of Fen's prison stared back at her, any pretence stripped away now, leaving only the bare truth carved on mouldering stones. Rose let out a trembling breath. What had it cost him to save her?

'I've got you.' Fen held her closer, stroking down her curls. 'You're safe now.'

'Sylvie and Callum.' Rose sat up, her eyes flicking over the dim cell. 'Are they—'

'They got out.'

Good. The thought sent a ripple of relief through her racing pulse. At least they were safe, even if she wasn't. Her gaze fell upon the rickety cot in the corner, no longer disguised in the comfort of Fen's four-poster bed. *What if you're not strong enough?* His last words to her echoed through Rose's mind, making her stomach sink. How right she'd proved him, in the end.

She pulled her knees up to her chest, barely able to meet his gaze. 'How did you find me?'

'I felt it when Ionas went to you.' Fen's hand fell from her shoulder. 'The mindscape they put you in made it easier for him to access you. But he got sloppy, and he left me an opening to come through, just for a moment.'

'Oh.'

Rose pulled at the torn fabric around her skinned knee. Was it sloppiness? Or did Ionas simply intend to lull her into a false sense of security with the warmth of Fen's presence? Letting her think she was safe until he inevitably found her again?

'I'm so sorry, Rose.'

Her head snapped up, her throat suddenly tight as she met Fen's gaze. But his eyes were so earnest as he took her hands between his, pulling her to her feet. His touch was so gentle as he tucked a stray curl behind her ear – his smile so soft as it spread sadly across his lips.

'I never should have said you weren't strong enough – it was careless. And it isn't true.'

Her breath caught in her throat as she stepped closer to him instinctively. 'What are you saying?'

'I – I think you could do it.' His hand dropped to cup her chin. 'I think you *could* bring me back. I was just too scared to hope.'

Rose's heart fluttered at the thought. What would it be like to have him back again? But doubt crept along the edges of her mind. That desire had led her astray once already. Mired in pride and doomed by so little thought, how could she trust now that it held any weight?

'But I failed.' Her voice cracked as she pressed a hand against his chest, almost fearing that he would disappear at her touch.

'No.' Fen caught her hand, holding it against the steady beat of his heart. 'I'm here. And I won't leave you again.'

Her breath hitched as Fen's eyes bore into hers, sparking with flames she never thought she'd see again. And then he leaned in, catching her in a kiss as if she'd set fire to his soul. Rose stumbled back in shock, even as warmth burgeoned in her heart for the heat in his embrace, kindling her memory. Of stolen kisses in dark chambers, whispered praise pressed gently into her skin.

But now his kiss was greedy – hungry. And so unlike him. Rose stilled, the sweetness of his lips souring against her tongue. She *knew* Fen. From the gentle spark in his eyes to the loving depths of his soul; she would always know him.

And this was not Fen.

Rose shoved away from him, her lips raw and aching. But her mind reeled, burning beneath a thousand rampant thoughts as her stomach heaved.

'Rose?' Fen's voice sounded as if it were leagues away, dampened by her own thunderous pulse in her ears. *No*. Not Fen's voice. 'Are you all right?'

She pressed a nail into the bed of her thumb, forcing her shallow breaths to steady. 'You're not him.'

'Pardon?'

She didn't step away as he reached for her shoulder. Didn't flinch beneath his touch. Instead, she straightened, each furious beat of her heart pouring into her magic, hardening it into a blade within her trembling palm. Before he could move any closer, she pressed it against the tender flesh of his throat. His eyes widened in the cool silver light of her summoned blade, and she couldn't help but revel in the shock that rippled through them.

'You're not Fen,' she bit out, louder this time. 'Are you?'

But she already knew the answer, even as he stared back at her all too innocently from Fen's lovely face. Even as his visage morphed and shifted. Until his dark eyes were replaced by startling white, and Fen's soft features sharpened into the very mask of cruelty.

The man before her didn't look much older than her: golden brown skin a few shades lighter than Fen's, and ash-brown hair with a streak of grey just along the peak of his hairline. Yet there was something so hollow about those cold milky eyes as they fixed on Rose. As if he'd looked upon the face of death, and death had stared back.

Bile crept up her throat. 'Ionas.'

'One and the same, my dear.' His smile widened as he straightened out his pearlescent robes. 'A pleasure to finally meet you. Face to face, that is.'

Rose's grip on her blade loosened. Had Fen always been a lie? Every touch, every whisper, every plea measured and calculated against the depths of her longing. Spun to draw her in, like unsuspecting prey to the spider's web.

'Where's Fen?' Her voice was barely more than a whisper – hollow and hoarse.

'Exactly where you left him.' Ionas pulled her in closer, the edge of her knife cutting into his ashen throat as he caught Rose's chin in a chilling grasp. 'Cold and dead.'

A wave of nausea rolled over her with startling acridity. How well he'd woven the illusion that even she had fallen for it. Letting him whittle her desperation into a blade that she'd plunged into her own foolish heart. And, all the while, Fen had remained bound to the death that she'd doomed him to.

'It was you the whole time.' She pressed the blade deeper, but no blood spilled from Ionas's wound, as if he were little more than a corpse playing at life. 'Masquerading as Fen. *Using* him.'

'Only as you did.' He plucked her knife away with ease, disappearing into shadow. 'But I apologize for the misdirection – I simply had to see if our goals aligned and you needed a face you could trust.'

Rose's eyes scanned the darkness as his voice bounced off every corner. He was a fool if he thought she would ever help him. If he thought that forging Fen into this grotesque mockery of his life would do anything beyond incur her ire.

'How are you here?'

'I've always been here, Rosera.' A chuckle rumbled through the shadows. 'Watching, wishing, waiting for my chance to slip through. And your foolish chancellor finally provided it.'

Rose's stomach sank. 'The dampening collar.'

'He thought it would temper your power, but it was little more than a dam holding back the raging tide of your casting. And it was all too easy for me to tap into.'

Of course. Rose bit down hard on the inside of her lip. Woodstone's meddling had never benefited anyone but him. And now it might be the death of her.

'Why? What do you want?'

He reappeared at her shoulder, a shiver creeping down Rose's spine as he stroked her cheek. 'Isn't it obvious? For decades, I've been trapped in this prison – left to rot with no one for company. Until you.'

Rose stilled as a shimmering mirror took form before her. Yet the reflection within was one she hardly recognized. Bright and clear – a shred of life mired in dark shadow. But she didn't feel so bright now, the cold grip of this wretched darkness leaching her power away.

'And you are exquisite.' Ionas's white eyes found her as he peered around the edges of the glass. 'You bring life, Rose, even in a place that only holds death. Do you know how rare that is – how extraordinary you are?'

Rose's lips curled in a sneer as he stroked the pane, her reflection beaming under the touch of his bony finger. Ionas stared at that empty version of her so longingly, as if she had hung the very stars upon the sky. As if she alone could tether him to life.

'Fen did.' Ionas's breath fell coldly across her cheek, and she flinched away from him. 'He loved every piece of you. He knew you down to your bones. Every thought and feeling. Every fear and failure. Every scent. Every sound. Every taste.'

The last word fell from his tongue in a soft hiss, sending a shudder down Rose's spine. He spoke as if he too knew the depths of her soul. As if he'd spent every moment he was buried within her mind simply watching. Studying.

'To him, you put the stars to shame, and he never even got to see you shine.' Ionas cupped her chin again, pulling Rose's gaze back to him. 'But I could give him back to you.'

And there, the milky white of his eyes softened to Fen's brown once more. But they didn't warm Rose now – they offered no comfort from behind the tenuous veneer. Her heart sank. Whatever fate Ionas had wrought upon her was nothing compared to what she'd done to Fen.

Trapping him between the foolish heights of her pride and the depths of Ionas's twisted desires, it was all she could hope for now that his soul still lay untouched in the peace of death. Clenching her jaw, Rose wrenched herself away from Ionas and slammed her fist into the mirror.

It shattered in an echoing cacophony, glass slicing through the flesh at her knuckles as it splintered into shadow. But Rose didn't slow at all, her heart hammering dully in her chest as she reached for one of the shards, slashing desperately through the air as Ionas vanished again.

'He's not yours to give.'

'But he was yours to lose.'

Ionas's whisper pierced her more surely than any glass as he stepped out of the shadow, still wearing Fen's face. Rose faltered, eyeing the mask with sickening judgement. How had she ever fallen for this dull imitation? It was a pale flicker of moonlight against the blazing sunshine she'd always known and loved. But, in truth, Fen's flame had been more of a candle. A steady glow, able to light up another's path, even when they couldn't.

Yet there was nothing to guide Rose now. Without him,

she was the raging blaze of an inferno, scorching through all in her path. As if the moment Fen had died, every soft piece of Rose's heart had been wrenched away from her, leaving only sharp edges and bitter fury.

And, oh, how they burned.

She stepped closer, blood pooling between her fingers as she gripped the jagged shard of glass. 'You're not Fen.'

'I am everything you ever wanted from him,' Ionas whispered. 'Everything you could still have.'

But Rose only shook her head. 'You're not *him*. And the only thing I want from you is death.'

Sucking in a sharp breath, she closed what little distance remained between them and sank the shard deep into his heart. Ionas staggered back, shock flickering across his gaze as his eyes sharpened back to milky white. He clutched his chest but didn't wrench the glass from between his ribs.

Instead, a slow smile spread across his lips as he reached out to stroke Rose's cheek one last time. 'Thank you.'

Rose reeled back, but the prison wavered before her eyes, vanishing in the din of shattered glass and screaming shadow. And then there was only light, bright and blinding against her eyelids as she blinked awake. A familiar figure loomed over her, hazy but still a balm to her racing heart.

Soren's muttering ceased as they both froze for a moment, his eyes searching hers as if he sought the very depths of her soul. But something dark and dangerous flashed through his gaze – there and gone. Rose frowned, almost reaching for him when Sylvie appeared at Soren's shoulder, shattering whatever spell lay between them.

'Oh, thank the gods.' She pushed past Soren, gathering Rose in her arms. 'I thought we lost you too.'

Too? Rose glanced back at Soren, who stared at her oddly, as if he couldn't quite believe she was there. Stomach sinking,

Rose's gaze caught upon Callum, whose eyes dropped to the ground.

'What happened?' She pulled back from Sylvie's embrace. 'What's wrong?'

'It's the others.' Sylvie gestured to Peiren and Oliv laying listless on their cots. 'They're dead.'

36. On Your Knees

The infirmary descended into a flurry of commotion, pulling at the trembling beat of Rose's heart. Mistralus and some healers scurried about, futilely trying to revive Oliv and Peiren while the Mamsella cradled a weeping Azalaïs in her arms. The Faceless stood pressed against the side wall, muttering among themselves and watching the chaos through their masked gazes. And, in the middle of it all, was Woodstone, who looked as if he were about to be sick.

For once, Rose felt much the same, as her gaze caught on the lifeless pair. So pale and listless as healing tonics trailed sticky lines past their still lips. But none of it was any use. Even her magic would fail them now, just as it had Fen. And it was all her fault. Her stomach heaved at the thought, her legs unsteady as she slipped off the cot. It was more than she could bear.

No one batted an eye as she darted out into the corridor, and she whispered silent thanks that they were so focused on the others. She just needed a moment to herself. To *breathe*.

But she was not granted even that.

Before she could blink, a hand reached out from the shadows, wrapping around her throat. Rose tried to scream, but a cloth was shoved over her mouth – coarse linen that smelled of sinfully sweet caramel and something altogether sharper. Her vision blurred, her lungs burning as her eyelids drooped and darkness welcomed her into its cold embrace.

When Rose woke, it wasn't to the sterile scents of the infirmary. Dark stone stared down at her as she lifted her head off a rickety table, her wrists were bound in glimmering cuffs. And there, staring at her from across the table, was the Aratis.

Bastard. Her mouth went dry. They must have been lying in wait, taking advantage of the commotion to strike.

'Welcome back, Messere Thenlif.' Their voice was as low and cold as ever. 'You'll have to excuse our rough approach, but I'm sure you can understand our caution. Necromancers are not to be trifled with, after all.'

Rose froze, her blood running cold. How could they possibly know that? Swallowing hard, her eyes darted to the door behind her. And it was only then that she saw the second figure lurking in shadow, silver-streaked hair and pale eyes gleaming in the dim light. *Imrys.*

Her eyes narrowed at the man as he peeled himself away from the wall. *Of course.* Ewan had warned her that the pair of them would try something at this trial. And clearly, they thought they had the winning hand if they were willing to lay it down now, abandoning all pretence of legality.

Rose turned back to the Aratis slowly, fighting to keep her voice even. 'I don't know what you're talking about.'

'I'm sure you do.' They clucked their tongue, as if scolding a small child. 'Messere Osiander had his life drained away from him, and you are the only one unaccounted for in the last trial.'

Rose frowned. 'I have an alibi.'

'Hardly credible.' Imrys sniffed. 'Your cohorts are all too eager to cover for you.'

'Just as you're so eager for my guilt?' The words fled from Rose's tongue like a sharpened blade before she could think better of them.

Imrys's eyes darkened as he rounded her shoulder, towering over her as if he could bend her will with his presence alone. 'You can dance around the truth all you like, but we will get it out of you.'

Rose recoiled from him instinctively. For it was no threat that lingered in his voice now but a promise. Cut away from any constraints that may have once bound him, there was no telling what lengths he might go to.

'Hmm, yes. The tonic we used to bring you here was no simple thing.' The Aratis's rasping voice pulled Rose's eyes back across the table. 'Brewed especially by one of the top alchemists in the capital, you'll find you'll have a hard time refusing our request for answers now.'

Rose's heart fluttered in her chest. Was that what Imrys had sent them to retrieve? Some insidious tonic meant to rend the truth from her tongue?

'What do you mean?'

'Compulsion in a bottle, Messere.' They waved a hand blithely. 'So, if you please, the truth, for once.'

In an instant, Rose's spine went rigid, her tongue heavy against her lips. A thousand different truths fluttered at the back of her mind, begging to be set free. It was enough to make her head spin. Yet there was no tether to this compulsion, no scent she could trace to break the cast. And Ionas still sat silent at the back of her mind.

'Did you attack Arden in the woods that day?' The Aratis's question barely found her over the pulsing thrum in her ears.

'I-I don't remember.'

Imrys grabbed her hair and wrenched her head back, eliciting a soft cry from Rose. 'Give us the truth.'

The Aratis made no move to curtail Imrys's brutality, and Rose's stomach sank, pain searing across her scalp. She'd seen the marks he'd left on Ewan when his patience ran thin away from prying eyes. She had no doubt he would meet her with the same mercy if she refused him. But she couldn't even think to try, her thoughts bound by the dulling grip of their wretched tonic.

Words burgeoned behind her lips, burning her throat, cutting and raw, until the metallic taste of blood pooled on to her tongue. She blinked back tears, her jaw clenched so tight it felt as though it would snap. Choking on her own lies, she had no power now to keep her lips from parting.

'That *is* the truth,' Rose bit out through gritted teeth. 'Someone possessed me – used my body to attack him.'

But Imrys didn't loosen his grip on her. 'And did this person kill your mother too?'

Rose willed her tongue to still. To fall silent against another word. But she couldn't, blood spilling from the corners of her mouth as she finally spoke. 'Yes.'

A slow, satisfied smirk spread across Imrys's lips before he released her roughly. 'Write it down.'

The Aratis slid a pen and paper towards her. 'Every last detail.'

Rose tried to keep her hand from grabbing the pen, from putting it to the paper. But her body refused to obey her, and every moment of resistance only cut deeper. She hissed as angry, jagged slits carved from her lips down her chin, blood pooling freely down her throat.

A scream coiled in her chest, but she refused to let it free – to give them the satisfaction. Her hand trembled above the parchment, blood mingling with ink as it dripped from her throat, as if to doom her with the stains of her own lies.

A loud bang at the door made Rose jump. She whirled around just as a blast of ice curled around the hinges, shattering the door beneath its grasp to reveal two familiar forms. Her fingers tightened around the pen as Sylvie and Callum strode into the room with such surety that it made her heart leap.

It was as if their presence brought even time to its knees, and it slowed to a crawl as Callum's eyes slid to Rose. What little light had flickered within snuffed out in a heartbeat; they were so dark now that it sent a shiver down her spine. He'd looked at her much the same way before shattering her collar in the trial, every ounce of kindness drawn away.

Yet Rose didn't recoil as he stepped forward. She didn't fear the anger etched into the furrow of his brow or the way the muscles of his jaw twitched with ill-concealed fury. She didn't fear *him*. Couldn't – even as he towered above her, the heat of his ire emanating off him in trembling waves as his gaze turned back to Imrys and the Aratis.

Whatever spell had held between them shattered in an instant. The dampening chains around her wrists snapped, the compulsion that bound her tongue fading to a dull ache at the back of her mind.

Sylvie rushed to Rose's side as the metal fell away. Warm hands curled around her face, the soft scents of plum and lilac filling her nose as Sylvie muttered a healing spell under her breath. But Callum's gaze didn't budge from Imrys and the Aratis, who shared a brief glance before the latter got to his feet.

'Messeres Avenhart, Belliaris, you cannot—'

'Sit down.' Callum's eyes locked on the Aratis. 'Do not move unless I say so. Better yet, don't even breathe.'

Rose winced as the Aratis slammed back into their seat, as rigid as the mask they wore. Familiar hints of chestnut and chicory stole over her, but they didn't hold the warmth she'd grown so used to. This was cloying and fierce – choking the air around them in a cruel grip.

'What is this?' Imrys demanded, drawing himself up to his full imperious height as he glared down at Callum. 'You cannot just—'

Callum took a slow step towards him, unfazed by his disdain. 'I think you'll find I can.'

'I beg your pardon?'

'If you insist.' A cold smile crept across Callum's lips. 'On your knees.'

Imrys's skin paled, his carefully schooled features flashing with something that resembled fear, if he were capable of such a thing. Then, stiffly, he bent, his knees sinking into the stones beneath their feet. It was as if an invisible grip had taken hold of him – some macabre puppeteer pulling at his crooked strings. But his eyes lost none of their edge as he glared up at them.

'Callum.' Sylvie's voice was low in Rose's ear – a gentle warning.

'Don't worry, darling.' His eyes didn't leave Imrys. 'I won't leave a mark.'

Rose's pulse leapt for the sharpness of his tone, even as her vision blurred. Some reasonable part of her mind warned her to stop him, but she brushed it away. There was something too delicious about watching him imposing his will upon theirs, as they so callously had done to her. About seeing their prideful egos bent to utter submission.

Callum stalked around Imrys, his gaze as sharp as steel, like a cat toying with its prey. Beside her, a choked noise echoed from the Aratis's blank mask, their body trembling.

'Callum,' Sylvie warned again, more firmly this time.

Callum's eyes slid to the Aratis, and he waved his hand. 'Very well.'

With a start, the Aratis collapsed against the table, gasping for air. Rose leaned away from them, but the effort made her stomach turn. Her head felt light, spinning as if it might free itself from her shoulders. Still, she blinked, desperate to keep her focus.

Imrys sneered up at the three of them, his eyes roiling with ill-kept fury. 'There will be consequences for—'

'Be silent.' Callum's voice was so low Rose could hardly hear it over the pounding in her ears, but it would brook no argument.

Imrys's jaw snapped shut, his lips pinched thin and his eyes widening as if he'd swallowed something sour. His own pride, perhaps. For a moment, Callum seemed frozen, looming over Imrys as if he held his fate on his next breath. Yet there was no sly mirth in his eyes now. Only ire, and a wrath that would consume any in his path.

But it was only when his eyes finally flicked back to Rose, meeting hers through the haze of pain and fatigue, that she noticed the tears lingering within. The raw, aching terror that echoed her own. And it nearly tore her heart in two.

'Leave, now. Both of you.' His voice cut through the stillness like a knife – a threat as much as it was an order.

Rose sagged against Sylvie as Imrys stood, her vision blurring at the edges. But his eyes didn't meet hers; they were fixed blankly on some point in the distance as he fell in step with the Aratis. They retreated like moonweed caught in daylight with not a thought left of their own to guide them.

But it was as if their departure took the very air from the room. The breath from Rose's lungs, the fire from her veins. Every scrap of will she'd had to resist them fled as they did. The dull ache of pain flared at the back of her mind, numbing her to any sight or sound. She had not the strength left even to stand, her knees hitting the stone floor with a dull thud as darkness once again enveloped her.

37. Stay

When Rose awoke again, it was dark beyond her window. She blinked groggily at her dorm, bathed in the soft glow of candlelight. And there, perched upon the mattress beside her, was Callum, his brow furrowed with such aching concern. She reached for him gently, trying to sit up.

'Easy, dal.' He pressed a hand to her shoulder to ease her back on to her pillows. 'That was quite the beating you took.'

Rose reached for her throat, but the painful ache of Imrys's compulsion had vanished, leaving behind only a faint soreness. She looked at the healing tonics that littered her bedside table and then back up to Callum.

'You healed me?'

'Don't sound so shocked.' He shrugged, avoiding her gaze. 'Sylvie and I didn't exactly trust leaving you at the infirmary.'

Rose cleared her throat, eyes darting around the empty room. 'Where *is* Sylvie?'

'She said she needed to take care of something.' He glanced up. 'That she'd be back in the morning.'

Rose's stomach lurched. 'She just left?'

'Well, she patched you up and then threatened bodily harm against me if I didn't keep an eye on you, so I wouldn't say she just up and abandoned you, but yes.'

In spite of everything, Rose almost smiled. That sounded about right for Sylvie. Still, what could possibly be so pressing that she couldn't at least wait for her to wake before leaving? It stung, if she were honest, the absence of her steady warmth. For there was a part of her that craved nothing more in that moment.

'Did she say what for?'

'Just that it couldn't wait.' Callum ran a hand through his curls, his eyes skirting past hers. 'And that we shouldn't worry.'

We. Rose's pulse fluttered. It was strange how the word curled around her ears, burrowing deep beneath her flesh and settling so easily in her heart. That Sylvie thought of them in the same breath. That Callum cared for them both. And that Rose craved them each in turn. For it was a truth she could no longer deny, even if it brought them nothing but pain.

Finally, she nodded, gently clearing her throat. 'Right. Well, thank you. For watching over me, I mean. And – er – everything with Imrys.'

Callum's face fell, his eyes flashing with such pain that it made Rose's heart flip. But it was gone in an instant. That gilded veneer covered his easy smile – the mask firmly back in place.

'*Now* we're even, dal.'

Rose recoiled with a scoff. 'Is that all it was? Evening some score?'

Callum paused, his brow softening before he leaned in, cupping a hand around her cheek. 'No.'

The word fell from his lips so softly that it stilled Rose. A shred of honesty that set her heart fluttering against her ribs like a caged bird as she leaned against his hand. 'Callum . . .'

He was so close now, his lips only a hair's breadth from hers. Rose glanced from his eyes to his mouth and back up again – a silent plea for him to close that distance and douse this unbearable heat that had bloomed between them. Yet he pulled away.

'You should rest.' An empty smile pulled at his lips. 'You've had a long day.'

And then he was gone, lifting himself easily off the bed and gliding to the door. Yet the thought of his absence pulled at some tangled knot buried deep within Rose's heart. A frayed thread desperate to be tugged loose, even if it unravelled her entirely. For she was tired, so very tired, of seeing him put that wretched mask back into place every time they approached the cusp of something real.

Rose was on her feet before she could even think about it, catching Callum's hand just as he reached the door. He stilled, his spine going rigid, as if her touch had rooted him to the floor.

'Wait.' The word tumbled out of her in a breathless gasp. 'Stay.'

'No.' His voice was softer than a whisper. 'I should go. Before we both do something we regret.'

Rose squeezed his hand, refusing to let him go so easily. 'I would never regret you.'

'Yes, you would.' He rounded on her so quickly that she stumbled back. 'The moment I was out of your sight and your thoughts were your own again.'

'Is that what this is about? You think you might somehow compel me? You know I can break through that.'

'Could you?' His voice cracked, his eyes glassy as they finally met hers. 'When you're angry, sure. But with my lips on yours? With my hands tangled in your hair and you screaming my name in pleasure – how could I ever trust a word you said was your own?'

Rose's pulse leapt, hungry desire pooling through her at the mere thought of it. Her breath coiled in her lungs as she took a step closer and Callum's throat bobbed, his eyes darkening with heady want. And yet he dropped her gaze, flinching when Rose reached out to cup his chin. Why did he deny himself this when he so clearly wanted it? But her memory flickered at the thought.

'Is that what you wanted?' she whispered. 'In the trial – what you said you could never have?'

'What I *can* never have.' His eyes flashed up to hers, desire now chased away by anguish. 'I would never put you through that. Either of you.'

Rose swallowed hard as she took another step closer. But she didn't break beneath the weight of his gaze, and she wouldn't look away. Not this time.

'Send me away.'

'What?'

'Compel me. Make me leave.'

At this, Callum recoiled. 'No, Rose, I just said—'

'I know. But I trust you,' she cut across him, stroking her thumb soothingly against his skin. 'So, please, trust me.'

Callum's eyes flicked back to the door before his shoulders sagged. As if the weight of what he was about to do had sapped all his strength away. Finally, he turned back to Rose with tears in his eyes.

'Leave. Now.'

Rose caught the telltale chestnut and chicory of his casting, but it only felt warm to her – loving. A tenderness so unlike him, for he was all sharp edges and jagged lines. But she knew now that he could be soft. That, for her, he would be.

She shook her head. 'No.'

'Go, please.' His voice broke. 'Before it's too late.'

'No.' Her fingers tightened around his. 'I'll stay – with you.'

He didn't drop her gaze this time, staring at her as if she were something precious and altogether unreal while tears spilled down his cheeks. Rose brushed them away gently, and he leaned into her touch.

'Rose...'

'May I kiss you?'

Numbly, Callum nodded. Ever so slightly but enough. Rose stood on her toes, leaning in slowly – giving him time to escape if he still needed. But he didn't, his breath hitching on the smallest gasp as she closed that final distance and pressed her lips to his.

It was the gentlest of kisses, yet Callum still melted beneath her, his hands curling around Rose's waist as he pulled her closer. But then he stilled, breaking away from her with a small frown.

'Wait. What about Sylvie?'

In spite of herself, Rose smiled. There would be no living with Sylvie when she found out about this. Not because she'd be angry, or even envious. *No.* She would be utterly insufferable, tossing out smug innuendoes and sly smirks in equal measure. And she would be all too eager to join them in the future, Rose was sure.

'Sylvie will enjoy gloating over the fact that she was right.'

'Oh?' Callum quirked an eyebrow. 'About what?'

A fierce heat crept across Rose's cheeks. 'That I had feelings for you.'

'Do you? Huh.'

'Shut up.'

She caught him in a bruising kiss, silencing him with a soft flick of her tongue. Callum moaned into her mouth as she led him back towards the bed. His grip around her tightened as his tongue delved between her lips, deepening the kiss. And it stirred something within Rose – a need she'd buried for too long. A heady jolt of desire that pooled low in her core.

Her fingers reached fervently for the collar of his robes, clumsily undoing the buttons and shoving the fabric away. Callum stilled as his onyx blouse caught on his shoulder, his breath catching in a small gasp when she finally pulled it free. Rose faltered, pulling back.

His eyes didn't meet hers, cast to the floor as her gaze sank to his chest. Scars littered his torso, pale against his cool brown skin – as if someone had used his flesh as the canvas for some horrid map. She'd seen a hint of them the other night, but this? Her heart ached as she reached for him, hesitantly skimming her fingers over the uneven flesh.

Callum flinched, still avoiding her gaze. As if he were waiting for Rose to pull away. To flee from him or curse him – call him a monster. But she didn't. And she never would. Instead, she lowered her head, brushing soft kisses against his marred skin. His shoulders eased as he leaned into her touch, his quiet exhale caressing her cheek. And it was that small tremor of insecurity that made Rose want to indulge him in such sweet mercy that his fear would buckle beneath it.

Though he spoke with the surety of one who'd lain with others before, Rose wondered if, in the malice that had mapped out his life, he had ever known such simple ecstasy as the warmth that blossomed between them now. The kindness of a loving touch – the compassion that could lie buried in a kiss. Likely not, she decided, her lips ghosting over his collarbone.

But she would show him. She would lead him gently to that precipice of pleasure and send him crashing over the edge until he was spent and weary. She would hold him close afterwards and smooth the worry away from his sweat-slicked brow. And she would never let a cruel hand touch him again.

Rose reached for the waistline of Callum's trousers, hooking her fingers around the ties when he caught her hand. She glanced up to find his eyes boring into her, something dark and daring dancing across them. Words brushed her lips but, before she could utter them, he grabbed her shoulder and flipped her around.

Rose let out a small gasp as he pulled her flush against him, the stiff length of him pressing into her back. *Oh.* She bit her lip as Callum's fingers inched up her thighs, pushing the hem of her nightdress up over her hips.

But as his touch traced over the lace edges of her underwear, he muttered softly. '*Abis imi.*'

Rose shivered as they vanished entirely, leaving her bare before him. She scowled. For someone who'd once claimed charms weren't his specialty, he seemed proficient enough with them now. But the thought fled from her mind as Callum slipped his deft fingers between her thighs, groaning softly in her ear when he found her slick and wanting.

His other hand rested at her throat, cradling her against his shoulder as he pressed featherlight kisses to the shell of her ear and down her neck. All the while, his thumb circled her gently, drawing her wetness up between his fingers as Rose's breathing grew more and more desperate.

Even such a gentle touch unravelled her quickly, guiding her ever closer to her peak. She nearly keened as he sank one long finger into her, then another. Slowly working her open – finding that perfect spot within her. But then a soft spark spread from his fingers, pulsing against her walls with a jolt that sent her hurtling over the edge. Rose came with a sharp cry, her breath stolen from her lungs as the molten climax coursed through her.

She whimpered and trembled against Callum's chest as his pace didn't slow at all. Circling her still until she was at the brink of overstimulation and had to pull his hand away. Warm scents of chestnut and chicory lingered in the air from his casting, lulling Rose as she came down from her peak. She sagged against him a moment, catching her breath before she turned.

Callum's eyes widened as she spun him around, reaching for his trousers. He stumbled back with a breathy laugh, catching himself on one of her bedposts, but didn't stop Rose as she went about undressing him. She cursed as her fingers fumbled over the buckle of his belt and the ties of his trousers.

Until, finally, he was bare before her, a glorious mix of harsh lines and softened eyes as he reached for her. Callum bit back a strangled groan as she caught herself against his chest with one hand, the other sinking low between them. He was already hard, his cock stiff against the dark hairs that trailed down his abdomen. Rose stroked him lightly, catching the beads of moisture that pearled at his head and rubbing them down his shaft.

She eased him back on to the bed with a small smile. They were almost eye level when he was seated, his nose brushing her chin before she bent to kiss it. But then she sank altogether lower, kneeling before him, and nudging his legs apart.

Callum gasped as Rose pressed a tentative kiss to the tip of his cock, his throat bobbing as he leaned back on his hands. His eyes fluttered shut at her delicate touch, barely more than a whisper as she teased him. Just long enough to make him squirm before she took him fully into her mouth.

He curled in on himself with a shattered groan, panting as Rose pulled her lips across his length with a few testing strokes. The taste of him made her shiver – a salty, heady mix of lust and pleasure and *him*. Callum's fingers coiled through her hair, almost absently pulling it away from her face. And it was that simple act of sentiment that made Rose abandon any teasing ploy she'd planned as she hollowed out her cheeks and began to suck in earnest.

His hips jerked and stuttered, and she pressed a hand to his waist to keep him from thrusting into her mouth. Lips quirking, her eyes flicked up to meet his, still keeping pace.

'*Vala nan*,' he panted out a breathy moan. 'Rose, I—'

The words died on his lips as she quickened her strokes. This time, she didn't stop his hips as they bucked against her. Until, after a few moments, he caught her hair, stilling her.

'As sensational as you are, dal, if you keep going like that, I'm afraid I won't last long.'

Rose smirked at this, releasing him with a soft *pop*. Getting to her feet, she pressed herself instead against the flush warmth of his lean chest, peppering kisses along his brow. Callum pulled the neckline of her nightdress down, laving his tongue against her breasts in turn. A low moan rippled from Rose's lungs, her fingers twisting through his silver curls.

But she pulled away, her pulse racing as she pushed Callum on to his back. He landed on the mattress with a quiet 'oof', his hands flying up to catch her hips as she straddled him. He quickly pulled himself forward to meet her, cradling her against his chest and pushing her nightdress off in one smooth motion.

Yet the heat within Rose's core had grown unbearable: a desperate longing to have him within her – inching her ever closer to the pleasure they could share.

Callum stilled as she reached once more between them, his eyes flicking up in the dim glow to catch hers. He searched her gaze so earnestly it cracked something deep within her heart. Even now, he sought her permission – proof that her mind was still her own. That this pulsing, furious heat between them would not fade come dawn. Slowly, Rose nodded, pressing a kiss into the shell of his ear as she sank slowly on to him.

'*Gods*, Rose.'

The stretch of him was delicious, filling her so thoroughly that she stalled there a moment to adjust before he began to thrust gently. Callum's fingers tightened in her curls, and she moaned against him as he caught just the right angle within her.

Until, in one smooth motion, he flipped her on to her back, bracing his arms on either side of her. Instinctively, her legs wrapped tight around his waist, pulling him in deeper as he stroked her temple. And it was there, in the heat between their bodies – the warmth burgeoning in their hearts – that he gently met her, magic to magic. Source to source. Life to life.

Every nerve in her body lit up beneath his touch, as if they'd been expanded. The slap of his flesh against hers filled the room in a filthy cacophony, sweat slick against Rose's brow as she neared her peak. And Callum was right there with her, his thrusts growing faster and feverish as they both danced along that precipice. Gods, he was beautiful like this – silver hair glowing in the soft candlelight and eyes squeezed shut in the throes of pleasure.

He was so close now. Teetering along the abyss of his climax yet holding himself back. *For her*, Rose realized with a pang. He was unwilling to lose himself in it if she did not fall alongside him. Hungrily, she sank her fingers between them, providing that last bit of pressure she needed to send her careening over the edge.

She came with a muffled moan against Callum's shoulder, drowning beneath wave after wave of pleasure. And it didn't take Callum long to follow her. His warmth pooled deep within her as he drove himself home again, again and again.

Finally, he stilled, collapsing against Rose with a deep sigh. For a while, they simply lay there, neither willing to move. Until, slowly, Callum pushed himself up and out of her, settling down beside Rose, his head pillowed by her breast. She stroked a hand idly through his curls, counting his ragged breaths. It took several long moments before her own heartbeat settled, the sweat at her brow cooled and her pulse lulling on the edge of slumber. But she shivered as Callum stirred, pulling away from her.

'No.' Rose reached for his arm. 'Stay.'

Callum stiffened, his breath hitching in his throat. But then his shoulders relaxed, his arms holding Rose in their steady warmth as they wrapped around her once more. She smiled as his lips found the shell of her ear, a contented sigh rumbling through his chest.

'As long as you like, dal.'

38. With Love

The pale light of dawn crept timidly through Rose's window, illuminating her room in a soft grey hue. She stirred lightly, her body sore but sated as she pulled her bedsheets tighter over her bare chest. But she stilled as a warm arm tightened gently around her middle.

For a moment, Rose's mind went utterly blank. Until memories came flickering back in hazy pieces. Her wounds wrought by Imrys's hands, the kindness in Callum's eyes as he cared for her. The heat of his touch as he'd poured his passion out upon her.

Rose's stomach flipped as echoes of her pleasure rippled over her skin with a shiver. Slowly, she rolled over to face him. He didn't wake at the movement, his silver curls lying a bit flatter against his forehead as Rose gently brushed them aside. Brow smooth and eyelids fluttering over some dream, he looked so at peace in his slumber that Rose was loath to wake him.

Slipping gently away from the bed, she left him to his peace and darted into her washroom to relieve herself and swallow a tonic to ensure there were no lingering consequences from last night. Rose shivered as it slid down her throat with a gentle warmth. She hadn't had to use these in years – not since Fen. Her heart flipped, but she shoved the thought away. She didn't want to think about that now.

Splashing some cool water over her face and combing through her mess of curls, she quietly tiptoed back to the bed. Callum stirred as she settled in beside him, his eyes fluttering open slowly. They blinked blearily around the room before landing on Rose, softening so thoroughly that it made her want to weep.

'Good morning, dal,' he mumbled, stretching out.

Rose smiled, stroking his cheek gently. 'You stayed.'

Calum stilled in an instant, his eyes flashing up to hers. 'Last night, you said – should I not have?'

Her chest squeezed for the tremor of uncertainty that lingered in his voice. As if he feared the light of day carried with it the bitter sting of rejection. Rose's stomach sank. Because he did – he'd told her as much last night.

Frowning, she snuggled closer to him, desperate to smooth away his worry as she rested her head against his chest. 'I'm glad you did.'

'So am I.' His shoulders loosened, his fingers running gently through Rose's curls.

They stayed like that for a long while, basking in the glow of each other's presence. Languidly counting each other's heartbeats and dancing upon the edges of slumber once more. But Rose's mind pricked with the familiar sting of unease as she traced her fingers idly over Callum's scars.

She hadn't wanted to ask about them last night – hadn't wanted to burden him with the weight of painful memories. But now questions swirled through her mind, brushing her lips.

She had a guess where they'd come from. She'd seen glimpses of it in his memories, after all. *His mother*, she thought darkly. But how could she impose such cruelty on her own child? Finally, Rose sighed, resting her chin on Callum's chest so she could meet his gaze.

'Your scars,' she murmured. 'May I ask about them?'

Callum stiffened, his eyes straying away from hers. 'Could I stop you?'

Rose sat up. 'Tell me to drop it and I will.'

Callum eased himself on to the pillows beside her, but still didn't meet her gaze. 'It's not a pretty story.'

'Maybe not.' She shrugged. 'But it's yours. You've seen the worst parts of me and never once turned away – how could I do any less?'

Callum watched her unsurely before he gave an almost resigned nod. Leaning forward, he propped his elbows against his knees and rubbed wearily at his brow. Rose gave him a moment to gather his courage in silence, brushing soothing kisses along his bare shoulder.

'I come from a long line of compulsionists,' he said finally. 'My parents were both in the personal retinue of the empress's brother, and didn't particularly like each other, or the idea of children, but their gifts were considered too great not to pass on.'

Rose frowned. It seemed such an empty reason to bring a child into the world. Such a lonely way for them to grow, without love or kindness. Her stomach lurched. Had she not been raised the same way? Ever the disappointment to her mother's grand expectations.

'I'm sorry.'

'Don't worry, dal – it gets far worse than that.' A dry scoff rumbled through Callum's chest. 'Turns out, having kids isn't so bad when you can just compel them to behave. For years, they kept me pliant and malleable to their will – the perfect heir to their insidious inheritance. I don't recall most of my childhood behind the haze of their compulsion, only the moment I finally broke free.'

Bile bit at the back of Rose's throat with a searing acridity. For all the cruelty her mother had bound her to through barbed words and bitterness, she'd never stolen her mind. Though did that really matter? While the methods were different, the intent was the same – affection doled out and withheld at whim like an ever tightening leash. An illusion all of its own. Of choice, of desire. Of freedom her mother never once granted her.

'I was seven when I first broke free.' Callum's voice jarred her from her thoughts. 'I should have run then, but I didn't understand what they'd been doing. I didn't know how much worse it could get.'

'By the time my parents tracked me down, they'd realized only a compulsion prodigy could've broken free of their spell and wanted to "train" me.' The words spilled from his lips as if they tasted foul. 'They compelled me once more, trying to get me to break free again. Mostly they just used the lure of that freedom I'd tasted to tempt me but, sometimes, they would lock me away with one of them for what felt like hours. They'd order me to harm myself in new and creative ways, trying to force me to break their compulsion, to unlock the true depths of my power.'

Rose's jaw clenched so tight it was almost painful, tears burning against her eyes as she trembled beneath the weight of her rage. *No* – not rage. This was no blind fury that lashed out with reckless abandon; it was the steady fires of wrath, etched deep beneath righteous ire and fuelled by each heavy beat of her heart. But then hot tears splashed against her arm, and her heart faltered, fury fading to grief as she held him tighter.

'Oh, Callum.'

'Please.' He shook his head, drying his eyes. 'Let me finish – then see what pity you have left.'

As if any words that fell from his lips could quell the warmth curling around her heart as she stroked his marred flesh. But it wasn't even pity. It was the soft blush of caring, the heady heat of desire – the tender ache of *love*. And it razed through Rose with such force that it was almost staggering. She pulled him closer, as if she could bury him in the depths of that feeling and hold his pain forever at bay.

'They carried on like that until just after my sixteenth birthday. I don't know what changed that day, but something in me snapped and finally I broke through. But I didn't flee or get myself to safety. No.' His voice broke. 'Instead, I threw their own compulsion back at them. I ordered them to cut themselves for every wound they'd ever wrought upon me. They bled out slowly, begging for mercy I never granted them.

'Even then, I didn't run.' A short laugh reverberated through his chest, but the sound was bitter – hollow. 'The royal guard found me hours later, sitting in the pool of their blood. After that is a bit of a blur, but I remember it never got to trial. Swept under the rug by the empress's brother and my grandfather, neither of whom wanted the taint of scandal. Instead, I was sent off to a sanatorium deep in the northern mountains and forgotten about.'

Rose frowned, a memory pricking her thoughts. 'Oliv – she said something about that in the bar.'

'"One mad killer drawn to another". Yes, I remember.' Callum nodded. 'After two years there, I was shipped off to Maalstrum on my grandfather's orders. Somewhat of a gamble on his part, but I was still a prodigy. And, having killed the best two compulsionists in the empire, I had somewhat of a debt to pay in his eyes. But I never compelled anyone again. Not intentionally anyway. Couldn't bring myself to – or trust myself if I did.'

'Until yesterday.'

'For you, yes,' he whispered. 'Nothing had ever been worth it before, but seeing you cuffed to that table, covered in blood and your fire snuffed out by someone else's will, it was . . .'

Rose fell silent as Callum trailed off, pulling his knees closer to his chest. How much pain he'd held within him all this time, burning beneath his skin with nowhere to cut save inward. The thought nearly choked her.

All alone in a world that only ever threw more cruelty at him without a shred of kindness. Not even from Rose, as she'd thoughtlessly pierced his heart with undue blame. And now, she wasn't sure she could salve it.

'I'm so sorry.' She nestled into the crook of his neck.

Callum turned to pull her close. 'You have nothing to apologize for, dal.'

But she did. For every lie she'd ever spun him, every accusation she'd ever tossed his way. How eager she'd been to paint him as a villain when he'd been guilty of no more sin than her own. Just another broken soul reaching out to her the only way he knew how. Not innocent, but entirely undeserving of the wrath she'd met him with.

Her heart wrenched as she leaned forward, pressing a gentle kiss to the scar upon his shoulder. Callum flinched at her touch, his eyes fixing on her as if he couldn't quite believe she was there.

'What are you doing?'

Rose didn't answer, instead brushing her kisses along the scarred stretch of his arm, and then across his chest. Callum shuddered beneath her, his fingers twining in her curls, but she didn't stop. Tracing each jagged line beneath her lips, covering them with gentleness she wasn't sure he'd ever known, desperate to fill the pain of them with something softer – kinder. With love.

A choked sob broke from his chest as she straddled his waist, her lips still dancing across his collarbone, and then up to the hollow of his throat. His arms curled around her, pulling her closer, as if she were the only thing that tethered him to this world. And, when she felt hot tears spill across her shoulders, she tilted Callum's head back and kissed those away too.

The salty taste of them lingered on her lips as her own throat tightened. Finally, she pulled back, daring to look up into those broken, beautiful obsidian eyes of his. But they were only filled with hunger now, held on a beat of silence before he captured her mouth in a bruising kiss. Rose's heart leapt, heat pooling low in her stomach as she broke away.

'What you did to them was no less than what they deserved, and no worse than anything I've done for even less reason.'

Callum frowned, brushing a stray curl away from her brow. 'From what I gather, your mother wasn't exactly innocent.'

'Maybe, but my mother isn't the only person I've killed.' Rose ducked her head, sitting back against Callum's thighs. 'That string of murders I mentioned – it was the local barman acting on a thirty-year-old grudge. Sylvie was one of his victims, as was my best friend, Fen. I was able to save her, but Fen didn't make it. Hollis, the barkeep, he stabbed him through the heart right in front of me, and my magic ate him alive, but it couldn't save Fen. *I* couldn't.'

'So you cast the Spell of True Revival.' Callum's voice was achingly soft now.

Rose nodded. 'And, in so doing, I set Ionas free. Every death since is on my hands.'

There was so much more to it than that – so many horrid truths she couldn't bear to utter now. Raw wounds that would be all too easy to split open. But Callum didn't seem to need them, pulling Rose close to catch her lips in a gentle kiss.

'Not just yours,' he murmured as they parted.

'Maybe, but I don't think that's the point.' She frowned. 'We're not monsters because others failed to love us or because we snapped under the weight of their cruelty. We were trying to protect what we loved most, even if that was only ourselves.'

The words felt hollow to Rose's ears, but there was a truth to them she could no longer deny. Even if she still sometimes struggled to believe it. But, *oh*, how she wanted to. Needed to, perhaps.

Yet Callum only shook his head. 'I don't know about that, dal. I'm not sure there's all that much worth loving about me.'

'There is,' said Rose before she could think better of it.

Callum didn't freeze or retreat from her admission. Instead, at long last, a slow, genuine smile ghosted across his lips. A fierce heat crept across Rose's cheeks, but before she could say anything else, there was a knock on the door. Her heart lurched as she froze.

'Are you expecting someone?'

'No.'

Unhooking herself from Callum's waist, she leapt from the bed. Her nightdress lay crumpled on the floor, but she hastily tugged it over her head, tossing Callum's blouse at him. She didn't look to see if he caught it before staggering over to the door and throwing it open.

Sylvie's bright eyes greeted her like eager rays of sunshine breaking through a storm, and a warm smile spread across Rose's lips. *She was all right.* The thought chased away worry Rose hadn't realized she'd been holding. Yet it simmered back to the surface as Sylvie's eyes flicked over her shoulder to her bed.

'By the Nine,' Sylvie muttered, pushing past Rose.

'Hello, darling.' Callum shifted awkwardly, still tugging his onyx blouse into place.

Rose's heart stuttered, suddenly racing. Sylvie had wanted this for them, hadn't she? So why did she suddenly feel like a child with their hand caught in the sweets jar? She licked her lips as her mouth went dry. Perhaps they should have talked about it more first, or gone in search of her last night?

'Sylvie, I—'

A sharp laugh cut across whatever paltry excuse Rose had been about to utter, and Sylvie's lips spread in the most obnoxiously smug smirk. 'I told you so.'

At this, Rose shot a glance at Callum, only barely resisting the urge to utter an 'I told you so' herself. His dark brows quirked, and he let out a breathy chuckle.

'Yes, I'm sure you're very pleased with yourself.' Rose scowled, her fear dissipating beneath the stirrings of annoyance. 'But where have you *been*?'

'Oh.' The smile slipped from Sylvie's lips in an instant. 'Right.'

'What's wrong?'

'I just—' Her eyes fell to the bag at her shoulder, and she clutched it tighter for a moment. 'I think I know who Ionas is possessing.'

'Who?'

With a sigh, Sylvie dipped her hand into the folds of her satchel and tossed a dossier on to the bed. 'Soren.'

39. Neither Living Nor Dead

For several moments, all Rose could do was stare at the dossier. Her heart hammered in her ears, rejecting Sylvie's words with every rapid beat. And yet she knew that Sylvie would never lie to her about this.

'What is that?'

Sylvie sank uneasily on to the foot of the bed. 'I found it in Soren's office.'

'You broke into his office?'

'Yesterday, after the trial, Soren was acting oddly.' Her lips pressed thin, as if she hated the idea of parting with this truth. 'When Callum and I couldn't find you, I asked him to help, and he just marched off. At first, I thought he was going to look for you, but—'

'But he never showed up,' Rose finished for her.

She hadn't even thought about it at the time, but she couldn't deny that it was strange. If Sylvie and Callum had feared for her safety, Soren never would've sat idly by. Rose swallowed down the growing dryness in her throat as her memory danced over the events of the trial. The way he'd stared at her – hollow, as if there was nothing behind his eyes at all. Or perhaps just nothing of *him*. And Ionas had been remarkably silent in her head ever since.

'Right.' Sylvie nodded. 'I thought maybe he was looking for you elsewhere, but something just felt . . . off.'

'Is that why you disappeared?'

Sylvie grimaced. 'I didn't want to worry you if I was wrong, so I followed him. He sat in his office until just before midnight and then stormed off towards the village. I followed as far as the cemetery, where I lost track of him and circled back to search his things.'

Rose's heart leapt into her throat. If Ionas had hold of Soren, his brutality could've been so easily turned upon Sylvie. Even when he was buried within Rose's mind, Sylvie's safety had hung by a thread – bound only perhaps by her love.

'By yourself? Sylvie, what if he had caught you?'

'But he didn't.'

'*Vala nan.*' Callum shook his head. 'And I thought Rose lacked all sense of self-preservation.'

'I was careful.' Sylvie rolled her eyes. 'And anyway, I found this, so I'd say it was worth it.'

'But what *is* this, Sylvie?'

Rose plucked the dossier from the bed, skimming through its pages. It was a chaotic mess of scribbled notes – harsh lines and hastily drawn formulas. She frowned, for she recognized Soren's hand within the madness.

'I think –' Sylvie's voice grew small – 'it's the alchemical formula he used to try to revive your aunt, all those years ago.'

Callum choked on a strangled gasp. 'Pardon?'

'I'll explain later.' Sylvie's eyes barely flicked to him before fixing again on Rose. 'Look at the front page.'

Swallowing hard, Rose did as she was told, her eyes landing on the bolded letters of a title. *Reath: Studis ab Salis ed Antasis*, it read. *Studies of Life and Resurrection*. And then, just below, in smaller print: *Authored by Ionas Tirecin, 1828*. Her pulse leapt, breath catching in her throat.

'He knew,' she whispered. 'Soren knew who Ionas was.'

Sylvie nodded. 'Look at his notes in the back. He must've started piecing it together after we visited him last week.'

Rose flipped to the back pages, squinting at the familiar scrawl. If anything, Soren's penmanship had worsened over the years, haphazardly jotted over the parchment. Still, Rose could just make out a few phrases. *Ionas Tirecin, born 1799, chief imperial necromancer* was underlined at the top of the page. Then, further down: *last historical record of Ionas in 1829; Edict of Ardalis passed 1830 – related?* And finally, at the bottom, circled over and over again until it had nearly torn through the page: *potential imperial cover-up; Ionas neither living nor dead??*

Rose stared at the page, tears blurring her vision. For there, beneath the note, was a series of symbols. Ones that flickered in her memory like a bad dream, half forgotten on the edge of dawn. *No.* Her breath hitched. It *couldn't* be.

'Sorry.' Callum's voice made her jump. 'Could one of you please explain what all this means exactly?'

'Well, Rose—'

'Explain on the way,' Rose cut across Sylvie, tucking the dossier under her arm.

'Er – on the way where, dal?'

But Rose didn't answer, hastily tugging on her coat over her nightclothes and fleeing out into the corridor. Furious tears burned against her eyes, but she didn't wipe them away. If Ionas wanted a fight, she'd be all too happy to give it to him.

Rose didn't slow at all as she trekked across campus. Sylvie and Callum followed a few paces behind her, whispering softly between themselves. She wasn't sure if it was kindness or trepidation that kept their voices from reaching her, but she was grateful all the same.

She didn't have it in her now to muddle through explanations – her only thought was for Soren. For finding him and seeing the truth in his eyes. And hoping she wasn't too late.

Finally, she came to a sharp halt before a small hatch tucked at the back of the School of Magical Theory. It was entirely innocuous to those who didn't know what it was. Rose herself never would've found it had Ewan not dragged her down there last year, and she'd grown up on the secret corridors and tunnels of Dunhollow.

Sylvie's gasp echoed behind her. 'Rose, no . . .'

But Rose didn't meet her gaze. Lifting the metal lid, she turned away as aged, musty air billowed out. Her eyes darted to the darkened depths below and she sucked in a steadying breath before descending. The ancient wooden stairs creaked beneath Rose's feet as she eased down them, the dank smell of wet earth and mildew hanging heavy in the air. The temperature dropped significantly the further she went, her breath coming out in small puffs.

Yet, as she reached the bottom, she stilled. Dim flickering lanterns came alive, casting eerie dancing shadows on the decaying walls. It looked almost unchanged from last year. Towering mahogany shelves, clearly once sturdy and grand, now sagged under the weight of aged tomes and lost history. Books and manuscripts, yellowed with age, lined the shelves in scattered disarray. Parchment scrolls lay still unrolled and untouched, protected only by a thick layer of dust. It was as if neither soul nor solid form had stepped through these halls since Rose herself had last set foot in them.

Her stomach churned, Fen's warm smile flickering through her memory. Her fists curled at her sides, the nails biting into her flesh. She wouldn't lose Soren the same way she had Fen. And yet, there was no sign of him now. Of anyone. Only an echo of magic – a faint scent of his signature, melded with something acrid and cloying. *Ionas.*

Rose glanced over the empty room. It was peaceful in a strange way. Secluded and serene. Held in a silence that was so far removed from the raging threads of her own thoughts. But it shattered in the great creak of aged wood.

Her eyes flew back to the stairs, where Sylvie and Callum picked their way down. She'd half expected them to stay above, somehow – Sylvie especially. Yet she held her head high, only her eyes betraying any shred of fear as they darted about the rancid space. Callum, however, only looked mildly perturbed as he ducked through the doorway to join Rose.

'What is this place?' His voice bounced off the stone walls.

'The archives.' Sylvie shuddered. 'Part of Dunhollow's old campus. We shouldn't be here, Rose.'

It was where Ionas had been hiding, by the looks of it. The same sigils and symbols that had been dotted all over Soren's dossier were etched faintly upon the rough stone walls. Last year, she'd thought them left by ancient members of the Order of Salix, but what if they'd been left by *him*?

If Ionas had been an imperial necromancer, then he must have been a student at Dunhollow once too. She chewed the inside of her lip, her gaze lingering on the russet bloodstains now painted overtop the sigils. That certainly hadn't been there last year. Was it Soren's blood? Her stomach lurched. Or her own?

Callum drifted from Sylvie's side, his fingers skimming idly over some papers on the rickety table. 'Looks like we aren't the only ones who've been down here.'

Rose inched forward, ignoring Sylvie's sharp huff behind her. That wasn't Soren's handwriting. Or rather, it was, but almost as if it had been drawn by someone unfamiliar with his hand, the marks thick and jagged upon fading parchment. Little sigils and poorly sketched diagrams of something he'd labelled a soul source. But it was the lone note at the bottom of the page that caught her eye.

Bearath still trapped, it read. *Reath within? Some chance remains for Aelra?*

Rose frowned. Aelra – she didn't recognize the name, but

the others? Reath was listed on the study Soren had had, and Bearath . . . She faltered, her blood running cold. Wasn't that the name on the grimoire she'd used in her spell? Her hands shook, the corners of the notes crinkling as her grip tightened.

'I should have seen it,' she muttered. 'Should have remembered.'

Sylvie stepped closer. 'Remembered what?'

'Gods, it was right there, this whole time.' A bitter laugh slipped past Rose's lips as she tipped her head to the ceiling. '*He* was.'

'Sorry, dal, but I think we'll need just a bit more to go on.'

'The Spell of True Revival.' Rose turned back to them. 'It was Ionas's grimoire I used – *his* spell. That's how he got in.'

Sylvie frowned. 'How do you know?'

'Look at Soren's notes.' Rose reached for Soren's dossier, tearing out a page and holding it up against the worn notes on the table. 'The book Soren used to revive my aunt was called *Reath*: *Studies of Life and Resurrection*; mine was *Bearath*: *Studies of Death and Necromancy*. They were mirrors of each other – life and death. And penned by the same hand.'

'By the Nine.' Sylvie's tawny skin went a shade paler.

But Callum only frowned down at the notes. 'Bearath and Reath – he talks about them as if they're people. And who's Aelra?'

'I don't know,' Rose admitted with a small shake of her head.

Yet her own voice sounded distant and dull beneath the heartbeat raging in her ears. All this time the answers had been right in front of her. Etched into every wretched spell that had ever plagued her. Whether spun by her hand, Hollis's or Soren's, they all led back to that insidious thread between life and death – to Ionas.

And how easily he had pulled her strings to his tune. Rose's stomach churned, something shifting in the shadows surrounding them. She stilled, rooted to the spot as a sickening chuckle whispered at the back of her mind.

Hello, Rose. Ionas's voice was silken and sinfully soft. *Did you miss me?*

40. Run

For a moment, the room hung with a stunned silence. Shadow fell over the three of them like a cloak, plunging the room into utter darkness. Vaguely, Rose could hear Callum's voice calling to her – could feel Sylvie's grasp around her shoulders, trying to shake her from this reverie.

But her memory only flickered over dark woods and masked faces – nameless bodies swarming out into a murky treeline. Her pulse leapt and skittered, lungs tightening around shallow breaths as if she were right back in that cursed forest, fleeing the dangers of the guildhall and all the horrors the Order of Salix had held. As if she were back in that rugged ravine, watching Fen slip away from her so easily.

Then, through shadow, a warm hand closed around hers. 'Rose, come on – we have to get out of here!'

Sylvie's voice crashed over her, unravelling the fear tangling around her thoughts. Her chest loosened, her breath slowing. But the cruel presence that lurked in these shadows was not content to let her go so easily.

Go ahead, Rose. Run, Ionas whispered, his voice like cool chains that bound her in place. *It's what you do best, after all, isn't it?*

The darkness shifted, Sylvie's voice fading once more to the quiet whisper of shadow. Rose's stomach dropped as she blinked, her eyes adjusting to the familiar silhouettes of Ionas's prison. And there, before her, was Soren, his warm brown eyes lost to the milky white of Ionas's gaze as it fixed on her with a keen hunger. She'd known that Ionas wore his form, yet nothing could have prepared her for seeing that face she knew and loved so well staring back at her with such malice.

'It's the simple truth, Rose.' His tone was almost saccharine with its dulcet timbre. 'If you'd acted sooner last year, maybe Fen would still be alive.'

His face flickered, shifting to Fen's soulful eyes and sweet smile. Rose turned away, gritting her teeth. Though she knew him to be nothing more than imitation now, the sight of Fen still pulled at something irreparably broken deep within her, some shred of grief she could not yet let go of.

But then those eyes darkened, russet skin shifting back to umber – ink-black waves stretching to long gold-cuffed twists. 'Even now, with Soren at my mercy, you'd rather flee.' Soren's visage faded as Ionas disappeared into shadow, leaving Rose stumbling over empty air. 'And how easily you've moved on too. Running straight from Fen's arms to Sylvie and Callum's. You just can't stop.'

Memories flashed before her eyes, twisted by whatever spell Ionas bound her in: Rose's hands tentatively ghosting over Fen's bare flesh, her fingers drawing cries of pleasure out of Sylvie as they sought gentle solace in one another, her legs wrapped firmly around Callum. Rose squeezed her eyes shut, trying to push the memories away, to keep them from the taint of Ionas's grasp. But he prised her eyes open, forcing her to witness each one.

'Perhaps it's because you know that the minute you stand still long enough, they'll see the truth of you and run themselves. Sylvie, who so desperately wants to see the strength in you. But what happens when she realizes that for all your newfound power, your courage is still a fickle beast?'

Suddenly, the memories twisted into flames consuming Sylvie. A wave of nausea washed over Rose at her haunting shriek and the agony blistering across her skin until all that remained of her was a charred, broken corpse.

'And Callum? Poor boy.' The scene shifted from Sylvie's charred body to silver hair and pleading eyes. 'He loves you for those dark stains upon your soul. He thinks he's finally found someone who can understand him – someone he's safe with. He would burn the world down to save you, but you'd do it just to feel anything at all. And that would scare even him.'

The image wavered beneath another anguished wail, Callum's scarred skin torn by thousands of cuts as his blood pooled beneath him. Hot tears spilled down her cheeks as he fell beside Sylvie, little more than flesh and bone brought to ruin by Rose's hand.

But the thought no longer rang with such truth within her mind. Rose swallowed hard, eyeing the ever shifting shadows. After all, it had been her strength that had brought Ionas back in the first place. Her power that had let him toy with her mind and make puppets out of those she loved most. And it would be her hand that brought about his end.

Because she would raze this world to the ground and carve his death out of the ashes before she let his cruelty claim anyone else. Clenching her jaw, Rose reached out through the shadows, catching Ionas by the throat as heat seared beneath her skin.

'Enough.'

His milky-white eyes widened just for a moment before his lips curled in a sickening smile. 'There you are.'

But the caustic fury that burned at her now could not be tamed. Silver flames spilled from her hands, yet Ionas watched her almost serenely, his smile never slipping, even as his form wisped away like little more than ash. *An illusion.* Her heart sank. He'd been nothing more than smoke and mirrors.

'Rose!'

A blast of cool ice jolted Rose back to the archives, now caught in the silver blaze. Though ragged crystals of ice dotted the room, fire licked greedily at the rotted wood, swallowing up the room as it devoured all in its path. *No.*

Her magic faltered as the gentle green light of Callum's barrier fell over them. The roar of the fire died down, though a few lone flames still licked at the floor, even as Sylvie's ice doused them with a soft sizzle.

Rose's stomach heaved, the acrid stench of smoke curling beneath her nostrils. How close she'd come to damning them alongside her. 'I'm so sorry, I—'

'It's all right, dal.' Callum coughed, waving away the smoke. 'What happened?'

'I-it was Ionas.' Her voice wavered. 'He was taunting me. Showing me what he would do to Soren. To you.'

'Oh, Rose.'

Sylvie reached for her, but Rose recoiled, staring down at the page in her hands, now little more than charred parchment. A victim of her flames like everything else in this cursed room – any proof of Ionas's crimes now lay scorched at her feet. It would come soon, though, whatever he planned.

But it didn't matter. Whatever Ionas hoped to resurrect in the bowels of this place, she couldn't let it happen. She might have been the tool by which he gained power, but she would also be the instrument of his demise. Of *his* end. Even if it was the last thing she did.

'We're going to get Soren back.' Her voice was barely more than a whisper as she slowly lifted her head. 'And whatever it is that Ionas really wants, I'll make sure all he gets are ashes.'

41. Tread Carefully

Rose stared up at the jagged swirls of the looming obsidian door of Woodstone's office. Her fury had led her this far, a burning heat fuelling her every step as she'd torn across campus. Yet, now that she was here, her hand stilled upon the latch, doubt seeping through the cracks of her anger.

Her eyes flicked to Callum and Sylvie making their way up the last of the spiral steps behind her, flushed and panting. What could she say to Woodstone? What words could she ever utter to sway him without spelling her own doom, especially without proof of Ionas's plans? And yet, to leave them unspoken – to abandon Soren to the mercy of a monster *she'd* unleashed – that would be the far worse fate to suffer, in the end.

Straightening, Rose gritted her teeth and shoved through the door. It hit the wall with a loud bang, but Woodstone barely flinched, his dull eyes lifting to rove over the three of them with ill-concealed disdain. As if their intrusion were a mere annoyance he did not have time for this morning.

Rose faltered as the chancellor's gaze slid pointedly from her to another figure looming over his desk, grey eyes sharp and lips twisted in a sneer. *Imrys.* She pulled up so quickly that Callum nearly crashed into her, cursing under his breath. Though whether that was for her or Imrys, she couldn't say.

'Messere Thenlif, what a surprise,' Woodstone drawled, leaning back in his chair. 'Though, I must say, not a particularly pleasant one.'

Rose's stomach fluttered as she tore her gaze from Imrys,

but she pushed the feeling down. She wasn't here for him. Marching to Woodstone's desk, she slammed her hands on to its surface. 'You need to cancel the tournament.'

Woodstone sighed deeply, looking more bored than anything. 'Imrys, would you excuse us?'

Imrys's sneer slipped as shock ricocheted over his sharp features. 'But, Everard, she—'

'We can speak further on the matter later.' Woodstone's voice was clipped, as if his patience were hanging by a thread.

Imrys seemed to sense this too, as he gave a curt nod. 'Of course, Chancellor.'

Straightening his ascot, he flashed Rose a truly withering glare that made her skin crawl and brushed past them. Callum and Sylvie stepped back to let him pass, though Rose was mildly surprised that the latter didn't stick her foot out to send the man sprawling down the spiral staircase. She pursed her lips. A pity, really.

'Now, then.' Woodstone cleared his throat, extending a hand before them. 'Do have a seat.'

'We're not here for a chat, Chancellor,' Sylvie snapped, her eyes burning as she moved to Rose's side. 'You need to—'

'Cancel the tournament? Yes, I heard,' Woodstone cut across her. 'However, I will need just a smidge more information to go on if it's all the same to you?'

Rose trembled beneath her fury, forcing her breath to steady. It was a fair enough request, she had to admit, but the condescending lilt of his tone did nothing to soothe her temper.

'Soren is missing,' she managed finally.

'Missing?' Woodstone leaned forward with a frown. 'Are you sure?'

Rose faltered, her mind stirring in trepidation. She could hardly give him all the details, not unless she wanted to incriminate herself. But she had to give him *something*.

'I—No one has seen him since last night.'

'I see.' Woodstone propped his elbows upon the desk, tenting his fingers beneath his chin. 'Well, that could all be rather innocuous.'

'Innocuous?' Callum stepped up to the desk. 'Every trial has been sabotaged, you've had four deaths, and now a professor has gone missing. You're deluded if you think that's harmless.'

'Deluded? No.' Woodstone shook his head. 'Determined.'

Rose blinked. Of course he didn't care. Not about Soren, not about them – about any of it. The only thing that drove him now was some strange, rabid need to see this tournament through. To bolster Dunhollow's rotten image with the thin veneer of victory.

'Gods, all you care about is Dunhollow's damned reputation, isn't it?' she snapped. 'Even if it gets us all killed.'

'Rather rich from you, my dear.' Woodstone chuckled. 'After all, it was your necromancy that sank us all into this mess, wasn't it?'

Rose's heart dropped straight into her stomach as she stumbled back. How could he know that? 'I—'

'Oh, don't look so shocked.' He tapped a finger to the leather-bound file at the edge of his desk. 'Imrys came to me with his suspicions after the first trial, and I was quite convinced by the time you attacked Arden. That's why he was here, encouraging me to arrest you.'

But Rose only shook her head, her heart hammering in her ears. This didn't make any sense. How could Woodstone have known all this time and have done nothing about it?

'Then why not let him?' Her brow knotted. 'Why let me compete at all?'

'For the same reason I don't cancel the tournament now.' Woodstone got to his feet with a gentle sigh. He was insidiously quiet as he straightened his robes, striding over to the window behind his desk. There he stood for a moment in utter silence, watching the rain patter against the glass. But Rose eyed him warily, like a serpent poised to strike.

Finally, he chuckled. 'You know, you remind me somewhat of your mother.'

'My mother?'

'We were friends once,' he mused. 'In our school days. Back before she got tangled up with Imrys and his vapid Order.'

Rose folded her arms over her chest. It was hardly surprising that they'd have gotten along, but still, she frowned. 'What does that have to do with anything?'

'Because, Messere Thenlif, much like your mother, you're far too wrapped up in your own pride to understand the full gravity of the situation.' He turned to face them. 'You see, when Araminta failed to keep that wayward barman in line last year, it shook the faith that every noble family had in this institution to the core.

'In the wake of your mother's disgrace, I was personally tasked by her eminence to ensure that faith did not shatter entirely.' Woodstone tucked his hands behind his back. 'Because our empress understands what you clearly do not: that Dunhollow is the cornerstone, and if it falls, it would only be a matter of time before all else followed in its ruinous wake.'

Rose recoiled. He couldn't possibly believe that — *could he?* But he did; she could see the truth of it plainly in his eyes. So dulled by his 'grand purpose' that he couldn't even see his own folly any more.

'So, no, it's not just this place's "damned reputation" that I am protecting, my dear.' He clicked his tongue gently, as if he pitied Rose's poor insipid mind. 'It's the fate of the entire empire.'

Rose swallowed hard, biting back barbed words. He could paint his inaction in as many pretty words as he liked, but it would make no difference. In the end, it all came down to Dunhollow's truest core values: apathy and pretension.

Silence held between them for several heartbeats before Sylvie let out a small scoff. 'Gods, you're a monster.'

'Believe me, Messere Belliaris, I've been called worse.' Woodstone pulled a tight smile. 'The truth cannot be dulled by sharp words, I'm afraid.'

At this, Rose lifted her gaze. 'You want the truth? Fine, I am a necromancer, but not the one you need to worry about. *He's* currently parading around in Soren's body, and even your beloved empress's directive won't keep him from turning this damned tournament into a bloodbath.'

'Rose . . .' Callum's tone was a low warning.

Woodstone's eyes narrowed. 'You have proof of this?'

'I . . .' Rose faltered. It shouldn't matter – the proof was all around him, if he only cared to look. 'His name is Ionas Tirecin; he was an imperial necromancer before it was outlawed. *He* killed my mother, Arden and the other competitors. We found his lair in the archives, and he's planning to cast something called a soul source. He's coming for Dunhollow, Chancellor.'

Woodstone regarded Rose coolly for a moment before he chuckled softly. 'That's quite the story. But even if I did believe you, that is a risk I'm willing to take.'

'Then you're a fool,' Callum snapped. 'You can't force us to compete.'

'I'm not quite so foolish as to try and compel *you*, Messere Avenhart, no.' Woodstone stepped closer, leaning against his desk. 'Though I wouldn't suggest you try either. Your Mistralus has kindly provided me with an anti-compulsion sigil.'

Callum's jaw tightened as he sank back on his heels but said nothing.

'Which leaves us at somewhat of an impasse.' The chancellor's smile was cold and empty. 'So, should Messere Thenlif decline the honour of competing, I would happily turn her over to Imrys to answer for her crimes. And I assume the two of you would be loath to let her compete alone?'

Sylvie and Callum shared a sharp glance before their expressions set in clear defiance. But Rose's stomach flipped. Perhaps turning herself in would be for the best – breaking this noose Woodstone held around her neck and keeping her from Ionas's grasp.

When none of them spoke, however, Woodstone clapped his hands together. 'Good, I'm so glad we've settled that. Now then, Mamsella de Prevath sent word this morning that Messere L'Espina will be dropping out of the tournament, so you three are our official finalists. Given the perils faced at the other trials, we will be pushing the final event ahead of schedule, which should please you. I doubt your errant necromancer can whip up too much trouble by tomorrow morning, after all.'

A sneer curled at Sylvie's lip. 'You can't be serious.'

'Quite.' Woodstone raised an eyebrow. 'I've cancelled classes for the week and the new timing will align with Harvestfest celebrations this weekend, which will allow us the chance to properly mourn those we've lost, including the victims of your mother's negligence last year, Messere Thenlif. I'm told you were quite close with one Fenil Hathorin.'

Rose's breath caught in her throat at Fen's name, her eyes pricking with tears, but she refused to let them fall. 'Leave him out of this.'

'If you wish.' Woodstone gave a gentle *tsk*. 'Now, was there anything else?'

Rose couldn't help the scoff of disgust that slipped out. If Woodstone wanted to cower behind tradition and formality, hiding his guile behind that wretchedly simple guise, then he deserved whatever cruel fate awaited him. And it would come. If not by Ionas's hand, then perhaps by Rose's own.

Gritting her teeth, she swallowed the urge to make him choke on his words. 'No, Chancellor.'

'Good, then I'll see you all tomorrow morning in the assembly hall.' He flashed a dull smile. 'Until then, tread carefully.'

Turning on her heel, Rose stormed out of the office without another word. If Dunhollow was the cornerstone of anything, it was surely only Woodstone's ambition. And he, in turn, was everything it could hope to produce in its charges. Shrewd, driven and utterly without a conscience. But the foundations of Dunhollow were built long before Woodstone, rotted and bowing beneath the weight of time. And maybe such a fragile, fickle structure deserved to fall.

42. Prized Instruments

Rose didn't slow at all as she burst through the obsidian door, taking furiously to the spiral steps. The door slammed behind her with a resounding thud, but she could barely hear it over the din of her own raging heartbeat, her gaze focused solely on the archway ahead. On fleeing this wretched place before she dissolved into her fury.

'Rose, wait!'

Sylvie's cry carried over her shoulder as a towering form stepped into her path. A dark cloud of ebony robes and shrewd grey eyes blocked out the light of the hall beyond and made Rose's stomach turn. She came to a sharp halt as a cold smile spread across Imrys's lips.

'Messere Thenlif. Just the person I was looking for.'

Of course he hadn't just left after Woodstone's dismissal, but had laid in wait for her in dark corners. Her heart sank. Somehow, she'd thought that his last run-in with Callum would've been enough to ward him off. A foolish notion really.

'What do you want?' Sylvie bit out breathlessly, moving to Rose's side.

'Nothing that concerns you.' His gaze flicked between her and Callum behind them. 'Either of you.'

'Somehow I doubt that,' Callum scoffed.

Imrys's smile widened as he held up a slip of paper. 'This is a writ of arrest, Messere Thenlif, direct from the capital. So you'll be coming with me, despite your dear chancellor's protestations.'

Imrys barely spared them another glance before he reached for Rose. But his fingers hadn't even brushed her skin before Callum caught his wrist in a cruel grip. Rose flinched, her eyes flying over her shoulder. But Callum didn't even look at her, his gaze burning with an ire so deep his eyes had lost all their light.

'You just don't learn, do you, Ambassador?' His voice was low as he placed himself between Rose and Imrys. 'Back away. Now.'

Scents of chestnut and chicory stole over Rose as Imrys went rigid, though he didn't obey immediately. His jaw was set so tight his muscles twitched, his eyes fixed on Callum, refusing to drop his gaze. A silent battle of wills warred between them as they both fought for control.

After a long moment, Imrys finally took a slow step backwards. Then another. Until Callum was forced to release him, flexing his hand at his side as though Imrys had left some foul substance upon it. Rose and Sylvie exchanged a charged glance, neither uttering a word.

'Now, you wanted the truth so badly from Rose, so how about you treat us to a little honesty yourself, hmm?' Callum's gaze flashed from Imrys back to Rose. 'What is it that you really want?'

Imrys's throat bobbed, his lips twisted in a snarl. 'Her ruin.'

'And a murder charge was the way to go?' Callum chuckled drily. 'Surely you could've just reported her necromancy?'

'No,' he said through clenched teeth, still trying to keep the truth at bay. 'Arden wouldn't cooperate – I had no choice.'

Callum sighed as if dealing with an unruly child. 'Do make things plain, Ambassador. You'll only make it worse for yourself the longer you avoid the truth.'

As if to punctuate his point, blood pooled at the corners

of Imrys's mouth. But even he was powerless against Callum's will, and the truth fled from him in a breathless whisper.

'*I* killed Arden.'

'*What?*' Sylvie gasped.

But Rose was numb, her head spinning as her pulse thrummed in her ears. 'Why?'

'When he woke, he was too cowardly to say a word of your attack.' Imrys's lips trembled. 'He was more use to me dead.'

Rose recoiled, something stirring in her chest that she couldn't quite place. Pity, perhaps? Though she couldn't fathom why. Arden had set sail with Imrys's success, even knowing his cruelty. And he'd killed him for nothing more than his own whim.

She almost wanted to be glad of it. That it wasn't her hand that had snipped that final thread of Arden's life. That it wasn't *her* fault. But it rang hollow now. It might have been Imrys's choice that had sealed his fate, but it was hers that had set this all in motion. That haunted them still.

'How very pragmatic,' Callum drawled. 'But why go to all this trouble? Why pin it on Rose?'

'She knew things.' He bit out the words. 'Things that could ruin me.'

Rose frowned. What, like his history with the Order and her aunt's death? Was that what this was all about? She flashed a glance at Sylvie. But why now?

'Yes, I'm sure a man like you has his secrets.' Callum leaned closer. 'But there's more to it, isn't there?'

Imrys's pale face was bright red now – bloated and strained. *Good*, Rose thought cruelly. Let him taste his own poison. Finally, his head bowed, the words spilling out so softly, she almost couldn't hear them.

'She took the one person I ever loved from me. And she needs to pay.'

Rose blanched. Her mother? Her heart dropped straight into the pit of her stomach, souring upon the thought.

How could he call that love? When all they'd ever done was wage bitter war between themselves – stealing life and purpose alike from one another? Carving wounds so deep into each other's hearts that they would never heal and all the while treating it like some insidious game.

Rose shook her head. 'That wasn't love.'

Imrys's eyes narrowed as he sneered at her. 'You wouldn't understand.'

But the saddest thing was that she did. She knew what it was to bear her mother's idea of love more than anyone, and she hadn't been left unmarred by it either. But she knew it now for what it was.

Not love, or any of the warmth that came with it, but a bid for control. Affection granted for as long as one danced to her tune and rescinded the moment one dared step out of line.

Those her mother had claimed to love most were merely her prized instruments. Like herself and Sylvie, who she'd used all too eagerly to chip away at the rough edges of each other, until all that remained was what she wanted of them. And, in so doing, she'd stolen parts of them that were never hers to take.

'Wouldn't I?' Rose said finally. 'People are never people in your eyes. We're just tools to you, there to perform our function and easy enough to discard when they break. But you can't love a tool. So, no, I didn't *take* her from you because she wasn't yours. And I was never hers.'

Imrys gasped as Rose stepped closer, watching her as if she were a blade poised to strike. But she had no fire left in her fight, no thirst left for vengeance. Not for him, anyway.

Finally, she turned to Callum. 'I've heard enough; do whatever you want with him.'

'Gladly.' Callum grabbed Imrys's chin. 'I want you to forget, Ambassador. Rose, her mother – this whole cursed endeavour. But, most importantly, I want you to forget every ambition you ever fostered. Every desire you've killed for. Everything that's ever brought you joy. Only an echo will remain, and every time you try to think of it, it'll wrench you open. A wound upon your frozen heart that'll never close, and you will never know why. Do you understand?'

'Y-yes.' The word slipped from Imrys's lips in a broken whisper.

'Good.' Callum leaned back with a cold smile. 'Then get out of my sight.'

In a heartbeat, Imrys straightened, sweeping past them and back out into the dim light of the courtyard beyond. But his gait wasn't so sure now; it was almost wobbly. As if he'd lost the part of himself that held him upright.

Rose watched him disappear before she turned to Callum. Words of thanks hung on her tongue. Of worry and love. But Callum didn't meet her gaze. Couldn't, perhaps.

'I'm sorry, I—'

'No,' Rose cut across him, reaching up to cup a hand around his cheek. 'Thank you.'

Callum's shoulders sagged, a gentle sigh escaping him. As if her acceptance set something free within him. In spite of everything, Rose smiled as he leaned down, resting his forehead against hers.

They stood there like that for a moment longer before Rose lifted her head, glancing back at Sylvie with a grimace. 'Come on. Let's get out of here.'

43. Not Everything

The dry weight of her wine lingered on Rose's tongue. She'd thought it might help – to chase away the pain of Ionas's illusions and the truth of Soren's fate at his hands. But it filled her almost numbly now, her mind racing too quickly for even alcohol to dull it.

Her gaze slid down to Sylvie, who lay nestled against Rose's stomach as she stared up at the canopy of Rose's bed above them. Callum had curled beside them, leaning against the pillows and sipping slowly at his wine. They hadn't spoken a word since fending off Imrys, returning to Rose's dormitory under the pall of dreadful silence.

If they were a painting, they would look so at peace. Just three lovers, caught in the heat of each other's arms – no shadows of wrath or ruin hanging over their heads. But peace was not for them.

Rose leaned her glass against her chest with a sigh, staring into Callum's illusory fire that crackled in place of her window seat. Its flames filled the room in a warm glow, its stone chimney blocking out the night sky. Still, her heart flipped. Was Soren out there somewhere? Scared and alone, suffering for Rose's mistakes? How many others would fall to them before the end?

Finally, Callum stirred, lifting his head to glance down at Rose. 'As much as I'm enjoying this little interlude, are we going to talk about what happened?'

'Which part?' Rose scoffed into her wine. 'Getting attacked by an undead necromancer, Imrys nearly arresting me or the fact that our esteemed chancellor is determined to send us all to our graves to pretend nothing is wrong?'

'All of it, I suppose.'

'Do you think they could be working together?' Sylvie said after a moment, rolling over on to her stomach. 'Woodstone and Ionas, I mean.'

Rose frowned. It seemed unlikely. Woodstone just wanted to keep his reputation intact, and Ionas wanted – what? Freedom? He had that already, even if it was bound to Soren's body. Her mind drifted back to those drawings in the archives. Clearly, whatever immortality he had at Soren's expense wasn't enough. He was planning something far worse, she was sure, but she couldn't fathom that it had anything to do with the blasted Ashwood Tournament.

She shook her head. 'I doubt it. Woodstone wouldn't help anyone who threatened to upend his precious tournament.'

'Unless he was trying to get you to the last trial.'

'I can't see why Ionas would want that – or why he would need Woodstone's help to do so.' Rose took a long sip of wine. 'No, Woodstone might be a monster, but I don't think he's a liar. He really does think he's upholding the empire with this nonsense.'

Sylvie's voice grew small. 'Then why bring up Fen? Why taunt you with that now, after Ionas already did?'

Because, for all Woodstone liked to pretend otherwise, his tenuous facade was crumbling quickly, and he would use any weapon in his arsenal to make sure it stayed in place. Or, at the very least, he would take out any who threatened it. Rose sipped her wine bitterly. A double-edged sword was aimed straight for her heart, reminding her that it could always sink deeper.

'To hurt me.' She shook her head, her throat tightening. 'To remind me of what he knows, and what he could use against me, should I misbehave.'

Sylvie's gaze dropped with a grimace, and she pressed a gentle kiss into Rose's stomach. Almost an apology, though she had nothing to be sorry for. None of this was *her* fault – only Rose's. Yet Callum watched the pair of them curiously, his brow drawn in a soft frown.

'Can I ask what happened last year?' He spun his glass between his fingers. 'I mean, I've gleaned pieces here and there, but not the whole picture.'

Sylvie blinked up at Rose, her brow furrowing. 'You haven't told him?'

'Neither have you.' She shrugged. 'And it's your story as much as mine.'

Sylvie's scowl deepened and, for a moment, Rose thought she might not answer. Finally, she sat up, downing the last of her wine before reaching for the bottle on the bedside table. When her glass was once again full, she settled herself back between Rose's legs and turned to Callum.

'I died last year.' She sighed. 'Well, sort of . . .'

Rose's jaw clenched as Sylvie recounted the sordid tale, her tone as dry as kindling as she explained Hollis and all his atrocities. The same atrocities that Rose herself had gone on to commit, all while claiming it was entirely different. But she knew now that it wasn't.

Despite the pretty lies she'd spun for herself, in trying to revive Fen she'd been just as bad as Hollis. Worse even, given what Ionas might still do. But it had to stop. Rose's fingers tightened around her glass. She couldn't let anyone else suffer again for some caster's vain notion of cheating death.

'I'm so sorry.' Callum's soft voice startled Rose. 'For both of you.'

Sylvie nodded, flashing him a watery smile. But Rose could hardly meet his gaze. Even so, Callum squeezed both their hands tighter.

'When we were in the infirmary,' said Sylvie once she'd gathered herself, 'you asked why I protected Rose, even knowing she's a necromancer. It's because without her I'd be nothing more than a footnote to history. She gave me back more than just my life that day, and she lost everything for her trouble.'

Was that really how Sylvie saw things? Rose frowned, stroking a hand down Sylvie's shoulder. She may have lost a piece of her heart that day but not the whole of it. For all that this wretched place had tried to tear them apart, Sylvie was still here.

'No,' she whispered, pressing a kiss to Sylvie's brow. 'Not everything.'

Sylvie leaned up, catching her lips. Her warmth lingered on Rose's skin – faint notes of her orchid and musk perfume hanging in the air as she pulled away. And then her eyes found Callum's, dark and fixed upon them with such exquisite longing that Rose's heart nearly burst.

'I don't want to lose you.' Her voice trembled as her eyes flicked from Sylvie to Callum, and she reached out to stroke his cheek. 'Either of you.'

'You won't, dal.' He leaned against her hand for a moment before pulling her into a kiss.

His lips were gentle against hers, his hand tightening around the back of her neck before he broke away. The smallest of smiles ghosted across his lips before his eyes slid to Sylvie, who watched the pair of them hungrily. Leaning down, Callum caught her chin in the crook of his hand before pulling her into a searing kiss as well.

Heat pooled low in Rose's core as Sylvie pushed herself up off the mattress, leaning into Callum's embrace before she eased him back on to the pillows at the head of Rose's bed. Slowly, Sylvie kissed down his throat, unhooking the buttons and laces of his robes as she went. This, finally, stirred Rose to motion, as she set about pulling Sylvie's blouse away from her shoulders while Callum pushed aside the straps of Rose's nightclothes.

It was a slow process, pulling each article of clothing off one another, prolonged in no small part by broken kisses and grasping touches as they explored each newly bared inch of each other's bodies. But there was a hesitance between Sylvie and Callum: all shy glances and fleeting smiles as they danced around one another, lavishing attention on Rose in turn. As if they were bound by her alone.

Her breath caught in her throat as Sylvie sank into the mattress, entirely naked now as she tugged Rose closer. She pitched forward unsteadily, her knees knocking against the bedframe when Callum caught her with a gentle hand around her throat, pulling her flush against his bare chest. His teeth skimmed the shell of her ear as Sylvie leaned forward, pressing tantalizing kisses down Rose's torso.

Perhaps this desire burgeoning between them was still too new. Too raw and fierce for anything more than a kiss here and a heated touch there. After all, only she had known them both. Only she had seen every sharp edge and jagged scar they hid away and still chose to love them. Though she had no doubt that they would grant each other the same grace given the chance. Still, for this moment, if she was the thread that bound them, perhaps that was enough.

But the thought fled Rose's head as Sylvie caught her in a bruising kiss, her tongue delving between her lips. Heat coursed through her, and she ran her nails along Sylvie's scalp, weaving her fingers through her gossamer hair before she pulled. Not hard, but enough that it earned the most delicious whine from Sylvie's lips.

Rose pulled back to press a heated kiss to the pulse point

of her lovely throat, her teeth scraping gently over her skin. Sylvie shivered against her, and Rose smiled softly before pushing her back.

Her eyes roved over Sylvie with a jolt of desire, tracing the stiff peaks of her nipples down to the dark curls at the juncture of her thighs, glistening in the low light. Gods, she wanted nothing more than the taste of Sylvie upon her tongue, writhing beneath her, Rose's name falling from her lips like a prayer as she came. The thought pulled at her as she pressed tantalizing kisses down the delicate skin of Sylvie's inner thigh.

But a flicker of motion caught the corner of Rose's eye, and she glanced over to where Callum stood behind her, stroking his fingers down the curves of her back. Almost as if he was unsure whether he was allowed to intrude. Rose grimaced at the tremor of insecurity that flashed through his eyes, mingling with a raw hunger. She reached to draw him closer, leaning back against his stiff length.

'I want you inside me,' she whispered, and Sylvie groaned eagerly in agreement.

'Wait.' Sylvie propped herself up on her elbows, her eyes hazy with desire.

Callum faltered at Rose's back, his fingers tightening at her hips. 'What is it?'

With a sly smile, Sylvie muttered softly and waved her hand, her spell falling over them with a gentle warmth that smelled of plum and lilac. 'Mirror charm.'

Rose bit back a grin as Callum nodded slowly. Sylvie's favourite spell these days, it seemed, though she hadn't thought it could extend past two people. Then again, Sylvie had always been an exceptional caster. She watched hungrily as Sylvie leaned back against the mattress, spreading her legs. Inviting her in. And Rose all too eagerly obliged.

She bent forward, the heat between Sylvie's thighs

enveloping her as she ran her tongue over her with a teasing lick. Yet the taste of Sylvie only spiked at her desire – a tangy mix of robust earthy sweetness and heady musk that pooled against Rose's tongue and echoed low within her. A phantom touch that left her aching for more.

Sylvie pitched forward, arching her back as Rose began to circle her lightly, but Callum remained utterly still behind her. Even with Rose laid bare before him and bent over the mattress, he didn't move, as if drinking in the sight. Rose squirmed against him, her tongue flicking over the pearl of Sylvie's clit, making her keen beneath her.

Finally, that stirred Callum to motion as he caught her hip in a bruising grip, holding Rose steady as he slowly sank one finger into her. Slick and pliant as she was, it wasn't long before he slipped another finger in, curling them at just the right angle.

She groaned, eagerly shifting her hips back against him, but Callum seemed content to torment her. Working her open slowly, making her wait. Still, Rose needed more.

She whimpered, her tongue faltering as Callum pulled back, resting the tip of his cock against her. She swallowed hard, waiting for him to sink within her, yet he simply stalled. As if he were drawn by the sight of Sylvie's legs spread wide before him – of Rose's head buried between her thighs.

Teasing, toying, sucking as Sylvie writhed beneath her, a moan catching in her throat as Rose dipped her tongue lower into her entrance. And it was that solitary sound that finally set Callum in motion. As if he could not bear it any longer, he sheathed himself within Rose in one slow stroke, his grip tightening around her hips.

'Gods, yes,' Sylvie cried as the echo of him stretched within her too.

But Rose couldn't have found the words even if she'd

wanted to, her mind buzzing. He stilled, hips resting against her for a moment, letting her adjust before he started to thrust gently. Rose pitched forward, every nerve on fire as Callum found his rhythm. She let out a pitiful mewl as he tangled a hand through her curls, her pleasure hanging by a thread.

Each thrust carried her closer to it, stroking that spot deep within her. Sylvie's fingers tightened around the bedsheets as Rose dipped into her once more, edging her ever closer to that precipice alongside her. Callum tensed within her as he inched towards his finish, bringing her so close to her own release that Rose could almost taste it. Tighter and tighter, it wound within her like a coil.

Until, all at once, it snapped and sent her careening over that precarious edge.

It took all Rose's strength for her jaw not to tighten. All her will for her teeth not to pierce Sylvie's fragile flesh as her pleasure washed over her. Stars burst behind Rose's eyes as Callum muttered fervent, feverish praise in her ears, coming only a few strokes later with a strangled groan.

His pleasure pooled within her, mingling with the tail end of Rose's climax almost before she could catch her breath. But it only quickened Rose's pace – setting her tongue to renewed purpose against Sylvie as that taut coil wound in her core once more. Callum sagged against her back, sated and utterly spent as Rose chased her second orgasm. Or third. It was hard to say through the haze of it all, their pleasures shared and amplified until the end of one was indistinguishable from the peak of another.

Sylvie tensed beneath her lips, her back arched into the mattress, her dark hair splayed across the pillows beneath her. She was close – so close now. Until, finally, with a shattering cry, Sylvie came undone.

The intensity of her climax crashed over Rose in a burst of colours as she squeezed her eyes shut. Behind her, Callum's hands gripped her hips tightly as their collective pleasure washed over him as well, elongating it into steady waves as it rolled over them. It seemed ages before they all came down from it, panting and thoroughly spent.

Pleasure rippled beneath Rose's skin in haunting echoes as Callum pulled out of her and collapsed on the bed beside Sylvie. Sweat clung to his chest, his lips curled in a satisfied smirk as he traced languid kisses over the peak of Sylvie's breast.

Her tawny skin darkened in a flush, her nipples hardening once more. But Sylvie gently tugged at Rose, pulling her up to lie between her and Callum. Rose pressed a lazy kiss to her shoulder, entwining her legs between Callum's before leaning back against his chest. And there, wrapped in the warmth of their arms and the steady beats of their still racing hearts, Rose felt the first stirrings of true peace.

Tomorrow, it might all be wrenched away from her. Whether by the apathy of the Faceless, the tournament itself or Ionas's cruel machinations, she knew now that the world would never let her keep such a fragile serenity as she found in their embrace. Not unless she fought tooth and nail to clutch it to her raw and bloodied chest. And she would. Tears pricked her eyes as a soft sigh slipped past her lips. For them, she would do so much worse.

44. Together

It was the distant rumble of thunder that finally woke Rose, soft and carrying over the mountains beyond her window; her eyes fluttered open to meet it with a frown. It almost felt like a warning somehow. The skies themselves were filled with foreboding, grey clouds that rolled ever closer.

Rose shifted gently as her eyes adjusted to the dim light. But whatever danger lingered beyond these walls faded beneath the heat of the bodies surrounding her. She grinned at Sylvie, who had stolen most of the blankets sometime during the night and shifted all the way to the edge of the bed. Callum, on the other hand, was pressed firm at Rose's back, his limbs draped over her as if trying to keep them both warm.

Her bed was not really made to fit all three of them, yet it didn't feel cramped at all. Rose stretched out languidly, enjoying the sleepy little moan it drew from Sylvie's lips. A scowl furrowed her brow as the low light of day flickered over them, and Rose chuckled. Sylvie had never been a fan of mornings.

But the sound set Callum stirring, his eyes blinking open blearily before they fixed on Rose. A slow smile broke across his lips then, and he wrapped his arms tighter, rolling on top of her to pepper her with lazy kisses. Rose squirmed beneath him with a laugh, squeezing him tight.

As if sensing she was missing out on something, Sylvie opened one eye to glower at the pair of them from beneath her makeshift burrow. But her gaze quickly softened as she inched forward to join them, pressing her lips to Rose's shoulder before sleepily catching Callum's in a kiss.

Finally, Callum rolled on to his back with a smile, rubbing the sleep from his eyes. 'Not a bad way to wake up, I must say.'

'Mmm,' Sylvie murmured into Rose's throat. 'If only we could stay here all day.'

'And miss out on the last trial?' Callum laughed drily. 'The scandal.'

Rose stilled. She'd almost forgotten about the damned trial. It seemed so far away – so insignificant against the threat that Ionas posed as to be laughable. As if they were trapped on a cavalcade that was hurtling off its tracks, blithely playing games while racing towards their own demise.

Sylvie slowly lifted her head. 'We could run.'

Rose frowned. Could they? Imrys had been cowed, but she doubted Woodstone would be content to let them escape his charade so easily. Nor would Ionas, for that matter.

'Sylvie . . .'

Callum cut across Rose. 'Where did you have in mind, darling?'

'Maybe somewhere near the coast?' Sylvie propped herself up on her elbow, her eyes flitting between the two of them. 'If you're amenable.'

Callum's eyes softened as his arms tightened, pulling them both close. 'I would be amenable to anything so long as it was with you two.'

For a moment, the idea filled Rose with such painful longing that she almost caved in. Flashes of Sylvie's mindscape came flooding back with a searing heat – the three of them carving out a sliver of peace by the sea. Building a home together. But then Rose's stomach lurched as her memory flickered over Fen's face. They couldn't just leave. Not with

Ionas out there, planning gods knew what. He'd already stolen any hope she had of bringing Fen back — she couldn't let him take Soren from her too.

'We can't,' she whispered, shattering any tenuous threads of that fantasy before they could take hold.

Sylvie frowned. 'Why not?'

'Because it's exactly what Ionas wants.'

Rose sat up, burying her face in her hands. She felt the mattress shift beside her as Sylvie and Callum sat up too.

'What do you mean, dal?' Callum asked after a moment

Rose swallowed hard. 'When we were in the archives, he said that even with Soren at his mercy, I would run away, just like I always do.'

Sylvie raised an eyebrow. 'And you didn't think to say anything last night?'

'My tongue was otherwise occupied, if you'll recall,' Rose scoffed, her cheeks flushing as the words slipped out.

Almost in spite of himself, Callum snorted on a laugh, but he quickly cleared his throat. 'And if you stay?'

'There is no *if*,' Rose snapped. 'He has Soren. And who knows what he still has planned. I'm the one who started this whole mess; I have to stay and see it through.'

'Dal, I—'

Rose clenched her jaw, leaning back to meet both their gazes. 'But you two should go.'

In any other circumstances, it might have been comical, the way shock splintered across both their faces in matching expressions.

'Absolutely not.' Sylvie shook her head adamantly.

'Without you?' Callum said at the same time. 'Not likely, dal.'

Rose sighed deeply. It would be so much easier if they both just left. But also lonelier, she realized with a pang. As if two halves of her were at war with each other — one loath to put them in harm's way, and the other wanting nothing more than to keep them close.

For the two of them were nothing less than the last of her failing strength. The breath in her lungs and the very fire of her fight. She couldn't do any of this without them.

Finally, Sylvie pulled her close. 'This won't be like last year, Rose. We know who we're up against this time. Whatever he throws at us — we'll face it.'

'She's right,' said Callum. 'You can't do this alone.'

Rose's throat tightened, and she leaned into the warmth of their arms. 'Together, then.'

The three of them walked in dour silence across campus, their heads bent and fingers locked tightly. Thunderclouds hung over the courtyard, their rumbling echoes sounding like a dirge. It was as if they were marching towards their own funeral.

Finally, they came upon the assembly hall, its imposing stone walls glowering down at them from darkened skies. Rose's heart flipped as they approached the arched doors, and Sylvie squeezed her hand.

'Are you sure you want to do this?' Her eyes held Rose's with a resigned plea. 'It's not too late to run.'

Rose forced a dry smile. 'I seem to recall you once telling me to *stop* avoiding my problems?'

A scowl flickered across Sylvie's brow before Callum placed a gentle hand on her shoulder. 'Come on then. No point in delaying the inevitable.'

With a sigh, Sylvie finally nodded and, together, the three of them pushed open the doors. Rose's heart leapt into her throat as they stepped into the shadow of the room. The hairs on the back of her neck prickled almost immediately, the silence pressing in all around them like a shroud. The room before them was cavernous, utterly empty, save for five figures standing at the far end of the hall. Rose's stomach squirmed as she took in their masked visages.

The Faceless.

But something was very wrong. Rose stiffened as she drew closer – close enough for her to catch the silver source wrapped around their throats like they were lined up at the gallows. *No.*

Sylvie pulled back a step. 'What is this?'

'It's like they've been . . . hollowed out,' Callum whispered.

'We need to get out of here.' Rose's blood ran cold, her eyes darting back to the doors.

Yet they slammed shut in an instant, a loud thud echoing through the room. Before Rose could even blink, a thick powder filled the air, choking them all under its haze. Her lungs burned, her vision blurring at the edges as she swayed. But then, as Rose's knees sank on to the cold stone floor, an all too familiar form stepped in front of her: all milky-white eyes and an insidiously cheerful smile. *Ionas.*

'Hello, Rose,' he purred. 'I was so hoping you would join us.'

Rose blinked back tears as she pitched forward on all fours, desperately fighting whatever poison he'd inflicted upon them. Beside her, Sylvie and Callum were faring no better, trembling and coughing as they reached desperately for one another. Rose gritted her teeth. Gods, she wished she could claw out Ionas's tongue, if only just to shove it down his wretched throat.

'I hope you don't mind me stepping in for the chancellor.' Ionas almost giggled. 'He was so busy preparing for the grand victory celebration in the main hall, so I thought I'd save him the trouble. After all, I'd so hate to ruin the surprise for him when he sees the full breadth of what his negligence has wrought.'

'Stop.' Rose choked out the words. 'This is between you and me.'

His smile was sickeningly empty. 'Not any longer, I'm afraid. In fact, you three will be quite safe in the trial I planned. Well, surrounded by your greatest fears, of course, and all too likely unable to escape. But still, far safer than the rest of this poor academy.'

His grip on the silver source around the Faceless's throats grew tighter, and they fell to their knees, wheezing and choking in an awful cacophony. 'Ah, well. If only they'd listened to you.'

'Please – don't do this.'

'Oh, it's far too late for that, my dear.' Ionas stepped closer as Rose collapsed fully on to the floor, the stones cool against her cheek as the world went dark. 'Best of luck to you all.'

45. Always Enough

Cold stones were the only thing that greeted Rose when she opened her eyes. Beyond that was utter darkness – and a sharp pain shooting through her skull. She groaned, pushing herself up slowly. *Sylvie and Callum.* The thought seared through her mind with a desperate heat.

But they weren't on the floor beside her. Rose blinked around the shadowy room, her heart sinking. Dampness and must clung to the stones, wet beneath her fingers. A strange dripping noise grated on her ears and a harsh scent hung on the air, almost like vinegar. Her stomach churned as her eyes adjusted to a sickly green glow casting eerie shadows across the stone walls. She knew this place. *Hollis's basement.*

A wave of nausea rolled over her as she staggered to her feet. Ionas had said they would have to face their fears, but this? Rose squeezed her eyes shut and shook her head, as if she might chase away the memory. She couldn't do it.

'Rose?'

'Fen!'

Her eyes flew open, the basement alight with the crackle of magic and the glow of Rose's own source. But it wasn't her that Fen spoke to. Rather, he cradled the Rose who had found him in that basement all those months ago. The one who'd trembled at the terrible choice before her, her eyes glowing silver and tears streaming down her face.

Save him, she wanted to scream. *Don't let go.* But she was just as powerless to help him now as she had been then. So much time – so much power and growth – and yet that one bitter truth remained.

Rose's throat tightened when her casting shattered, hurtling the room into darkness once more as Fen's form faded. But then it flickered to life before her, watching her with those brown eyes she knew so well. Yet they were laden only with sorrow now.

'Why didn't you choose me, Rose?' Fen whispered. 'Why did you let me die?'

'I didn't.' Her voice cracked as she reached for him.

'Yes, you did.' He shook his head. 'You chose *her.*'

Sylvie. Rose's heart lurched. The life she'd saved, the love she'd chosen. Still, the thought rankled. Did Fen truly think he meant any less to her? Or perhaps he simply wanted an apology – a small sliver of atonement for what her choice had cost him.

Yet she couldn't give it.

Because this wasn't Fen. Rose's nails bit into her palms as her fingers curled into fists. It was nothing more than her own fear, shaped by the grief that still tore through her heart with every beat. But she couldn't hold on to it any longer.

'And you chose death.' The broken whisper fell from her lips. 'You *begged* me to save myself. You made your choice, and now I have to live with it.'

The echo of Fen recoiled, some last shred of sadness splintering in his eyes before he smiled. And then he was gone, leaving Rose alone in the dark. But the shadows weren't done with her yet.

They flung her forward, hurtling her into their ravenous abyss as images flashed past Rose's eyes. Her mother's screams as fire razed her flesh, Arden's terror as the silver webs of Rose's source caught him in their grip. Peiren's pale skin as his life faded. Dirt beneath her nails as she dug and dug and dug – deep beneath the earth and calling death back to her will.

She was weightless and buoyant, bound only to the burden of her memories. For they were hers, she knew, even if her body hadn't been at the time. Her hand had been bent and broken beneath Ionas's will, as he moulded her into his weapon. But for what?

The scene shifted, forming hazy fractures of skeletal fingers reaching through dark waters and flesh sloughing off freshly risen corpses. Rose's head spun. There were dozens of them – hundreds even. Bodies and bones that should have been left to the peace of death drawn by a deft hand and bound in the grip of bolstering magic. *Her* magic.

Her life source tied them all together, dragging them forth from water and earth. Forming them into an army for Ionas. Rose could see him now in horrid flashes, making a puppet of Soren's form as he welcomed his ranks gladly with open arms. Rose squinted at the sigils glowing behind him, carved into burnt echoes of aged chambers.

The archives.

But then the vision faded and Rose hit the ground with a dull thud. Pain didn't ricochet up her shins at the impact, but she stumbled all the same, blinking as a soft glow surrounded her – not eerie green but full and flickering, from an oil lamp hanging from a thick chain at the centre of a cell. Tiny and cramped, it was little more than the stones at her feet and the rusted iron bars that marked her only exit.

She stumbled forward, shaking them frantically. But then a chuckle lilted over her shoulder, and Rose's blood ran cold. Whirling, she found herself standing face to face with . . . herself? The Rose standing before her wasn't a reflection but was not quite her either. Bent upon the edge of shadow there was a keen cruelty to her hazel gaze.

Her shadowed self only smiled. 'Look at you. Even with all the power in the world, you haven't even learned a simple unlocking charm.'

Rose flinched as the figure drew closer, tucking an auburn curl behind her ear. She could count the same freckles that dusted her own nose, the same flecks of green within her eyes. But they were so very empty now.

'Perhaps you don't want to learn.' Her shadow pulled away. 'Because if you had knowledge and power, you'd finally have to admit to yourself the truth you've always known – that you are not enough.'

Rose blinked as the other her vanished, then reappeared at her side. Her jaw clenched tight. It almost reminded her of Ionas in a way. Perhaps it *was* him. But something within her mind rejected the notion automatically. Because, deep down, she knew it was only her own fear, taking form in the shadow that had followed her the longest.

'Not for your mother, not for Sylvie, not for Fen.'

'You're wrong.' She shook her head, but her voice came out hoarse and unsteady – unbelievable even to her own ears.

'Am I? I know all of you – your secrets, your hopes. Your fears. I *am* them.'

And it was for that reason alone that Rose knew this wretched creature could only have been born of her own mind. For all that Ionas had tormented and taunted her with the faces of those she loved, he'd never understood that which she feared most was the one that stared back at her from every reflection. Fragile and fleeting and so often unrecognizable.

Even so, furious flames licked at the back of Rose's mind, though they faltered as the figure's eyes shifted. No longer meeting hers at level, but staring up at her, wide and wavering. Peering out of a younger visage of chubby dimpled cheeks and tiny furrowed brows.

Yet there was hope lingering amid the malice of that gaze that Rose hadn't known since she was a child. It was a bright light she'd snuffed out long ago and never even realized. And now looking back at her with all the innocence she'd left behind.

'*You* are your worst fear.' The younger Rose's voice was soft and sweet but no less piercing. 'That time and time again you'll destroy the ones you love most, and you'll never be enough to save them.'

Rose gritted her teeth, her grip loosening. Perhaps she was right. This thread of fear had bound her for so long that she'd lent truth to it all on her own.

It was a noose that had been wound and woven many times over the years. Tied tight by people desperate to keep her small and pliant. And all the while, she'd danced over the ledge of those gallows they'd built for her, taking on the burden from others of keeping that knot firmly in place. But it was long past time that she cut it loose.

Because she would never grow as long as she kept denying parts of herself. Her anger, her pain. Her fear. Burying them all away to meet the expectations of others, to save herself from their cruelty and apathy. And never once had it worked.

She could no longer swallow the poison of others and call it her own, letting it fester in the gaping wounds within her heart. So she did the only thing she could. Staring down at those burning hazel eyes spread wide in fear and such deep, desperate longing, she pulled herself close and wrapped her in the warmth of her embrace.

And, as a choked sob caught in Rose's chest, she whispered the only words no one had ever thought to give her, and now which only she could give herself. 'Thank you for keeping me safe. But we were always enough, and I can protect us now.'

With a small smile, Rose's younger self faded into nothing more than memory. It was a piece that still lived within her but was sated and safe now amid the racing beat of her heart. The bars beside her clicked open with a great creak, beckoning her out into a well-lit hall. Sucking in a sharp breath, Rose steeled herself and then stepped out into her freedom.

A dull pulsing rang in Rose's head as her eyes flickered open to the looming heights of the assembly hall. She groaned as she pushed herself up, her back stiff from lying upon the cold stone floor. But the thought fled as her eyes landed on Callum and Sylvie, who lay prone beside her.

They were so pale and listless upon the stones that her heart leapt into her throat. Scrambling towards them, she reached out, checking their pulse. She could feel Ionas's insidious spell twisting around them, burgeoning at the edges of their consciousnesses. *No.* She couldn't lose them now. Not to him.

Her magic flowed out of her in silver tendrils, seeking the familiarity of their minds and the noose tied tight around them. It flared brightly, slashing through the corded thread that held them, bound by their terror. For fear was a brittle thing, and it shattered with so little resistance beneath the weight of her love. With a jolt, the spell faltered, Rose's magic snapping back towards her as their eyes flew open.

'Rose?' Tears shimmered against Sylvie's cheeks as she sat up with a start, staring at Rose like she wasn't sure she was real. 'You were—I saw—'

'I'm here.' She cradled Sylvie's face between her palms.

Callum's soft groan cut between them as he pulled himself upright, his skin ashen. 'Are you both all right?'

Words brushed against Rose's lips. Gentle soothing assurances that faded on her tongue as a low growl echoed through the room. She stumbled to her feet, peering through the lingering haze of Ionas's poison. Something shifted in the shadows – a prostrate form dragging itself across the ground. *One of the Faceless.*

Rose hesitated. It disgusted her that mercy was still her first instinct. Drawing her forward on some strange urge to help, whether or not they deserved it. But the feeling quickly faded as their mask slipped, revealing swollen grey skin that hung on the edge of undeath.

Rose recoiled with a cry. What had Ionas *done* to them? But she had little time to ponder it as the figure lurched forward with a grating shriek.

'Rose!'

A blast of ice cut through the hall, crystal shards spiralling up from the floor and impaling the Faceless straight through the jaw. A soft gurgle cut through the air as they twitched upon their skewer. *Could they not be killed?* Rose blinked, swallowing the urge to retch as her heart hammered in her ears.

'We need to get out of here,' she said finally, her eyes flying back to Sylvie, who stood trembling beside her. 'Find Ionas and put a stop to whatever he has planned.'

'That may be harder than you think, dal.'

Rose followed Callum's gaze, stumbling numbly towards the window. The faded outlines of fleeing students darted past the mottled panes, their footsteps thundering against the stones. But then her eyes slid to the forms that followed them and her blood ran cold.

Corpses – dozens of them. Shambling hollow echoes of a life once lived, now twisted into little more than rotting flesh and bone, the hollow sockets of their eyes alight with an empty silver glow. And all bound under Ionas's spell.

46. Don't Hold Back

As Sylvie heaved open the great doors to the assembly hall, the first thing that struck Rose was the smell. Not the screams that rent the night air nor the spells that whizzed and ricocheted off the stone walls, but the fetid stench of decay.

It permeated the air with a sickening haze, punctuated by the uneven shuffling of Ionas's army. His *undead* army. Rose's stomach churned. They swarmed the campus like maggots crawling in filth – most little more than bones and dust, while a few still clung to bloated greying skin. Yet a subtle white glow hung in all their eyes, whether hollow socket or half-decayed flesh.

Her pulse burned beneath her skin in restless tremors. This must have been his plan all along. To trap her in her worst fears so there was no one to stand against him as he spun his sick magic. Was *this* the soul source he'd written about? Sucking the life away from every student to fuel his own power? Power she herself had given him . . .

Rose was jolted from the thought as a crowd of her peers raced past. They flowed in a haphazard stream, pushing and shoving one another as undead chased after them. Sylvie darted into the crowd without hesitation, summoning her crystal cat and slinging ice with deft ease at the encroaching corpses.

But there were so many of them. So many that *she'd* helped to raise. Though they answered to Ionas, it was her magic that bound them all. And hers alone, perhaps, that could undo it.

'Watch out!' Callum's cry halted Rose as a bolt of his

lightning shattered upon a corpse only inches away from Sylvie's throat.

'Thanks,' Sylvie panted.

Callum gripped her arm, shoving her gossamer hair away from her face before his eyes darted over the carnage. 'We need to get out of here.'

Rose nodded. 'The main hall is closest – Ionas said Woodstone was preparing there.'

Taking them each by the hand, Rose dragged them down the slick cobblestone path, darting and weaving around the charging undead. The corpses were slow, at least, their grasping fingers not particularly clever as they lumbered after the fleeing students. Still, many were caught in their clutches – overwhelmed or simply unlucky.

Where were the professors? Rose's eyes darted left and right. Woodstone, she knew, had been preparing for the post-trial festivities when Ionas attacked, but most students should have been safe behind the walls of the main hall, not caught out in the open. And why had the faculty seemingly abandoned them?

Blasts of source magic cut through the night air in splinters of silvery blue as Sylvie fought to clear their path of the wretched creatures, but she couldn't protect everyone. A few paces ahead, a pair of younger students – first-years, likely – raced hand in hand, clutching one another tightly, until one of them stumbled. They hit the ground with a muted crash that made Rose falter as three undead descended upon them. Their screams pierced her heart, as they scrambled futilely back.

Releasing Sylvie and Callum, Rose's source was at her fingertips before she could think better of it, silver and shining as it sliced through the air, latching on to the grotesque corpses with a fierce heat. And then she wrenched it back, leaching away every perverted shred of life that clung to them until all that remained were hollow bones that crumpled to the ground. The first-year leapt to their feet hastily, their green eyes wide as they darted between Rose and the fallen undead.

'Th-thanks.'

'Don't mention it.' Rose pushed them and their friend towards the courtyard. 'Get to the main hall – now.'

Callum took Rose's arm as the pair stumbled back into the fray ahead of them. Grabbing hold of Sylvie, the three followed the other students' lead, quickly coming upon the chaos of the courtyard.

The campus green was ruptured and littered with corpses struck down by her peers' spells. But they rose again all too quickly, undeterred by death as they clawed their way through the dirt and grass. Students swarmed in from every direction, heading towards the safety of the main hall. A raggedy green barrier stood before its oaken doors, a familiar voice piercing the night air.

'Quickly!' Briony cried out. 'Quickly now. Everyone inside!'

'Briony!' Relief flooded Rose at the sight of her sage-green hair glowing like a beacon in the midst of the pandemonium beside the white-haired Professor Saoloris.

'Oh, Rose, thank goodness!' Briony wrapped her in a fierce hug.

Sylvie came to a panting halt beside them, her eyes darting back to the courtyard. 'Professor, what happened?'

'The undead – they came out of nowhere.' Briony shuddered. 'Most of us are sheltering within the hall, but they're about to barricade the doors.'

Rose glanced back at the turmoil raging in the courtyard. 'What about the people still out there? Trapped in the dorms or the outer buildings?'

Briony shook her head grimly. 'I don't know. Come on, I'll take you to the others. They were coming up with a plan.'

Briony took Rose's hand, muttering something to Professor Saoloris before leading Rose, Sylvie and Callum inside. The sight that met them within wasn't pretty – haggard students sagging over the long tables and barely uttering a word. Most held a hollow haunted look in their eyes, and were either covered in bruises or trembling furiously as other professors tried to comfort them. Or both.

They looked so young like that – the sharp edges of their insidious smiles faded to tenuous misgiving and fear. And all because of her. Her spell had summoned Ionas; her life had fuelled him. Yet it wasn't her that had freed him. At least, not her alone.

Her jaw tightened, her eyes darting to the far end of the hall, to where Mamsella de Prevath, Professor Troidilis and Woodstone stood huddled. Rose frowned. Of course the chancellor had survived Ionas's attack. Like a persistent mould clinging stubbornly to life, they would never be rid of him so easily. But she had little time to think on it now, as their voices spilled out over the silent hall.

'Barricading now would leave too many students unaccounted for,' the Mamsella snapped, her cerulean eyes bright with uncommon fire.

Woodstone only scoffed. 'And if we don't, we risk everyone gathered here instead. With the Faceless gone, there aren't enough of us to hold them off.'

Rose blinked, drawing up short. Did he know that Ionas had killed his beloved Faceless? Her jaw tightened. That he could have so easily joined them in their undead fate if he wasn't so busy setting up his facade? Her eyes roved over the streamers and bunting lining the ceiling, all of which hung almost eerily still now.

'Even so, we must fight them.' Troidilis's voice cut through Rose's thoughts, their arms folded tight across their chest.

'How?' Woodstone shook his head. 'They're undead – nothing can kill them.'

Except necromancy. Rose chewed the inside of her lip. *Except her.* Only she could counter Ionas and whatever spell he'd woven, but she wouldn't be able to if her magic were drained by the time she reached him.

She frowned, looking out over her peers. They seemed so defeated and helpless in the gloom of the hall. Even Ewan and Azalaïs, who sat near the end of one of the long tables, smiling grimly as Rose passed. Delia too, as she trotted up to her wife's side, silently checking Briony for any injury. But the sight only kindled the fierce heat alight in Rose's veins.

'We can't just cower in here.'

Woodstone turned slowly, a sneer already on his lips. 'I don't recall asking *your* opinion, Thenlif. For all we know, *you* summoned these beasts.'

Rose's jaw snapped shut. Of course he'd sell her out so easily. His precious tournament had been ruined and his fragile pride was bruised – there was nothing left to save her from his cruel whim. Sylvie stepped forward to shield her in an instant, as if those gathered might descend on her as surely as the horde outside. The Mamsella and Troidilis eyed her curiously, while Briony and Delia looked chagrined, and Ewan and Azalaïs crept closer to their group.

'You're a necromancer?' Mamsella de Prevath said finally.

Rose's tongue lay thick and heavy, caught on the edge of truth. It would be so easy to fall back on old lies. To bury this part of herself behind subterfuge and guile, as she always had. Yet she found she had no strength left to care.

'Yes, but this wasn't me.' She shook her head.

Troidilis pushed past Woodstone before he could protest. 'But you *can* fight these undead?'

Rose flinched at the intensity of their tone. She shouldn't have been surprised, she supposed. Troidilis had always been pragmatic above all else, and they recognized, perhaps, that Rose was the best weapon in their arsenal.

'If I can take out the necromancer controlling them, the spell should unravel. But I'll need a distraction to get to him.'

A slow smile spread across Troidilis's lips. 'What did you have in mind?'

'They're an undead horde attacking a campus full of magical dangers – I say we let them come up against a few.'

'Such as?'

'The College of Untamed Arts has enough alchemical solutions stored up to burn through this horde twice over.' Rose shrugged before turning to Delia and signing quickly. 'And we could unleash the books on them.'

The librarian frowned. 'They'd start a frenzy at this hour. We'll never get them back inside and ordered, or—'

'That's the point,' Rose cut across her with quick gestures. 'Let them cause a bit of a fuss for once.'

Delia tugged at the ends of her short lavender hair. But finally, resignation flickered through her eyes and she nodded.

'And, Briony –' Rose's gaze slid to the professor as another thought occurred to her – 'can you release the carnivorous *convallaria* and the *solanaceae*?'

The professor's tawny skin paled as her eyes widened. 'That's quite a risk, Rose.'

'More so than letting undead run rampant, Professor?' Sylvie quirked an eyebrow.

'No.' She nodded weakly. 'You're right.'

Sharing a glance, Briony and Delia leaned in for a quick kiss before casting two glimmering portals and stepping through to their respective domains. Rose gave a short nod before turning back to the others, who all watched her expectantly.

'And what are the rest of us to do?' asked Ewan.

The Mamsella drew herself up to full height. 'We fight.'

'You cannot ask the student body to fight a hopeless battle,' Woodstone all but whined, still desperate to hold some shred of command over this situation.

But Rose had no patience for him, and no threat hung over her to dull the sharp words that bit at her tongue. 'We're students at the most prestigious magical academy in the empire, *Chancellor*. If a few undead is all it takes to render us useless, then we're hardly deserving of the title, are we?'

Woodstone's lips thinned, his dull eyes fixed on Rose with unfettered hatred. But there was one value that Dunhollow had instilled in all of them. Not valour or anything so sentimental as loyalty, but pride. And every student here would rather die upon their sword than admit to the cracks in their shields.

Rose gritted her teeth. It wasn't kind or pretty pulling at that fragile cord. But it was what worked, and it snapped all too easily beneath her words. Even now, some students circled closer to them – the defeat in their eyes replaced by indignation. Every single one of them was drawn by the need to prove they held no weakness.

'I will gather the third- and fourth-years willing to fight and tell Saoloris to fetch supplies from the alchemy wing.' Troidilis's hawkish eyes slid towards Woodstone with no small amount of disdain. 'The first- and second-years can stay here with you, Chancellor.'

In spite of everything, a cruel smile tugged at Rose's lips. Clearly, she wasn't the only one who saw straight through to Woodstone's craven centre. But she shook the thought away, eyeing the others gathered.

'Troidilis, can you and the Mamsella keep the horde's focus in the courtyard? Hold the line there, while Ewan and Azalaïs evacuate everyone who didn't make it out of the dorms back here.'

'Caring for the weak and defenceless, Thenlif?' Ewan's blue eyes danced with wry amusement. 'I'm almost impressed.'

'I aim to please,' she said drily. 'Now go.'

'And be safe!' Sylvie added.

Mamsella de Prevath gave a short nod. 'We'll make sure that they are. The people of Arbelis do not surrender easily.'

With that, she, Azalaïs and Ewan turned for the great doors at the front of the hall, a small crowd of students following them. But Troidilis hesitated, eyeing Rose with something akin to . . . respect.

Rose squirmed under their gaze. 'You don't have to pretend to care for my safety, Professor. I'll be fine.'

'I'm sure you will.' Their lips quirked. 'Just don't hold back, Thenlif. You've done that for far too long already.'

Before Rose could respond, they turned and swept off with the others, leaving her to stare after them in utter shock. After a moment, Callum huffed a small laugh.

'You know, dal, I almost think that was a compliment.'

'As close to one as they'll ever give, anyway.' Sylvie shrugged. 'Now where are we going?'

'Back to the archives.' Rose's jaw clenched. 'Once the others distract the horde, we can slip through to the entrance. Just stick close out there – both of you.'

Sylvie's eyes softened and she leaned in to catch Rose in a quick kiss. 'We're not going anywhere.'

Fierce, desperate longing took hold in Rose's heart as she pulled away from Sylvie and embraced Callum in turn: to keep them both safe and whole, even if it cost her the one thing that was hers to bargain in all this – her life.

47. Two Sisters

The night air greeted them coolly as Sylvie, Rose and Callum burst out of the main hall. Spells still shot and ricocheted off the pillared colonnade and the din of shuffling undead footsteps remained, but they were no longer punctuated by helpless screams.

Instead, shouts and cries echoed through the courtyard, fluttering on the wings of ruthless, sleep-deprived books as they whizzed and darted through the fray. Some chomped down on any bit of flesh or bone they could find while others dived in a dizzying array around the muddled horde – screeching obscenities and taunts that would make even the dead blush.

On the other side of the courtyard, venomous vines and insidiously singing blooms crept towards them from the greenhouse. Ensnaring any undead in their lethal grasp, they allowed Troidilis and their sorcerers to cut them down with deft ease while Saoloris lobbed explosives at them. It wouldn't kill them, but it would slow them down well enough.

A roar drew Rose's gaze to the centre of the green as Mamsella de Prevath wrapped herself in root and thorn, her cerulean eyes aglow, until her form was more bark and branch than flesh – a towering, living embodiment of the forest as she barrelled through the undead with ease.

Two figures darted through the chaos behind the Mamsella, rallying straggling students to safety before they ducked into the nearest dorm hall. Unease pricked at Rose as she watched Azalaïs and Ewan disappear, but she shoved it aside. She couldn't help them now – not while Ionas still lived.

'Come on.' She tugged at Sylvie and Callum, leading them towards the School of Magical Theory.

'Why are we going back to the archives?' Sylvie panted as they came to a stop before the trapdoor, slinging a blast of ice at a nearby corpse.

Rose dived around the grasping venomous plants. 'I saw visions of Ionas in my fears, welcoming this horde. I think we're still bound in some way.'

Callum grunted as he dodged out of the grasp of a half-rotted skeleton. 'Then how do we get you unbound, dal?'

Rose didn't answer immediately, crouching to lift the metal door, which opened with a great creak, before she glanced back up at Callum and Sylvie. 'We cut the snake off at the head.'

Without waiting for their response, Rose jumped through the hatch. The wooden stairs creaked as she landed on them, the only thing, perhaps, that survived her flames. Her vision swam for a moment as her eyes adjusted to the dim light, and she buried her nose in the crook of her arm, swallowing a gag.

The rancid scents of scorched wood and festering decay pierced her nostrils, burning in her lungs with a cloying weight. Above, the exposed beams hung like a burnt rib-cage of some strange corpse, ash sprinkling Rose's hair. She coughed, waving a hand in front of her face as Sylvie and Callum followed her descent.

Yet something stirred in those cursed tunnels beyond the scars of her rage. Muttering voices and the echo of magic that lingered in the air. It drew Rose forth towards the myriad of hollow doorways that lined the corridor ahead like holes in a honeycomb. But one at the very end of the hall flickered with the soft glow of flame. It was Ionas – it *had* to be.

Rose glanced back at Sylvie and Callum before moving towards the light. Yet she couldn't shake the feeling that she was a fly following the spider to the very centre of its web, willingly walking herself right into the trap that spelled her own end.

Still, she couldn't just leave him to his grotesque machinations — she had to face him. For Fen. For Soren. For every bit of carnage Ionas had wrought from her stolen power. And maybe, in the end, for herself too. Even if her life were the cost of such courage.

For it was clear to Rose now that she was at the centre of all of it — the knot that held together this tangled tapestry Ionas wove. Her hubris had awoken him, her anger had freed him, and her magic now bolstered his strength. If her life was the thing that would bring it all crashing down around him, then she would pay that price in an instant.

Finally, she rounded the crumbling doorway and stilled in her tracks. Soren stood before a great altar, his umber skin a shade paler and his cheeks a bit more gaunt, as if Ionas's presence had hollowed out more than just his mind. But it was the milky white of his eyes that made Rose's skin crawl. Proof that not a shred of him was left behind that gaze.

'Ah, Rosera.' Ionas gave a soft sigh, as if he'd been waiting for her to show up for a cup of telka and a chat. 'I should've known you'd break your way out of that trap.'

Her jaw tightened. He sounded so calm, so unconcerned with the carnage that raged above. 'Should've made a better trap then.'

'I was only trying to keep you out of harm's way.' He clicked his tongue. 'And yet here you are. Come for our final confrontation, I'm sure. But there's no need for us to fight. You wouldn't want to hurt your father, after all.'

Suddenly, Ionas's gaze faded back to the deep brown of Soren's. Realization flickered there for a moment — understanding bound in the weary burden of grief and anguish — and then his eyes slid to Rose as his face fell.

'Rose, you have to stop him; he'll—'

Soren's words died in a shattering crack as his neck twisted at an unholy angle. A scream wrenched from Rose's lips as he cried out, his bones snapping and joints popping as Ionas jerked him beneath his sadistic grasp.

'Stop!' Rose lurched forward. 'Leave him alone.'

White hollowed out Soren's gaze once more as Ionas chuckled, rolling his neck from side to side. 'That I can't do, I'm afraid. But he is fascinating, isn't he? He was the first to open my prison, you know. Chasing after lost love, just like you.' Ionas hummed. 'For sixty years in that prison, there was simply nothing. No time, no fear, no life or death. Until your dear Soren prised it open and stole one of the very foundations that held it in place, and suddenly I knew every agonizing minute of it. Three decades, I remained trapped there, slowly losing all sense of even my own mind. And then, through that void, there was you.'

Rose's lips curled in a sneer, but she said nothing. Her eyes flashed to Sylvie and Callum, who lingered behind her just beyond the doorway. Perhaps if she could keep Ionas talking, she could find a way to get them out of here alive.

Ionas stepped closer to her. 'You gave me hope, Rose; you gave me a connection to this world I'd long thought lost. And when you reached out again, seeking your lost friend with a spell I myself had crafted, well, I couldn't resist. I stayed with you, seeing light and life again for the first time in so long.'

'You *used* her.' Callum's voice rumbled over Rose's shoulder, low and filled with ire.

'Just as I was used, yes.' Ionas waved a hand blithely. 'How do you think I ended up in that prison in the first place? Because our illustrious emperor sought a way to defy death and my soul was the price he was willing to pay to get it.'

'Of course. You're the victim,' Rose scoffed.

'Victim, villain.' A sickening smile spread across Ionas's lips. 'The world makes monsters of us all, eventually. As you well know.'

'No, *you* turned me into a monster.' She closed in on him, a furious pulse pounding in her ears. '*You* murdered innocents by my hand. I only wanted my friend back.'

Ionas nodded, unfazed by her fury. 'I told you we were the same. All my research, every spell and sacrifice, it was to return my daughter, Aelra, to me. But, as you found with your Fen, my magic only led to that hideous space between life and death, never to true revival.'

Aelra. A gasp slipped past Rose's lips, stirred by the briefest sting of pity. The name in his notes. Her stomach twisted, her eyes roving over him as if he were some dark reflection of herself. Because whatever he was now, he had once been no worse than her – a fool driven by love. She winced. And what a cruel thing love was to keep them reaching across this chasm, ever hopeful, even as they fell to their doom.

'The emperor preyed upon my grief, pushing me to seek a way past those barriers by binding Life and Death within it.' Ionas turned away from her. 'But they did not care to be trifled with and they shattered their bonds with their realms, caging me alongside them in that wretched prison.'

Rose frowned. 'Them?'

'Reath and Bearath – the spirits of life and death,' he mused, toying with the flame of one of the sconces that hung on the rough-hewn walls. 'Sisters bound in their endless dance, never to meet, yet one always follows the other. I summoned and caged them, and they trapped me for that crime until Soren here came crashing through that barrier.'

How could that be? Rose's breath caught in her throat. Spirits had been gone from this world for centuries. And even then, they weren't like ghosts or the undead. They were entities of pure magic, moulded by the concepts and beliefs of the mortal world and more like gods in their power; they couldn't simply be bound to a necromancer's whim. Not least those of Life and Death.

'Reath – Life – saw her chance at escape and took it, latching on to him. What you so blithely call Soren's curse was nothing more than Life herself clinging to him – strengthening him.' Ionas straightened, his gaze keen as it fell back upon Rose. 'And you too.'

Rose blinked, stumbling back. 'No. That's not possible.'

'Oh yes, my dear.' He chuckled. 'When your mother bound what she assumed was simple necromancy, why do you think it was that life was the only magic that transcended her curse? Because you grew in Reath's shadow – you touched the original source. And then you brought her back to me.'

Rose's heart hammered against the cage of her ribs. Had she ever truly mattered in all of this then? Or had these ancient shreds of magic and myth used her just as the emperor had done with Ionas, nothing more than vessels for another's purpose? Patterns of cruelty and pride that echoed again and again over time, always sacrificing those beneath them upon their poisoned pyre.

Tears pricked at Rose's eyes, but she swallowed hard against them. 'And now you're using her to achieve immortal life yourself? How are you any different from the emperor who used you?'

'All I wanted was my daughter,' Ionas snapped, as if his patience hung by a frayed thread. 'Once, I would have taken the grace of death in a heartbeat to join her, but you changed that, Rose. You brought Life back to me, and now her power will ensure I never meet Death again. That only *I* will control that delicate thread.'

No. Rose's chest squeezed at the thought. 'Please, you can't.'

She almost thought he would laugh. Scold her for begging, perhaps. But Ionas looked solemn now. He was so serene in his surety that it dulled his malice as he bowed his head.

'For what it's worth, I am sorry for what comes next.'

With a flick of his wrist, silvery tendrils shot forth, stretching past Rose to coil around Sylvie and Callum with a caustic grip. They cried out as one as Ionas's magic bit into their skin, binding them with his power, bringing them to their knees. Rose's source was at her fingertips in an instant, but Ionas's magic tightened around their throats as she raised her hand.

'Ah, ah. Careful, Rosera.' His shrill voice stilled her in her tracks. 'I'm not some clueless barman playing around with alchemy he doesn't understand. One false move and I could snip away the lives of everyone you love.'

Her heart skipped a beat as the silver tendrils coiled around Callum and Sylvie's mouths, their eyes wide and pleading, desperate for her to save them. But she couldn't move. She could barely even breathe with the keen sting of fear piercing her every thought. Already the colour was fading from their cheeks, their lives at the mercy of his malice.

Rose's breath caught in her throat, her gaze flitting back to Ionas. He would never stop, no matter how many lives he took. Their souls would bolster the strength of his magic and their bones would build his craven throne. And she couldn't let that happen.

In another time – another life, perhaps – she might have felt pity for him. One caged bird crying out to another from behind their bars. But Ionas was no songbird trapped to put on a beautiful show. He was a serpent, confined only to keep his venom at bay.

Rose's jaw clenched tight. Perhaps something broke him within that prison, making him grasp greedily at any shred of life. Perhaps he had always been that way deep down, his love overshadowed by a craving for power and influence, like so many others in this wretched empire.

But it mattered little now. She wouldn't let him bind her power to that purpose, and she couldn't condemn those she loved to whatever fate he would bring upon them. Whatever hold Life had on Rose was a tether that went both ways. It had always bound her, but maybe she could set it free. One final thread to cut, in the end.

'Take me instead.' The words fell numbly from her lips, spurring muffled noises of protest from Sylvie and Callum that Rose ignored. 'You said yourself that my magic was spurred by Reath. If you want control over all life, then you'll need me, not them.'

Ionas's eyes narrowed for a moment as he considered her. 'Very well,' he said finally. 'Come here.'

Stepping closer to Ionas, she reached for him. Tears burned at her eyes as she searched that milky-white gaze for any hint of Soren, though she found none. Ionas flinched at her touch but didn't pull away. Whether it was shock or surprise that held him as she cupped his face in her palms, Rose couldn't say. She didn't care now.

Instead, she glanced back at Sylvie and Callum one last time, so many unspoken words still hanging between them, lost to the memory of a life they would never have. But they would survive – as would Soren.

'I'm sorry,' Rose whispered, the words drenched in such bitter grief as she tightened her grip and let her magic fly freely.

'No!' Ionas's cry shattered the air, but it was too late.

Silver tendrils coiled out of Rose's palms, latching into Ionas's skin – leaching away that life he'd stolen. Blistering heat pulsed into her veins, yet it didn't burn her. No flame could touch her now, sizzling to little more than smoke beneath the weight of her power.

But it was too much. It seared behind her eyes, a blinding light that made Rose's head spin. Still, she couldn't let go now – not when she was so close.

Ionas, however, would not release his hold on life so easily, his face twisted in a hideous snarl as he pressed a cruel hand to Rose's chest. Her silver flame buckled and wavered beneath his rage, turning as dark as a moonless night. Until, all at once, it shattered, splintering into a shadowed shard that shot straight through Rose's heart.

48. Every Day Since

A soft light burgeoned behind Rose's eyelids. Cool and dim, but steady all the same, it drew her from the dregs of shadow as she blinked awake. Rough grey stones greeted her first, slick with moisture and decay. Cobwebs clung to the corners, their gossamer strands gleaming in the dim light like spun silver.

Rose's lungs burned beneath the thick scents of damp earth and rot, her head spinning as she sat up. Had she died? The thought twisted within her as her eyes roved over the dank chamber veiled in such darkness and despair. Shadows danced upon the walls, their movements erratic and frenzied, as if they were alive with insidious intent.

No. Rose swallowed hard. This wasn't death – it was a prison. *Ionas's prison.*

Her heart took up a rapid pace in her chest. But if she were here, that meant Ionas was still back in the archives – alone with Sylvie and Callum. And Soren. *No.* She scrambled to her feet. She had to find a way back.

Her eyes roved desperately over the space. It was cold and cruel, just like Ionas himself. And yet, amid the loneliness and anguish that lingered deep within these stones, there was a certain beauty. A haunting elegance that transcended the boundaries of life and death.

Rose's gaze slid to the centre of the room, where the soft glow of a shimmering cloud fell upon her: a cold light, like that of a dying star, but still rippling with raw, untamed power. She inched towards it, squinting as it quivered and twisted upon the air.

It was a deep midnight blue threaded through with glints of silver – like starlight mapped across the night sky. So serene amid this darkness. So beautiful.

'Rose?'

The voice shattered Rose's thoughts – weak and breathless but so familiar all the same. Her heart leapt as she turned to meet it, her breath coiled in her chest.

'Fen?'

His face lit up at the sight of her, his eyes sparking from behind his glasses. But Rose didn't run to greet him this time – her heart was too weary to watch him disappear again beneath a crumbling facade. Still, his smile seemed real. So warm and bright amid this darkness that encroached upon them.

But he was weaker, somehow. Rose's eyes narrowed at the hollow curve of his gaunt cheeks and the ashen tinge to his russet skin. Even his raven hair had lost its lustre. She chewed the inside of her lip. Was this another of Ionas's tricks?

'You came back,' Fen whispered, startling her.

'Back? I – I don't understand.'

'I've been here all along. Waiting.'

Rose's stomach turned as she backed away. 'No. I-it was just Ionas masquerading.' *Wasn't it?*

'Not at first.' Fen took a step closer to her. 'Your spell worked. But after Ionas saw our reunion, that's when he stole my form – used it to trick you.'

'And how do I know that's not what's happening now?'

'You don't.' Fen's shoulders sagged, his eyes broken beneath the weight of Rose's mistrust. 'But I promise it's not. I don't want anything from you, Rose. Not life, not freedom – not even love. Not if it will drag you down here with me.'

Rose's heart fluttered in her chest. It sounded like something Fen would say. But then, so had Ionas's last mockery of him, and she wouldn't be so easily fooled again. Reaching out with her source, she was surprised when silver tendrils still spilled out of her trembling fingers.

Somehow, she'd imagined life would have left her – fled from Rose's failing form as she was doomed to face her fate. Yet here it was, warm and wistful as it curled around Fen's skin, searching his essence for any shadow of Ionas. But all she found was him. Weary and unsteady but utterly real.

'It's really you.' Her voice cracked as she launched herself into his arms, a broken sob wrenching from her chest.

'It's me.' He pulled her closer with a muffled breath. 'I'm here.'

After a long moment, Rose pulled away, her eyes flicking over his wan features once more. 'This place.' She stroked a hand over the hollow of his cheek. 'It's killing you, isn't it?'

'I'm already dead, Rose.' Fen grimaced. 'But if I stay here, eventually it will eat away at me. *She's* been keeping the worst of it at bay.'

'She?'

He jerked his chin towards the midnight cloud behind her. 'Bearath – Death.'

'Ionas said she was trapped, but I didn't think . . .' Rose trailed off, reaching out to touch the swirling threads. 'She's beautiful.'

She'd expected Death to be cold and draining. Or a malevolent force of grim fate. But the fragment before her was none of those things. Weakened and bound by constraints woven by a craven hand but still strong. And utterly inevitable.

She was as steady and sure as stone, yet warm and kind, like sun-stained sands shifting beneath her feet. And there was a fire within. A spark of life kindling in her broken depths – desperately, greedily. And it echoed now in Rose's own heart, begging for release.

For freedom.

'She's been . . . protecting me somehow.' Fen's voice made Rose jump. 'She said I reminded her of someone she used to know.'

Rose turned back to him, one eyebrow raised. 'Who would Death know?'

'Everyone, eventually.' He shrugged. 'But she was mortal once, and she still holds that in her heart.'

Rose's eyes flicked back to the starlit shadow. Bearath and Reath, Ionas had called them. *Sisters.* She'd thought he was simply being poetic. After all, life and death were so vast in concept that it was hard to think of them once being contained by mere fragile flesh.

And yet, what could possibly *be* more mortal? Did not every soul bear the burden of one and the promise of the other? It was almost tragic seeing what she'd been reduced to by Ionas's machinations. Stripped bare of her power and caged with no hope of release. And that, at least, Rose could understand all too well.

'She's been trapped,' she whispered. 'All this time.'

Fen nodded. 'She needs to be freed. *You* can free her.'

'And you?' Rose's throat tightened as she turned back to him. 'What will happen to you if I do?'

Fen's gaze fell, his throat bobbing weakly. 'Rose . . .'

Her breath coiled in her chest. She knew the truth that would fall from his lips already and how it would pierce her heart more surely than any blade. But it couldn't stop the desperate whisper as it slipped from her tongue.

'Come with me.'

'No, Rose.' Fen shook his head. 'I can't.'

'Yes, you can.' She clutched his hands between her own. 'I'm stronger now. I can get you out of here – we can defeat Ionas together.'

But Fen only pulled her closer, cupping her chin between his palms as he tugged her gaze up to meet his. Glassy and weak, his eyes filled with such painful longing that it nearly tore Rose's heart in two. Yet he didn't beg or plead. He only smiled sadly. And somehow, that was so much worse.

'I loved you till the day I died,' he whispered, tears spilling down his cheeks. 'I will love you for every moment you live on without me, and for aeons after you join me in death. But I can't leave here any more than you can stay.'

'Please.' Rose trembled against his touch. 'I can't lose anyone else.'

'Then don't.' His fingers tightened around her face ever so gently. 'Fight.'

'I can't.'

'You *can*.'

'Not if it means losing you.' The words fell from her lips, cracked and broken beneath the weight of tears. 'I can't bear it again.'

Fen pressed his forehead to Rose's before peppering kisses along her brow. Soft soothing reminders meant to steel her courage and send her back into the embrace of life. But all they did was tear ever further into her heart. Finally, he pulled back, his brown eyes meeting hazel in the agonizing silence held between them.

'Let it go,' he whispered, stroking tears away from Rose's cheek. 'Whatever guilt you're still clinging to, you don't need it. I was happy in death – I was at peace. And, one day, after you've gone out and lived, truly lived, I'll be there, waiting for you with a bottle of wine to hear all about it. So hold on to your love, Rose, but let me go. Please.'

Rose stared up into those eyes she knew so well, wordlessly begging Fen to change his mind. To choose life. Her heart skipped a beat. To choose *her*. But she knew he wouldn't.

Because he'd chosen himself – his happiness. His peace. And she couldn't wrench that away from him again.

Instead, she only nodded, wiping the tears from her eyes as she closed the distance between them and pressed her lips softly to his. Fen stiffened beneath her for a moment, but then he melted, cupping Rose's face with aching tenderness as he sank into her kiss.

And, etched into each second of it, was everything that still hung between them. Every aching pain that had torn through Rose's heart, leaving bloodied scars in its wake. Every goodbye they never got to say – every shred of life and laughter and love that they would never get to share with one another. All of it fell to the heat of their embrace. Unspoken, yet known all the same.

Until, finally – *finally* – with bitter resignation, Rose pulled away. She searched the warmth of Fen's eyes, letting them hold her steady for just that little bit longer above the abyss she was about to launch herself into.

'I love you too,' she whispered, setting that last truth free between them. 'I always will.'

Aching, bittersweet joy flashed through Fen's eyes before it dimmed to resignation. He pulled away from her, but held on to her hand. One last moment of connection even he seemed reluctant to release.

Finally, he nodded. 'Go, please.'

Gritting her teeth, Rose pulled away from him with such sorrow that it nearly broke her. She didn't know how she would free Bearath – if she even could. But if this pulsing grief in her heart could've grown wings, it would've carried them to freedom all on its own. Or to some kinder fate altogether.

Wiping away her tears, she turned back to the pulsing shadow of death and stretched out a trembling hand. It met her almost eagerly but it did not cool the fire that had taken root within her. Instead, it stoked those flames with a hand that had clearly known such pain – a soul that had once known the ravenous abyss of grief.

Oh, child. Bearath's voice filled Rose's mind with such staggering warmth. *Just hold on a little longer.*

Before Rose could blink, the world around them swirled and shifted. Desperately, she turned to catch one last glimpse of Fen – an easy smile pulling at his lips as the darkness around him shattered and he simply faded away. Lost to her once more.

Tears streamed down Rose's cheeks as Death carried her away from Fen's embrace and back to the dank corridors of the archive, where life bloomed in her lungs once more. Back to Ionas's cruelty and Sylvie and Callum's cries as his magic drained their lives away. Back to the pulsing heat of fury as it razed through Rose's veins, fuelled by the gnawing grief in her heart.

Bearath stirred within Rose's mind – not caustic and cloying, as Ionas had been, but a bolstering strength for her weary veins, a balm to the haggard beat of her heart. The fire to her fight. For the scent of death was gentle, her touch warm and her hold tinged with kindness. But her wrath was a dreadful thing to behold. And so too was Rose's.

Ionas turned on her with a snarl, his magic coiling around her. But it slipped away from Rose all too easily. The insidious tendrils could no longer find purchase in her.

For she was beyond the fear that held him tight in its poisonous grasp. With death on the wings of her fury and life pulsing through her veins, she was beyond *him*. Source fled out of her in a searing torrent – life, flame and something entirely Rose's own. Pure unadulterated energy that scorched the ground beneath her feet, tearing apart the very seams of the earth.

It slammed into Ionas with a shattering crack, wreathing him in starlit shadow, mingling with the silver tendrils that poured out of him in turn. Life and Death turned upon their captor, their vengeance wrought in the heat of their fury.

Silent, useless prayers splintered Rose's mind, pleading for Soren to be all right. For whatever thread of life that bound them still to shield him from the onslaught. Yet Rose could no longer see him behind the glow of silver flame, nor the shadow of death. She couldn't hear Sylvie and Callum's cries or Ionas's screams. There was simply nothing beyond the raging beat of her heart and the fires of life burning in her lungs as her own mind buckled and the world around her faded away.

49. Live

In the space between life and death, there was only darkness. Not cruel or frightening – desperate to drag Rose into some cold, ravenous abyss of shadow – it simply hung around her, warm and safe. Her limbs lay heavy and numb, her pulse thudding in her ears, yet she'd never felt more at peace.

Everything had slipped away from her. Fear. Worry. Pain. A touch of mercy in the echoes of Bearath's wrath as she led Rose softly to her end.

But death was not for her.

A dim light pulsed behind her eyes, distant and dull at first, then furiously bright. Rose gasped, breath searing through her lungs as hands curled around her shoulders. Faintly, she could hear someone calling her name, but it faded to the beating of her heart as it raged against her ribs.

Thoughts flickered through her mind like fleeing shadows, leaving her barren in their wake. Around her, colours sharpened and began to take shape. Slowly, at first. Then all at once like a fog swept away with the breeze.

Beyond her, rolling verdant hills met a violet sea, a star-stained sky draped overhead like a shimmering curtain. Rose blinked against a silver sun, weakly holding a hand up to its pale light. But no warmth fell upon her skin, and no ground stood beneath her feet.

It was strange, she thought, like peering into another realm, even as the cold stone floor pressed at her back. As if her body were anchored in one world, while her spirit yearned to soar beyond the confines of her broken flesh. To touch death, even as life raged desperately against that fate.

And something in it tethered her here. Callum's gentle touch as his hands skirted over Rose's skin. Sylvie's voice ringing in her ears. Fen's smile flashing across her memory. Pieces of her heart and soul that rooted her to this place, drawing her back from that ledge on only the ghost of a hope.

Not yet.
Let me go.
Come back.
LIVE.

50. What We Fear Most

The sky held in a grey silence. Damp earth lay beneath Rose's feet, moss-laden and covered in clover. Their delicate leaves danced and shivered as her tears fell upon them, rolling on to the soil beneath. There was little beyond memory here, nothing more than this paltry stone to mark his life.

It stared back at her, darkened and dour beneath the gentle mist of rain that drizzled upon it. Rose swallowed hard. All the many parts of him that had lived and loved – that *she'd* loved – had gone in the blink of an eye. His choice had been death, but hers had been life.

And she knew now that she wanted more from it than these broken shards of pain and anguish. More than the fear that had once bound her and the sorrow that had driven her. She wanted to live well. And she could never do that here.

Rose sniffled, laying her hand upon the top of the stone. 'Goodbye, Fen.'

Her voice fell upon the wind as no more than a whisper, swept away from Rose just as Fen had been. She hoped it reached him, somehow. That it curled around his ear as he enjoyed his peace and made him smile even from worlds away. That he knew Rose would never forget him, no matter how long they were apart.

Wiping away her tears, Rose straightened with a shaky breath. Fen's courtyard was still quiet at this hour – miraculously free of the debris and corpses that littered the rest of campus. Two days on and even non-stop cleaning spells couldn't get the stench of decay out of the stones.

Though the death toll hadn't been as high as she'd feared, the pall of it still hung over Dunhollow. By some stroke of luck, Azalaïs and Ewan had managed to save more than Rose might have counted on, and those they hadn't been able to had met a quick end at the Mamsella's hands. By all accounts, it was the library books that had done the most damage, though not to the students, luckily.

But it didn't matter now. The buildings they could mend, but the lives lost? Not so easily. Nor the ones that remained, for that matter. Rose shuddered and then jumped as leaves crinkled behind her.

'Thought I might find you here.'

She whirled to find Soren beaming down at her, his brown eyes bright behind the sway of his own mind once more. All at once, every foul thought and dreadful whisper at the back of her mind vanished, chased away by the warmth of his smile.

'Soren!' Rose launched herself into his arms at full tilt, making him stumble back. But she faltered as he winced. 'You should still be in the infirmary.'

'Don't worry.' His chest rumbled with soft laughter as he kissed the top of her head. 'They released me.'

Rose nodded, curling herself further into his sweater. It had been touch-and-go for a while there. Sylvie and Callum had dragged both her and Soren from the depths of the archives to the overcrowded infirmary. She'd woken not long after, but he'd remained ashen and feverish – barely conscious for over a day before his body came back to him.

A smile ghosted over Rose's lips. She still wasn't sure how he'd survived exactly, but her best guess was that it was Reath. One final 'thank you' for carrying her all these years, perhaps, before she finally graced him with the gift of death.

Pulling back, Rose's eyes roved over Soren's frame. If she

squinted a bit, he almost looked his age now. Still quite young for just past fifty, but his ink-black twists were now threaded through with grey and crow's feet had taken up residence around his kind eyes. His curse had been broken – his life was finally his own at last.

And something of that hung about him now. Something in the warm tilt of his smile or the loosened collar of the wrinkled white blouse tucked beneath his russet sweater. Peace, she thought. Or perhaps just the swell of freedom. Either way, it suited him.

'Well,' Rose said finally, 'I'm glad you're feeling better.'

'Much.' Soren's smile widened, eyes flicking about the alcove. 'Where are Sylvie and Callum? I thought they'd be here with you.'

Rose shrugged, dropping Soren's gaze. 'I needed to do this alone.'

It hadn't been terribly difficult to slip away. Though Sylvie had been reluctant to let Rose out of her sight in the last day, for this she'd relented. Or she would've if Rose hadn't elected to sneak out before eight o'clock, when waking Sylvie would have been the greater sin than leaving her behind.

Callum had shot her a knowing look as she'd left, but he, of all people, was content to let her keep her secrets. Rose chewed the inside of her lip. Deep down, she knew they'd understand. While she was overjoyed that they'd made it through Ionas's attack safe and sound, part of her couldn't yet celebrate everything she'd saved beneath the shadow of what she'd lost.

'Are you all right?' Soren's voice made Rose jump as she lifted her eyes to meet his.

'I will be. Given time.' She forced a wan smile, stepping back from his embrace. 'What about you? After everything with Ionas, well, I'm here if you need to talk.'

Soren sighed, sinking on to the damp seat of one of the benches. 'Mercifully, I don't remember much. But I know something of what I did – what I wrought upon this place.'

'It wasn't you.' Rose sat beside him, taking his hands in hers.

A ghost of a smile flickered across his scarred lips. 'No more than any of Ionas's deeds were your own. But the burden of it still weighs heavy, even so.'

'I know.' Rose nodded, her voice small.

Silence settled between them. Worn and familiar, there was a comfort to its steady beat, broken only by the pattering of rain against golden leaves and the quiet rhythm of their own breaths. Until, finally, Soren shifted.

'Fiorella said Woodstone told everyone about your necromancy.' His fingers tightened around Rose's. 'Bastard.'

But Rose only sighed. 'Is it strange that I feel relieved? Not that it was him who did it or the circumstances of how it came out, just that it's no longer mine alone – another fear I can let go of, in the end.'

'You're not worried at all?' Soren's brow furrowed. 'What if he calls in the capital inquisitors?'

'Oh, I expect he will soon.' Rose shrugged. 'The only reason he's delayed is because he's too busy fielding letters from enraged parents and trying to save face. But, according to the Aratis, the empress has known about my necromancy all along. I'm sure she'll have Woodstone collect me soon so she can turn me into her pet monster, just as her forefather did to Ionas. The more things change and all that.'

The empress would likely even see it as a kindness. Offering her a gilded prison rather than a forgotten cell. Lauded and pampered but caged all the same – bound to the vapid whims of another who simply wanted to cheat death. Just like Ionas. But Rose was done languishing in any prison imposed by another, and any hand that tried to tame her now would find itself burned.

'And that doesn't scare you?'

She sighed deeply, measuring her words before she answered. 'I've seen what fear does when we don't grow past it. My mother, so afraid of losing control that she tormented everyone else to keep it. Woodstone, so frightened of losing his reputation that he nearly sentenced all of us to death for it. Even Ionas, so caught up in trying to undo death that he brought it upon himself. But I've been scared of myself for far too long – terrified of living with blood on my hands and all the mistakes I've made. In the end, it was life itself that I feared. And I can't any more.'

Soren fell silent for a long moment before he lifted his gaze. 'You're leaving again, aren't you?'

All Rose could offer him was a sad smile, squeezing his hand gently. He wouldn't understand – not fully. But she had to go all the same.

'I can't stay.' She shook her head. 'I never should have come back, really. But I had to prove I could, I suppose.'

Tears welled in his eyes. 'And now?'

Rose's heart cracked beneath the weight of his gaze. Gods, she wished he could come with her. That they could set out together once more and enjoy everything the world had to offer. But Soren's life was finally his own again – she couldn't ask him to join her in going on the run. Even if she was running towards something just as much as she was running from it.

'Now we simply get to be.'

'We?' he echoed. 'Sylvie and Callum are going with you then?'

Rose nodded, tears of her own burning against her eyes. For all her sins, they still longed to be at her side. And it frightened her somewhat if she was honest. Because once she ran, she could never come back, and if they bound themselves to her now, neither could they.

Her heart skipped a beat. What if in a year's time they grew to hate her, or they all simply drifted apart? Would they regret the fate she'd doomed them to? *No.* Rose shook the thought away. She'd made her choice, and they'd made theirs. There was nothing more she could ask of them. And it was well past time that the world owed them a little peace – whatever that might look like.

'When do you leave?'

'Tonight.' She swallowed the lump in her throat. 'And don't ask me where; we don't know yet.'

She wouldn't tell him even if she did. It seemed cruel, but she knew he would try to follow her. To the ends of the world and back – to the edge of death itself. As any good parent would. But she couldn't ask him to sacrifice any more for her.

'So soon?' Soren's voice was choked but he collected himself quickly. 'Then I suppose I should wish you well.'

'This isn't goodbye.' Rose wrapped her arms around his waist. 'One day, I'll find you again. And until then I'll write.'

Soren chuckled against her, thick hot tears splashing down on to Rose's forehead. 'You'd better.'

Epilogue

The little village of Hova was not a place that asked questions. Tucked away on the Rebel Isle of Eohad, the people here didn't much care for the petty politics of their Na Qisan neighbours. Mostly, they were fishermen, farmers and crafters, whittling away their humble lives in the rugged beauty of the isle, barely taking any note of the travellers and traders that passed through. The perfect place, in short, for three people hiding from the empire's cruel grip.

Though it didn't feel much like hiding any more. Rose sighed, her eyes flicking to the little stone cottage on the other side of the garden. Six months on and their haven had become a home.

Colourful flowers sat beneath the windows of their cottage, framed by hand-painted shutters and climbing vines of ivy. The front door stood out as a shock of sunshine yellow, while the stone wall that surrounded the garden had become little more than a canvas for Sylvie's half-finished murals. Full of laughter, love and light – all the things they'd been denied for so long.

And Rose felt that most out here in her garden, with soil beneath her fingers and all things green and growing surrounding her. Where the wind danced past and the distant rhythm of waves crashed against the shore like a steady heartbeat. Where life and death were held only in the passing seasons – sisters bound in their endless dance but no longer trapped. They flowed gently through Rose as she stretched her hand over one of her struggling melon plants. It was rare for her to use magic these days. Flame to tend their hearth, life to bolster their garden and death to occasionally help the villagers speak with their lost loved ones. But the power no longer burned beneath a searing grip.

Rose released the plant as new blooms sprouted from its stem, wiping her hands on her apron as she stood. Shielding her eyes from the summer sun, she gathered up her basket full of eggs and herbs and made her daily walk down the path for the post. There was something quite peaceful in the steadiness of this routine, her steps measured by the lowing cattle and bleating sheep who grazed upon the red hills carved across the skyline behind her.

As she reached the letterbox, Rose slowed, running her fingers over the painted letters that curled across it, somewhat faded now. *Fen's Rest* – the name they'd chosen for this place. A little piece of him that could share in their peace, even beyond the bonds of death.

With a sad smile, she collected the post and ambled back up the path. Not much today – the local newsletter, a thank-you note from the family she'd held a seance for last week and a piece of parchment tied up with a writhing vine. *From Soren.*

Rose's heart skipped a beat, and she hurried into the cottage, only slowing when she heard a breathy moan cut through the air. Her gaze flew to the bedroom door, a fierce warmth blooming in her core as the sounds of Callum and Sylvie's lovemaking carried out into the kitchen. They'd been bickering and bantering since yesterday – it was only a matter of time before it boiled over to a heated breaking point.

For a moment, Rose considered joining them, but she quickly decided against it. Let them sate whatever hunger they had built with one another. By the sounds of it, they were close to finishing anyway.

She set her basket on the counter and pulled a bottle of dandelion wine and some melon water out of the ice box before grabbing three glasses. Sylvie and Callum would need something to cool down when they were done, and it had been a long hot day in the garden for Rose as well.

Settling into one of the chairs at their tea table with a full glass, she tore into Soren's letter, her eyes scanning his jumbled scrawl. Most of it was just idle musings, though she wrinkled her nose at his update on Woodstone's trial.

When the three of them had disappeared, things had quickly crumbled to dust around the chancellor. Between the disaster that was the Ashwood Tournament and the influx of irate parents demanding he step down, his beloved empress seemed to have abandoned Woodstone. According to Soren, he'd been stripped of his position and put under inquiry; he was due to stand trial before the year was out.

A cruel smile tugged at Rose's lips. She didn't imagine it would go his way. She was just reading the final lines when the bedroom door clicked open. Rose barely even looked up – not until Callum's warm arms wrapped around her shoulders.

'Hello, dal. You didn't want to join us?'

'It sounded like you two were having quite the time of it on your own.' Rose chuckled, tilting her head back to catch his lips in a kiss.

Sylvie snorted as she moved past them, giving Rose a quick peck on the cheek. The pair of them were all sated, languid touches as they moved about the kitchen. Callum, dressed in one of Sylvie's paint-stained robes, reached eagerly for the melon water, pouring himself a generous glass before he plopped down beside Rose and propped his feet on the table. Meanwhile, Sylvie in her misbuttoned sundress reached past him to grab a bowl of olives, munching away as she hopped on to the counter.

After a moment, her eyes dropped to the letter in Rose's hands. 'From Soren?'

'Who else?'

'Mmm. I got one from Ewan yesterday.' She popped another olive into her mouth. 'Apparently their father finally broke from Callum's compulsion; they've been elected his conservator.'

Callum flashed a sly grin, tipping his glass forward as if in cheers before taking a sip. 'Can't say he didn't deserve it.'

'He deserved far worse,' Rose muttered, though there was little heat in it. Imrys and all his poison seemed too far away to truly pierce her any more.

'*Anyway*,' Sylvie said, pointedly glancing between the two of them, 'Ewan sounds happy. They're thinking of using their newly acquired funds to open a law practice in Tol Qilius for those who can't afford it.'

'How generous of them.'

'Half of it is spite,' Sylvie scoffed. 'They know their father would hate it, were he lucid.'

'Of course.' Rose couldn't help the small smirk that bit at her lips. That did sound more like Ewan.

'So,' said Callum, after a moment, 'how's Soren faring?'

'He's finishing up the year at Dunhollow and then transferring to a position at DeVoil with Fiorella. But he sends his love.'

Callum quirked an eyebrow. 'Not coming for a visit then?'

'Not yet.' Rose shook her head. 'He thinks the capital inquisitors might still be watching – he doesn't want to lead them here.'

'They wouldn't dare set foot in Eohad.' Sylvie frowned. 'They couldn't justify breaking the treaty for three paltry criminals.'

Rose fiddled with the browning petals of the wild flowers

at the centre of the table. It was true enough, but their timely escape had only bought them so much freedom. She didn't imagine the empress would be content to let the power to extend her life slip so easily from her grasp. Given the tumultuous history between Eohad and Na Qis, she likely wouldn't risk a direct attack, but Rose was sure that wasn't the only blade in her arsenal. It had been a risk to even tell Soren of their location – he couldn't be caught visiting them.

'It would be safe enough for us, sure, but not Soren.'

'Safety is overrated,' Callum drawled as he refilled his glass.

'Is it?' Rose's tone was sharper than she meant it, and she winced as Callum stilled. 'Sorry.'

She dropped her gaze to the cheery yellow wine in her cup. She wouldn't trade anything for their little life here, truly, but there was a part of her that still felt restless some days. Anger for all that the world had taken from them, guilt that they'd fled to this tenuous peace while others still suffered in the cruel system that had raised her. Raw wounds that had yet to heal. And perhaps they never would.

'Rose?' Sylvie's voice jolted her from her thoughts. 'Everything all right?'

Rose startled at finding Sylvie now standing above her, reaching for her hand. 'Yeah, fine.'

'You want to go back, don't you?' Callum's eyes narrowed as his feet slipped off the table.

'No.' A bitter scoff slipped past Rose's lips.

Sylvie frowned. 'But you think we should.'

Rose resisted the urge to glower at her. Sometimes, she wished they couldn't read her *quite* so well. But she couldn't deny that they were right.

There was no part of her that wanted to return to Dunhollow, that missed those insidious halls in the slightest. Because any return they made would spark the fires of more than just Rose's rage, and she knew Dunhollow would only be the beginning. She chewed the inside of her lip. Some days, the thought of lighting that match fed her more than anything else. But not today. *Not yet.*

'No.' Rose shook her head. 'Not unless it's in ashes.'

Glossary of Terms

Places

Abis imi (*Ah-BEESS ih-MEE*) A vanishing charm.

Aelvide intes ealorpus (*EYEl-vee-deh in-TES eh-yah-LORE-pus*) An alchemical diagnostic spell.

Allian (*AH-lee-yahn*) The westernmost of the three continents in the world. Known for its unregulated and powerful magic, it is split up into twenty-two different cohabiting countries across its vast mountains and coastlines, which include the birthplace of necromancy and dreaming magic.

Ashurd (*Ah-SHERD*) A city at the south-western tip of the empire. Known as one of the oldest cities in Na Qis, it was the ancient capital of the older Qisan empire, and is still a popular destination with the upper echelons of the current empire, thanks to its decadent ancient architecture and pristine beaches. Also, Fen's home city.

Bearath: Studis ab Mord ed Necromancie (*BAY-ah-wrath: STOO-diss ahb MOREd edd NEH-kroh-man-see*) Literally translated, the title reads *Bearath: Studies of Death and Necromancy*, as this grimoire was a personal study on history and practices of necromancy, death magic, and ancient spirits throughout the world.

Belel (*beh-LELL*) The smallest of the three Southern Trading States that make up the eastern half of the continent of Teonar. Known for having some of the most ancient architecture outside Na Qis, it is widely considered a centre of arts, culture and courtly love. It produces a number of spices and luxury perfumes, and is a popular vacation destination in no small part because of its gorgeous beaches.

Carnivorous Convallaria (Con-vah-LHA-ree-yuh) A flowering plant known to 'sing' in order to lure in their victims, as they strangle any caught in their grasp before slowly devouring them. Used medicinally in small doses, it is incredibly useful at treating bacterial infections.

Dunhollow Academy (Dun-HALL-oh) The largest and most prestigious of the empire's three most elite magical universities. Located a short distance from the capital of Tol Qilius, its curriculum is the most challenging and varied, covering practical spellcraft, illusion and invocation, magical theory, herbalism, sorcery and alchemy.

Eohad (EH-oh-had) Also known as the Rebel Isle, Eohad is a large island off the north-east coast of Na Qis. Once a part of the Qisan empire, it is best known for rebelling under the rule of Queen Isolde and bringing Qis to ruin. Known for its red hills and rugged landscapes, Eohad is also the birthplace of divining magic, and is currently presided over by the Motherhood of Diviners, who keep any Na Qisan overreach at bay.

Hova (HOH-vah) A small fishing village in Eohad, located not far outside the larger city of Port Righainn *(REE-yahn)*.

Ir Taril (EER TAH-rill) A large region in the north-western mountains of Na Qis. Known for both its rugged landscape and specialty with mental and compulsion magics, it's generally viewed as a less than friendly place by the majority of the empire. However, the imperial family makes great use of the region's skilled compulsionists in their personal court. Rose's family hails from the Outer Isles of this region.

Isle of Arbelis (Ahr-BEH-liss) A forested island off the south-eastern coast of Na Qis. A more recent addition to the empire's ever-growing lands, it's known for its wild grasp of natural magic – particularly as the birthplace of herbalism and botany. It is also well known as the site of the Arbelian Wars.

Maalstrum Institut (MAHL-strum IHNS-tih-toot) Another magical academy and one of Dunhollow's rivals, commonly referred to simply as Maalstrum. Located in the mountains of Ir Taril, it specializes in mental magics, specifically compulsion.

Miral neris (*MEE-rahl NEH-riss*) A mirror charm.

Monsorel (*MOHN-soh-rell*) The capital city of Ir Taril.

Na Qis/Na Qisan Empire (*Nah KEES/Nah KEES-awn*) The name of both the easternmost continent upon which Dunhollow is located and the empire that rules it. Meaning 'New Qis', it is a continuation of the much smaller Empire of Qis that was brought low centuries before and has now been restyled by its descendants. It covers all corners of the eastern continent, and many of its outlying islands, though it is still expanding. It is well known for its more rigid views of magic, and for coveting new magical forms from its conquered territories.

Old Pelanghe (*Peh-LONG-heh*) Located on the easternmost shores of Teonar, Pelanghe is the oldest continuous city in the world. As the site of the Great Calamity, ruins of its ancient iteration lie beneath volcanic ash on a shattered coastline, but the city has rebuilt itself many times over the millennia. Currently, its harbour is a popular stop on trade routes between many countries in the continent of Allian and the Southern Trading States of eastern Teonar.

Pentarchy of Etanhe (*Eh-TAHN-heh*) The Pentarchy is a coalition of trade cities in the far western ports of the continent of Allian, while Etanhe is its capital city and the seat of power. Run by a cadre of wealthy merchant families, it is known for being a somewhat lawless place with a long history of piracy and spiritual activity, as well as being the birthplace of necromancy.

Prevans (*Pre-VAHNCE*) The capital city of Arbelis.

Ques (*Kehss*) The Arbelian word for 'what'.

Qis/Qisan Empire (*Kees/KEES-awn*) The original empire that claimed much of the lands around Dunhollow. Much smaller in scope, it spread from the southern city of Ashurd and reigned for three hundred years before a rebel queen and diviner brought it to its knees in the late sixteenth century (roughly four hundred years ago).

Reath: Studis ab Salis ed Antasis (RAY-ath: STOO-diss ahb SAH-liss edd Ahn-TAH-siss) Literally translated, the title reads *Reath: Studies of Life and Resurrection*, as this grimoire was a personal study on history and practices of revival, life source, and ancient spirits throughout the world.

Rhal (RAHL) The westernmost of the three Southern Trading States that make up the eastern half of the continent of Teonar. Known for its ruggedly beautiful mountainous landscapes and bounteous mines, it produces some of the most sought after gemstones and weaponry in the world.

Salirel/Salirelean (SAH-lih-rell/Sah-lih-REH-lee-an) Located on the eastern coast of the westernmost continent, Salirel is known for being the birthplace of dreaming magic, and for hosting the gateway into Ionaen (the Realm of Dreams) itself. As such, it boasts a strangely ever-shifting landscape and some of the most robust libraries in the world (even if some sources are questionable).

Savoissanta DeVoil (Sah-vwah-SAHNT-ah duh-VWAHL) Another magical academy and one of Dunhollow's rivals, commonly referred to simply as DeVoil. Located on the Isle of Arbelis, it specializes in healing magics, namely botany and herbalism, and boasts a renowned student hospital.

Solanaceae (Soh-lah-NAH-see-eye) A plant with venomous vines that is known to produce a variety of fruits, berries, and even some vegetables across its many species. However, one in ten of its harvest is known to be deadly to any who eats it, making it a risky endeavour to try. Also, its vines have a potent paralytic effect, so it is generally left alone, or grown in strictly controlled environments.

Tai filha ese'aici (TIE FEE-lah ESS-eh'EYE-see) A phrase in the Arbelian language meaning 'Your daughter is here'.

Telemestra (Teh-leh-MEH-strah) A hilly region in central Na Qis known for its vineyards, fine wines and luxury scarves.

Teonar (TEH-oh-nahr) The southernmost and oldest settled continent in the world. It is widely considered the birthplace of magic, though these days, the grand ancient empires and powerful magics of its western half have largely faded. Its eastern half is ruled by the Southern Trading States, a powerful collection of three countries whose alliance has long fended off the conquering ambitions of Na Qis.

Tol Qilius (Toll KILL-ee-yuss) The capital of Na Qis. Known for being incredibly opulent, the city seamlessly blends ancient architecture with modern magical advancements. It is both the seat of imperial power and the birthplace of source magic, as well as Sylvie's home city.

Other Terms

Arbelian (Ahr-BEH-lee-ahn) Of or referring to the people, language, culture or customs of the region of the Isle of Arbelis.

Arbelian Wars (Ahr-BEH-lee-ahn) A series of three wars drawn out over a century between the Isle of Arbelis and the Empire of Qis, which eventually saw Arbelis conquered and brought into the empire.

(The) Ashwood Tournament An ancient tournament hosted once a decade for the last three hundred years and held between the three most prestigious magical academies in the empire: Dunhollow, Maalstrum and DeVoil.

Bahalan (BAH-ha-lahn) A type of woodland creature native to the forests of Arbelis. It looks a bit like a cross between an incredibly large wildcat and a sentient tree, with long canines, antlers and a body plated by thick vinewood.

Bearath (BEH-ah-rath) An old word in the tongue of spirits meaning 'One of Death'. Literally, the primordial spirit of death who was once mortal and sister to her counterpart Life.

Calamity/Great Calamity Though many records of this period are now lost, most extant ones agree that it was the last great clash between gods and mortals nearly one thousand years ago, in which those gods were ultimately destroyed. By all accounts, it occurred in the ancient city of Pelanghe and led to its destruction, as well as the very downfall of magic for a time.

Convallaria (Con-vah-LAH-ree-yuh)

Dal/Dalissan (DAHL/DAH-lee-sahn) A common term of endearment in Tarilian, meaning something akin to 'darling' or 'sweetheart'. Originally, the name belonged to a popular dessert in the region.

Dia vhal (DEE-yah VAHL) A common curse that literally translates to 'sacred blood', and can be used to express shock, awe or anger. Range of intensity includes everything from the relatively inoffensive 'oh damn' to the more vulgar 'fuck's sake', depending on the intonation of the swearer.

Edict of Ardalis (Ar-DAH-liss) An edict passed about one hundred years before Rose's time that codified in strictest detail the illegality of necromancy alongside dreaming magic and divining, which had unofficially been outlawed centuries earlier.

Messere (Meh-SAIR) A common honorific and form of address.

Motherhood of Diviners The spiritual order in Eohad that preserves the magic of divining, which has largely been lost to the world. For the most part, they provide prophecies and predictions of the future, though some tales claim the more powerful diviners can cut their enemies' futures out of time altogether.

Order of Salix (SAH-licks) A secretive order founded in the early days of Dunhollow. Most recently run by Imrys Elaegius, though it suffered great scandal after Fen's death and was disbanded.

Queen Isolde/The Rebel Queen The last queen of the Qisan Empire, originally from the Isle of Eohad. A powerful diviner, she is famous (or, rather, infamous) in the current Empire of Na Qis for turning traitor and leading a rebellion against their predecessors that ultimately led to their downfall.

Queen of Pelanghe (Peh-LONG-heh) According to legend, its last queen was responsible for the Great Calamity, in which she struck down the corrupted old gods, destroyed her city and became the embodiment of death itself.

Reath (RAY-ath) An old word in the tongue of spirits meaning 'One of Life'. Literally, the primordial spirit of life who was once mortal and sister to her counterpart Death.

Sumar mimsoia (SOO-mahr Mim-SOY-ah) A type of strangling vine native to the forests of Arbelis that releases toxins that can lead to fever, hallucinations or even death.

Tarilian (TAH-rih-lee-yun) Used to describe either the people, language, culture or customs of the region of Ir Taril.

Telka (TELL-kah) A bitter drink made from the root of the telka plant, which helps increase one's magical reserves. Usually consumed with milk and honey or sweetened cream.

The Nine The nine gods who founded both the Qisan and Na Qisan empires according to legend. In the modern day most within the empire no longer worship them as gods but rather as folk heroes or powerful casters of old. The old churches and temples to The Nine do, however, still hold some ceremonial sway, and are used by the imperial family to manipulate the lower and middle classes of Na Qisan society, who still largely keep the faith.

Vala nan (VAH-lah NAHN) A common curse in Ir Taril; similar in meaning to *dia vhal*.

Dunhollow Schools

College of Healing and Herbalism (CHH) Focused on the healing sciences. Available specializations include: Herbalism, Physiology, Potioncraft and Somatics.

College of Illusion and Invocation (CII) Focused on the mental magics. Available specializations include: Compulsion, Illusion, Channelling and Goetic Studies.

College of Untamed Arts (CUA) Focused on alchemy and experimental magic. Available specializations include: Alchemical Functions, Transmutation and Esoteric Studies.

School of Defensive Arts (SDA) Focused on source magic. Available specializations include: Sorcery, Battle Magic and Elemental Applications.

School of Magical Theory (SMT) Focused on academic magic. Available specializations include: Magical Philosophy, Historical Sciences, Sigils & Symbolism and Linguistics.

School of Practical Spellcraft (SPS) Focused on practical magics. Available specializations include: Charmwork, Magical Law and Justice, Summoning and Apotropaic Studies

Cast of Characters

Araminta Thenlif (*Ah-rah-MIHN-tah *THEN-leaf*) she/her – Rose's mother and former chancellor of Dunhollow Academy

Arden Osiander (*AHR-den Oz-YAN-der*) he/him – Rose's peer and rival

Arvir Mistralus (*Are-VEER Miss-TRAH-luss*) he/him – lead professor of the Maalstrum competitors

Aveline Goarsbel (*Ah-veh-LEEN GORES-bell*) she/her – one of the students murdered last year in a necromantic ritual

Azalaïs L'Espina (*AH-zah-lay Less-PEE-nah*) she/her – a competitor from DeVoil

Briony Burroak (*BRI-yuh-nee BUR-oak*) she/her – head of the College of Healing and Herbalism at Dunhollow

Callum Avenhart (*CAH-luhm AH-venn-heart*) he/him – a compulsion prodigy from Maalstrum and Rose's lover

Delia Droosberil (*DEH-lee-yuh DROOS-bare-ill*) she/her – the librarian at Dunhollow Academy

Everard Woodstone (*EH-ver-ahrd WOOD-stohne*) he/him – the current chancellor of Dunhollow Academy

Ewan Elaegius (*YOU-wan Eh-LAY-**ghee-yus*) they/them – Sylvie's ex and Rose's former rival turned frenemy

Fenil (Fen) Hathorin (*FEN-ill HAH-*thor-in*) he/him – Dunhollow's former golden boy and Rose's best friend, who was murdered last year in a necromantic ritual

Hollis Tipill (*HALL-iss TIP-ill*) he/him – former pub owner, who murdered Fen and Aveline and kidnapped Sylvie before he was killed by Rose

Imrys Elaegius (*Ihm-REES Eh-LAY-**ghee-yus*) he/him – Ewan's father, head of Dunhollow's board and a long-standing rival (as well as a former lover) of Rose's mother

Ionas Tirecin (*YOH-nuss TEE-reh-sin*) he/him – formerly: the personal necromancer to the Na Qisan emperor one hundred years past. Currently: obsessed with his own revival

Mamsella Fiorella de Prevath (*Mahm-SELL-ah Fee-yoh-RELL-ah duh PREH-vath*) she/her – lead professor of the DeVoil students

Oliv Ivyssen (*OH-lihv IH-vih-sehn*) she/her – a competitor from Maalstrum

Peiren Havillande (*PAY-rehn AH-vee-lahnd*) he/him – a competitor from DeVoil

Professor Saoloris (*Say-LORE-iss*) they/them – head of the College of Untamed Arts at Dunhollow

Revan Troidilis (*REH-vahn TROY-dill-iss*) they/them – head of the School of Defensive Arts at Dunhollow

Rosera (Rose) Thenlif (*ROE-zeh-rah *THEN-leaf*) she/her – student at Dunhollow, secret necromancer, object of obsession to Ionas, and lover of Sylvie and Callum

Soren Sylverfir (*SORE-en SILL-ver-feer*) he/him – head of the School of Magical Theory and Rose's father figure

Sylven (Sylvie) Belliaris (*SILL-ven Bell-ee-YAR-iss*) she/her – Dunhollow's star caster, a source prodigy and Rose's former academic rival turned lover

The Aratis (*Ah-RAH-tiss*) gender unspecified, they/them – the head member of the Faceless

The Faceless – the group of five judges presiding over the Ashwood Tournament

---

* 'Thenlif' and 'Hathorin' have a harder 'th' sound, as in 'thin', rather than 'then'.

** 'Elaegius' has a harder 'g', as in 'golly', rather than 'gee'.

Acknowledgements

Thank you so much to each and every person who has been involved in the publication of this book, and to all those who stuck around for Rose's journey through Dunhollow. I truly cannot express how much your support has meant to me.

To my amazing agent, Nina Leon, without whom this series would never have been born: thank you so much for all the brainstorming, sweat, and tears that you poured into these books and this world (and sorry again for scandalizing you with *those* scenes). I'm so grateful to have you in my corner championing my work!

To my wider team at Pérez Literary & Entertainment, endless thanks for your incredible support and encouragement.

To Ruth Atkins and Jorgie Bain, I can never express how much it means to me that you gave my little witchy book a chance, let alone that you let me turn it into a duology. Ruth, thank you so much for trusting me to wrap up this sordid tale and for not immediately chucking that beast of a first draft in the bin. I'm so glad you were able to see the diamond in the rough! Jorgie, thank you for encouraging me not to pull my punches on the story beats and for being the first to fall in love with the world of Dunhollow. I'll always be so grateful to you both.

Thank you also to my wider team at Penguin Michael Joseph, especially Beatrix McIntyre for managing everything with such patience (even when I was sporadically chucking new fantasy words into an already overflowing glossary), Nina Elstad for my gorgeous cover, and Jennie Roman for catching all my repeat words!

A huge thank you to my amazing US team at Arc Manor Books.

And, to all of my incredible critique partners, thank you so much for not immediately dropping me as a friend when I sent you this mess of 150k words. Leah, thank you for consistently reminding me how the English language works. Ann, thank you for providing the spiteful motivation to make this book the emotional mess that it is. And Makayla, thank you for always pointing out that I have no concept of spatial awareness, even in fiction.

To all my friends, thank you for cheering me on the whole way through – I owe you so much more than I can say. Also, special thanks to the PMJ author group chat for keeping me sane in this wild industry.

And to my wonderful best friend, digital artist, and personal perfumer, Gabrielle – I'm so lucky to have you in my life for all the wine nights, rambling conversations, fan art, and perfume profiles that led to this book being more than just some beast bouncing around in my head. The way you're able to bring my characters to life through your art will never cease to amaze me!

To my whole family, thank you for turning a little feral child into a voracious reader by regularly leaving me to my own devices at the local library. Your support over the years has made so much of this series possible, and I'm eternally grateful. Also, for the sake of being able to look at each other at the next family dinner, please avoid reading chapters 24, 37, and 43, thank you.

Last, but certainly not least, to anyone who read or listened to this book, thank you from the bottom of my heart! Know that you have made my dreams come true, and I hope you were able to see a bit of yourselves in these pages. And if any of you have a bone to pick about the endings of either book, please reach out to my dearest agent, Nina, because it was all her idea.